More praise for

Lifelines

"[A] spot-on debut . . . a breathtakingly fast-paced medical thriller."
—*Publishers Weekly*

"Forget about your plans for the day and prepare to be swept away on a pulse-pounding adventure. This is my favorite kind of medical thriller—harrowing, emotional, action-packed, and brilliantly realized. CJ Lyons writes with the authority only a trained physician can bring to a story, blending suspense, passion, and friendship into an irresistible read."
—*New York Times* bestselling author Susan Wiggs

"A pulse-pounding adrenaline rush! . . . Reminds me of *ER* back in the days of George Clooney and Julianna Margulies."
—*New York Times* bestselling author Lisa Gardner

"Have we got a prescription for you . . . a tense thrill ride that feels like all the best episodes of *ER* and *Grey's Anatomy* squeezed into one breathtaking novel . . . [an] impressive debut."
—*Hilton Head Monthly*

"CJ Lyons writes with both authority on her subject and a down-to-earth reality for her characters . . . Engrossing, intriguing."
—*New York Times* bestselling author Heather Graham

"CJ Lyons' debut medical thriller is a fantastic and wild journey through the fast-paced world of a big-city ER. With rich, fascinating, and complex characters and a thoroughly compelling mystery, *Lifelines* is an adrenaline rush and an all-around great read."
—*New York Times* bestselling author Allison Brennan

continued . . .

"Lyons captures the frenetic setting of the ER with a smooth style that demands the reader move forward to keep up with the pace, but she also creates winning portraits of the supporting players set to anchor the series . . . Sets the table well for the next adventure at Angels of Mercy." —*Newsday*

"If this debut novel is any indication, [Lyons'] decision [to write books] could be a gift to readers of multiple genres . . . Lydia is a well-drawn heroine, the writing is strong, and the plot could have been taken out of today's headlines." —*Pittsburgh Post-Gazette*

"Lyons' first book is a winner, too, giving us terrific characters and a compelling plot. An excellent book for fans of the medical thriller." —*Fresh Fiction*

"It takes a real emergency physician to write this excitingly about an emergency ward. CJ Lyons has been there and done it. The pages are packed with adrenaline. I can't recall a hospital novel that so thrilled me."
—*New York Times* bestselling author David Morrell

Titles by CJ Lyons

LIFELINES

WARNING SIGNS

WARNING SIGNS

CJ Lyons

JOVE BOOKS, NEW YORK

THE BERKLEY PUBLISHING GROUP
Published by the Penguin Group
Penguin Group (USA) Inc.
375 Hudson Street, New York, New York 10014, USA
Penguin Group (Canada), 90 Eglinton Avenue East, Suite 700, Toronto, Ontario M4P 2Y3, Canada
(a division of Pearson Penguin Canada Inc.)
Penguin Books Ltd., 80 Strand, London WC2R 0RL, England
Penguin Group Ireland, 25 St. Stephen's Green, Dublin 2, Ireland (a division of Penguin Books Ltd.)
Penguin Group (Australia), 250 Camberwell Road, Camberwell, Victoria 3124, Australia
(a division of Pearson Australia Group Pty. Ltd.)
Penguin Books India Pvt. Ltd., 11 Community Centre, Panchsheel Park, New Delhi—110 017, India
Penguin Group (NZ), 67 Apollo Drive, Rosedale, North Shore 0632, New Zealand
(a division of Pearson New Zealand Ltd.)
Penguin Books (South Africa) (Pty.) Ltd., 24 Sturdee Avenue, Rosebank, Johannesburg 2196, South Africa

Penguin Books Ltd., Registered Offices: 80 Strand, London WC2R 0RL, England

WARNING SIGNS

A Jove Book / published by arrangement with the author

PRINTING HISTORY
Jove mass-market edition / February 2009

Cover image of Empty Hospital Bed by Dana Neely / Taxi / Getty Images; cover image of "Amanda, Gina, Lydia, and Nora" by Claudio Marinesco.
Cover design by Rita Frangie.
Text design by Kristin del Rosario.

For information, address: The Berkley Publishing Group,
a division of Penguin Group (USA) Inc.,
375 Hudson Street, New York, New York 10014.

ISBN: 978-0-515-14583-0

JOVE®
Jove Books are published by The Berkley Publishing Group,
a division of Penguin Group (USA) Inc.,
375 Hudson Street, New York, New York 10014.
JOVE® is a registered trademark of Penguin Group (USA) Inc.
The "J" design is a trademark belonging to Penguin Group (USA) Inc.

PRINTED IN THE UNITED STATES OF AMERICA

10 9 8 7 6 5 4 3 2 1

Thanks to my readers,
who have made this dream-come-true of
writing for a living so fulfilling,
to my critique partners for keeping me on my toes,
and to my family for their patience.

This book is for Jeff,
lost too early,
but still an inspiration and never forgotten.

ONE

Thursday, 5:21 A.M.

AMANDA MASON TILTED HER FACE TO THE wind, trying in vain to detect any hint of the ocean in the predawn darkness. Nothing. Only the rancid odors of diesel fuel and machine oil.

It was warm enough to feel like home, even out here on the Allegheny River, the sun not due up for another two hours. Going in this direction, away from the Ohio and upstream to the boathouse on Washington's Landing, the wind was full in her face, sharp enough to bring tears.

It had to be the wind. She was twenty-five years old, a grown woman, a fourth-year medical student who daily held lives in her hands. There was no way she was homesick.

The scull passed beneath the Roberto Clemente Bridge, accompanied by the rumble of a truck passing overhead, echoing through the dark. Amanda emerged on the other side in time to watch the firefly sparks of a discarded cigarette somersault and vanish. A horn sounded on the riverbank, followed by the scream of a siren. Definitely not home. But she most definitely wasn't homesick. Not at all.

She finished her trip up the Allegheny and pulled the rowing shell from the water. She already felt the effort in her shoulders—would feel it more by tomorrow, she was certain. It had been a few months since she'd had the chance to row. The life of a medical student doing clinical rotations was anything but predictable—especially as she'd had some of her most difficult rotations this summer and fall: emergency medicine, oncology, pediatric surgery. But not this month. This month should be a cakewalk. Neurology. Strictly consults, no overnight call in the hospital. This month she'd take her life back. She vowed to find more time to go to the boathouse; she'd forgotten how invigorating it was to start the day out on the water.

"Here, let me help you with that," Jared, the boathouse manager, said, appearing from the shadows of the large overhead doors that led into the boathouse.

"What are you doing here so early?" Amanda asked, grabbing the oars as he easily lifted the shell. Jared was short and stocky with red hair that had earned him the unimaginative if apt nickname of "Carrot-Top," but he was always helpful and ran the boathouse with admirable efficiency.

"My girlfriend is training for another marathon, gets up around four, so I figured why not come in early? No sense trying to go back to sleep."

Together they stowed her shell, and he followed her up the stairs to the locker rooms and social hall. "Do you have any more of those flyers about the research studies over at Angels? Folks have been asking for them."

"Yes, I brought some. Wasn't sure where to post them—" She gestured at the black-framed photo that had replaced the usual collection of flyers, announcements, and advertisements on the community bulletin board next to the locker rooms. In it was a picture of a smiling girl, the boathouse's assistant manager. Below it was a memorial plaque.

Amanda reached out and stroked the side of the frame.

"I didn't even know about Shelly until I came in this morning and saw this."

"We posted it on the e-mail loop."

"I went nomail when things got crazy at school. What happened?"

Jared shrugged, his lips tight as he regarded Shelly's photo. "Don't know. Her husband isn't really talking about it. It was so sudden," he said, straightening the frame she'd knocked crooked.

Amanda sighed. She saw grieving families every day—and still hadn't gotten used to it. "I'd better get changed or I'll be late." She pushed open the door to the women's locker room and stopped, looked back. "I'll leave the flyers on the desk."

Jared said nothing, but merely nodded, his gaze fixed on Shelly's bright smile.

A SHORT TIME LATER, HER HAIR STILL DAMP from her quick shower, Amanda raced down Pittsburgh's Angels of Mercy Medical Center's east stairwell, the echoing sound of her clattering heels reminiscent of rain tap-dancing on a tin roof, taking her home to rocking chairs, sweet tea, and her mother's veranda.

Her pager screeched, obliterating the illusion. The pulse-jarring noise propelled her into an instant state of alertness. *Worse than Pavlov's dogs,* Amanda thought, hating the gut-twisting adrenaline surge that hit her stronger than any caffeine jolt.

She silenced the pager and clutched the stethoscope jostling around her neck, barely catching herself as she rounded the landing. Her coat pockets bristled with notebooks, index cards, and neurology manuals. The books were heavy enough to swing the coat like a pendulum, throwing her off balance as she dashed down the stairs to the ER.

The ER, which would *not* stop paging her. She quieted

the beeper again. "I'm coming, I'm coming," she said aloud, startling the janitor mopping the landing below her.

He glanced up, but didn't bother to move out of her way once he caught sight of the short lab coat marking her as a mere medical student, or "scut-monkey" in hospital parlance. The lowest of the low, actually paying for the privilege of running labs, starting IVs, jabbing poor unsuspecting patients for blood, and stroking attending physicians' egos.

Amanda skidded across the wet floor, grabbing the door handle to stop herself before she slammed into the concrete wall. Her short heels were comfortable but not designed for galloping down stairs in response to a summons from the ER for a stat neurology consultation.

A lady never rushes. Her mother's oft-repeated instruction returned to her. Amanda took a breath, smoothed her lab jacket, and straightened her stethoscope. She closed her eyes for a moment, trying to recapture the serenity she'd felt out on the river, rowing in the predawn mist that huddled over the Allegheny.

Then she calmly strode through the door—with three older brothers to keep up with, her mother had never been successful in getting her to glide like a proper lady—and entered the vortex of humanity that was Angels of Mercy's Emergency Department.

"What are you doing here?" Nora Halloran, the ER day-shift charge nurse greeted Amanda, glancing up at the clock.

"You called for a neurology consult?" Amanda tried to sound confident, as if a fourth-year medical student could actually contribute something useful. She still broke out in palpitations every time she remembered that this time next year she'd be a real-life, full-fledged doctor. How could one person ever hope to learn everything she needed to know in such a short time?

"Not me, I'm not on the clock yet." Nora's hazel eyes gleamed as she took in Amanda's dress and heels. "You aren't either—not until seven. Trying to impress someone special?"

"Please." Amanda's Southern accent drew the word out into two syllables. She straightened her posture, tucked an errant strand of blond hair behind her ear, and attempted to look calm, cool, professional. "No, I have a doctor's appointment later, is all."

"Pretty nice dress for a doctor's appointment," Nora continued. "Who's the doctor, George Clooney?"

Amanda smiled at the compliment. She'd chosen the blue linen dress to match her eyes, and she felt good wearing it. After spending her last rotation mainly in the OR, stressed out and sleep-deprived, wearing scrubs and blood-splattered Reeboks, she had rejoiced in the opportunity to dress like a real person again, pulling all her favorite girl clothes from her closet.

"No, it's Dr. Nelson. Last time I saw him, I was working the ER, hadn't slept in two days or had a chance to shower. I wanted him to see that I know how to take care of myself." Another reason why she'd gotten up before dawn and headed over to the boathouse on River Avenue. She'd neglected her rowing—or any exercise—for several months, and she was determined to put herself and her health ahead of her studies for once.

The door to the resuscitation room banged open. A dark-haired woman craned her head out, her gaze sweeping across the ER, looking for trouble. Dr. Lydia Fiore, the youngest and newest ER attending, gave Amanda an abrupt nod. An alarm blared and she vanished back into the room.

"Guess I know who paged me," Amanda said, leaving Nora for the resuscitation room, her heels clacking against the linoleum with an authority she didn't feel.

She liked Lydia, enjoyed working with her, but the attending's boundless energy and ability to make diagnoses with minimal information could be a bit overwhelming and intimidating. Even the regular ER staff was polarized by

Lydia—either in awe of her apparently magical abilities or scornful, waiting and hoping for her downfall. Lydia didn't seem to notice or care, instead focusing all her energy on her patients with a self-assuredness Amanda envied.

Pushing open the door to the treatment room, Amanda entered a symphony of chaos. Nurses and lab techs swarmed around a motionless black girl, maybe twenty years old, who lay on the exam table, colored wires leading from her chest to a monitor, two IV lines in place, a respiratory tech adjusting a nonrebreather oxygen mask over her face. Elise Avery, the flight nurse who must have transported the patient in on the hospital's helicopter, was directing traffic, a scowl on her face.

The only oasis of calm was Dr. Fiore herself, who stood motionless at the head of the bed, one hand resting against the girl's shoulder as if giving comfort. Except Lydia wasn't really still. Her gaze was in constant motion, devouring everything in its path, and one foot tapped an impatient staccato that mirrored the beeping of the heart monitor.

Gina Freeman, an emergency medicine resident and Amanda's roommate, had once compared Lydia to a hand grenade—not much to look at on the outside, but ready to explode when triggered.

"Nineteen-year-old collapsed during a cross-country run this morning, transported in from Millvale," Lydia told Amanda. "On arrival, she was unresponsive, noted to have hypernatremic dehydration with an elevated sodium of one fifty-one. Vitals were normal, but patient grew increasingly nonresponsive with myoclonic movements of her extremities and eventually exhibited a descending paralysis. I was just getting ready to intubate her, but thought you might want to do a quick exam first."

"No elevated temp?" Amanda knew heatstroke could cause similar symptoms.

"Not here." Lydia raised a questioning eyebrow at Elise, the transport nurse.

Elise shook her head, her usual calm, commanding expression clouded by the mystery of why the girl had gone downhill so fast. "None at the scene either."

Descending paralysis? Amanda had never heard of that—usually paralysis hit one side of the body as in a stroke, or started at the feet and moved up the body as with Guillain-Barré. It didn't start at the head and work down.

"Normal temp on scene," Elise continued. "The sodium is coming down nice and slow, so you can't blame that. Besides, according to her friends, she had the neuro symptoms before she collapsed. Complained of trouble swallowing, uncontrollable muscle tremors, blurred vision."

Amanda pursed her lips and checked the patient's reflexes. Nothing. Except the girl did have a normal Babinski reflex, which meant her nerve impulses could make it from the brain to the big toe and back again. She appeared to be sleeping, although her respiratory rate was a little slower than normal.

Amanda stepped back out of Lydia's way, clutching her stethoscope with uncertainty. If Lydia couldn't figure it out, what chance did Amanda, a lowly medical student, have? "I think I'd better call my attending."

"Already paged," Elise told her.

"Drop an NG," Lydia ordered. A nurse grabbed the nasogastric tube designed to prevent aspiration. "There's nothing on exam. I can't find a reason for this girl to be unresponsive." Lydia glanced at Elise. "Any past medical history? Drug use? Current meds?"

Elise shook her head. "Friends didn't know of any. Sorry." She sounded genuinely regretful that she didn't have the answers needed to help their patient.

"We'll have to wait for a tox screen. What else? Tick paralysis? Botulism? Miller Fisher variant?" Lydia muttered, drumming a reflex hammer against her palm in time with her words. She quickly gained control of the situation, completing a head-to-toe assessment of her patient and ordering repeat labs.

Elise moved to one side, leafing through her paperwork as if searching for an answer from her records. If the girl on the gurney in front of them hadn't been so sick, Amanda might have been pleased to see the transport nurse flustered for once.

Instead, Amanda looked down at their patient and had the sudden image of herself lying there lifeless.

The door banged open and the neurology attending barged into the room, shattering her reverie: Lucas Stone, the one person she'd been hoping to avoid.

TWO

Thursday, 6:52 A.M.

GINA FREEMAN SHIFTED HER SHOULDERS, shrugging the weight of her bulletproof vest into place. The living room walls spun around her as a sudden urge to run to the bathroom, a need to feel the cool, reassuring, porcelain toilet hugged against her body, jolted through her faster than lightning.

Jerry's arms curled around her, pressing his body against hers, and she was able to beat back the panic, ignore the sweat gathering at the small of her back.

"You don't have to go," he told her, planting a kiss along the side of her neck, resting his face against her shoulder-length mass of frizzled ebony curls.

"I do if I want to finish my residency." She'd already traded all the shifts she could in order to postpone her EMS rotation.

All she'd dreamed of for the past two years was the chance to get out on the streets, to see real action. Now she was a third-year emergency medicine resident, finally able to run with the med squads, and the dream had turned to dust.

Getting shot at during her first time riding with an ambulance crew probably had something to do with that.

Jerry stiffened. She knew he was thinking of the shooting as well. If he hadn't given her a Kevlar vest, hadn't insisted she wear it, she'd be dead.

Her toes curled with the need to purge the dark memories, these crazy, out-of-control feelings threatening to consume her. She tried to pull free of Jerry's embrace, but he held her tight.

"So don't finish your residency." His voice caught. "Marry me, Gina. Be Mrs. Jerry Boyle. You don't have to work, you don't have to do anything you don't want to. Stay with me, stay home, safe and sound, have my children, lots of beautiful children who will be as gorgeous as their mother." He wove his long, pale, slender fingers between her dark ones as if weaving their futures together.

Gina's breath snagged in her throat, banishing memories of ambulances and riots and gunfire from her mind. Jerry had asked her before, had done the traditional bended knee, candlelight, roses, and wine last month—despite her parents' forbidding it. A fact Jerry didn't know she knew about. A fact that before the shooting would have sent her racing into his arms.

She'd answered by asking for time. Almost dying had changed everything. She just had no idea what it all meant yet.

The rest of the world seemed the same, everyone picking up and moving on, cleaning up the mess the riots that overwhelmed the city on July 4 had left in their wake. All Gina had survived was a near miss by a drive-by shooter. A single bullet, that was all. Yet nothing was the same.

She could fake it during her shifts in the ER, where there were other residents and attendings to take up the slack. But riding in an ambulance . . .

"I can't," she whispered, her voice torn. "I can't."

Jerry's sigh vibrated against her body, and he released her. He obviously thought her words were meant for him and his proposal of a happily-ever-after life with a great guy who loved her. She missed his warmth immediately, turned to explain, but then clamped her mouth shut. As she watched him check his gun and holster it, clip his badge onto his belt, and shrug into his suit jacket, sorrow weighed her down.

Jerry was the hero, a real hero. How could he love her, a coward, a fake, a liar?

Gina watched helplessly as the thought branded itself into her brain. Then he was gone. And she was alone once more.

This time when the urge to run and hide in the bathroom struck, she surrendered.

AMANDA'S RELIEF THAT HELP HAD ARRIVED quickly morphed into dismay when she saw who it was. Dr. Lucas Stone strode into the room, ignoring the flurry of activity and focusing on their patient.

Lucas was a thin, sandy-haired man who exuded intensity. He also had the most gorgeous blue-gray eyes, eyes that reminded Amanda of the ocean back home after a storm had blown through, gleaming and clear and yet with hidden depths. Not that she'd noticed or anything. In fact, she'd been trying hard to forget everything about Lucas Stone. When they'd first met, it had been a disaster.

"What are you doing here?" she blurted out without thinking.

He raised his face enough to meet her gaze from across the bed. "Switched with Campbell."

There was a moment of silence before she could force a polite smile, but his attention had already returned to the patient lying between them. Did he even recognize her? Remember who she was?

Following Lucas into the room was Jim Lazarov, an emergency medicine intern with aspirations of someday evolving into a Neanderthal. Jostling Amanda aside, Jim plowed his way directly through to the head of the bed, where Lydia was preparing to intubate the patient in order to take control of her breathing.

"Hey, can I tube her?" Jim asked, grabbing the laryngoscope.

Lucas paused in his exam. "Give me a moment."

He was talking to Lydia, but Amanda knew it was her job to bring the attending up to speed. She quickly gave him a report, ending with, "Now she's lost her gag reflex as well."

"And her sats are dropping," Lydia added, reaching past Jim for a bag-valve mask to force oxygen into the patient. "She's hypoventilating."

Lucas was efficient, quickly completing his examination and stepping back to give Lydia room. Then he glanced at Amanda. "Maybe my student could do the intubation?"

Wow, maybe he did remember her after all. It wasn't usual to allow a mere medical student to perform an intubation in a patient this ill. But she hung back. Not that Jim Lazarov deserved any consideration from her—he'd given her hell the last time they'd worked together in the ER—but, as odious as he was, he had asked first. "That's okay."

Jim nudged her and said in a voice too low for the attendings to hear, "Yeah, scut-monkeys should be seen and not heard. Don't try poaching my patients or procedures."

So much for altruism. Jim clearly still resented her having been assigned the "better" patients while she was on her ER rotation.

Nora pushed the door open and stuck her head in, gesturing to Lydia, releasing the sounds of a woman screaming and the clatter of metal on metal into the room.

"You've got things covered here?" Lydia asked Lucas.

"No problem. Go." Lucas stood over their patient, arms crossed and one eye squinted, thinking hard.

Jim leaned forward, ratcheting open the girl's mouth

with a twist of gloved fingers. He began to slide the lighted metal laryngoscope blade over her tongue when Lucas lunged and grabbed the intern's arm.

"Stop." Lucas kept hold of Jim's arm, his gaze fixed on the monitor. The patient's heart rate was in the eighties, then as Jim backed away it dropped to the seventies. Her oxygen level remained the same, but her blood pressure, which had gone up a small bit, also dropped.

"What's the problem?" Jim demanded, shaking free. "Her heart rate's dropping. I need to tube her now." He bent over the patient again, but Lucas swung his arm to barricade the patient.

"I said stop." Lucas's voice was low but intense enough that everyone in the room was now staring at him. "Give her two milligrams of Versed and start a Propofol drip. Now!"

The nurses jumped to obey him. From the looks they gave him, Amanda had the feeling Lucas didn't shout orders very often.

"Why are you putting her under?" Jim argued. "She's already gorked."

Lucas ignored him, surprising them all by squatting down so that his mouth was almost touching the girl's ear. He whispered something Amanda couldn't hear. Everyone in the room stopped what they were doing to stare at Lucas, the nurses with curiosity, Jim Lazarov with disdain.

Amanda edged closer, one hand on the girl, absently stroking her hair as the nurses gave her the sedatives.

"She's an athlete; her resting heart rate is probably in the sixties or lower," Lucas explained.

"Okay, so technically she's not bradying down, but why snow her more than she already is?" Jim asked, pinching the flesh of the girl's upper arm. There was no change in her vital signs. He arched an eyebrow at Lucas, who nodded his consent and allowed the intern to proceed with the intubation.

"With those drugs on board, you're going to lose your neuro exam until she wakes up," Amanda noted as Jim inserted the artificial airway.

"That's the problem," Lucas said, pulling Amanda away, out of earshot of the patient. "She *is* awake. Probably has been all along."

Amanda stumbled and looked over her shoulder at the girl. "You mean, she's paralyzed but she can see and hear everything?"

A grimace passed over Lucas's face. "Yes. Can you imagine?"

She could. All too well. Being buried alive, unable to communicate with anyone, was a recurrent childhood nightmare. The dreaded "locked-box" syndrome defined Amanda's greatest fear.

"Lucas, we have to help her. What are you going to do?"

"Wish to hell I knew." His voice was low enough that she was sure she was the only one in the room who heard him. He turned away, his shoulders hunching.

Amanda stepped forward, pivoting to face him square on. "What did you tell her? Before you put her under?"

His eyes darkened to a stormy shade of gray as he looked past her to their patient. "I told her everything would be all right. I told her, 'Don't be afraid.' "

She could tell from his expression that he didn't believe his own words.

THREE

Thursday, 7:26 A.M.

LYDIA EMERGED FROM THE RESUSCITATION room and immediately shoved thoughts of her puzzling neuro patient aside. In her short time here at Angels, she'd worked with Lucas Stone enough to know she could trust her patient to him, and right now there were plenty of other patients to focus on. The stocky well-tattooed man throwing punches and kicking at the two police officers and the security guard trying to restrain him was the most obvious.

Nora circled the quartet at a safe distance, a syringe of Haldol at the ready. Two other men, an EMT and a nursing assistant, jogged down the hall, eager to join the fray.

Lydia ignored the ruckus. The cops muscled their captive into an exam room where he wouldn't be a threat to anyone. And from the way his bellowed curses seared the air, it was obvious his lungs and heart were working just fine.

She wasn't so sure about the very pale gray-haired woman slumped in a chair in a curtained bed space, her palms pressed against the arms of the chair, fingers curling and uncurling with every breath. A boy, maybe ten or twelve, sat on the exam bed, anxiously watching the woman.

Lydia grabbed the EMT, a guy named Williams who was working part-time in the ER. He gave her only the briefest of frowns. Most of the EMS guys knew her because she was their new medical director. The fact that she also happened to be involved with Trey Garrison, their district chief, didn't hurt either. She pulled Williams into the woman's bed space. The medic scooped the boy from the bed to clear it and turned the monitor and oxygen on while Lydia knelt beside the woman, feeling for her pulse as she patted her hand.

"Can you tell me what's wrong?" she asked.

The woman's eyes were wide as she struggled to breathe. "Not. Me." She reached her other hand out to the boy. "Deon."

"I'm fine, Gram," the boy said, a single tear escaping as he grasped her hand. "I only said my stomach hurt so you'd come see the doctor."

The woman frowned and sent a stern glance at the boy only to have it deflected as Lydia and the medic hauled her up and onto the gurney. She started to bat their hands away, feebly protesting, then sank back against the head of the bed, greedily sucking in the oxygen Lydia attached to her via a face mask.

"Room air pulse ox is seventy-eight percent," Williams said, attaching monitor leads to the woman. "With O_2, it's up to ninety-four percent, respirations sixteen, heart rate eighty-eight, but her blood pressure is only sixty-eight over forty-four."

"Get me cardiac enzymes, a CBC, and chemistry panel," Lydia said, stethoscope in her hand. "Start a liter of saline and get an EKG as well." She listened to the woman's chest. Clear, no murmurs, no abnormal heart rhythm. "Do you have any medical problems?"

The woman nodded, obviously more comfortable with the oxygen. "Blood pressure and diabetes."

"Do you take insulin shots or the pills?"

"Pills." Before she could say more, the boy, Deon, had opened his knapsack, spilling out several changes of underwear, a rain poncho, clean socks, a well-loved copy of the first Harry Potter book, a tablet and some broken crayons, a plastic bag filled with wipes, shampoo samples, toothpaste and two toothbrushes, and another bag brimming with loose pills and medication samples.

"Here," he said, emptying the pill bag into Lydia's waiting hands. "These are her sugar pills. And these are for her heart. And these"—he pulled out the sample medication, sealed in its plastic bubbles—"are the new ones the clinic gave her last week."

He met Lydia's gaze with an expression that brimmed over with hope, despair, and helplessness, as if he simply didn't have room to keep any more emotions bottled up inside. She gave him a smile. "Good work, Deon. My name's Lydia and we're going to help your grandmother."

"Actually," he said in a whisper, "she's my great. But we don't say that."

"Okay, her secret's safe with me."

As Lydia examined the pills, Deon efficiently repacked his knapsack. She winced at the familiar sight. She and her mother had spent the first twelve years of her life on the streets of L.A. How well she remembered hauling everything important to them in a small bag that seemed all that separated them from total destitution. As long as they had clean underwear and toothbrushes, they weren't really homeless. Just occasionally without a roof over their heads.

Better that way, Lydia's mother, Maria, used to say, making a game of it all, preferring to camp on Venice Beach whenever possible. Stars above, no one to tell you when to turn out the lights, and the ocean was better than any lullaby.

Of course, in L.A. they never had to worry about snow like folks here in Pittsburgh did. Thank goodness it was still warm out, the city enjoying an Indian summer that felt more like August than October.

Deon zipped up his bag, slinging it onto his shoulder, and grabbed his great-grandmother's hand once more as the medic wheeled up the EKG machine. "What's that?"

"A machine that's going to record the electricity in your gram's heart."

Deon watched the ink needles dance across the pink-and-white-checked paper, riveted by the small squiggles they produced.

"Did you know it takes electricity to keep your heart beating?" Lydia asked as she scrutinized the EKG results. ST elevation and T-wave inversion in the precordial leads. Not good. "Are you having any chest pain?" she asked the woman.

"No. Never. Just dizzy all the time, past few days. Nothing to worry about." She frowned at Deon, but her eyes were filled with pride. "Wouldn't even have come in if he hadn't said his stomach was paining him so."

"I'm glad you did."

The admission clerk wheeled her computer to the bedside and hastily registered the woman, Mrs. Emma Grey. Lydia distracted Deon while the medic drew blood and started an IV.

"What's wrong with her, Lydia?" Deon asked, his voice tight and high-pitched.

"It looks like her heart might need a little help."

"Don't listen to her, Deon, I feel better already," Mrs. Grey protested.

"The fluids and oxygen did that. But I need to monitor you. You could be having what we call a STEMI; it's a type of heart attack."

"Told you, my heart feels fine." Mrs. Grey sat up, pulling the oxygen mask away from her face. "And this air blowing in at me smells disgusting."

Lydia switched her to a more comfortable nasal cannula. "I really need to watch you for a few hours. We'll get lunch for Deon; he can stay with you."

Too late she realized that Nora Halloran stood behind her. Providing food for patient's families was against the rules—as was allowing unaccompanied minors to remain with a patient.

"Dr. Fiore, I need a word," Nora said.

Lydia winked at Deon, handed him an extra copy of the EKG to ponder over, and closed the curtain behind her before joining Nora. She spotted Lucas Stone and Amanda escorting her neuro patient down the hall.

"Lucas was able to get her into an MRI slot," Nora explained.

"Helps to have a neurologist pulling strings." Lydia grabbed Emma Grey's chart and began signing off her verbal orders. No matter how urgent a case, there was always paperwork to contend with—and now with all the charts computerized, also additional time spent with the electronic medical record.

"You want me to call social services?" Nora asked.

"For what?"

Nora stopped short of rolling her eyes. They both knew Lydia wasn't that dense. "When they signed Deon in, they used an outdated medical assistance card and gave a fake address and phone number. We don't even know if the grandmother has legal custody."

"Do you think social services is going to magically find them health insurance, a home, and a phone?" Lydia was jaded when it came to the power of social workers to cause more good than harm.

Nora blew her breath out, twisting her fingers through her shoulder-length red hair. She ignored the clerk trying to hand her a phone. "Odds are the grandmother—if she even *is* his grandmother—will be admitted. What's going to happen to Deon then? He can't stay with her in the ICU. Not even on the regular floor."

"Let me see what I can do." Lydia hated that Nora was probably right. She didn't want to think of separating Deon from Emma. "In the meantime, since Deon *is* technically signed in as a patient, why don't you order him a breakfast tray. And a lunch one."

Nora shook her head and shrugged in surrender, taking the phone from the clerk. Lydia moved on to her next patient, but couldn't resist a quick peek at Deon and Emma as she passed their curtained space. Deon was curled up in the hospital bed with his grandmother, reading Harry Potter to her as she patted his shoulder in encouragement.

Maria, Lydia's mother, would never have allowed anyone to take Lydia away from her. Lydia closed the curtain and drew in a deep breath. The scent of the hibiscus tea Maria brewed whenever she found a client willing to pay for her "psychic" services wafted through Lydia's mind. She could almost imagine the feeling of Maria's hand rubbing the back of her neck, soothing her tension and fears.

If only it could be that easy . . .

Alarm bells shrieked from one of the telemetry beds across the hall. "Dr. Fiore!" a nurse called out. "We need you."

NORA HALLORAN JUGGLED NONSTOP PHONE calls, a waiting room stacked with patients, the cops now camped out with Mr. Crackhead—aka John "It Ain't None of Your Damn Business" Doe—in Exam Four, the acute coronary syndrome in telemetry, and the three admits waiting for beds upstairs. Kind of slow for a Thursday morning.

Best of all, there hadn't been any traumas—which meant no trauma surgeons, including her ex-almost-fiancé, Seth Cochran, who was a fourth-year surgical resident doing his trauma rotation. Things were still awkward, though to tell the truth, awkward was an improvement after her initial meltdown when she'd found Seth cheating on her.

"Hey, Nora," Elise Avery called as she restocked her flight bag from the medication room behind the nurses' station. "Got a minute?"

Nora nodded, hung up from the permanent hold sixth-floor med/surg had put her on, handed a stack of labs to the desk clerk, asked him to page the nursing supervisor to expedite the patients waiting for admission, and steered a lost OB-GYN intern in the right direction before joining Elise. "What's up?"

Elise raked her blond hair back from her eyes. A sure sign she was upset—usually Elise looked like she just stepped from the pages of a fashion magazine: tall, blond, and perfect.

"I'm not sure, just a feeling I have, but . . ."

It also wasn't like the flight nurse to hesitate. Elise had definite opinions on just about anything and usually wasn't afraid to speak up.

"That girl this morning, the neuro case," Elise began again, "Tracey Parker?"

Nora didn't know the girl's name, but she remembered the case. "Lucas Stone is doing an MRI-angio on her right now. Said maybe it was a thalamic stroke. But he didn't seem too certain."

Another weird thing about the Tracey Parker case—first Elise and Lydia Fiore were puzzled, and now Lucas. Elise and Lydia were both smart, but Lucas was a bona fide genius.

"It's Lucas Stone I'm worried about." Elise's voice sounded more certain. And more than a touch hostile.

"Lucas?" Nora leaned against the counter, crossing her arms in front of her, waiting for Elise to air her grievance. As charge nurse, she'd heard many a complaint about doctors, but Lucas?

The man couldn't hurt a fly—literally. Every August he would tear down the adhesive fly strips the maintenance guys hung in the ambulance bay, proclaiming them cruel and unjust. Strange behavior for a man who washed his hands a hundred times a day or more—even if he hadn't touched a patient. But that was Lucas.

"Why are you worried about Lucas?" she asked Elise.

"Back in July, I brought in another patient, similar symptoms to Tracey. Stone was her doctor. She died the next day."

"I remember her. Becky something—"

"Sanborn. Becky Sanborn."

"Right. I was in the ICU when she died. Lucas worked his butt off trying to save her." Nora's cheeks grew warm—that had been the same day she'd found Seth in the call rooms upstairs, in bed with another woman. Something everyone in the hospital was still talking about.

"Maybe." Elise zipped her bag closed, the sound tearing through the air. "But there was another girl, Michelle Halliday, with the same weird symptoms a few weeks ago. Another patient of Stone's. And she also died within a day of his admitting her."

Elise paused, leaning her weight on the bulky transport bag between them, jutting her chin forward. "For no good reason, Nora. For no good reason, they both died."

FOUR

Thursday, 8:49 A.M.

AMANDA WATCHED THEIR PATIENT THROUGH the thick glass of the MRI suite while Lucas juggled the phone and the computer, rapping on the monitor screen with impatience whenever he needed the radiologist's attention.

While the rest of the hospital attempted to project a bright and cheerful atmosphere, the radiology department seemed to take pride in providing its suites of rooms with the least amount of illumination possible. Every time she came here, Amanda felt as if she were entering a different realm, one made up of small, dark, enclosed caverns. No wonder Gina called radiologists vampires, saying they were allergic to sunlight and came out only at night—or to play golf.

"What's that?" Lucas pointed to a minuscule speck of white that looked like a stray flake of dandruff clinging to the monitor. "In the thalamus?"

The radiologist huffed at Lucas's intrusion into his carefully scheduled workday and scrolled back and forth, zooming in. "Nothing. Just a ditzle, a movement artifact."

Lucas leaned forward, squinting, still holding the phone to one ear. He took control of the computer and rotated the image. "Hmm. Okay, I guess. I can't find it on any of the other cuts."

He slumped back and focused on the phone. "It's about time," he snapped into the receiver, making Amanda—and, she was certain, the person on the other end of the line—wince. "I want a continuous EEG, nerve conduction velocity, and EMG all waiting for me when we get up to the ICU. I don't care if the tech is working with Hansen in the clinic today. Get me the machines, I'll run the damn things myself."

He hung up, dialing a new number as Amanda's cell phone blurted out a tinny rendition of "Dixie." Damn, Gina had reprogrammed her ringtones again. Amanda grabbed it, answering the call simply to shut off the annoying music. Lucas, the radiologist, and the tech all swiveled to stare at her. Her cheeks warmed with a flush that turned scorching when her mother's voice greeted her.

"What time will you be here on Saturday?" Amelia Mason's dulcet tones sang out. "The earlier the better, I'll need help with the icebox cookies and thought you could bake the red velvet cake. Plus the china will need cleaning, and—"

"Mama, this isn't a good time. I'm with a patient." Amanda turned to the corner, wishing she could crawl through the drywall and vanish. The MRI suite was too small to escape the attention of the others—there were only two chairs at the console and scant room behind them. On the other side of the thick glass wall, the scanner filled the room like a great gray whale, ready to swallow anything that came within range. It clanked and boomed, making the walls and floors shake.

"You're always with a patient. Never any time for your own flesh and blood anymore. Well, this is an emergency too, Amanda. Your family needs you."

Amanda frowned, trying to piece together what her

mother was talking about. Mama always assumed other people were as involved with her life as she was herself—and if not, they'd best hurry and catch up, 'cuz the train wasn't stopping. "Are you talking about the wedding shower? I already told you I can't come home for it."

Home was a fourteen-hour drive away, a small town on the coast just south of Beaufort, South Carolina. There was no way she could make it there and back just to attend a silly bridal shower.

"Of course you can. Andy's your last brother to get married, you have to be there."

"Why? Andy won't." Andy, her father, and her two oldest brothers were all going on their annual hunting trip—three days shacked up in a remote cabin, drinking beer, and telling dirty stories.

"All the more reason why you need to come. I can't do this by myself. Lord knows I've tried, but the honest truth of the matter is that I'm not as young as I used to be. I think I spoiled all you children, you expect I can perform miracles . . ."

Amanda turned back to the monitor, watching her patient's vital signs as her mother droned on. Mama could teach a doctoral-level class in guilt, but distance helped diminish its effect on Amanda.

"Mama, I'm sorry. We'll talk about this later. I really need to go."

"Amanda Camille Mason, whatever has happened to your manners? You do not speak to your own mother that way. We need to discuss this now."

"Good-bye, Mama." She flipped the phone shut, shoving it deep into her lab jacket pocket. Guilt trickled through her and she knew she'd regret her actions, probably end up driving all night Friday to make it home for the bridal shower from hell and even then wouldn't receive absolution.

The boys would be boys, could get away with anything short of mass murder, but a lady—well, according to

Amelia, her only daughter, Amanda, had little hope of ever becoming a lady. Even less now that she'd moved away from home and decided to embark on a career instead of settling down and giving her parents more grandchildren like a dutiful daughter should. Amanda tried to focus on her patient, shaking her mind free from her mother's recriminations, as clinging and invasive as kudzu.

Lucas had swiveled back to the computer screen, peering past the radiologist, the phone wedged between his ear and shoulder. "No leakage at all, no bleed, no clots."

The radiologist smirked. "Sorry, Stone. Looks like you wasted your time. Her brain is perfectly normal."

"Take a quick look at her cervical spine and neck for me. Include the thymus."

"I have patients waiting—"

"Are *they* paralyzed, trying their best to die?"

Everyone in the control room stared at Lucas. He hung up the phone, rubbed a hand over his face, and took a deep breath. "Look, I know you're busy, but it will save you time to do it now instead of me bringing her back later."

The radiologist scowled, seeing his ten o'clock tee time vanishing with Lucas's implied threat, and nodded. "Okay, we'll need to recalibrate."

"She doing okay?" Lucas asked Amanda without looking at her, his eyes focused past her to what little of the patient they could see.

"Vitals are stable, no sign that she's waking up." Given the terrific noise banging around inside the MRI machine, that meant the drugs had worked. Amanda shuddered, hoping they kept working. To be trapped in your own body, alone, unable to speak—or scream. . . .

"When we get upstairs to the ICU I'll need to wake her."

"Why? You can't extubate her," Amanda protested. "Not until she regains her reflexes. Why would you let her wake up? It's cruel."

"She has sudden onset of general paralysis preceded

by difficulty swallowing and speaking. We've ruled out anatomic causes; so far her labs show no sign of any infection or toxic reaction. Even her spinal tap was normal. What's left on our differential diagnosis?"

"Rabies, botulism, Miller Fisher variant of GBS," Jim Lazarov said from behind Amanda. She whirled around.

How the hell did he do that, always sneaking up on her? He reminded her of Andy, her youngest older brother and chief tormentor—he was constantly jumping out at her, scaring her, calling her a baby if she told anyone.

At least Jim didn't throw clumps of Spanish moss, riddled with spiders and chiggers, in her face. Instead he flung her own research at her—straight from the admission note she'd dictated before they left the ER.

Lucas nodded in approval. "Anything else?" he asked Amanda, obviously expecting more from her.

Like what? Jim had used everything she knew—unless . . . she thought back to what Lucas had said earlier. Difficulty swallowing and speaking followed by generalized weakness. And he'd forced the radiologist to examine Tracey's neck.

"Myasthenia gravis?" she ventured.

"No way," Jim scoffed, leaning on the console between her and Lucas. "The onset was too sudden and generalized."

"She's right. It can happen. Rarely." Lucas ignored the tug of war between Jim and Amanda, focusing instead on Tracey's form beyond the glass. "It will take days to get antibody results back. If the EMG and nerve conduction are consistent with myasthenia, I'll have to risk it."

"A Tensilon challenge? Cool." Jim was practically drooling.

"She'll need to be awake when you give her the Tensilon," Amanda argued. "And it will only work if she does have myasthenia gravis."

"Hence the name, 'challenge,'" Jim put in.

"But if it doesn't work, she'll still be paralyzed. And

awake." A sudden shudder raced up Amanda's spine. Ghosts waltzing on her grave, they'd say back home. She glanced into the darkened room. Tracey had been repositioned for the neck scan; now only her naked feet could be seen, the rest of her body sealed into the machine.

Like a body in a coffin.

Amanda's stomach felt empty, as if it had been turned inside out. Andy had once locked her inside an attic trunk. How much worse to experience that feeling of being buried alive for real? "Isn't there something else we can try first?"

"Find me something and I'll do it," Lucas replied grimly.

Jim smirked, happy about adding a new procedure to his repertoire with the Tensilon challenge. Amanda wanted to wipe the grin off his face almost as much as she wanted to help her patient. She thought about another patient she and Jim had shared during their ER rotation. Another young, healthy woman with strange neurological symptoms. Myoclonic movements, numbness, weakness that appeared and disappeared without warning.

Symptoms frighteningly similar to the ones Amanda herself had exhibited on occasion. *But not lately,* she reminded herself, looking down at her own feet as if verifying that they weren't twitching. *Not for weeks.*

"What about Becky Sanborn? Are all the results from her autopsy back?" She should have recalled that case earlier. The gross examination of Becky's body hadn't revealed a diagnosis, but often tissue analysis took longer to complete.

"Who's Becky Sanborn?" Jim asked.

"You know," Amanda told him. "Our patient with the strange paralysis. From this summer?"

He glared at her, remembering. Jim still blamed Amanda for "poaching" Becky's case—which was totally unfair; she'd just been in the right place at the right time. "The college girl? Oh yeah, I remember now. She died?"

"Yes." Lucas grimaced. He straightened and turned to them. "You two go track down Becky Sanborn's path results. All of them—no excuses about work backlogs or whatever else the pathologists come up with. And go through her chart, compare it to Tracey's. Question everything, question everyone who knew these girls. Find me something to work with."

"Certainly, Dr. Stone," Jim said. "We'll get right on it."

Amanda knew what *that* meant. She would do all the work and Jim would take all the credit. She gathered her notes, glancing one last time through the window at Tracey.

"This is a fascinating case, Dr. Stone." Jim put the finishing touches on his boot-licking. "I'd love to write it up for the *Annals*."

He threw his shoulders back, obviously excited by the prospect. Amanda wasn't sure if it was the potential publishing credit or the opportunity to avoid scut work in the ER that was more enticing to the intern.

"Don't you have patients waiting in the ER?" she said to him.

Jim merely smiled at her—a smile that was more a leer than anything, revealing his too-white-to-be-natural teeth. "I'm on neurology this month, just like you."

Great. Not only was she doomed to spend the month with Lucas Stone, who seemed unable to remember her name, she now had to deal with Jim "I Love to Use and Abuse Scut-Monkeys" Lazarov.

"Guess you'd better get to work, Amanda," he said, obviously relishing his role as her "boss." "Why don't you start down in pathology? I'll let you know if anything exciting happens with our patient."

Relegating her to the musty basement and even mustier pathologists—they all seemed dried out or pickled from inhaling too much formalin—while Jim got to do all the exciting stuff.

The MRI started up again, quaking the floor beneath them. Amanda glanced through the window. The machine had swallowed Tracey whole. This wasn't a competition. She didn't care if she had to do all the work and give Jim all the credit—which given his track record was exactly what would happen. It was all meaningless unless they discovered what was killing their patient.

FIVE

Thursday, 8:57 A.M.

"ELISE, YOU CAN'T BE ACCUSING LUCAS STONE of deliberately hurting his patients?" Nora's head ached at the thought, the very idea of a doctor doing something like that. *Any* doctor. But Lucas Stone? Never.

Besides, Lucas was a friend—well, technically he'd been Seth's best friend—but he and Nora had grown close while Lucas was struggling through his divorce. Who inherited the friends after you found your boyfriend sleeping with someone else, anyway? "I can't believe it."

Elise looked serious, crow's feet bracketing her eyes in an otherwise flawless face. Much like Nora, Elise took anything that affected her patients personally. "I don't know that it's deliberate."

"Glad to see you're keeping an open mind before accusing a doctor of being a serial killer." Nora glanced through the window in the closed door, making sure no one at the nurses' station was within hearing distance. "Get serious. We're talking about Lucas Stone. Not some stranger lurking in the shadows."

"All I know is that I reviewed the charts and there's no reason why these two girls died."

"What was the official COD?"

"The only thing listed under cause of death was cardiopulmonary arrest, origin indeterminate."

Pathologists were second only to radiologists when it came to the fine art of doublespeak. Nora tugged her fingers through her hair, yanking on her scalp as if the pain might counteract the headache squeezing her brain in a vise. "What do you want me to do?"

"I thought maybe you could pull the charts for the monthly ER QA review. See what a physician, an objective pair of eyes, says."

Part of being charge nurse was to collect charts for a quality assurance review by an ER attending. "This month's QA attending is Lydia Fiore. She's as suspicious and paranoid as they come—if there is something going on, she's the one to find it."

Elise's face relaxed slightly. "Good. In the meantime, I'll try my best to keep an eye on Tracey Parker."

"I'll talk to Amanda, she's on neuro this month. Maybe she can help."

"Isn't she only a medical student?"

"She's good. You can trust her." Nora scowled as the trauma radio on her belt squawked. Motor vehicle collision, multiple casualties. "I've got to go."

"T-BONE MVC, INTRUSION INTO THE PASSENGER side, adult driver, restrained, two kids aged seven months and two years in car seats," Lydia's trauma radio squawked, the sounds of sirens almost drowning out Med Seven's report. "We've got the baby; her car seat flipped, trapping her between it and the front seat. Unresponsive, initial respiratory arrest but heart rate of one sixty-two, we're tubing her, no IV yet. No obvious injuries except petechial hemorrhaging around the face. ETA two minutes."

Lydia left her sore throat and muscle aches—a guy in his twenties who wanted a note to skip work—and sped down the hall to the resuscitation rooms, where she was glad to find Nora already there dividing the troops.

"We've got three coming in, one adult, two peds, at least one critical," Nora was telling the staff as they set up the first room with pediatric equipment.

Kids were always tricky. They came in so many sizes and shapes that it was hard to predict ahead of time what you would need. And this baby sounded bad off—unresponsive in an infant often meant very bad things, usually involving brain damage.

"Get me the cooling equipment from the NICU," Lydia ordered one of the nurses. "And see if the PICU has anyone they can spare."

Rapid hypothermia had been shown to help adult stroke patients with hypoxic brain injury as well as newborns. From Med Seven's report, it sounded as if her patient had been asphyxiated when she was pinned inside the car—making her a good candidate to try the protocol.

If there was a protocol. Which there wasn't, not for kids beyond the newborn period and not for traumatic asphyxiation.

Nora was quick to point that out. "There's no standard of care, and it's experimental. How are you going to get consent?"

"Not even sure if we'll use it," Lydia said, arranging her airway equipment and inserting the pediatric needle into the EZ-IO drill. Kids were notoriously hard to get rapid venous access in, so the intraosseous device provided a quick alternative by using the bone marrow cavity instead. "I like to have options."

"Options? That's no option, it's a million-to-one long shot."

Lydia didn't wait to hear any more from the by-the-book charge nurse. Her two minutes were almost up. She strode down the hall, trauma gown billowing behind her, to meet Med Seven in the ambulance bay.

Sirens sliced through the crisp October morning before the red flashing lights appeared. They hadn't had time to call in any more of a report, but she wasn't surprised—in a scoop-and-run situation like this, the medics would be scrambling to assess and treat simultaneously.

There was a screech of brakes and the *beep-beep-beep* of the ambulance backing up. Lydia jumped forward, opening the rear door as soon as it stopped. She was pleased to see that two of her favorite medics, Gecko and Ollie, were working today. And not so pleased when she realized that they were alone except for the firefighter they'd drafted to drive. Gina Freeman, one of her residents, had been scheduled to work with them today.

Lydia pushed aside questions about her errant emergency medicine resident and focused on her patient, helping them lift the stretcher out. Scott Dellano—aka Gecko, nicknamed that for his rock-climbing skills—was bagging oxygen into the baby through an endotracheal tube. There was no IV, but she could see that they'd tried. As the new medical director for Pittsburgh's EMS, she wanted to get the EZ-IO drills onto all the units, but they were still working on funding.

"Idiot father put her car seat in the front seat and didn't secure it," Ollie was saying as he pushed the gurney. He was a rotund man who usually had a perpetually sunny disposition—except when his patients were kids. "When the front seat gave, she flipped forward, choked on the car seat straps, and was pinned upside down until we could extricate her."

"She was apneic and bradycardic when we got her out," Gecko continued the report. "Heart rate came up with bagging, we never had to start CPR, and I tubed her with a four-point-oh uncuffed tube. Couldn't get a BP on her, heart rate has been steady in the one-sixties, pulse ox ninety-four percent."

Lydia flicked her fingers against the bottom of the baby's naked foot. No response. Despite the good oxygen level, the baby's color was ashen, making the dark purple-red dots of petechiae, the broken blood vessels on her face, stand out like flecks of red paint splattered against porcelain.

"Good work, guys," she told them as they whisked the stretcher into the trauma room. She meant it—another minute down and the baby probably would have been in full arrest. "Any word on the other victims?"

"Should be right behind us. The dad seemed okay, the older sister was screaming but I didn't see or hear what was going on with her."

They moved the baby onto the ER's bed and quickly attached her to their monitors. "Get me c-spine, chest, abdomen, a trauma panel, and blood gas," Lydia ordered.

The neonatal cooling blanket and chilled saline were ready and waiting just as she'd instructed earlier. *Might just come to that*, she thought as she quickly drilled an intraosseous into the girl's leg bone and started fluids running directly into the marrow cavity. The baby didn't flinch or respond in any way to their interventions. *Not good.*

Her team worked efficiently, moving in and around the patient in well-rehearsed steps as the X-ray techs arrived and shot their films, lab techs hustled away with their specimens, and Lydia completed a head-to-toe examination. No signs of anything except the traumatic asphyxiation.

The X rays confirmed her findings. As did the blood work. Which meant everything they did to keep this baby alive might be in vain if her brain was already dead or dying.

"We're going to cool her," Lydia announced to the crowd. "Someone warn the peds ICU—but we're not going to wait for them, we'll start down here. Set me up for a femoral central line; in the meantime, switch the IO to chilled saline, and let's get a core temperature probe in her and the cooling blanket around her head."

To their credit, none of her team hesitated even though they all knew she was flying blind. But they also knew that without the unorthodox treatment the outcome would be worse than dismal.

Lydia ran her fingers through the baby's sparse curls before turning to snap on a fresh pair of sterile gloves and prepping the groin area for the large intravenous line that would carry the chilled saline directly into the baby's heart.

She didn't look up as Seth Cochran, the trauma resident on call, entered. Nora stiffened beside her, clenching the bed rail.

"You guys okay?" Seth asked, stopping a few feet away from the bed. Or more likely, a few feet away from Nora. "I've got the dad and sister. Sister has a few bumps and bruises, her car seat saved her from worse. Dad's asking to see this one."

"Do we even have a name yet?"

"Alice Kazmierko," Nora supplied. "I'll call social services to help with dad."

"You guys clear him already?" Lydia asked Seth.

"Yeah, he got away without a scratch. Not too happy about his police escort, though."

"DUI?" Drivers without significant injuries in a serious crash like this were often intoxicated, the drugs or alcohol relaxing their bodies on impact.

"Definitely," Seth said. "Cops say the accident was his fault, ran a red. Refused a Breathalyzer, we're still waiting on a BAC. Trust me, he's loaded. My money's on at least a point two-oh."

Lydia didn't have to look to know that Nora would be frowning at Seth for joking about a patient's labs. Nora was a no-nonsense charge nurse, but she was only in her midtwenties, still in that earnest, play-by-the-rules stage of her career—and her life. Lydia had outgrown that stage in her early teens when, after trying desperately to fit in with the alien world of foster "family life" her mother's death had thrust her into, she'd learned that playing by the rules was strictly for suckers—one of the few things that Maria, her fake-psychic con artist mother, had been right about.

Lydia finished the delicate job of threading the catheter into Alice's femoral vein. Vitals were stable, peds were on their way, not much more she could do down here. It was up to time, and the resilience of an infant brain, to decide Alice's fate.

Well, maybe there was one more thing. Her back to everyone else as she stripped her blood-stained gloves free and washed her hands, Lydia sent a quick prayer winging into the ether. Not exactly a prayer, more like a wish, a hope. Not that she was convinced that there was Anyone up there listening—or Who gave a damn. But it never hurt to hedge your bets—something she'd learned on her own since moving here to Pittsburgh and starting her life over.

The peds ICU fellow arrived, an entourage of residents following him. "We'll take it from here," he said dismissively, his skepticism of Lydia's use of the cerebral cooling protocol evident. "You heroes have done enough already. Don't you realize it only makes it harder for the family to let go when we have to declare them brain dead upstairs? It wastes our resources."

"Don't rule her out yet."

He shrugged his answer. "We'll see. But I wouldn't bet on it."

Hah. People had bet against Lydia her entire life and look where she'd ended up. But she said nothing to the ICU fellow; instead she merely smiled at baby Alice, ignoring the tubes sticking out of her mouth and nose, the IV lines, the monitor leads, the tape sealing her eyes shut. It was a miracle Alice had made it this far alive; Lydia wasn't going to rule out anything.

She stepped outside to find a man charging down the hall. "Where's my baby?" he was shouting. "You can't keep me from her."

Nora and Seth joined her outside the trauma room, Nora standing on Lydia's opposite side as if she needed a buffer between herself and Seth.

Lydia squared off, stopping the man from entering the resuscitation room. "Are you Mr. Kazmierko?"

"Yes. Where's Alice? I want to see my baby."

"The pediatric intensive care doctors are with her now, Mr. Kazmierko. We'll get you inside as soon as possible. In the meantime, let's go down the hall to a private room where I can tell you what's going on with Alice."

He blinked rapidly as if warding off her words, then tried to push his way past her. "Like hell. I'm not going anywhere until I see my baby."

Lydia was close enough that she could smell the alcohol on his breath. Southern Comfort. She hated that stuff—it had been one of her mother's favorite "indulgences."

"You need to calm down first, Mr. Kazmierko." She understood his need to see his daughter, but she couldn't let him near Alice if he was so out of control that he might interfere with her care.

"Don't you tell me to calm down! That's my baby in there. You let me in there now, you bitch!"

His fist shot out in a lumbering right hook that would have caught Lydia square in the jaw if she hadn't seen it coming and stepped aside, pushing Nora out of the way. Kazmierko stumbled forward, the momentum of his missed punch carrying him off balance. A uniformed cop appeared down the hall, jogging toward them.

Seth, his own fists up, made an easy target as the cop plowed into Kazmierko from behind. All three men fell to the floor, a mass of flailing limbs until the cop restrained Kazmierko and hauled him to his feet.

"You okay, doc?" he asked Seth, who was sitting with his back to the wall, massaging his chin.

"Yeah, just bit my tongue."

Nora was beside him in a flash, helping him up, offering a gauze 4×4 to wipe the blood from his lip.

"C'mon," the policeman said, handcuffing the distraught father, now sobbing incoherently. "Looks like visiting hours are over for you."

Nora and Seth walked off together, presumably to get the surgeon an ice pack. Lydia watched them go—she didn't understand what was going on with them. She'd heard the rumors, but she wasn't one to put much stake in gossip. Seth wrapped his arm around Nora's shoulders as they walked. Nora shrugged him away, spinning on her heel, and glaring at him.

Clearly, whatever had come between them wasn't going to be healed anytime soon.

"WHAT THE HELL WERE YOU THINKING, JUMPing in front of him like that?" Nora asked as she sat Seth onto an exam table and mopped the blood from his mouth. He flinched when she touched his lip. It was already swelling but hadn't split.

"What was I supposed to do? You could have gotten hurt."

"The guy was stumbling drunk, blind with fear about his daughter. Besides, Lydia and I can handle ourselves."

He wrapped his hand around her wrist, keeping her at bay before she could touch his lip again. "I worry about you."

That was all he said. Just four words. Four words that almost broke her resolve.

Her arm trembled in his grasp. She yanked free from him and rummaged through the supply cabinet, searching for some gel foam for his cut.

She swallowed hard. "Stop it, Seth. You have no right to worry about me. Not anymore."

His sigh circled through the room. "You're right."

The thud of his jumping down from the exam table hammered through her. She held her breath, surprised by how disappointed she was when his footsteps headed toward the door. She turned around, holding out the small packet of gel foam as if it were a peace offering.

He stopped and took it from her, their fingers brushing. "Thanks."

"Please, Seth—" She stopped. She *wanted* to forgive him, to start over. She *needed* to end this, move on. "Don't send me any more flowers."

He froze, mouth open as he held the tiny strip of gel foam against the edge of his tongue, stanching the bleeding. His eyes darkened, a V-shaped frown forming on his forehead.

"Flowers?" He removed the gel foam and spat out a glob of blood and saliva into the piece of gauze he held. "Who's sending you flowers?"

GECKO AND OLLIE APPEARED, COFFEE CUPS IN their hands, on their way out to the ambulance bay. "Jeez, Lydia, whatcha do now?" Gecko teased her as the cops dragged Kazmierko, still screaming, out to their car. "Start another riot?"

"Where the hell is Gina?" she asked, ignoring their gibes. Both paramedics had been with Gina in July when she'd been caught in the riot and drive-by shooting—which was why Lydia had assigned Gina to them for her ride-alongs. She thought the emergency medicine resident would feel safer with the men who had gone through the experience with her.

Obviously she was wrong.

Ollie shrugged. "Dunno. She never calls, never writes." He heaved a melodramatic sigh. "What's a guy to do?"

"Seriously, doc, is she okay?" Gecko put in. "I tried to call her, but she doesn't answer."

"Can't be that she doesn't want to work with us. We're the freaking A-Team."

"Don't worry, guys, I'll look into it. Gina will be out

on the streets tomorrow if I have to put her in four-point restraints and tie her to a stretcher."

Both men laughed. "As long as you let us watch." They continued back out to their ambulance.

The doors swished shut behind them. Lydia knew it wasn't easy facing the streets again after being shot at, but Gina couldn't avoid it forever. Although, in her short acquaintance with Gina, Lydia had noticed that avoidance and denial seemed to be the resident's most enduring qualities.

What the hell is going on with Gina? Lydia wondered as she made her way back to the nurses' station.

SIX

Thursday, 10:11 A.M.

GINA WAS PROUD SHE'D ACTUALLY GOTTEN HERself cleaned up, changed, and functioning. If you could call devouring everything on Eat'n Park's breakfast menu functioning.

A brainless steam shovel, hauling in all the food she could, that was her. Shame only fueled her cravings. As if food could actually fill any of the emptiness.

She knew better, had fought this battle before and won—but all that just made it worse. As she twisted her fork into a mound of French toast, ignoring the maple syrup and powdered sugar dripping down her chin, her phone rang again.

Not rang. Sang. The opening notes of Bette Midler's "The Rose"—the pun was so obvious and the song so inappropriate that it made her smile every time. Too bad her mother never heard the ringtone Gina had assigned to her.

LaRose Freeman would never have understood the joke, much less find it amusing. LaRose found very little in this world amusing—though she knew how to smile on cue. When Gina was young, she'd read an Isaac Asimov story about androids and had spent months trying to prove that her mother wasn't one. Some days she still wasn't sure. She couldn't remember the last time she'd heard her mother actually laugh.

Gina spat out her mouthful into a napkin, swiped the syrup from her mouth, and answered her phone. You did *not* let LaRose Freeman go to voice mail. Not if you knew what was good for you.

"Good morning," she sang out, wincing at her artificial cheerfulness. Surely even LaRose wouldn't buy it?

"*Buon giorno*, pet," LaRose's equally saccharine tones replied. "I think it's time for a mother-daughter trip to Antonio's."

Gina squeezed her eyes shut. Play hooky for a few hours and already Fate was smiting her. Not that she wouldn't love to spend a few hours being pampered in the exclusive Shadyside salon. But when those hours would also put her under LaRose's scrutiny, Gina's every gesture, every word reported back to her father? Fate wasn't playing fair.

"I do happen to be off today." She managed to get the words out without sighing.

"Wonderful. I'm here with Antonio already, I'll tell him you'll be right over." LaRose hung up without waiting for confirmation—after all, who could say no to her? Certainly not her daughter.

Gina pocketed the phone, picked up her fork and knife once more, and dove back into the stack of French toast, setting a new world record for speed eating. Her throat hurt from swallowing so fast and furious, she didn't taste a bite, and her stomach rebelled, contracting like a rubber band stretched too far and snapping back.

None of that mattered. Five minutes later it would all be flushed down a toilet, forgotten. What mattered was that for these miraculous few moments, Gina was in control.

* * *

AMANDA'S PAGER WENT OFF BEFORE SHE COULD leave the MRI suite to start collecting information on Becky Sanborn from the pathologists. "It's the ER. Again."

"Probably another consult," Lucas mumbled, focused on the monitor revealing thin slices of Tracey's neck tissues. "You go ahead; Jim can run to pathology and get those results."

Jim scowled, and she resisted the urge to wrinkle her nose at him. She turned to leave, then stopped as she glanced at the clock above Lucas's head. Ten-twenty already?

"Dr. Stone, I have a doctor's appointment at eleven. Is it okay if I leave as soon as I see what the ER wants?"

Lucas jerked his head up, squinting his blue-gray eyes as if examining a particularly nasty microbe. Those damn eyes of his that saw everything.

Including an embarrassing dizzy spell she'd had during the summer. It was nothing, mere fatigue, a typical med student's poor diet and lack of sleep, but Lucas had insisted that she get further evaluation—despite the fact that her own doctor, Dr. Nelson, had found nothing wrong with her.

She'd signed up for this neurology elective months ago and had been thankful at the time that Lucas wasn't assigned to be her attending. No way she could spend a month with him watching, waiting for her to stumble or drop something, diagnosing a devastating disease behind every little tremble or quake. Only she hadn't counted on his switching with Dr. Campbell.

"Something wrong?" Lucas glanced at Jim, who was listening with undisguised attention. At least he had the decency not to mention her so-called symptoms in front of Jim.

"No, of course not. It's just a routine checkup with Dr. Nelson. I'm in one of his research studies."

Lucas frowned, then looked away to turn his concentration on their patient. "Sure, whatever."

Jim, as usual, took the opportunity to pass off some of his work. "Hey, if you're headed over to the clinic, stop by pathology on your way. Check out Becky Sanborn's results."

She hadn't intended to go through the tunnels that connected the hospital buildings—the bowels of the hospital, rumbling with strange noises, alternating hot and cold, always muggy with the stench of mildew. She hated them, would much prefer to take the longer path outside around to the research tower.

But Jim was right, it would save time. And she felt possessive of Becky, didn't like the idea of Jim pawing through her life, even if it was just an examination of her pathology results.

The MRI resumed its scanning, a harsh thrumping noise only partially buffered by the thick walls. Lucas's attention was fixated on their patient. Amanda wished she could stay, make sure everything was okay with Tracey's scan, but she couldn't be in two places at once.

She closed the door behind her and glanced at her watch as her pager went off again, its high-pitched bleep bouncing off the tile walls and into her head. Make that three places at once.

She took off down the hall to the ER, the books and instruments crammed into her pockets thumping against her hips with every step.

LYDIA BANGED THE RECEIVER ONTO THE PHONE base. She couldn't get anyone to answer their pages today. Nothing more irritating—except maybe Gina going AWOL.

"Someone paged?" Amanda Mason asked, bouncing to the nurses' station with her sunny blond hair and chipper smile. Usually Lydia could handle Amanda's terminal cheerfulness, but today wasn't the day.

"Where's Gina and why isn't she answering her phone?"

Amanda did a double take and shoved her hands into the pockets of her short lab coat, threatening to dislodge several books, a reflex hammer, and a sheaf of papers. "She should be riding with Med Seven today. I think. Aren't you in charge of the EMS ride-alongs, Dr. Fiore?"

Lydia almost smiled at the "Dr. Fiore"—the formal politeness was as close to snippy as she'd ever seen Amanda. "Exactly why I'm trying to find your roommate. She didn't show for her ride-along."

Amanda shifted her weight, looking around her at the bustling ER as if searching for an escape. "Maybe Jerry knows. She was at his place last night. Been there a lot lately. You know, since . . ."

"Since the drive-by. Yeah, I know, I asked him already. Boyle thinks she made it to her ride-along and I'm not going to worry him. Why don't you try calling her, see if she answers?"

Lydia had hated lying to the detective—even though her mother had taught her that lying by omission and lying to the cops didn't count. Two of the many life lessons Maria had lived by that Lydia grew to despise. But what could you expect from a woman who could spin a new life story for both of them faster than a Popsicle melted in the L.A. heat?

Amanda pulled out her cell and dialed. "Gina? Hey, where are you?" Ahhh . . . the magic touch, or rather the magic Caller ID.

Lydia snatched the phone from Amanda's hand just in time to hear Gina's reply. "Wouldn't you like to know?"

"I would," Lydia said.

"Lydia, uh—" Gina sputtered into a coughing fit melodramatic enough to warrant a TB quarantine. "Sorry I couldn't make it to my ride-along today." Another coughing jag drowned out her words.

"Right," Lydia interrupted Gina's performance. "Just like the four shifts you switched last week. Let me make this easy for you, Gina. Either you show up with a note from a physician—a physician I can call and discuss the intricacies of whatever debilitating disease you have—before I finish my shift, or I'm dropping you from the program until you get counseling."

"You can't—you have no right—"

"Can and will. I'm off at seven." Lydia snapped the phone shut without waiting for Gina's answer. She handed it back to Amanda, who stared at her gape-jawed.

"You hung up on Gina."

"Yep." Lydia punched up a patient's lab results on the computer.

"And you told her what to do—Gina hates that."

Lydia leaned back in her chair, frustrated by the less-than-helpful lab results as well as her less-than-cooperative emergency medicine resident. "If Gina plans to keep her residency slot, she'd better get used to it." She glanced up at Amanda again. "Speaking of which—why did you let Jim do that intubation this morning?"

"He asked first. It was the polite thing to do."

"Polite has no place in the ER. You need to grab every procedure you can."

"It's not a competition."

"It is. Not between you and Jim, between you and experience. I once worked with a medic in L.A. who used to say experience is the best university around—except the tuition is mighty high."

Amanda's lips thinned as she rocked back on her heels, considering. "Still, there's no need to be rude."

"So that's all it was? I thought maybe there was something else going on. You didn't seem so happy when Lucas Stone showed up instead of Dr. Campbell." Lydia's instincts were rewarded when Amanda's face flushed and her fidgeting increased.

"Well now, I don't know what gave you that impression."

"Oh, you don't, do you?" Lydia stared at Amanda, even though the medical student suddenly seemed fascinated by the linoleum.

"Didn't you ever feel like that around an attending? Wanting so hard to do everything right and instead ending up all thumbs?"

Lydia smiled. She vaguely remembered the feeling—not that she'd ever admit it. "Just calm down and focus on your patients, and you'll be fine," she counseled. "Oh, and how's the baby doing?"

"What baby?"

"The MVA entrapment. Seven-month-old. I started a therapeutic hypothermia protocol on her. Didn't the PICU call you yet for a neuro consult?"

Amanda's pager went off. She squinted at the readout. "This is them now. Guess I'd better run."

Lydia watched as the med student sped away, her long blond hair escaping its barrettes. Amanda was a smart student, very good with patients, but she needed to learn how to prioritize and handle the demands of the job.

"Dr. Fiore," Nora said, leaning across the counter to get her attention. "We need to talk. Now. In private, please."

Talk about handling demands. Nora had been in a snit since the trauma this morning. And it never paid to have a charge nurse aggravated with you. Never.

SEVEN

Thursday, 10:34 A.M.

GINA HUNG UP HER PHONE AND SHOVED IT back into her pocket without looking. Normally she'd be fuming about Lydia's imperative tone and abruptness, but today she had something else to occupy her attention.

Like picking out exactly the right shade of nail polish guaranteed to make her mother twist her face into that look that revealed all of her crinkles and wrinkles. Hmmm . . . that outrageous blood red from OPI should do the trick.

"That one?" LaRose said. "Really, Regina." Her voice dripped with disdain, but her face remained placid.

Gina slumped back, splashing water from the whirlpool her feet sat in. Botox had stolen so much of the fun from her life. She sipped at the pomegranate mimosa Antonio had supplied her with as soon as she arrived at the exclusive Shadyside salon. LaRose had a full day planned here; she was dressed in a gold robe that hugged her enviable curves.

People often suggested that Gina looked like a model—but LaRose far outshone Gina's beauty despite having crested fifty a few years ago. Even though Gina had worn her tightest skinny jeans, an off-the shoulder Vera Wang blouse that accentuated her décolletage, and her favorite Jimmy Choos, she felt like a frumpy suburban housewife next to LaRose.

"So, Mom"—LaRose hated being called "Mom" almost as much as Gina hated being called "Regina"—"what was so urgent?"

"Can't a mother simply enjoy a morning with her daughter?"

Uh, no. Not unless said mother was getting ready to try to take over said daughter's life. Again. "Is this about Jerry?"

"Now, Regina, you must understand your father's view on that. It's quite out of the question."

"No, it's not. I don't understand what you two have against Jerry." Her father, the great and mighty Moses Freeman, noted for his genius-level knowledge of the law and his take-no-prisoners approach to trials, had quickly vetoed Jerry's marriage proposal—which her mother had rushed to tell Gina, absolving herself of any responsibility.

"I would think that would be obvious." LaRose arched an eyebrow at the manicurist, who had slipped with the cuticle clipper.

"No, it's not. Not to me."

"This isn't the time or place." LaRose's tone said the subject was closed.

Gina didn't try to hide her smile. You'd think her mother would realize by now that Gina's one joy was in provoking her. Something Gina would never dare to try with Moses—any argument with him was a blood duel to the death, family or no.

"Surely it's not because Jerry is white," she blurted out loud enough to draw attention from the blue-haired matrons on either side of them.

"Regina! Lower your voice, please. Of course it has nothing to do with color. Your father doesn't approve because he feels that man—"

"His name is Jerry. Detective Gerald Boyle of the Pittsburgh Police Bureau's Major Crimes Squad."

"Exactly. I rest my case."

"You don't like Jerry because he's a cop? How can you say that?" Gina had spent the last decade of her life bringing home increasingly disreputable boyfriends—the street artist who used feces and trash for his masterpieces, the tattooed and well-pierced songwriter, the paranormal investigator who tried to resurrect a ghost in the family's Sewickley Heights mansion, and a handful of out-of-work, flat-out bums.

All that changed after she met Jerry. She'd had to swallow her pride, thinking her parents would embrace his all-American respectability. "Jerry's one of the good guys."

"I'm sure he is very good at his job," LaRose allowed, as if it were another strike against Jerry. "However, your father feels—and I agree—that anyone pursuing a career in law enforcement shows an innate lack of ambition. There's little opportunity for advancement—"

"He doesn't care about promotions or corner offices. He cares about getting criminals off the streets, about protecting—"

"I'm sure that's all very altruistic. But seriously, what kind of adult pursues such a low-paying job with long hours, high risk, not to mention the type of people he must associate with on a daily basis? It's juvenile."

Gina twisted in her chair, tearing her hand away from the manicurist. "Juvenile? You realize you also just described my job as well."

To her surprise, LaRose actually smiled. "That's exactly the reason why I wanted to speak to you." Her eyes were as wide as Botoxed lids would allow, sparkling with anticipation. "Your father has devised a wonderful exit strategy for you, Regina. By the end of the year you can leave Angels of Mercy and embark upon a real career, one that will give you the prestige and lifestyle you deserve."

NORA LED LYDIA INTO AN EMPTY EXAM ROOM and shut the door behind them. Lydia paced to the far end of the room, then whirled around. "If this is about Deon and his grandmother—"

Typical of Lydia, striking first. Best defense and all that.

"It's not," Nora said, although she made a mental note to call social services. "It's about the neuro case from this morning."

"Tracey Parker?" Lydia's stride broke. "Why all the cloak-and-dagger about a routine neuro case?"

"Because Elise Avery doesn't think her case is routine. And, after listening to her, I'm not so sure either." She couldn't believe she was even saying this much. It was all coincidental—it had to be. Lucas was an excellent physician. Sure, he'd been a bit moody, maybe even depressed since his divorce, but that was normal—he'd never let his emotions affect patient care.

"Why not?"

"Because Elise found two other cases similar to Tracey's. Both admitted, both deceased." She bit down, refusing to tell Lydia the rest of Elise's suspicions. She wanted Lydia to review the charts with an open mind, draw her own conclusions, not start a witch hunt.

"I don't remember any cases like Tracey's."

"You weren't the attending. But since you're in charge of QA this month, I thought I'd pull their charts."

"Definitely. Tracey's symptoms didn't make any sense; maybe with more information we can piece something together." Lydia's radio blared; the medics needed orders for a trauma patient. She walked past Nora, then paused before opening the door. "Can you get me copies of everything by the end of the shift?"

"Sure. How about if I bring them over to your place?" Nora would have liked nothing more than to have somewhere to go tonight.

After moving out of the town house she and Seth had shared, Nora had jumped at an opportunity to exchange some light nursing care for room and board, and she'd moved into the top floor of a house owned by a lawyer with MS. Despite her wheelchair, Mickey Cohen, the lawyer, was mostly self-sufficient—in fact, she needed so little help that Nora felt guilty for not paying rent—but she was wise enough to realize that having someone around was a good idea. And Nora found that having someone to talk to, eat with, just be there in the house had helped her avoid facing the emptiness of life without Seth. But now Mickey was out of town with her sister on a two-week cruise, leaving the house and Nora's nights vacant. "Unless you and Trey have plans?"

"Nothing special. Yeah, tonight works." Lydia opened the door and Nora followed her out.

"We still need to talk about Deon Grey," she reminded Lydia.

"I've got it covered," Lydia said without looking back. Her shoulder blades hunched together defensively, and Nora knew better than to pursue the subject.

While Lydia went to the med command phone, Nora tapped Jason, the desk clerk. "Page Tommy Z for me. We need him in the ER to evaluate a child for placement. Thanks."

Nora didn't know what Lydia had against asking for help. Didn't matter. Sooner or later she'd come to see the value of having friends and co-workers watching her back.

EIGHT

Thursday, 10:38 A.M.

AMANDA TREATED HERSELF TO AN ELEVATOR ride up to the PICU on the fourth floor. Not because she was tired or thought the elevator would be faster than the stairs. Rather, sandwiched in the corner between a man pushing an IV pole with one hand and fumbling his cigarettes back into his pants pocket with the other and a couple obviously on their way up to OB, it gave her a few minutes to feverishly search through her pocket guides.

None of them mentioned hypothermia as a treatment for hypoxia, but the newest guide had been published last year (which meant it was actually written at least two to three years ago). Forget about a protocol for a seven-month-old.

Her vision swam as the elevator lurched to a stop and she elbowed her way out. She was so very much in over her head, like walking through a marsh only to find the ground shifting beneath her and sucking her down. The kind of muddy marsh where alligators liked to hide in wait for their prey—that was Jim Lazarov with all those shiny teeth of his. World-class alligator on the prowl.

Good thing she knew a thing or two about alligators. If only she knew what in the hell she had to offer a little baby trying hard not to die.

The doors to the pediatric ICU swished open, discharging a smell reminiscent of her great-aunt Nellie's attic. Not dirty or moldy, but stale. As if even the air didn't dare move too much in fear of disturbing the children who lay within. There was a chemical aftertaste to the scent as well, a hint of alcohol and iodine, biting against the back of her throat.

Amanda stepped inside, and the doors slid shut again. Nurses and doctors hustled and bustled, no one running but no one moving slowly either. Neon lights of monitors cast strange glows on the reflective surfaces surrounding the children—all of whom appeared much too small for their beds. Parents slumped in rocking chairs, wearing the haunted expression of the sleepless and hopeful.

It was a place where miracles occur—and where those same miracles could fail, come crashing down to earth with shattering speed.

Avoiding anyone's eyes, especially any parents', Amanda walked to the nurses' station and retrieved her new patient's chart. Alice Kazmierko. Alice in Wonderland.

An alarm sounded across the room—muted compared to the noise in the ER, but loud enough to bring several people running. They gathered around a child, but not a baby, so at least she knew it wasn't her patient causing the panic. She took Alice's chart into the dictation room behind the nurses' station and began to read.

She hadn't gotten far when her pager bleeped. The medical ICU. She dialed the number, hoping Tracey Parker hadn't taken a turn for the worse. "Amanda Mason, someone paged."

"Tracey Parker's boyfriend is here and he'd like to talk to someone about her," the clerk answered.

Damn. Jim must have given the ICU Amanda's pager number. Like she needed more to take care of. She glanced at her watch. She was due at Dr. Nelson's in twenty minutes. "Right. Where's he at?"

"He's in the family room." The clerk hung up before Amanda could ask any more.

She left Alice's chart in the dictation station, hoping to return to it in a few minutes. It wasn't as if she had any answers for Tracey's boyfriend—and even if she did, she wasn't sure how much she was allowed to tell him. He wasn't a relative. And she wasn't a doctor—what if she told him the wrong thing?

Her shoulders hunched with additional worry, she walked across the hall to the family waiting area. When her father had his stroke last Christmas, Amanda had spent too many frustrating hours of waiting, crammed into a small room just like this one, with bright shiny holiday decorations all around, thinking about the worst that could happen.

She paused before entering the waiting room, not sure of exactly what to do. The clerk hadn't given her Tracey's boyfriend's name, and she hadn't thought to ask. She stepped inside and cleared her throat. A middle-aged couple sitting together on a love seat, holding hands, looked up, their faces tightening at the sight of her white coat.

"Blackman?" the man said, a weary croak in his voice.

"No. Sorry. I'm looking for the friends and family of Tracey Parker?"

The couple shook their heads and looked down. The room was in the shape of an L with a vending area around the corner. Chairs and love seats were scattered about; two TVs hung from opposite corners, dueling soap operas playing across their screens. She turned the corner to the vending machines and was surprised to see a short, stocky man with curly red hair and thickly muscled forearms bending to reach for a cup of coffee.

"Jared. What are you doing here?" He wore a dark blue hoodie over gray sweatpants with the Allegheny Rowing Association logo adorning both.

"Amanda. God, I'm glad it's you. How is she? What happened?" His fingers tightened on the foam cup in his hand as he strode toward her, anxiety radiating off him.

"Tracey Parker is your girlfriend?" Elise had said Tracey was a long-distance runner; Jared had mentioned his girlfriend training for a marathon.

Jared nodded, confirming Amanda's fears. "Her running partners called, said Tracey is here. Said they had to Lifeflight her." He paused as if waiting for her to fill in the blanks but then changed his mind and rushed on. "They won't let me see her, tell me anything—no one will tell me anything."

In an effort to look professional and knowledgeable, Amanda put her hands behind her back, using the motion to wipe her sweaty palms on her lab coat.

"Can you get me in to see her? What happened? When can she come home?"

His questions were making her dizzy, especially as she couldn't answer any of them. "We'll know more in a little while," she said, borrowing a line from Lydia. "In the meantime, can you tell me more about Tracey's medical history? Does she have any allergies to medication? Has she been sick lately?"

"Tracey? Sick? No way. She's about to run a marathon." He shook his head, appeared stunned at the idea.

"Does she take any medications?" She reverted to the typical med student litany of thorough history taking, relieved that her questions distracted him from asking about Tracey. "Even vitamins or over-the-counter?"

Again he started to shake his head, then stopped himself. "Oh. Yeah, she does have some stuff from the health food store. And she sees a doctor here every month. He has her on some kind of special pills."

"What kind?"

"I don't know—they're in a big brown bottle, the label just has a bunch of numbers and a bar code on it."

Sounded like a research protocol. With the medical

school and several research labs here at Angels, thousands of Pittsburghers were recruited each year to participate in studies. Even Amanda was on one—the two hundred dollars a month it paid was her food budget. "Do you know which doctor she saw?"

He shook his head again, noticed the coffee cup in his hand, and turned to toss it away, untouched. "I don't know—she told me once, I know, I just can't remember." He spun around, muscles knotting his forearms as he tensed. "Amanda, tell me, what the hell is going on? What's wrong with Tracey?"

"I'm sorry, Jared. We just don't know very much yet."

"Why not? She's bad off, isn't she? I mean, she must be if she can't answer any of this herself."

"Right now we have her sedated. We couldn't find any next of kin."

"There isn't any that I know of. Except maybe a cousin—down in Virginia somewhere near D.C., I think. I can go through her things, take a look."

"Thanks, we'd appreciate it. When you go home, would you collect her vitamins and medicines and bring them in? All of them?"

"Sure. No problem." His mouth twisted. "Do you think I can see her? I really need to see her."

Amanda patted his arm. No one had ever told her how hard this was when you knew the patient or their family. "You wait here, Jared, and I'll see what I can do. It will take a while."

She left him feeding more quarters into the coffee machine and returned to the PICU and her other patient. As she pulled up Alice Kazmierko's ER summary on the computer, she opened the baby's chart across her lap. Because of the need to document verbal orders and events such as resuscitations, the ICUs and ER were the only areas of the hospital that still had paper charts in addition to the electronic medical record.

Even though the Institute of Medicine touted the EMR

as the solution to many patient care problems such as medication errors, Amanda still thought there had to be a better way. Unlike most other twenty-five-year-olds, she wasn't completely enamored with technology, still believed in talking face-to-face with actual people, and had a niggling feeling that despite all the safeguards, trusting a machine with patients' lives was a mistake.

"That our new patient?" Lucas's voice startled her, and she fumbled the chart.

"No. Our patient is a seven-month-old baby girl, not a chart," she snapped, irritated that he'd seen her clumsiness. Next thing you knew, he'd be ordering an MRI on *her*.

He leaned against the doorjamb, a chuckle escaping him at her insubordinate answer, making her flush with embarrassment. She buried her face in the chart, flipping through the ICU orders.

"Alice Kazmierko," she began again in a neutral and hopefully more professional tone, "is a seven-month-old, previously healthy girl suffering traumatic asphyxia after prolonged entrapment and extrication from her car seat in a T-bone collision. Patient with no other injuries, unresponsive at the scene, hypothermia protocol begun in ER—"

"Really?" he interrupted her, sliding the chart from her hand and lowering himself into the chair beside hers. Their legs brushed. Lucas didn't seem to notice; he was concentrating on the chart. But Amanda did notice, immediately swiveling away, then cursing herself for noticing.

Why did Lucas always make her feel like a clumsy schoolgirl with a crush on her teacher? She smoothed the fabric of her dress, tugging it lower and crossing her ankles like a lady.

"Lydia Fiore began the cooling process down in the ER," Lucas said. "Leave it to her—that's a pretty bold move." He snapped the chart shut and looked up at Amanda. "You did a neonatal rotation, right?"

"In the spring."

"Tell me about neonatal hypoxia." He leaned back in his seat, legs crossed, gaze unwavering, focused on her as if they had all the time in the world.

Amanda stole a glance at the clock. They didn't—well, she didn't. She had to be at the clinic by eleven, not to mention checking on Tracey Parker; getting the pathology results on their patient from last month, Becky Sanborn; and finishing her note on Alice. It'd be nice if somewhere in there she had time to eat, drink, or pee.

"For a variety of causes, both intrautero and during the delivery process, neonates can suffer hypoxic events, leading to decreased cerebral blood flow. Once blood flow is reestablished, more harm can be done with secondary swelling and inflammation, adding to the damage. For this reason, selected cerebral hypothermia was developed in the hopes of slowing the inflammation and subsequent damage. Studies—"

The sound of a car horn blaring out a rebel call blasted through the tiny space. Amanda jumped, almost falling off the rolling chair, but Lucas steadied her.

"I think that's coming from your pocket." He grinned as the sound repeated.

"My roommate, she reprogrammed my ringtones," she said sheepishly, grabbing her cell phone. She opened it to glance at the readout and see who Gina had assigned the General Lee's horn sound to. Adam. Her oldest brother. Great, Mama was pulling out the big guns.

"Go ahead," Lucas said, typing on the computer, reading through Lydia Fiore's dictation of Alice's resuscitation.

Amanda hesitated, tempted to just turn the phone off, but the annoying ringtone began again and the easiest way to shut it up was to take the call. "What?"

"Well hello to you too, Baby Girl," came Adam's rumble of a voice. If she hadn't seen the phone number, she would have sworn it was her daddy, they were starting to sound that much alike. "Is that any way to greet your big brother?"

Adam, the oldest, was seven years older than Amanda and considered himself the boss of all of the Mason children. Boss of the world.

"I can't talk now, Adam. I'm with a patient."

"It's an emergency," he went on without giving her a chance to interrupt. "Mama said you're not coming home for Andy's wedding shower."

"It's not Andy's shower. Andy won't even be there. He'll be out hunting with the rest of y'all."

"Is that what this is about, Baby Girl? You're still upset that we won't take you on our hunting getaway?"

"I shoot better than any of you, especially Tony."

"Hell, Aunt Nellie can outshoot Tony. We only bring him along because he doesn't whine about cleaning and skinning—"

"That's beside the point," Amanda cut in when she noticed Lucas staring at her, obviously listening with amusement. "I can't make it home this weekend. Tell Mama I'm sorry. I have to go. Good-bye."

"Wait! Don't you hang up—"

Amanda flipped the phone shut, hanging up on him. A rush of adrenaline surged through her. She'd just stood up to her oldest brother for the first time in her life. And she'd hung up on him!

Oh, hell, she'd hung up on Adam . . . triumph was quickly washed away by guilt and fear. What had she done?

"Sounds like your family is about as understanding as mine," Lucas said.

She shoved the phone back in her pocket, wishing she could hide the flush of embarrassment creeping up her neck.

Lucas ignored it, tapping his pen against the computer screen. "What do you think about Lydia starting the hypothermia? Was it a mistake? Should she have stuck to conventional trauma protocols?"

He wanted her opinion? What did she know, she was just a med student. But he seemed truly interested in what she thought. "I worked with Dr. Fiore during my ER rotation. I think she's an excellent clinician, and she knew that if hypothermia was going to have a protective effect, it's best to start as soon as possible."

His eyes crinkled as he stared at her for a moment longer before nodding. "I agree. It was a gutsy move, but the right one. What are the drawbacks of hypothermia?"

"You need to monitor the temperature closely, give benzodiazepines to avoid shivering, maintain the caloric intake, avoid acidosis, and watch cardiac and renal function."

"And?"

She glanced beyond him out the door to the patients in their beds. "And you need to keep the patient sedated and paralyzed, so you lose your neuro exam."

"Correct. Making our job that much harder. So what do you recommend?"

"Initial CT was clear, so I'd continue the hypothermia at least twenty-four hours, do an MRI, and if that shows no signs of any diffuse neuronal damage, I'd let her wake up." She paused. "Depending on how long blood flow to the brain was compromised, there's still a significant risk she'll remain in a persistent vegetative state. Or worse."

"Or worse." He sighed. "Good work. Let's go find the parents."

"The nurses said the cops arrested Dad for DUI, after he assaulted Seth Cochran."

"Seth's all right?"

"I think."

"We'll try to find Mom, then. She's probably down in the family room."

"I have that appointment—"

"Right. I don't know why, of all the research studies out there, you'd sign on with Nelson." He'd buried his face in the chart, but even in profile, his disdain was obvious. The muscle at the corner of his jaw was practically snapping with tension.

"Dr. Nelson is helping lots of people with his nutritional supplements—"

"Dr. Nelson is helping himself get rich." Lucas jerked his head up and opened his mouth as if ready to say more, but she didn't give him a chance.

"You don't know what you're talking about. Dr. Nelson doesn't have to do the studies on his supplements—the FDA doesn't require them. He does it because he's a scientist, because he wants to create the best product designed to help the most people—"

"Who are you, his poster girl?"

"No." She pushed out of her chair, stood, straightened her shoulders, and glared down at him. "I happen to be a friend. I was there when he and his wife lost their baby two years ago. Now, if you'll excuse me, Dr. Stone, I'm late for my appointment."

To her surprise, he stood and blocked her way.

"Amanda, if there's anything wrong—" It was the first time he'd used her name all day.

She shook her head vehemently, not sure what to make of the sudden concern. "No. It's just a routine check. Honest."

He narrowed his eyes as if cataloging her missteps. "You're sure? You've seemed a bit on the clumsy side today."

"Anyone would with you looking at them like they're a bug under a microscope. It's unnerving."

A ghost of a smile flitted across his face before he assumed a mock earnest expression. "I will try to avoid looking at you in the future, Ms. Mason. Although I confess it may be difficult."

With his last words hanging in the air—did he mean that because he found her attractive? or because she was an annoyance?—Lucas left. Most likely he was making fun of her because he knew she had a crush on him. He was probably used to it, thought her hopelessly naïve. Or worse, gullible.

Amanda shook her head, glanced at the clock, winced, and hurried out of the ICU. She hated to keep anyone waiting, especially Dr. Nelson.

LYDIA FINALLY MADE IT BACK TO EMMA GREY just as the tech was finishing her follow-up EKG. Deon stood beside the tech, watching the machine with rapt curiosity.

"It looks the same," he said, holding up his copy of the first EKG. "That's good, right?"

How was she going to explain the nuances of ST segment elevation to a ten-year-old? "Good eyes, Deon. It is the same." She took Emma's hand, felt her pulse. "How are you feeling, Mrs. Grey?"

"Fine. And call me Emma." She tugged at her nasal cannula, pulling it free from her nose. "I don't need all this. I'm fine. We should be going now, let you take care of some sick folk."

Lydia watched as Emma's oxygen level began to drift down, then reached over to adjust the nasal cannula back into place. "I don't think that would be a good idea. Your oxygen is still low."

"Is she having a heart attack?" Deon asked, his voice quavering up an octave. "You said she might be."

"Actually, I have good news. Your labs are normal. I'm not seeing any changes that indicate a heart attack."

"Great, then we can go back home." Emma acted as if they had a welcoming committee waiting on them "back home" even though they both knew that wasn't true.

"Hold on now. I still don't know for sure what's causing the dizzy spells and your low blood pressure. But I have some ideas. I want the cardiologist to see you."

"More fancy doctors? Can't I just go to the clinic like always?"

If Lydia was right, it was the clinic doctors—although

with the best of intentions—who had caused Emma's symptoms. Which might have saved her life.

"No." Lydia perched on the side of the bed, Deon climbing up to lean against her, peering over her shoulder as she showed Emma the repeat EKG.

"See these bumps here and here?" Emma and Deon nodded in unison. "There's a rare condition called Brugada syndrome that can cause those changes without a heart attack."

"Brugada?" Deon asked, trying the word on for size.

"You got medicine for that, right?"

"It was your new medicine, the beta-blockers, that unmasked it."

"So I won't take those no more and problem solved. Let's go home, Deon."

Emma reached to disconnect the oxygen again, but Lydia stopped her with a gentle hand on her arm. "It's not that simple. We're lucky we found it in time."

"You make it sound like cancer or something."

Deon jerked his head up at that, edging closer to his gram, reaching for her hand.

"It's not cancer, it's a heart defect. Something you were born with that over time has gotten worse."

"Nonsense, I'm as healthy as a woman half my age—the doctors always say so."

"This isn't something the doctors would have known about—not until you showed symptoms. It tends to run in families, usually hits young men without warning. Is there any history of sudden, unexpected deaths in your family?"

Emma leaned back against her pillow, her color draining. "Two brothers. One died while playing basketball; the other was just eating dinner. No one ever knew why."

"Brugada causes your heart to beat abnormally—there's no test for it on autopsy."

Emma's face narrowed with concern as she stroked Deon's back. "If I have this, could Deon?"

"Maybe. But we need to see if you have it first. Do some tests."

Her mouth opened, then closed. Finally she nodded. "Do them. Do whatever it takes. You gotta promise me one thing, though."

"What?"

Emma clasped Lydia's hand with a strength that surprised her. "You gotta promise that you'll look after Deon. He's all I have left and I'm all he has. You understand what I'm saying?"

Emma's eyes blazed so intensely that Lydia had to fight to meet them. Deon watched, statue-still, holding his breath. Lydia forced herself to face Emma's gaze and nodded, swallowing hard.

"Yes, ma'am, I do."

NINE

Thursday, 10:58 A.M.

"MOSES HAS A PLAN?" GINA WAS PRACTICALLY sputtering with anger and shock, but LaRose was smiling and nodding her head as if Gina had just agreed to relinquish her future to her parents' control. As if she were ten years old again.

"When he saw the media coverage of how you rescued those children this summer, he put things in motion. I'm so excited to tell you that he just learned that the city will be presenting you with their highest civilian honor, a Carnegie Medal. Congratulations, Gina! You've made us so very proud."

Damn if LaRose didn't pat away a few tears. Gina was stunned, didn't even feel the cold air hit her bare foot as the nail technician pulled it out of the whirlpool and dried it. She couldn't feel anything, as if she were drifting outside her body, far away from all this.

"Mom, that wasn't me who saved those kids." Well, she'd helped a little, but that was just being in the right place at the wrong time. Ken Rosen, another doctor at Angels, was the real hero. He'd risked getting shot to save half a dozen kids. All Gina had done was carry one to safety.

"Of course it was, dear. Don't be so modest—your picture was all over the papers and TV."

"Yeah, but—"

"No buts. The presentation will occur at the Winter Gala in December. Which of course I'll be presiding over, since I'm chair of the foundation. It will be lovely—even more so when you accept the award and announce your retirement from the ER in order to work with me at the foundation, raising money for charity." LaRose clapped her freshly manicured hands in delight. "What could be more perfect? Finally, an opportunity for you to pursue a meaningful career and meet the right kind of people."

"I can't—leave the ER?" Gina hated to admit that ever since the shooting she'd spent sleepless nights wondering if she was cut out for emergency medicine. But to just walk away? She looked around, spotting the nearest exit. Damn, she'd kill for a cigarette. A cigarette and ten minutes alone to think. "I'm not sure."

LaRose patted her arm. "Of course you are, Regina. You know this is the perfect opportunity. And your father—" She batted her eyes, tilted her head back as if sunshine were bathing her face, smiling. "Your father, I've never seen him so proud. It will mean the world to him. And to me, to see you two patch up your differences. Think what it will mean to our family."

To Gina's amazement, LaRose actually began to weep. "Oh dear. Please excuse me, I'll be right back." She accepted the attendant's hand, stepping delicately from the chair, and made her way to the powder room, the gold-colored robe fluttering around her.

Gina swallowed against a wave of bile, feeling trapped. Something in the perfumed air was making it hard for her to breathe. She shook her other foot free of the whirlpool.

"Please, just finish. I don't need two coats. I'm in a hurry, I need to get out of here."

AMANDA WAS PRACTICALLY JOGGING THROUGH the empty tunnels leading to the research wing where Dr. Nelson's clinic was housed. Not because the dimly lit, spooky tunnels frightened her. Not at all. She just hated to keep anyone waiting—it was rude.

Casting a guilty glance as she passed the pathology lab—no time to stop now, she'd have to get Becky's results on her way back—she rushed around the corner, crashing into a linen cart parked against the wall. She pushed off before it could topple and kept on going, eventually leaving the damp and musty tunnels for the sun-filled atrium of the research wing.

She patted her hair and smoothed her lab jacket as she waited for the elevator. She was perspiring in a most unladylike fashion, so when the elevator arrived empty she took the opportunity to fan her lab coat in the hopes of drying off before sweat stains marred her dress.

The elevator stopped at the fifth floor of the research wing. Dr. Nelson had half of the floor all to himself in recognition for the money he had donated to Angels. Amanda turned left and entered his clinic waiting room.

Despite Dr. Nelson's wealth—he'd made a fortune about ten years ago developing a new way to encapsulate medications, known as a perle, and quickly became renowned as the physician to the stars for his custom-tailored nutritional regimens—he kept his office space simply appointed. Staff was minimal. His wife, Faith, a pharmacist by training, was his main assistant and handled all the record keeping.

Dr. Nelson was always asking Amanda's opinion on new baubles to buy for Faith. In some ways he seemed desperate for material ways to show Faith his affection, even as he'd become obsessed with his research ever since their baby died.

But Faith didn't need the fancy jewelry; she was devoted to Dr. Nelson. And to his work. Which was why Lucas's accusations that Dr. Nelson was just looking to make money were more than unfair—especially after the pain Faith and Dr. Nelson had suffered when they lost their son.

Amanda had met the Nelsons during the start of her second year in medical school while shadowing a neonatologist as part of her Introduction to Clinical Medicine course. She'd been feeling homesick, but that was nothing compared to the tragedy that had befallen Faith and Dr. Nelson.

After trying for years to conceive, they had had an extremely premature baby boy who hovered for weeks on the edge of death.

Amanda had bonded with the couple, stopping by the NICU where they held constant vigil over their son, Joey. She'd tried her best to offer some kind of comfort. Although Faith was only thirty-five at the time, after Joey died she had decided to not pursue their dream of building a family. Instead, she and Dr. Nelson made his research the center of their lives—and had more or less taken on Amanda as a surrogate child, encouraging her to follow her dream of becoming a pediatrician even though that specialty made a lot less money than most.

"Amanda!" Faith Nelson greeted Amanda before the door to the waiting room closed. Faith was a skinny, intense woman who embraced perpetual motion—a stark contrast to her pudgy but genius husband who would think nothing of sitting and staring at a computer screen for hours on end. "You're never late. Is everything all right?"

Faith reminded Amanda of Mama. Only without the guilt.

"Sorry to be late," Amanda apologized. "I had a patient—"

"That's all right, let's go ahead and get your vitals."

Faith gently but efficiently hustled Amanda into the exam room and took her blood pressure, pulse, and measurements.

"Any problems you need to tell us about? Norman's notes indicate that you had some sort of dizzy spell?" She stared at Amanda with concern.

"It was nothing. I've been making sure I eat better and get more sleep and I've been fine ever since."

Faith nodded, head bent, as she transcribed Amanda's answer into the chart. Amanda felt a tinge of guilt and wondered why. She always tried to be scrupulously honest with Dr. Nelson. Not only in appreciation of the two hundred dollars a month he paid her for being a part of his study on a new vitamin and mineral formulation specifically designed for women, but also in recognition of the need to provide accurate data so that his study results would be valid.

She admired him for doing the research in the first place. The FDA didn't require it, but he felt his work was about more than making money. Dr. Nelson was convinced that someday he would discover the secret to eternal health—well, if not eternal, at least lifelong health and vitality.

He wanted to save the world, give everyone a long and prosperous life. "Riches aren't worth anything unless you share them," he'd say, usually reaching to give Faith's hand a squeeze as he did.

Amanda loved Dr. Nelson's enthusiasm and zeal. It was inspiring to see someone still excited by his work and not solely focused on the income it provided. She frowned, remembering Lucas's scorn and derision about Dr. Nelson's work. He'd acted as if the fact that she was a patient of Dr. Nelson's were a personal attack on him.

"Amanda?" Faith was standing now, asking something she had missed.

"Sorry, I was thinking about a patient." Should she tell Faith about Tracey Parker—would that be a violation of patient confidentiality? But of all people, Faith would know how to track down which of the many studies at Angels Tracey might have been a part of.

"I asked if you wouldn't mind giving us a urine sample now, since we're running a bit late? By the time you're done, Norman will be ready for you."

"Sure, no problem." No problem except she hadn't had anything to drink since before coming to the hospital early this morning. Good thing she hadn't had time to pee either.

Faith left, and Amanda used the private bathroom in the exam room to collect the specimen and change into a patient gown. Amanda sat back on the exam table, trying in vain to arrange the folds of the gown into a position that would allow some modicum of modesty without creating a draft.

She was a little disappointed. Usually she and Dr. Nelson chatted first before she changed. She'd even chosen her blue dress today so he could see how much better she looked than last time, when she'd showed up in scrubs, rumpled and dragging after being up all night.

"Morning, Amanda," he said as he breezed into the room, wearing a black silk polo shirt and crisp white slacks she was certain Faith had bought him. Left to his own devices, Dr. Nelson was more of a flannel-shirt-and-rumpled-khakis kind of man. "How's my favorite medical student?"

He shut the door behind him and sat on a stool. "No more of those dizzy spells, right?" he asked in a low voice as if they were sharing a secret.

She started to say no, but she couldn't force the word free. He looked up at her, a concerned and caring expression on his face—just like her dad's when she'd scraped her knee on the dock or put a fishhook through her finger. She couldn't do it, she couldn't keep lying—not to him or to herself.

Tears welled up in her eyes and she blinked furiously, refusing to give in. Dr. Nelson frowned, then stood, placing a hand on her arm. "Amanda, what's wrong?"

"I'm scared," she finally admitted, knotting the cotton gown in her fist as she spoke. "I had this patient, a few months ago, she had the same symptoms as I did, and she died. Then this morning another patient came in and now she's paralyzed."

"Amanda, calm down, everything is going to be all right." When he talked like that, his eyes staring into hers, his face so calm, so strong, she felt reassured. "Tell me about your patients and we'll get to the bottom of all this."

She nodded, swallowed back her tears and quickly told him about Becky Sanborn and Tracey Parker. "Now Tracey's paralyzed—in a locked-box syndrome. What if something like that happens to me?"

"First of all, you know that these symptoms could be caused by any number of things. Why do you assume that you have the same thing as your patients? If you even do have anything wrong with you?"

"I don't know. I'm sorry. It's just I can't believe Lucas can't find out what's wrong with them. And since I had some of the same symptoms—"

"Lucas? Lucas Stone?" Dr. Nelson's face shut down, lips curling with distaste.

"Yes. He's the neurology attending who took care of Becky and now Tracey."

He turned away for a moment before speaking. "I would never disparage a colleague, but well, maybe Lucas Stone isn't the best physician for this case. But that's not our problem—we need to know if something is happening to *you*. You told me you would call if you had any more symptoms."

She hung her head. "I know. I kept telling myself that it was nothing—just clumsiness, fatigue. But after seeing Tracey, and hearing that we're both involved in research studies, I guess I panicked."

"Let's put that fear to rest right now. I have no idea which study Tracey was involved with, but you know that this medical center is currently running thirty-two clinical trials as of the last IRB review. And half the patients in each trial are really only getting placebos—so there's little chance of you and her both getting the same medication. Don't start jumping to conclusions, Amanda. You're a smarter scientist than that."

"I know, I know."

He pulled out his stethoscope, began warming it against his palm. "Let's check you out, head to toe. I'm sure it's your imagination run wild. When I was a medical student I thought I had lymphoma, Alport syndrome, cat scratch fever, and Crohn's disease—all at the same time."

"You did, really?" she asked, reassured now that she'd been truthful about her fears.

"Really. Know what I really had? A severe case of medical-studentitis. My clinic preceptor advised a weekend of reading nothing but *Sports Illustrated* and *Field and Stream*. No medicine at all. Worked wonders."

He checked her lungs and heart, her abdomen, and her lymph nodes; looked at her retinas; and then had her close her eyes as he tested her sensation and reflexes. Amanda relaxed as he regaled her with tales of being a medical student "back in the old days" and how he and Faith had met one night in the library while he was studying for a pharmacology final.

"Not only was she cute, she was smart. Helped me pass, then inspired me to go on and get my Pharm.D. as well as my medical degree. Wouldn't be where I was without my Faith." His voice trailed away. "Let's try that again." She felt the dull thud of the reflex hammer against her elbows, then her knees. "Hmm . . ."

Amanda opened her eyes. "What's wrong?"

"Hang on a second." He opened the door and called for Faith. She joined them almost immediately. "Faith, would you be a dear and check Amanda's status for me?"

"You mean break the double-blind code? Norman, if I do that—"

"She's out of the study, I know." He glanced at Amanda. "It's for the best, Amanda. I want to put all your fears to rest."

Amanda gulped. Suddenly she was less afraid about some vague dizzy spells than she was of losing two hundred dollars a month. That money was her food budget. "Really, it's not necessary."

"I think it is." He nodded to Faith, who disappeared out the door with her usual efficient stride.

"Your reflexes are abnormal," he explained to Amanda once they were alone. "Hyperactive in your triceps and absent in your patella and Achilles. And you've some areas of decreased sensation, along the soles and sides of your left foot. Have you noticed any clumsiness, difficulty with balance lately?"

"A little—but nothing consistent," she was quick to add. A shiver crawled down her spine as the air conditioner blew onto her bare back. She hugged the gown tighter around her, but the cold feeling didn't go away. "Just when I'm rushed, or nervous."

"Hmmm. Might be nothing but a little electrolyte imbalance." He looked up as the door opened again and Faith returned. "What did you find, Faith?"

"Amanda is in the placebo group." Concern for Amanda was etched on her face. "I hope that helps."

"Well, at least we don't have to worry about any of the supplements being the cause of these symptoms. I still want to do some tests."

"Norman, if she's out of the study, you can't continue as her physician," Faith quietly protested. "I'm sorry, Amanda. But we have to follow the rules—"

"I can ask Lucas," Amanda said, although she dreaded the thought of admitting that there might actually be something wrong with her. Especially to Lucas Stone. "Or one of the other neurology attendings."

Dr. Nelson hesitated. "Let me at least get the basics,"

he said. "I'm sure I have a much better handle on these things than Lucas Stone. Besides, who's going to tell me who I can see as my patient and who I can't, right?" He grinned and patted Amanda's arm reassuringly. "Don't worry, Amanda. We'll get everything sorted out and it will be fine."

TEN

Thursday, 12:27 P.M.

LYDIA WAS STAPLING A SCALP LACERATION WHEN alarms sounded from the bed space across the hall. She quickly placed the last two staples, leaving the dressing for a nurse to take care of as the sounds of a woman shouting propelled her from the suture room and into Emma Grey's bed space.

"What's going on here?" she asked, raising her voice to be heard over the blaring alarm.

Emma had removed her oxygen and climbed out of bed. Across from her, Nora held Deon, her arms wrapped around his chest. A man, a stranger to Lydia, stood beside the bed. He had dark, wavy hair, rugged Eastern European good looks, and a wide mouth stretched into an "aw shucks" grin.

"You must be Dr. Fiore," he said, his smile never losing any wattage when she didn't shake his hand, although his face blushed beet red. More than just a blush, he had a bad case of rosacea marring his otherwise good looks. "I'm Tommy Zwyczaje. Sorry we have to meet under such circumstances. Don't worry about trying to pronounce my name, everyone just calls me Tommy Z."

"You're not taking my Deon." Emma's voice sliced through the air with the strength of an ax swing. In contrast, her body quivered with rage and fatigue. "Let him go. We're leaving this place."

"Calm down. No one's going anywhere. You're both still my patients; no one has the right to take Deon from you." Lydia reached past Emma to silence the alarm.

Emma's heart rate was slow—too slow, given her agitation, and there were a few irregular beats. Exactly the kind of rhythm that could trigger the Brugada syndrome. "Please Emma, lie back down."

"No. Not until he leaves. You promised, Dr. Lydia, you said you'd see to Deon."

"I will."

"I'm afraid Dr. Fiore is in no position to make any promises of that nature," the man, Tommy Z, said.

"Who the hell are you to tell me how to run my ER?" Lydia snapped at him.

Nora came to his defense. "Lydia, Tommy's from social services."

"I didn't call social services."

"Any staff member can consult social services," Tommy said. "If they feel their patient's needs aren't being adequately addressed."

"I'm addressing these patients' needs just fine."

"Lydia," Nora protested, "you can't keep Deon registered as a patient when there's nothing wrong with him. And he can't stay here while his grandmother is admitted."

Nora was right. Lydia had no idea how she could keep Emma and Deon together if Emma needed surgery, but she would figure something out. Without the meddling of an overzealous Good Samaritan like Tommy Z.

"Cardiology is on their way; we'll come up with a game plan for everyone after they make their assessment."

She turned her back on Nora and Tommy. Emma was

barely standing, both hands now grasping the IV pole like a lifeline. "Emma, I promise, I'll take care of this. Please get back into bed."

Lydia reached an arm around Emma to guide her back to the bed. Suddenly, the older woman's entire weight fell on her. The monitor screeched. Lydia was barely able to protect Emma's head as they both slid to the floor.

"Get me the crash cart. Now." She glanced up at the monitor. Emma's heart was beating in an erratic fashion, *torsades de pointes*—a lethal rhythm. "No pulse."

"Gram!" Deon cried out, trying to crawl over the bed to reach his grandmother. "What's wrong with her?"

"She'll be all right, Deon. But you need to leave." Shit, shit, shit. She was not going to lose this woman, not in front of her grandkid, not lying here on the floor.

Deon cried out and struggled as someone pulled him away, Lydia didn't see who—maybe Tommy Z had finally made himself useful. Running footsteps and the rumble of the crash cart coming down the hall sounded behind her.

She couldn't wait for the cart. Lydia raised a fist high in the air and struck Emma midsternum. The thump was audible even over the roar of the dueling monitor alarms.

She felt for a pulse, her gaze fixed on the monitor as the jagged lines went flat and then slowly reassembled into a slow but regular rhythm.

Emma's pulse echoed the beats on the monitor and her eyes fluttered open. "Deon," she gasped, her fingers scratching at Lydia's wrist.

"He's fine. Let's get you back into bed now."

Several people had gathered by now, providing enough muscle to lift Emma back into the bed. Lydia put an oxygen mask back on her while Nora took a complete set of vitals.

"Did that ACS patient go up to the cath lab?" Lydia asked.

"A few minutes ago."

"Good. Move Mrs. Grey into the telemetry room. I'll call cardiology again and get their butts down here."

Emma gasped in the oxygen and wrapped a hand around Lydia's. "What happened?"

"It was your heart. It began to beat erratically and couldn't get enough oxygen to your brain. But the cardiologists can fix it—it takes a simple operation. They implant a pacemaker that can keep your heart beating regularly."

"Operation?" Emma's eyes closed for a moment as she shook her head so vigorously the oxygen mask almost flew off. "I can't. What about Deon?"

Lydia squeezed her hand and looked around. Tommy was holding Deon back beyond the curtain as everyone milled around Emma. Lydia gestured to him to let Deon go. The boy ran the few steps to Emma's bedside but stopped short of touching her.

"Is she okay? I'm not going to hurt her, am I?" he asked in an earnest quaver. Tears streaked his face.

"She's going to be fine. And you didn't do anything to hurt her." Lydia crouched so that she was at eye level with Deon. She wiped his tears with the side of her thumb. "You saved her life by making her come in today, Deon."

He nodded slowly, as if reluctant to believe her words. Poor kid. She wondered what had happened in his life to make him feel responsible for the adults around him.

She hoped it was nothing like what had happened when she was a kid, but odds were it was probably something just as bad.

Lydia couldn't resist the urge to wrap her arms around him in a tight bear hug. Then she lifted him up to sit beside Emma on the bed, ignoring Nora's frown of disapproval as the movement jostled the monitor leads, triggering a bleep from the alarm.

"Emma, we're moving you to a room across the hall. It's a private room with special heart monitors. If this happens again, we'll have the equipment to fix things. The heart doctors will be down soon to talk to you."

"Deon can stay with me?"

Both Emma and Deon stared at her with matching dark brown eyes and fearful expressions.

"Yes. For now, he can stay with you in the telemetry room. I'll try to figure out what to do after that; just give me time, all right?"

Emma lay back against the pillows, drained of color and the energy to fight. Deon stroked her hair, taking care not to disturb her oxygen mask.

"All right," she said in a tone of surrender.

Lydia left her and Deon only to be ambushed by Tommy Z in the hallway and Nora from behind as the charge nurse followed her.

"Lydia, you can't—"

"Dr. Fiore, I have to call Children and Youth—"

Lydia whirled on them both. "Don't spout the rules and regulations to me, either of you. They're my patients and I'll deal with the situation. We're short on telemetry beds upstairs, so I'm sure cardiology won't mind if we keep Mrs. Grey down here tonight. Deon can stay with her."

"It's against policy to board admitted patients down here in the ER," Nora said. "What if we need that bed for someone else?"

"You don't even have documentation that she's the boy's legal custodian," Tommy put in. "Even if she is, CYS needs to be involved. That boy can't keep living out on the street, with or without Emma Grey."

"All I know is that if you separate those two now, the stress will probably kill her. I for one am not willing to risk that. So to hell with the rules."

They both opened their mouths to protest, but Lydia silenced them by raising her palm. "Don't say it, I don't want to hear another word. Write me up, fill out a complaint, do what you need to do, but Deon and Emma are staying together."

She whirled on her heel and strode to the nurses' station to call cardiology and convince them to agree to her plan. It wouldn't be hard; the CCU was short staffed and short on beds, and they'd love to let the ER do their work for them.

Which would take care of the problem tonight. But if they took Emma to surgery tomorrow, what was she going to do with Deon then?

ELEVEN

Thursday, 12:52 P.M.

"HEY, NORA, HOW MUCH YOU WANT TO BET Lydia gets another rip?" Jason the desk clerk asked once Nora had finished moving Emma Grey to the telemetry room and Tommy Z had left a terse and disgruntled note on Deon's chart. "Tommy Z's sure to write her up."

"Don't you have work to do?" she asked as Jason simultaneously played a handheld video game, rocked to whatever music was being drilled into his skull by his iPod, and meddled in things that didn't concern him.

"No, but you do." He nodded to the ambulance bay where medics appeared, wheeling in a teenaged girl, bundled in a blanket despite the heat, her face bruised and swollen.

"Trauma Two," Nora directed the medics. She was surprised to see Trey Garrison, the district chief for EMS, and Jerry Boyle, a detective with the Major Crimes Squad, accompanying the girl. "VIP?"

"Yes," Jerry said.

"Not her," Trey answered. He jerked his head at Jerry. "Him."

Jerry ignored him and followed the girl into the trauma room. Trey leaned over the counter at the nurses' station. "Lydia around? Damn fool got cut and wouldn't let me do more than dress it at the scene. If it wasn't for department regs and his partner, he would have refused treatment entirely. But I'm worried about a tendon laceration."

"I'll call her," Jason said with a knowing grin. Although they seldom engaged in public displays of affection, it was common knowledge that Trey and Lydia were involved.

"Thanks."

Trey joined the others in the trauma room, standing in the doorway—to prevent Jerry from leaving without treatment, Nora guessed. Both men were about the same height—a little over six feet—but Trey definitely had a weight advantage, and it was all muscle.

"Dr. Fiore, Trauma Two." The overhead page went out and she wasn't too surprised to see Lydia emerge from Emma Grey's room to answer it. Lydia was guarding Emma and Deon as if she had to protect them from the rest of the ER staff. Nora had hoped that Tommy Z could persuade her to see the wisdom of the rules about minors and protective services, but apparently Lydia was the one person in Pittsburgh on whom Tommy's charms failed to work.

Which also wasn't endearing Lydia to the rest of the staff. She shook her head; Lydia would just have to learn the hard way, as so many other new attendings did.

Trey moved aside to let Nora enter the trauma room, his broad face lighting up in a smile when he looked past her and saw Lydia.

Now that Nora was closer, she could see that the sleeve of Jerry's dark gray suit jacket was saturated with what looked like blood. He held his arm snugged close to his chest but otherwise ignored it, his focus on the girl on the stretcher.

"Tanesha, it's going to be all right," Jerry was telling the frightened and battered teen.

He had crouched down to meet her at eye level but looked a bit wobbly. Nora steered a wheeled stool up behind him. He sank down onto it. "Yancy is not going to hurt you. Never again."

"You don't know him," the girl wailed, tears streaking her glittered blue and black mascaraed eyes, leaving a glistening path through layers of rouge. "He's going to kill me."

"What happened?" Lydia took charge of the situation, reaching for Jerry's arm.

"Take care of her first," he insisted. "Bastard beat her pretty good before we got there."

"You mean before you charged in like a fullback in a 'roid rage. I told you to wait for backup." Janet Kwon, Jerry's partner, stood in the doorway. She was a petite woman but intimidating—even if she weren't carrying a gun on her hip. She nodded to Lydia. "He gonna be okay?"

"We'll see." Lydia finished her examination of Tanesha. "Nora, why don't you take Tanesha down to radiology? We'll need a full facial series and a Panorex."

"Janet, you go with her," Jerry said even as the teen began to panic and grabbed his arm. It was the wrong arm; he went pale with pain and swayed. Trey stepped forward and caught him, supporting him as Lydia took his good arm, and between the two of them they led him to the other gurney.

"I want to stay with him," Tanesha complained. "Yancy's gonna come after me, he's gonna kill me."

"Not while I'm around," Janet said, but her attention was on Jerry, not their witness.

"Tanesha, let's get you into a wheelchair." Nora tried to distract the girl.

Ignoring trauma protocol, Lydia hadn't cut away Tanesha's clothing. Nora could forgive her that infraction; it had allowed Tanesha to retain a small amount of dignity. Not that there was much clothing to get in the way of the exam: a Lycra micro-miniskirt and a metallic fringed crop top that barely qualified as a bra, much less a shirt.

Nora hoped that during the trip to radiology she might get a moment to ask the girl about possible sexual assault as well as her physical injuries—at the very least, she would need STD screening.

"It's okay, Tanesha," Jerry said from where he sat on the gurney opposite. "I'll be here when you get back."

"Everything will be fine," Dr. Nelson had said. His words rang through Amanda's brain as she walked down the steps in the secluded and empty stairwell of the research tower. How many times over the past few months had she told herself the same thing?

She hated it when her mother pasted on a sugary smile and denied anything was wrong with the world. Like when her father had had his stroke. Now it looked like Amanda had inherited at least one thing besides Amelia Mason's blond hair and blue eyes . . . the art of denial.

Amanda stopped, clutched the handrail, and banged her left foot against the side of the step below. Dr. Nelson was right. She could barely feel it. How could she have missed that?

Of course, how often does anyone go around sticking pins in the bottom of their feet to see if they can feel? She sank down to sit on the steps, not caring if her lab coat got dirty or how unladylike it looked. What if there really was something wrong with her? What if she had the same thing that had killed Becky and left Tracey paralyzed?

Stop it! Her mother's voice rang through her, more real than the sound of her own breathing echoing against the cement walls of the stairwell. Mama was known for her hypochondriasis—always had to be the center of attention—but she also had a steel-willed resistance to anything intruding into her reality. In the best Scarlett O'Hara tradition, Mama would think about anything bad tomorrow.

Amanda stood up, brushing off the back of her lab coat. This time Mama was right. No sense worrying when she'd have to wait to get the lab results back.

She started down the steps again, resisting the urge to watch her left foot, scrutinize its every movement. She continued down to the basement tunnels and began to travel the dark and twisty tunnels to pathology. The morgue was here too, along with the autopsy suites—as was the original hospital infrastructure: the crematorium, boiler room, laundry facilities, mechanical room, storage, and so on.

This main building of the hospital had sections that went back more than a hundred and fifty years. As the building was remodeled and expanded and remodeled again, the tunnel complex grew into a maze combining the occasional brightly lit, recently painted corridors with the original tile-walled, cement-floor tunnels.

Once when she'd taken a wrong turn down here, she'd even found an area of painted brick walls—some of the original passageways rumored to connect the hospital with the cemetery across the street.

Amanda shivered at the thought and hugged her coat around her tighter. Her footsteps rang out on the concrete. It was lunchtime and the tunnels were deserted. Her stomach rumbled as she thought about lunch, but she needed to get Becky's pathology results first.

She rounded a corner, trying to breathe shallowly. She could swear the closer she got to pathology the more she could smell the sweet stench of decay.

It was just her imagination. Pathology was in one of the newer sections, and the lab workers took pride in the fact that modern technology helped them eliminate 99 percent of the odors associated with their work. But still she swore she smelled something . . . overripe, like peaches left in the sun too long.

One more turn and she'd be back in the well-lit, modern

length of tunnel. A steam pipe burped overhead and she jumped. She quickened her steps, turned the corner, and plowed into a man rushing from the other direction.

She recognized Lucas Stone just as her heels skidded out from under her. Her hands flailed about, knocking against him. He kept his balance, but the sheaf of papers he carried went flying in all directions as Amanda landed flat on her butt.

The impact thudded through her, almost as bad as when she'd done a banana-peel slip on the ice last winter. Worse was the humiliation.

As she struggled to catch her breath, Lucas was chuckling even as he knelt beside her. "Are you okay?"

"Yes." Ouch. *No*. She resisted the urge to massage her bruised hip and tugged her dress down in attempt to regain some dignity. "I'm fine."

"Really? Sounded like you hit pretty hard."

Damn it, if only he'd stop looking at her. She started to push up to her knees. "I said I'm fine."

He wrapped his hands around her wrists to help leverage her to her feet, bringing them both up to standing in one smooth motion. She felt his breath against the top of her head, her face almost touching his chest for one brief moment. Then he dropped his hands and stepped back.

"Took me twenty minutes to get these results in order," he said, crouching to collect the scattered papers.

"What are they?"

"Becky Sanborn's path results—most of them at least. Ken Rosen still has some micro sections."

Now guilt added to embarrassment. It was her job to take care of stuff like paperwork—not her attending's. "I was going to get those for you."

She bent down to grab a stray sheet of paper and her left leg began to quiver. *Damn it, not now.*

Carefully, she retrieved the lab result and stood again, hovering close to the wall, hoping he didn't notice.

"You were at your appointment and I left Jim monitoring Tracey. I don't mind; I wanted to look at the slides myself anyway." His voice trailed off as he leaned over to grab a sheet that had skittered across the hall to land beside her feet.

She would have backed off but she didn't trust her leg to move. Strange electrical shocks raced through the side of her calf, and she bit her lip to keep from crying out in pain.

Lucas knelt at her feet, the paper forgotten as he touched a finger to her calf, eliciting a lightning strike of pain. "Amanda." He rocked back, looked up at her. She had her fist against her mouth, trying to fight back both pain and fear. "What the hell is going on?"

Amanda gulped in two deep breaths. "Dr. Nelson is running some tests, but he said everything is going to be fine."

His shoulders hunched, and he practically bared his teeth at the mention of Dr. Nelson. "Fine. Right."

He stood and faced her, his expression twisted with a strange mix of concern and annoyance. "Wait here; I'll be right back. Then we're going to have a long talk."

If she had had the strength she would have walked away, leaving him. She hated the way he presumed he was smarter than Dr. Nelson or that he had any right to order her about. Hated even more that he had seen her weakness. But her left leg was now quivering uncontrollably and wouldn't hold her weight, so walking away wasn't an option.

Even more frightening was that when she looked down she could see muscle fasciculations—abnormal contractions that writhed below the skin like a nest of riled-up copperheads. Oh boy, that wasn't good. Tracey Parker had had muscle fasciculations; so had Becky Sanborn, a day before she died.

Before her morbid thoughts could proceed down that path any further, Lucas returned with a rolling office chair from the lab down the hall.

"Sit," he directed, giving her no choice as he took her elbows and steered her into the chair. Then he gathered the rest of Becky's results and thrust the papers at her to hold while he pushed her down the hall.

"I'm fine," she protested as the cramping and electrical shocks faded. She glanced down at her leg. The fasciculations had stopped as well. Tentatively she flexed her foot. Everything seemed back to normal. "Dr. Nelson said it was probably an electrolyte imbalance—I haven't had anything to eat or drink all day."

Lucas shoved open the door to the lab. It was one of the small conference rooms, equipped with a table, an electronic microscope, and a large monitor. No one else was using the room. He rolled her chair over the threshold and parked her at the table.

"It's after noon. When was the last time you had anything to eat?" he demanded, sweeping through the room and bringing her a glass of water from the cooler in the corner.

She had to think. She'd grabbed a peanut-butter-and-banana sandwich on her way to the boathouse this morning. "About four-thirty or so. I'm fine, Dr. Stone. Really."

She pushed out of the chair and stood, stomping her foot up and down to prove her point. She didn't tell him about the numbness. No need to stir him up again.

He peered at her as if she were under the microscope rather than standing in front of it. "Sit. Drink this. I'm going to find you some food, and when I get back you're going to tell me everything about your symptoms. Everything," he added when she opened her mouth to protest. "From the beginning."

He stepped to the inside door leading into the main lab complex. "Don't even think of leaving—unless you want to fail this rotation."

He started to close the door behind him, then stopped to look back around the frame, again scrutinizing her intently. Intense. That was Lucas Stone, she thought as he finally closed the door behind him. As intense as an owl eyeing a mouse, deciding whether it was worth the effort of catching and eating.

She was *not* a mouse. She gulped down the rest of the water, stood, and tested her balance. A few black spots washed over her vision, and then she was fine. She took a few experimental steps, staying close to the table. Just fine.

Her pager blared, sending a jolt of adrenaline through her. Damn thing. She glanced at the screen. The PICU. Alice Kazmierko.

She *was* fine—just needed to take better care of herself, was all. And there was nothing Lucas Stone was going to say that would make her stop doing her job. She didn't care what kind of threats he made.

Besides, she already had a brilliant doctor taking care of her—who needed Lucas Stone, anyway? She marched out of the room, taking Becky's misarranged chart with her. She'd take care of Alice, grab a candy bar from the vending machines, and dissect Becky's chart so that by the time Lucas tracked her down, she'd already have the work done for him.

And maybe she'd find some clues to help Tracey Parker along the way. She made it to the elevator without trouble—except for the occasional scuff of her left toes against the floor. The elevator doors opened onto the fourth floor. As she turned the corner toward the PICU she stumbled slightly, easily catching her balance.

The doors to the PICU whooshed her inside, and she saw a man leaning over Alice's bed, pushing the nurses away, inconsolable. Amanda shoved Becky's lab work into her coat pocket and rushed over to help.

AS SOON AS NORA, JANET, AND TANESHA LEFT, Boyle collapsed back against the gurney. "Aw, shit."

Lydia glanced at Trey, figuring he'd be more forthcoming with answers than the stoic detective. As she used her trauma shears to cut away the blood-soaked jacket sleeve, she asked once more, "What happened?"

"Janet and Captain America here were interviewing a witness over in East Liberty when they heard a commotion. Turns out some pimp—"

"Yancy Gates," Boyle supplied, closing his eyes as the fabric of his suit parted. Wrapped around his left forearm was a compression bandage stained with blood.

"Was beating one of his girls," Trey continued, helping to ease Boyle free from the remnants of his jacket. Underneath he wore only a T-shirt. Trey had undoubtedly removed Jerry's dress shirt at the scene before applying the dressing. "Jerry rushed in, saved the girl, and got sliced for his trouble."

"Surprised Janet didn't shoot Yancy. Or did she and the guy's DOA?" Lydia began to cut through the layers of the dressing.

Trey hooked Boyle up to the monitor, ignoring his feeble protest at the "fuss over just a cut."

"Janet couldn't get a clear shot," Trey continued. "Guy got away."

"Hmm. What'd he use? Must have been sharp. This looks pretty clean." The wound sliced down the inside of Boyle's arm; now that she had removed the compression dressing, blood flowed in a steady stream from it. "Deep, but clean."

"Straight razor," Boyle answered, his face pale. A thin bead of sweat covered his upper lip, and his heart rate was on the high side. "Son of a bitch carries it on his belt, like a pocket watch, chain and all. It's his trademark."

"Lovely." Lydia assessed the damage.

Trey pulled the exam light over for her and inflated the blood pressure cuff above the wound, giving her a clear field to examine.

"You got off lucky. I don't see any permanent damage. We'll do a two-layer closure, update your tetanus, and you'll be good to go. First, let me get you some pain meds; this is going to take a while."

"No meds, I need to stay sharp."

Lydia knew he'd say that. "All right. You're still going to need some fluids. I'll have a nurse start an IV, we'll get some volume in you, then I'll be back in a few minutes."

"Check on Tanesha. Make sure Janet hasn't scared her to death."

"Anyone living the life Tanesha is, she isn't going to be scared easily."

Boyle opened his eyes and glanced up at her words. He knew about Lydia's background—more than Trey did, even. She stood and stripped off her gloves, ignoring his expression of concern.

"Just check on her. I don't want to lose her as a witness when we nail Yancy."

Right. They both knew how good the odds were of a teenage prostitute staying clean and sober and in one place long enough to testify. But unlike his partner, Lydia knew Boyle's main concern wasn't his case—it was his witness. For a cop, the guy had a soft heart. "Sure thing."

"Can't believe I was so stupid," Boyle muttered. "Good thing it wasn't Gina who showed up in the ambulance—she would have killed me for sure."

TWELVE

Thursday, 1:11 P.M.

AFTER BRIBING THE MANICURIST TO TELL LaRose that Gina had been called away and turning her phone off, Gina had driven aimlessly through the streets of Shadyside and East Liberty, chain-smoking her way through half a pack of Gitanes, trying to decide what to do about her parents' latest bombshell.

She'd ended up at Angels. As she pulled into the visitors' parking garage—officially forbidden to students and residents, but where Gina routinely parked—she considered the best way to sneak into her own hospital.

Avoiding the ER—where if Lydia didn't spot her, Nora was certain to—Gina walked around the memorial gardens, past the patient tower and outpatient clinics, and ended up at the research tower. She glanced up at the steel-and-glass building, a starkly modern contrast to the older brick patient care wing connected to it via two skywalks. The research building was sleek, bold, promising answers with its confident stance.

Answers were exactly what she needed—and the man

who held them, Dr. Ken Rosen, had his lab here in this building. Gina pursed her lips, then yanked the glass door open.

Ken Rosen's seventh-floor immunology lab resembled a cross between a frat house and Frankenstein's laboratory. Gina paused inside the doorway, assaulted by dueling boom boxes—one blaring Bach's Fugue in G Minor, the other Drowning Pool.

No one was around to lay claim to the noisemakers or to the coffee boiling over on a Bunsen burner, the leaning towers of petri dishes, reams of paper wadded into fist-sized balls, the collection of Steeler bobbleheads, a mountain of empty soda cans spilling out from a recycle bin, or the pair of mice with their noses pressed up against their cage as if welcoming Gina as their savior.

As an ER doc, Gina prided herself on her ability to thrive on chaos, but this OSHA inspector's nightmare—how could anyone work here?

She clicked off one of the boom boxes. Drowning Pool's impassioned plea to let the bodies hit the floor never sounded so good.

Immediately a man bounded out from an office in the rear of the lab. "Who turned off that music?" Ken Rosen demanded. He lunged across the room, swiping at the boom box, reinstating the cacophony. "Are you trying to sabotage two years' worth of work?"

"No," Gina yelled above the din. "Just trying to hear myself think."

He blinked at her as if she were one of the specimens stacked in the glass cabinets lining the wall behind her. He was average height, wiry but solidly muscled, with dark hair that curled below the collar of the denim shirt he wore over a Godsmack T-shirt. "Gina."

That was it, just her name. A man of few words. He turned and walked back to his office, never looking to see if she followed. Which of course irritated the hell out of her because, sure as sure, here she was following him. And admiring the way his ass fit his well-worn Dockers.

Stop it. She thought of Jerry. The worried, exhausted look on his face the last time she'd seen him, how his hands felt on her body. The way he believed in her—despite knowing the worst about her. He was the man for her.

Ken Rosen was merely an annoyance, but an annoyance she hoped could help her find the answers she needed.

Somehow the thought wasn't enough to totally erase a smidge of guilt as she stepped into Ken Rosen's office and he closed the door behind them.

"What can I do for you?" he asked, his smile welcoming.

Gina squirmed. "Maybe this was a mistake."

Actually, she was certain it was. She'd had this same weird reaction to Ken the first time they met—huddled together beneath a barrage of bullets. This twisty, Jell-O feeling that made her toes curl.

Ken merely stared at her, waiting.

"The EMS guys are no help," she blurted out, not bothering to explain. "They act like this kind of thing happens all the time." The mandatory counseling session her residency director had sent her to after the shooting was equally worthless. She'd stayed only long enough to tell the shrink what he wanted to hear and get her chit signed.

It had been almost as bad as sophomore year at college when her parents found out she'd been seeing a counselor. That had rated a triple D on the Gina Freeman Parental Disgust Scale. They'd been dismayed, distraught, and disappointed.

"What do you need to see a counselor for?" LaRose had whined. "You know you can tell us anything, that we'd do anything for you."

Right, anything except postpone a trip to Barbados or, let's get really radical, listen to their daughter for once.

"We taught you how to stand on your own two feet, to have some pride," Moses had preached as he sipped his third martini of the afternoon. "There's nothing you can't handle on your own, young woman. Not if you get off your lazy ass and put your mind to it. Remember, what you do reflects on your mother and me as much as it does on you."

Somehow "putting her mind to it" hadn't stopped the nightmares or cold sweats of terror that overcame her at the thought of returning to the streets. "Putting her mind to it" seemed poor protection against a bullet.

Attitude was everything in this business. And somewhere back on that street in Homewood she'd lost hers.

But not Ken Rosen. He'd ignored the danger, ignored the bullets—almost getting himself killed as he tried to save an innocent bystander. And had done it all with the same calm, placid, Zen monk demeanor he had now as he waited for her to continue.

No one could be that content, complacent. At least no one in Gina's world. She burned with a sudden urge to shatter his calm, to prove to herself that he was as human and fallible as she.

"So," he finally said, a slow smile simmering across his features, "you dodged any bullets lately, Gina?"

"Smartass," she snapped, leaning up against the wall and crossing her arms in front of her, leveling her best she-who-must-be-obeyed stare on him. Usually it worked on everyone except her father.

He kicked back, perching on the edge of his cluttered desk. The music from the other room was muted, but the bass line rattled the wall she leaned against, marching its imperative beat into her bones.

Their staring contest lasted long enough for Gina to realize she had met her match. Mr. Inscrutable didn't seem to need to blink. He simply met her gaze, placid, unwavering.

"I need the answer to a question." Gina finally broke

the silence. He inclined his head in a regal nod, granting her permission to continue.

"Why?" She began, then paused, trying to gather her thoughts, strip them of all emotion. "When those gang-bangers shot up that car and it crashed, you risked your life running out to try to save the driver even though it was pretty certain that he was a goner. I need—" No, the last thing she wanted was to admit that she needed anything. "I would like to know why."

Ken finally blinked, slowly, like a cat. He tilted his head, skewering her with his emotionless gaze as if she were one of his lab rats. "Why did you run after me? Men shooting guns, and you leave the ambulance to run after me."

"That was different. Don't avoid the point."

He pushed away from the desk, took two steps forward, and stopped, hovering just beyond reach. "It's the same question, Gina. Answer one and you'll answer the other."

Music crashed through the door as he opened it and stepped through. He closed it behind him, leaving Gina alone.

She stood frozen in indecision. She hated this feeling, spinning her wheels, out of control. She was used to being in control; she needed to be in control—of her patients, her choices, her fate.

"Goddamnsonofabitch!" she shouted into the empty office.

The door cracked open again and Ken poked his head inside. "I thought you wanted some answers. You coming or not?"

NORA OFTEN FELT AS IF SHE NEEDED A PASSport when transporting patients down the hallway for X-rays. Like most of the nurses she knew, she had a love/hate relationship with radiology. They performed an irreplaceable service for her patients, yet they also often kept patients waiting, cooped up in tiny holding areas with no privacy, often returning them to the ER without having a procedure done only to wait some more until it was convenient for the radiology staff to fit them into their schedule.

The worst thing about this strange land of radiology was that people died here. There was rarely anyone around to help when you needed them. Mix sick people in tiny spaces far from anyone who had the equipment and know-how to help them, and it was a recipe for disaster. Nora's greatest patient care nightmare was trying to run a code or resuscitate a patient in the tiny confines of the CT scanner or, even worse, the MRI, where the magnetic field was never turned off and so you couldn't even approach the room with anything metallic on your body.

The trip to radiology did little to calm Tanesha. She gripped Nora's hand so hard it was quickly drained of blood. As they waited in the patient holding area, Janet Kwon wisely held back, hovering just out of sight but listening closely.

"I'm dead, I'm dead, I'm dead. Just like the others, he's gonna kill me." Tanesha's voice had faded to a low chant.

Janet nudged Nora's rib cage. Nora sat on a plywood coffee table facing Tanesha. "What others, Tanesha?" Nora asked, matching her voice to the scared girl's plaintive whisper, not loud enough to rustle the air between them.

"The ones buried in the backyard." Tanesha was rocking, her gaze fixed on an invisible point beyond the walls of the waiting room. "He's gonna kill me just like he did them."

Behind Tanesha, Janet straightened with excitement, circling her hand in a "more, more" motion. Nora knew the detective was eager for details, but the state Tanesha was in, it was going to take patience and finesse, not bullying and scare tactics.

Before she could ask more, the radiology tech emerged

from the back. She pulled down the blanket Tanesha was wrapped in to check Tanesha's ID bracelet against the computerized orders and nodded. "Pregnancy test?" she asked with a frown. "I don't see it documented."

Damn, Nora had meant to get a urine specimen from Tanesha before they left the ER but Jerry had distracted her. "We haven't gotten one yet."

"Well then, I'll need you to pee in a cup for us," the tech told Tanesha, looking askance at the teen's clothing. "Nora, you can help her with that, right?" The tech's tone made it clear that she wasn't about to touch Tanesha or get anywhere near her body fluids.

"No need." Tanesha's voice was louder, filled with anguish. "I'm pregnant. That's why I'm going to die—Yancy's gonna kill me and my baby."

"It'll be all right, Tanesha," Nora said, taking both of Tanesha's hands in hers.

"No. No, it won't." Tanesha was crying now, scaring the tech back into the dark caverns of radiology. "I saw him—I saw him kill Angie. He's gonna do me as well."

Janet couldn't hold back. She stepped forward, inserting herself into the teen's field of vision. "What did you see, Tanesha?"

Tanesha gulped and snuffled back some tears. Nora extracted one of her hands long enough to grab a tissue from the box on the table beside them. Tanesha blew her nose, shoved the dirty tissue into Nora's hand, and finally met Janet's gaze.

"We all knew he was mad at Angie for letting herself get pregnant. Told her if she didn't get rid of it, he would do it for her. Then a few nights later, I snuck back home to grab a"—she faltered, glancing at the detective—"a smoke, and I saw them. Yancy carrying Angie out to the backyard. She was floppy like a rag doll. He dumped her on the ground and grabbed a shovel, started digging. And that's when I knew she was dead."

Tanesha hung her head, rocking again, refusing to look

up at Nora. Janet's eyes had gone wide with excitement as she grabbed her cell phone. "Man, if she's right," she said breathlessly, "I'd better tell Boyle to cancel any plans he has for tonight."

THIRTEEN

Thursday, 1:37 P.M.

LYDIA LEFT BOYLE IN THE GOOD HANDS OF ONE of the nurses and walked into the hallway with Trey. She wanted to ask him if Gina had called him about missing her shift, and because Boyle still thought Gina had made it to her ride-along, she couldn't do it in front of the detective.

She hated this lying and misdirection. Hated even more how easily lying came to her.

Trey led her into the stairwell and shut the door, bracing his back against it. With a glance to make sure no one was coming down from above, he snagged her by the waist and pressed her against the cement block wall for a quick kiss before she could say anything.

"We still on for our dance lesson tonight?" he asked when they parted.

Lydia brushed her lips against his again. "Can't. Promised Nora she could come over—she's worried about some patients, wants me to review their charts."

He did a shuffle step. "You're choosing charts over learning how to cha-cha?"

In addition to his job as a district chief for Advanced Life Support, Trey moonlighted as a dance instructor for his sister's studio, just as he also worked as a handyman for his mother's real estate firm. He didn't give Lydia a chance to reply, but instead nuzzled her neck, his palms pressed against her hips, the heat of his touch radiating through her scrubs. "I thought after, maybe we could finally break in that new bed of yours."

Lydia laughed as he reached the sensitive spot behind her ear, his tongue tickling her. They'd had sex on pretty much every horizontal surface in her house and a goodly sampling of the vertical ones as well. But even she hadn't slept in her new bed or used the bedroom yet, preferring the couch.

Her house was fourteen hundred square feet, more than twice as large as any place she'd ever lived before. She still wasn't used to all that space. It felt claustrophobic at times—as if too much space could imprison you as much as too little.

"Did Gina talk to you about missing her shift today?" She didn't want to break the mood—wished there were more time for fun—but they both needed to get back to work. And, she hated to admit, she was worried about Gina.

Trey's hands remained on her waist, but he straightened to his full six feet, nodding solemnly. "No, she did not. What the hell's going on with her anyway?"

"A lot of things—getting shot at didn't help any."

"She's not the type to talk. She'll try to keep it bottled up inside." He lowered his forehead so it touched hers. "A lot like someone else I know."

Lydia shrugged that small reproach aside, instead grabbing his impeccable uniform shirt in her fist and tugging him closer, planting her lips against his, savoring his warmth. The kiss deepened, his thumbs sliding up, flicking across her breasts, raising her nipples as heat surged through her.

One of them made a noise deep in their throat; Lydia thought maybe it was her. She rubbed her ankle up the back of his leg, feeling his hard muscles through the polyester of his uniform slacks. Finally they parted for air.

"I'd better be going," she said, wondering at the hint of regret in her voice.

This thing she and Trey had, it was tricky, hard for her to define, falling somewhere between the no-man's-land of lust and the dangerous shoals of something more serious. At times the intensity of her response to a single glance from him made her feel as if she were drowning, pulled down by a riptide and unable to come up for air.

"Sorry about tonight."

"Hmmm." Trey pulled his hands away, shoving them into his pants pockets and slouching his shoulders. "I guess I'll just go home to my swinging bachelor pad, call up one of my other girls—"

She punched him in the shoulder, hard enough to rock him back.

"Er, I mean, take a cold shower and microwave a dinner." Then he smiled. "Better yet, I'll head over to Mom and Dad's—nice weather like this, Dad will have steaks going."

"If I know your mom, more likely it will be soy burgers. Guess you won't be missing me at all."

He took his time, looking her up and down and up again, his gaze settling on her mouth. "Who me? Mr. Independent? Nah, won't miss you at all."

"Liar." She walked with him out to the city-owned Suburban he drove when on duty. The SUV was white with yellow and red stripes and was as polished as Trey's shoes and badge. "Can you do me a favor tomorrow?"

"Maybe." He pulled her in for another quick kiss. "It'll cost you."

"Name your price, Chief."

* * *

AMANDA APPROACHED THE DISTRAUGHT MAN AT Alice's bedside warily. She'd heard about what happened in the ER—the guy had tried to punch Lydia Fiore. He was lucky Lydia hadn't hit back.

Nancy, the charge nurse, sidled up to her. "The cops couldn't keep him—he posted bail. I called security, but I'm thinking a guy in uniform is just going to set him off again. His wife is no help, made things worse—said she's taking the other kids and leaving him."

"Great. So you called me."

"Your beeper number is on the chart. I have a page in to your attending as well." She shrugged. "Just give him some of that Southern charm, sweet-talk him. As long as he's calm and no danger to my staff or his daughter, he's welcome to stay. If he follows the rules."

"Right." Amanda heaved out a breath and straightened. Looked like her vending-machine lunch would have to wait.

She walked over to Alice's bed, trying to look casual. Standing at the foot of it, she took in the monitor readings and saw that the baby was stable, normal—if being in a medically induced coma with your body temperature dropped to thirty-four degrees Celsius could be considered "normal."

"You can touch her, if you want," she said in a soft voice, demonstrating by rubbing Alice's toes between her fingers, stroking them gently.

Mr. Kazmierko drew back, shaking his head vehemently. "No. She feels cold, dead." He turned red-rimmed, sunken eyes on Amanda. "She is dead, isn't she? I heard them talking—that ER doctor, she killed her, you all are just keeping her heart beating so that doctor won't be blamed. Probably want to sell her organs or something. And then when she's gone, I'm the one everyone is going to blame."

Amanda had to bolster herself against the force of the father's accusations. "Dr. Fiore is trying to help Alice.

Cooling her body is the best way to try to save brain function—if any can be saved. You must understand how sensitive a baby's brain is to any lack of oxygen—"

"I understand that you all are trying to save yourselves from a lawsuit. The cops just want to pin everything on me."

"Mr. Kazmierko—"

"This wasn't my fault—I'm a good father, I would never do anything to hurt my baby girl." He was pleading now, a stray tear slipping unnoticed from his eye. "This wasn't my fault."

"No one said it was."

"It's that ER doctor, she's the one. Trying an experimental treatment on my little girl—someone needs to stop her, she shouldn't be allowed to keep treating patients." His voice rose, and the charge nurse glared at them. He hung his head and lowered his voice, his palms gripping the edge of the Lucite panels that surrounded Alice's tiny crib. "It's her fault, not mine. She killed my baby."

Amanda laid a hand against his shoulder and felt the rhythm of his jagged sighs move through his body. "How's your other daughter?" she asked, hoping to distract him from Alice's uncertain and precarious condition.

"Fine. My wife took her home—won't let me see her, got an emergency restraining order. She's going to leave me. I can't make it alone, I can't. Why is this happening?" He raised his head, the odor of Southern Comfort wafting off him. He looked to Amanda as if she had the answers. "Why me? First that stupid driver who cut me off, then that ER doctor, now I have nothing . . ."

"We're doing everything we can for Alice," she said uncertainly, knowing it wasn't the answer he wanted.

He glared at her, his eyes narrowing to sharp slits. "You doctors. You're all the same. Always protecting each other. Just leave me alone. Leave me and my baby alone."

Amanda's mouth went dry as she searched for an

answer to his accusations. Finally she simply gave Alice's foot another squeeze and stepped away.

"There you are." Jim Lazarov's accusing voice greeted her as he burst through the PICU doors. "Should have known you'd be here with all the pygmy patients. Did you get those results Stone wanted?"

"I need to get them organized." She pulled the thick sheaf of papers from her pocket. "Unless you want to."

"God, no. That's scut-monkey work. Just let me know the highlights so I can present them to Stone on rounds this afternoon."

Maybe it was hunger, frustration over her visit with Dr. Nelson, or her encounter with Mr. Kazmierko's despair, but Amanda was sick and tired of being pushed around. "I can present them."

"No, I have something better for you to do. In fact"—he gave her a superior smile—"you're going to thank me for it. A consult came in—kid on peds, needs his seizure meds double-checked. I know how much you love hanging out with the other pygmy docs."

She started to protest, then thought better of it. Spending the day down on pediatrics would keep her far away from Lucas and the unnerving attention he paid to her every fumble and misstep. Not to mention prevent him from asking her questions about her symptoms—they were the last thing she wanted to think about. And it would give her time to go through Becky's results and maybe even do some research on hypothermia and hypoxic brain ischemia.

"Okay," she told Jim, who looked pleased at her acquiescence. They both knew that whoever got the consult page was the one who was supposed to do the work.

"Great. Here's the info." He handed her a piece of paper, and she started back toward the PICU doors. "Hey! Don't forget to call me with those results before Stone and I make rounds."

Right. Like hell she would. If she found anything important in Becky's results, she'd call Lucas herself. Even if it meant making Jim look bad in front of the attending—if he did his own work, he wouldn't have to worry about it.

With one last look at Alice Kazmierko and her father, who had already given her up as dead, Amanda left the PICU.

FOURTEEN

Thursday, 2:02 P.M.

"CAN YOU WALK IN THOSE SHOES?" KEN ASKED as they rode the elevator down from his lab.

Gina raised a foot, inspecting her Jimmy Choo open-toe wedges. "These shoes cost six hundred dollars."

"That doesn't answer my question. I ride a bike to work, so it's either walk or double up on my handlebars."

"What's wrong with my car?" She refused to ask where they were going—refused to expose any weakness.

"No way am I going to waste gas and pollute the environment to travel less than a mile and a half." He held his arms out as if steering a bicycle. "So which is it? Walk or ride?"

She scowled at him, but it took an effort. She wasn't really angry. In fact, the knot that had taken up permanent residence in her stomach was beginning to relax for the first time in months. "You are the strangest man I've ever met."

"Okay, walk it is." The doors opened and he led her out of the building. The air was hot and muggy, the sun dimmed by hazy clouds trapping the heat below them.

The route he led them on took them past the ER entrance and ambulance bay. Gina sped up, hoping no one was stepping outside for a cigarette break. Good idea. She reached for her own cigarettes, but Ken stilled her hand with a touch and shook his head. She obeyed without protest—something that sparked another wave of irritation at him. Damn the man.

"You haven't been sleeping much, have you?" he asked, as if talking about the weather. "And having nightmares when you do, right?"

She opened her mouth, ready to lie, but instead she just shrugged, picking up her pace despite the fact that her feet were already pinching and feeling rubbed raw. He caught up easily, his long legs matching her stride effortlessly.

"Have you been back to work since the shooting?"

"In the ER," she found herself answering. "But I'm supposed to be out on the streets doing my EMS rotation. I just, I can't. I'm—" She stopped herself before she said the dreaded word.

Ken didn't let her off so easy. He stopped and placed one palm on her arm, halting her as well. He stood still, ignoring the traffic beside them; the handful of street kids behind them, tossing quarters against a wall; the shopkeeper sudsing his windows. He kept his gaze locked onto her face, pinning her down.

"I'm scared." Gina felt the words pass her lips but didn't believe she'd actually said them until they reached her ears.

A long silence passed after her admission. Everything around them faded into the background; there was just her and Ken.

Finally, he nodded as if accepting her fear, respecting it. And her. "I know. I am too."

She stared at him. He was scared too? Why would he admit something like that to her, a virtual stranger?

"I just want—I need—to learn how to get on with my life." Gina swallowed hard as they resumed walking.

She'd already revealed more to Ken Rosen in a few minutes than she had to anyone in months. Even Jerry.

Fear sparked through her nerve endings in a fight-or-flight rush. She'd said too much, left herself vulnerable, exposed. She faltered, wanting to run back to her car, drive home, and dive into a gallon of Peachy Paterno ice cream. Instead she hastened her pace to catch up with him. "This was a mistake."

He ignored her and they kept on walking. Gina faltered, searching for a neutral topic. "Sorry about the whole Hero of Angels thing in the news."

Even though Ken was the real hero and had saved several kids during the riots, it was a chance picture of Gina helping him by carrying a single baby out of harm's way that had ended up on TV and in the papers.

"It doesn't matter."

"Yeah, it does. They're going to give me a Carnegie Medal for it. I didn't ask for it or anything, but that's kind of why I needed to come talk to you . . ." She trailed off, not sure at all about what she wanted from him.

"Congratulations. Your father must be very proud of you." His tone held no rancor or sarcasm. Instead, he seemed genuinely pleased for her.

"You know my father?" she asked, bracing herself for the inevitable. Snide remarks, vitriolic attacks on her becoming a doctor, asking if her father gave her a bonus for every physician she ratted out . . .

"Moses Freeman? Yeah, we've met." A shadow crossed his face, almost too fast for her to see.

Most people—especially fellow physicians—had much more dramatic reactions to her father's name. She hated that she couldn't read Ken; he was like a koi pond on a windless day. You knew there was a lot going on beneath the placid, unruffled surface but you just couldn't see it.

"So your dad's the lawyer who single-handedly started Pennsylvania's malpractice crisis." His lips quirked in an almost smile. "I'll bet that leads to some interesting discussions at family dinners."

"My father doesn't believe in discussing anything. He believes in verbal warfare."

It was the truth. You didn't try to discuss religion, politics, philosophy, the arts, literature, medicine, or the law with Moses Freeman unless you were prepared to battle to the death. Gina had learned at a very young age that she could never win with her father; too many times she'd abandoned the bloody carcass of her ego on the battlefield of the dining room table.

"How did you and my father meet?" she dared to ask.

"In a courtroom, of course." His tone was light, but again that shadow darkened his eyes. Suddenly he looked older, crow's-feet worried into the corners of his eyes, a crease lining his forehead.

She'd long ago vowed never to apologize for her father—after all, she hadn't chosen her parents. But Ken's expression looked mournful, as if he'd lost something important to him. "I'm sorry."

He shrugged, and the mask of geniality returned. It was a relief to know it *was* a mask, and that he was as human as the rest of the world.

She glanced around and realized they'd walked a long way from Angels. They were in the heart of Homewood, a neighborhood so riddled with violence that school buses refused to enter for fear of getting children caught in the crossfire that the bright yellow government-sponsored targets attracted. The same neighborhood where she and Ken had almost died last July. Gina should have fit in, been comfortable in this black neighborhood, yet the hairs on the back of her neck prickled as she imagined the eyes of a hundred faces focused on her. "Do you know where we are?"

"Of course," he laughed. "I live here—we passed my building a block back."

They stood in front of a brick rowhouse with a sagging porch at the top of a steep set of crumbling concrete steps. The cement-block wall below the porch was pockmarked, the missing chunks leaving white scars behind. A flutter of deflated Mylar balloons cascaded along the gutter, tied with faded ribbons to a telephone pole.

Panic surged through her, sweat cascading down her back. She shivered uncontrollably. Gina wanted to run, to hide, but she was frozen, locked in place by fear. A car turned the corner down the block, cruising toward them. Her heart pounded so hard in her throat, she couldn't swallow.

In her mind gunfire raged around her, ricocheting from the cement wall, the sidewalk, pinging against the car that had crashed against the phone pole, thwacking into the grass . . . and one bullet found its mark, right between her shoulder blades.

Her hand rose to rub the spot at the base of her neck. The spot where the bullet hit her hadn't hurt at the time—the pain blitzed by adrenaline and terror—but ever since, it had ached and throbbed. Sometimes she swore she could feel the bullet wedged between her vertebrae, as if her own flesh had caught it rather than the bulletproof vest Jerry had insisted she wear.

She closed her eyes, trying her best to force the memories away. Ken took her hand in his, squeezed hard, and tugged her forward. "You're all right, Gina."

When she said or thought those same words, they came as a plaintive wail. When he said them, they came out like a statement of fact, carved into stone.

"Gina." Ken's voice pulled her back and she opened her eyes. A woman, maybe in her forties—it was hard to tell with her gray hair and worn expression—was slowly making her way down the porch steps. "This is Angela Hardesty. It was her son driving the car."

Oh, him. The guy with his brains blown out, splattered

all over the windshield. The one Ken had risked his life to save—and the reason Gina and the ambulance had been out there in that firestorm of bullets.

"Is this her?" Angela asked, taking one of Gina's hands in both of hers. "This the doctor who tried to save my Ronald and who helped all those beautiful babies?"

Gina winced at her words. She hadn't tried to save the driver—if anything, she'd urged Ken to abandon him as the SUV with the shooters came after them. Her body shook as if bullets were flying again. The urge to flee became even more overwhelming. Gina knew her palm was drenched in sweat, but Angela didn't seem to notice.

"This is the one." Ken's voice had a trace of—what? pride?—in it. "Meet Dr. Gina Freeman."

"Oh, honey, it is so good to meet you."

To Gina's chagrin, Angela pulled her into a fervent hug. She smelled of lilac talcum powder and Windex.

"Come inside, please. I want to hear everything."

Ken nodded his encouragement, but the thought of staying here, where she'd almost died, one more moment sent Gina's stomach spinning into a tailspin.

"Sorry, I can't stay." Gina yanked her hand free from Angela and spun on her heel, almost tripping over a twisted root poking through the sidewalk. It took everything she had not to run. Inside her skin it felt as if her muscles and nerves, her stomach, her lungs, her heart were already in the flight of their life.

Ken caught up a few moments later, his long strides effortlessly keeping up with her. She beat back the tears blurring her vision, waiting for his reprimands. *Coward, liar, gutless wonder*—there was nothing he could say that she hadn't already told herself.

But Ken was silent, simply keeping pace with Gina. That was almost worse; it meant there was nothing to drown out the sounds of her guilt.

* * *

"SO, HAVE YOU SEEN GINA TODAY?" BOYLE asked as Lydia placed a row of vertical mattress sutures. His color was better after a liter of saline and his heart rate was back to normal. "She doing okay?"

Lydia kept her head low so that the detective wouldn't be able to read her expression. "I was going to ask you the same thing. I'm in charge of the EMS ride-alongs, so I heard about Gina switching shifts last week. I thought you said she was better."

Boyle's large, dark brown eyes always reminded her of a puppy dog's, all sweetness and compassion. But now they narrowed in concern. "She was. She is. Except . . ."

"What's wrong?" Lydia asked.

"She just seems so . . . empty. I don't know what to do."

"Is she sleeping?"

"I think so. The nightmares seem to have stopped. And she's been eating, even laughs, smiles at my jokes." He made the goofy face of a man in love, his voice wistful. "It's just—"

"Be patient. Gina's never had to face anything like that, being shot at, never had anything go wrong in her life."

"Nothing her folks couldn't buy their way out of, at least." His tone was bitter.

"Did you talk to them?"

"I tried." An uncharacteristic scowl darkened his features. "They didn't want to hear anything. All they care about is what they read in the news. And of course that idiot reporter, Pete Sandusky, made her front-page news, talking about how she saved those kids."

Everyone knew that Gina hadn't saved the children alone. The main credit went to another physician, Ken Rosen. But Gina, tall and as photogenic as a fashion model, was the one the public had dubbed the Hero of Angels. More pressure the resident didn't need.

Lydia sighed. She liked Gina, she really did, but the resident was one of those people who were like lightning rods, attracting chaos around them. "I'll talk with her."

Boyle nodded his thanks. "I appreciate it."

Lydia tied off the last subcutaneous suture and switched to 4–0 nylon for the skin. She wanted to ask Boyle more about Gina, but before she could, the door banged open and Janet Kwon returned, talking into her phone as she swept into the room. Behind her came Nora, pushing Boyle's witness, Tanesha, in the wheelchair, an envelope of X-rays in her lap.

"Get the ADA working on a warrant, and Boyle and I will meet you there," Janet was saying. "Yeah, and have those guys at CMU bring that ground-searching radar-gizmo of theirs." She hung up and beamed down at Boyle. "You're not going to believe this one."

AFTER FINISHING HER CONSULT, AMANDA found a quiet hidey-hole in the procedure room of the peds floor. There was a desk for charting along with a computer and, as long as no kids needed spinal taps or other invasive procedures, she'd have some time to examine Becky's chart without interruption.

One of Amanda's extra-cash jobs had been as a medical records data-entry clerk two summers ago when the hospital began its conversion to paperless charts. So it was easy work for her to quickly distill the ream of pages to the essentials: Becky Sanborn, age nineteen, student at Carnegie Mellon University, presented with several weeks of intermittent numbness and tingling of her hands and feet, followed by sudden onset of fasciculations and paralysis. Died thirty-six hours later, cause of death: cardiorespiratory arrest, cause unknown.

Those were the facts. Frighteningly stark when Amanda printed them onto a sheet of chart paper. Not to mention familiar—she'd had the same symptoms off and on for months.

Just an electrolyte imbalance. She heard Dr. Nelson's reassuring voice in her head. She was getting too personally involved; she needed to stand back, be objective. Okay. So what else did they know about Becky?

No meds, no allergies, no previous health concerns other than asthma as a child. Not so helpful. She remembered they'd never been able to get a family history—Becky had died before her parents made it to Angels. And the roommate who brought her in hadn't been very helpful; they'd only been together since the start of the summer session, didn't know each other well at all.

Would it be wrong to call the parents, now, months after Becky's death? It might upset them, bring back bad memories. She grabbed the phone but hesitated before dialing. But if she'd lost someone, she'd want to know people still cared, were still looking for answers.

Amanda licked her lips; she couldn't believe how nervous she was about calling Becky's parents. Once she was a pediatrician, a real doctor, she'd be responsible for actually telling parents their child had died. If she couldn't handle a simple follow-up phone call, how was she ever going to handle that?

She took a deep breath and dialed their number. A woman answered after two rings. "Hello, Mrs. Sanborn?"

"Yes?" She was wary and sounded like she was ready to hang up.

"I'm Amanda Mason from Angels of Mercy Medical Center." Amanda forced herself to slow down. "Um—I'm calling about Becky."

"Becky?" The woman's voice caught. "Have you found something? I know there were more tests they were waiting for. I never thought it would take so long, but it will be a blessing to finally know for sure—"

There was a sudden pause as the woman ran out of words. Amanda could feel the weight of her grief even long-distance.

"I'm sorry, ma'am. I don't have answers, but I did want to let you know we're still looking into her case and as soon as we do have answers, we will let you know."

"Then why did you call?"

"I thought it might help if we knew more about Becky as a person. What she liked to do, any hobbies she had, things like that. And I wanted to ask about any family history of illnesses or problems."

The ragged edge of a sob shuddered through the phone line. "I'm sorry," Mrs. Sanborn said after another pause. "This is very difficult. But if you think it will help, please go ahead, ask your questions."

FIFTEEN

Thursday, 7:14 P.M.

LYDIA SIGNED OUT HER PATIENTS TO MARK Cohen, who was the attending coming on shift, and began to make her patient rounds.

Most emergency medicine physicians loved the shift-work aspect of their jobs—as soon as their replacement arrived and they had their patients ready to sign out, they were free to go home. Lydia enjoyed not being on call overnight in the hospital, but she liked to follow up on her patients. Some of the ward attendings complained about her "spying" on them, but she thought of it as the opposite; it was her chance to learn from them what worked and what didn't.

Deon and Emma Grey were at the top of her list of patients to visit. Mark Cohen was also her boss, the director of emergency services, and he'd reluctantly agreed to her plan to keep them together tonight—much to Nora's chagrin and disapproval.

"You two set for the night?" she asked Emma after entering the telemetry room. Here Emma was constantly monitored, but still had some privacy.

"Yes, thank you, Dr. Fiore." Emma looked much more comfortable; her color was better and the rhythm on the monitor was nice and regular. She'd even been able to take the oxygen off.

"And the cardiologists explained everything?"

"Yes. It's worrisome, having surgery, but they explained how it's all done through a vein. They don't need to cut into my heart at all. Still . . ." Her gaze settled on Deon, who was immersed in the world of Harry Potter. "You remember what you promised?"

"Yes ma'am." Lydia restrained herself from sighing. What the heck was she going to do with Deon while his grandmother was in the hospital, much less if something happened to Emma?

Instead of dwelling on it, she patted Deon's arm. Startled, he looked up from his book, holding his place by sandwiching the pages around his finger.

"And you, you're not going to leave this room until I come for you tomorrow morning, right?" He nodded. "All right then, I'll see you both in the morning."

She only hoped she came up with a plan by then. One that didn't involve Children and Youth Services or foster care placement.

Under the radar—if there was anyone who should be able to do that, it was Lydia. She took the stairs up to the ICU floor to check on her other patients: Tracey Parker and Alice Kazmierko. As she jogged up the steps, she remembered that Nora was meeting her tonight to discuss Tracey's case and the other patients Elise had found with similar symptoms. It would be nice if Lucas had found an answer already. Then maybe she and Trey could still get together tonight.

She paused on the fourth-floor landing. Gina hadn't come by—damn, one more thing to deal with tonight. She considered asking Amanda to take her roommate a message. No, it wasn't fair putting Amanda in the middle again. Lydia had to stop thinking like Gina's friend and start acting like her boss.

Pushing the door open, she headed to the PICU first—all those sick kids freaked her out, so best to get it over with first, before she found some excuse to avoid it.

She wasn't surprised to find Amanda at Alice's bedside. Looked like it had been a long day for the medical student—her eyes drooped with fatigue, and her once-crisp linen dress was now baggy with wrinkles.

"How's she doing?" Lydia asked. The baby was swathed in equipment, making her look like some kind of infant cyborg mutant.

Amanda stood, stroking Alice's foot—about the only naked skin not attached to a monitor or medical device. "We have her paralyzed and sedated, so hard to say. Lucas is going to risk waking her up tomorrow. If her EEG looks promising, we'll warm her up. If not . . ."

If not, Lucas would follow standard brain death protocol: an MRI with angiogram. Lydia pursed her lips, glancing beyond the infant's bed to the nurses' station, where the PICU fellow was glaring at her, challenging her now that she was here on his turf.

"If things look bad, I'd like a chance to talk with the parents, explain why I did what I did."

"I don't think that's such a good idea. The cops let the dad out this afternoon. The mom blames him for the accident and is leaving him, taking the kids. He kinda blames you—"

"Me?" Lydia rocked forward on the balls of her feet, unconsciously assuming a fighting stance. "He blames me?"

"It's just too scary for him, seeing Alice like this—not knowing . . ." Amanda gave the baby's foot a quick squeeze as if trying to reassure the comatose infant that she wasn't alone.

"Does Lucas think I made a mistake? Starting the cooling?" Lydia hated to ask; she felt sure she'd do the same again given the circumstances. But she also knew that she might have saved Alice's life only to condemn her to a life in a persistent vegetative state.

"Lucas likes to think things through—guess that's why he's so good at his job. But he said that what you did was innovative. I think he wished he'd thought of it."

"If it was going to work, I needed to move fast. Down in the ER we don't always have the luxury of thinking things through." Lydia wasn't defending her actions, merely stating a fact of life—a fact that many of the floor attendings conveniently forgot when it was the ER docs down in the trenches fighting for their patients' lives. Maybe she could explain that to Alice's father, once he sobered up. "How's my other mystery patient, Tracey Parker?"

Amanda scrubbed her hands with the antibacterial foam at the patient's bedside. "I was just going to check on her."

As they walked down the hall to the medical ICU, Amanda explained that Lucas still didn't have a diagnosis for Tracey. "He's planning to wake her for a Tensilon challenge in the morning. I hate the idea of what will happen if it doesn't work—can you imagine being in a locked-box syndrome like that?"

"Lucas will just sedate her again. Even if the Tensilon doesn't work, Tracey won't be awake all that long, maybe an hour or so."

"Even that's too long." Amanda shuddered, hugging herself. She seemed more than tired; she was dragging.

"Are you all right?" Lydia asked.

"I just haven't had a chance to eat much today. I think it's catching up with me."

Lydia remembered the long days of living on caffeine, chocolate, and peanut butter crackers swiped from the nurses' stations. Unlike residents, who were limited to an eighty-hour workweek, there were no regulations on how many hours a week medical students could work, so they were sometimes pushed beyond their limits—although usually a consultation service like neurology was a "cush" rotation with predictable hours.

"You know Tracey's case better than anyone. Why don't you come over to my place for dinner? Nora is bringing Tracey's chart and those of a few other patients that she and Elise Avery discovered who had similar symptoms. Kind of like a book club, only instead we're trying to solve a medical mystery."

"Other patients?" Amanda stopped outside the doors to the medical ICU and looked both ways down the hall as if worried someone would hear. "Besides Becky Sanborn?"

Lydia shrugged; she didn't know their names. "Nora said there were at least three. She was going to do a records search and pull copies of the charts."

Amanda looked down at her feet, scuffing one of them against the floor.

"Amanda, is something going on?"

"No. I'm fine, everything is fine." She brightened and stood up straight again. "Dinner sounds like a great idea. I'd love to help Tracey if we can find the answers before Lucas has to do the Tensilon challenge tomorrow."

AMANDA FOLLOWED LYDIA DOWN THE STEPS leading outside, glad she'd run into the emergency medicine attending. Her conversation with Becky's mother had been unenlightening except for one small item that just didn't seem to fit. Either it was a coincidence or—no, it had to be just coincidence. The only way it wasn't would be if Amanda was part of the pattern, had the same thing as Becky and Tracey.

And that just wasn't so. But still, it had given her chills when Mrs. Sanborn mentioned that Becky had been staying in Pittsburgh for the summer because she was on CMU's crew team.

Which meant Becky rowed out of the same boathouse

as Amanda. The same boathouse where Jared worked. Too weird.

She'd stopped by to ask Jared about it, but he was gone—leaving Amanda puzzled but no closer to an answer.

Maybe Lydia would find one and she could relax, stop worrying. More important, if Lydia found an answer, they could still save Tracey before it was too late.

LYDIA OBVIOUSLY WASN'T HOME YET. NORA shifted the stack of printed patient records in her arms as she approached the small Craftsman-style bungalow that sat behind the Angels cemetery.

It was against the rules to take charts outside the hospital, but if Elise was right about Lucas, then the last thing Nora wanted was to be discussing the possibility inside Angels. Hospital walls had ears, and nothing was sacred or spared from becoming grist for the gossip mill—as Nora knew from personal experience. Careers and lives could be ruined with less . . . if Elise was right.

Which she wasn't. Still, it wouldn't do to be speculating about a doctor's possible involvement in patients' deaths, not where they might be overheard. So Nora had broken the rules—something she was certain Lydia hadn't considered when she suggested they meet here tonight. Must be nice to never worry about little things like rules and regulations and JCAHO and HIPAA laws and the like.

She knew where Lydia kept the key, on a hook behind some paint cans in the carport, but it turned out she didn't need it; the door leading from the carport to the kitchen was unlocked. She rolled her eyes—apparently Lydia didn't worry about security either. Nora hoped she never learned how fragile that feeling of being secure was.

A sleek, oversized caramel-colored cat slinked past her into the garage. He curled between her legs, sat back, and looked her up and down, his head coming up past her knee. The gleam in his green eyes made Nora wonder if he was sizing her up as a would-be intruder or as dinner.

"No, I'm not Lydia," she told the cat, whom Lydia called No Name. "You'll just have to wait for her."

The cat blinked slowly. It was larger than any cat Nora had ever seen, squared off in shape, resembling a small panther. It had been living here before Lydia moved in, some kind of stray from the cemetery that stood between the house and Angels.

No Name rolled back onto his feet, twining his way between the wheels of the vintage motorcycle parked in the carport, then disappeared into the overgrown hedge on the other side. Nora eyed the bike with distrust—Lydia had inherited it, but any ER doctor knew the dangers of motorcycles—"donorcycles," as they were called in the hospital. Why hadn't Lydia sold it or given it away? She wasn't riding the damn thing, was she? That's all they needed, one of their own attendings coming in DOA one night. Surely even Lydia wasn't that reckless.

She shook her head and stepped into Lydia's kitchen. It was spotless and spartan—the only things on the counter were a microwave and a motorcycle helmet. Good Lord, she *was* riding it.

There were two chairs and a round table, too small to spread out all the documents from the three patients, so Nora continued through to the dining room. It had beamed ceilings like the rest of the Craftsman-style house and was painted a soft apricot color that reflected the sunlight from the wide French doors that ran along the outside wall. But there was no furniture—unless you counted the tall surfboard propped up in the corner, a remnant of Lydia's previous life in Los Angeles.

A large archway connected the dining room with the living room. Here there were at least a few pieces of furniture, which Nora recognized because she had helped move them in—a few photos arranged on the fireplace mantel; an overstuffed chair angled out from the front windows; a worn leather sofa; and a small TV/DVD combo perched on an end table wedged into the far corner.

Trey's contribution, Nora guessed. The paramedic was a Pittsburgh native and wouldn't risk missing any Steeler or Pirate games. Lydia didn't seem like much of a TV person. Instead there was a proliferation of books that hadn't been here the last time she'd visited—two crooked stacks, leaning ominously to one side beside the couch. All from the library.

Despite its lack of furniture and personal items, somehow Lydia's empty house felt more like a home than Nora's own place, even though her apartment had rooms filled with possessions she'd moved from the town house she and Seth used to share.

Nora dumped the stack of files onto a coffee table. She was tempted to continue her exploration of Lydia's house—had she bought any bedroom furniture yet? What did she and Trey do if she hadn't?—when the sound of the carport door opening prevented her.

Nora turned, her heart pounding, experiencing a strange déjà vu, expecting to see Seth bounding through the door.

She placed one palm over her chest, hating that her body still insisted on reacting as if she and Seth were together. Of course it wasn't Seth coming in—and why would she want to lay eyes on his lying, cheating face anyway? Was she becoming that desperate or lonely?

She told herself it was just that Lydia's home reminded her of how much she missed living in the house she and Seth shared—how much she'd lost. She shook her head, banishing the thought, as Amanda followed Lydia through the door and into the kitchen.

"Roses and peonies along the side of the carport. Maybe some lavender too." Amanda gestured with her hands to emphasize the garden she was planning for Lydia. "And camellias—not sure if they'll grow this far north. I'll check with Mama."

"So how much is this going to cost me?" Lydia asked, nodding to Nora and absently bending to pet No Name, who had appeared again from out of nowhere. "I've never gardened, so I'd definitely need your help."

"No charge, a garden is a labor of love," Amanda protested, draping her lab coat over a kitchen chair.

As Lydia scrutinized Amanda, Nora had the feeling she could tell the balance in Amanda's bank account down to the penny. Lydia had a gift for noticing things and adding them up into surprising insights.

"I'm going to give you a budget," she told Amanda. "You spend as much as you want on the plants, keep the rest for your troubles."

Nora hid a smile at the way Lydia ensured that Amanda would take her money without it seeming to be charity. Amanda's stubborn streak when it came to asking for help—financial or otherwise—was one of her greatest weaknesses.

"I brought the patient charts; they're in the living room," Nora said, leaning against the back of a chair as Lydia opened the refrigerator and without asking handed her a Yuengling and Amanda a bottle of Dr Pepper.

"It's so nice, maybe we could eat outside?" Amanda asked.

"Good idea," Nora said, noting how pale Amanda looked. The girl definitely needed to get out more often.

"It might be a light supper," Lydia said, emerging from the refrigerator with an armful of fresh vegetables. "Trey's back on his health kick. Grilled veggies, salad, bread—oh, but I found some chorizo down at the Strip; that will spice things up a bit."

The door opened again without any sound of a knock.

"How about steaks?" Gina asked, holding two bulging Whole Foods bags out to Lydia as if they were peace offerings. "You guys don't mind if I crash this party, right?"

SIXTEEN

Thursday, 7:49 P.M.

LYDIA LOVED HER KITCHEN. IT WAS SMALL enough to be comfortable, large enough that she could spread out when she cooked, and with its maple cabinets and the bright blue paint that glistened like the Malibu surf at sunset, it felt warm and inviting.

Through the window above the kitchen sink she could see Amanda and Nora setting the picnic table. She turned and glanced over to where Gina sat at the table, slicing tomatoes, her nail polish matching the brilliant sheen of the beefsteaks. Painted nails? Not a good sign. You didn't take care of patients in the back of an ambulance with a fresh manicure.

Gina finished with the tomatoes, and Lydia tossed her a towel. It was so typical of Gina to show up here instead of coming to the ER as Lydia had instructed. Gina always had to do things her way, on her terms. Which was one of the reasons she was this close to losing her residency slot.

As Gina wiped her hands clean, Lydia got a closer look at the other woman's knuckles. She'd noticed the calluses over both middle fingers when she'd first met Gina, but now they were raw, freshly abraded.

"Give me your hands, Gina." Lydia held her own out, palms up, as if she wanted to admire Gina's impeccable manicure.

Gina lay her hands on top of Lydia's. "You like? It's a new shade by OPI."

"When was the last time you purged?"

"I don't know what you're talking about." Gina jerked back, but Lydia held her fast.

"Purge. As in stick your finger down your throat until you vomit." Lydia squeezed Gina's hands even harder, rubbing her thumbs over Gina's knuckles. "When was the last time?"

Gina glared at her, but Lydia met her gaze effortlessly. After a few moments of a silent tug-of-war, Gina surrendered.

"This morning," she whispered, head sunk as she stared at the floor.

"And before then?" Lydia persisted.

"A few weeks ago. I have it under control." She jerked her chin up at Lydia, defiant.

"So instead of joining Med Seven on a ride-along and saving lives, you decided to stay home, make yourself vomit, and get a manicure. That seemed the best way to make use of your time?" Lydia kept her voice steady. There was no way she was going to let Gina off easy. The resident was only two years younger than Lydia, but she had a helluva lot of growing up to do.

Gina gave her a hard stare, eyes narrowed, head tilted to one side. "I don't know what you want from me. But whatever it is, I just can't give it to you, I can't do it. I'm sorry that I'm not as perfect as you are, Lydia. Not a superhero. I'm doing the best I can."

Lydia dropped Gina's hands and stepped back, a short, derisive laugh escaping from her. Gina's eyes bulged with anger. "Nicely done. When did you start giving mommy and daddy that speech? High school? Give me a break."

"You have no right—" Gina's neck muscles tightened into twin delicate ribbons.

"I'm your boss. I have every right," Lydia interrupted her. "Sit down."

Gina balked, glancing down at the chair, then twisted her mouth into a well-practiced pout.

"Sit. Now."

Grudgingly, Gina slid into the chair.

"When did you start?" Lydia asked, taking the chair opposite from Gina. The sliced tomatoes and knife lay between them. "How old were you?"

"Twelve," Gina said without meeting her gaze.

"And you'd give that little speech to your folks, who would then take their assigned roles of being disappointed and concerned, willing to do anything to get their perfect little daughter healthy again, right? Which put you in control, just the way you like it."

Gina flicked a stray bit of tomato pulp along the table's surface with the tip of her fingernail, frowning as if it took more concentration than putting a man on the moon.

"Well, guess what. That was then and this is now. This is your life, Gina—not your parents'. You get to decide how you want to live it. You're in charge of what happens next."

"I—I can't," Gina mumbled, her head still hung low. "I just can't—"

"Sure you can. But first you have to promise me, no more of this bullshit." Lydia reached across the table to take Gina's hand once more. "If you feel like binging or purging or cutting or anything like that, you need to promise me that you'll tell either Boyle or me. Right away. I mean it, Gina. That's a deal breaker."

Gina's gaze crept up to almost meet Lydia's. "Jerry knows?"

"He loves you, of course he knows."

"You guys have been talking about me? Behind my back?" Gina bristled like a toddler ready to stamp off into a tantrum.

Lydia chose her words with care. What Gina did with them was up to her. "You have people worried about you, people who care. In my book that puts you ahead of most folks. Now, do we have a deal?"

Gina looked away for a long moment, then nodded.

"Did counseling help you before?" Lydia asked. "I can set you up—"

"No. I just end up playing mind games with them; it makes it worse." Gina sat up straight, clapping a hand over her smile. "Oh my God, I never told anyone that before. You must think me a real queen bitch."

"Can you talk with Boyle?" Lord knew Lydia wasn't counselor material, but if anyone was, it was Jerry Boyle.

"He's swamped with a case right now. But I've got people." Gina gave a little shake of her head. "Not Amanda, though. Don't tell her—the kid's got enough on her plate, I don't want her worried about me."

Lydia smiled and nodded. Empathy for someone else had to be a good sign. "You're going to want to scrub that polish off tonight, because tomorrow you're back out on the squad."

"I'm not ready."

"Trust me, Gina. You are. Trust yourself."

Gina slanted a look of doubt Lydia's way but finally shrugged noncommittally. Lydia decided it was time for a little tough love. "If you're not on board Med Seven tomorrow morning, you're out of the residency program."

"You can't. Lydia—"

"Sorry, kid. The real world doesn't stop and wait while you get your shit together."

AMANDA HELPED NORA CARRY OUT THE STEAKS and vegetables and set the picnic table on Lydia's patio.

The cat followed them out, eyeing the thick ribeyes Gina had brought. Amanda gave a small shake of her head. Gina should have known Lydia couldn't be bribed. She was glad she couldn't hear their conversation—there was sure to be plenty of yelling, at least coming from Gina.

"Think Lydia will actually fire her?" she asked Nora, who was trying to fish a dropped slice of red pepper from between the grill's grates.

"No. But Gina might wish she had. I don't get the feeling that Lydia gives up on anything or anyone very easily." Nora cursed as the fork she was using fell between the grates as well.

"Yeah, but Gina's the most stubborn person I know. She always gets her way."

"That's part of the problem, isn't it?" Nora lifted the grate free and used the tongs to rescue the pepper and the fork. "Okay," she said when she had replaced it and had everything arranged to her liking. "Ready to fire up."

"Don't you want to preheat it?" Amanda asked. She'd almost said something sooner, but Nora had been so focused on arranging everything on the grill that she didn't want to interrupt. "At least, that's how my daddy does it."

Nora's mouth twisted in a frown. "Yeah, guess that's how Seth did it too." She grabbed a platter, transferred all the veggies she'd arranged on the grill back onto it, closed the lid, and started the grill. "What do you think, high to preheat, then medium to cook?"

"Sounds good to me. Anyway, that will give them more time to talk." She nodded toward the kitchen window.

Nora grabbed her beer and dumped herself into one of the chaise longues. "I think Seth is trying to make up or something."

Amanda sat in the other chaise, tugging her hem down. She kicked off her pumps, watching as the cat began to nudge them with his paws. "Did he ask you out?"

"No. But the last few nights when I've gotten back to Mickey's place there were flowers waiting for me—no card. Then today he put his arm around me and acted . . . well, I'm not sure how he acted."

"Do you want to go back to him? I mean, he and Karen—" She stopped when she saw the wince cross Nora's face. Amanda hadn't ever told Nora, but she'd also spotted Karen and Seth together herself.

"He keeps trying to deny it, but I saw them, together, naked, in her call room. Does he think I'm that stupid?" She blew her breath out in a sigh and took a drink from her bottle of Yuengling. "Men."

"I've been living without for over a year now, and it stinks," Amanda said. Nora glanced at her in surprise, and Amanda clapped a hand over her mouth, trying to suppress her giggle. Back home she'd never talked like this—her few girlfriends would have been aghast, and her brothers would have teased her endlessly.

Enjoying herself, she abandoned her Dr Pepper and grabbed a bottle of beer. Why not? She wasn't on call. "Between you and Seth, Gina and Jerry, and now Lydia and Trey, I've felt like a third wheel. Or a seventh. I'm so tired of being too tired to even think about trying to find a guy, much less never having the chance to meet anyone outside the hospital."

"What about you and Lucas?" Nora asked with an arch smile. "I saw the way you look at him. Except you know it's against the rules."

"Actually, I thought about that." She took another swallow of beer, the alcohol already buzzing through her system, making her feel giddy and reckless. God, she couldn't believe she was talking to someone about this; she'd barely admitted it to herself. "I did some research. It's only against the rules for him to date anyone he supervises or grades. So if I were an intern or resident, it'd be impossible, but as soon as I finish my neurology rotation and he's no longer grading me. . . ."

"He's fair game? Poor Lucas, he's not going to know what hit him." Nora reached across and clinked her bottle against Amanda's. "It will be good for him. He's been moping ever since his divorce. You just have to promise me you'll be gentle with him, let him down easy when you're done with him."

"Nora! I would never—" She stopped when Nora began to laugh and she realized Nora was joking.

Nora patted her arm. "I know, sweetie, that's why you two would be so good together. Lucas needs someone to take care of him almost as much as he needs someone he can take care of."

"I don't need taking care of by anyone, thank you very much."

"We all need taking care of, Amanda. You'll see." Nora sat up and turned away to set her bottle down, but not before Amanda saw the look of pain cross her face. "I think the grill is hot enough now."

As Nora fiddled with the grill, Amanda watched the cat stalk imaginary prey along the arborvitae hedge that stood between the yard and the wrought-iron fence that marked the boundary of the cemetery. Beyond the hedge, the top half of the towers that made up the medical center could be seen in the distance. Other than that they had complete privacy. It was nice, felt a little like sitting out on her own back porch, back home.

"What's with Lucas and Dr. Nelson?" she asked. Seth was Lucas's best friend, so Nora might know. "Why don't they get along?"

Smoke billowed around Nora's face and she waved it away. "I forgot you were helping Dr. Nelson with one of his studies. For godsakes don't tell Lucas, he'll flip."

"Too late. He called Dr. Nelson a quack, but that's not fair. Dr. Nelson has a Ph.D. in pharmacology and is double-boarded in allergy and internal medicine. And he and his wife have been so kind and helpful to me—it feels weird being caught in the middle."

Nora finally got the heat where she wanted it and placed the vegetables on the grill. "It has nothing to do with what kind of doctor Dr. Nelson is. It's about what kind of man he is."

She closed the lid to the grill and sat back down. "Lucas and Seth grew up in Monroeville. Blue-collar, working-class—Lucas's father is a sanitation worker, and his mom worked the checkout at Giant Eagle. You can imagine how a kid with a genius IQ like Lucas fit in around there."

Amanda nodded—about as well as a girl fit into her male-dominated family.

"At least Lucas was good at sports; that helped him make friends. Still, he graduated high school at sixteen; went to Pitt on a scholarship, and Emory for medical school. When he came back to Pittsburgh to start his internship, his mom got sick—ovarian cancer. He postponed his residency and went to work in Nelson's lab. This was before Dr. Nelson hit it big with his patents that let him take those vitamin horse pills and compact them into one small, easy-to-swallow perle."

"What happened?"

"Well, according to Lucas, the perle delivery system was his design, not Dr. Nelson's."

"Dr. Nelson stole it?" Amanda sat up. No, she couldn't see it happening—Dr. Nelson honestly didn't seem to care about the millions his delivery system brought him. She remembered when she had met him and Faith for the first time in the neonatal ICU, their grief over losing their baby, their generosity in donating a large amount to the NICU afterward, funding a grief counselor to help other parents.

"Worse," Nora continued, "when Lucas confronted him, Dr. Nelson claimed he had evidence that Lucas had tampered with his research results, and they almost kicked Lucas out of his residency program."

"Lucas would never tamper with research results. If anything, he'd repeat them twenty times to verify them." Of course, the same could be said for Dr. Nelson—otherwise, why would he spend so much time and money on his clinical trials when he didn't have to?

Nora shrugged. "It all happened almost ten years ago—who knows the truth now? I think what hurt Lucas the most was that Dr. Nelson had been his mentor. Lucas thought he'd finally found someone who understood him, who wasn't threatened by how smart he is."

"He felt betrayed." No wonder Lucas was so touchy about her trusting Dr. Nelson. But what happened all those years ago had to be a mistake, some kind of clerical error or misunderstanding. She couldn't believe either man would actually have done the things they were accused of.

"The divorce last year didn't help. Lucas actually met Stephanie because of Dr. Nelson. She was the lawyer he hired to defend him, to get him reinstated in the residency program. They married after he finished his internship, but then she left him because she didn't think he was ambitious enough. Engaged to a rich lawyer now."

"Ouch."

"Ouch is right. So when I ask you to be gentle with him, I'm not kidding, okay?" Nora sent one of her "mother hen" looks Amanda's way.

"Don't worry. Right now I'm not exactly on his radar anyway. He's focused on his patients. Took him all day to even remember my name."

"Oh, you're on his radar all right. Lucas doesn't miss a thing, believe me. If it weren't for the fact that he plays by the rules, and that he's probably a little gun-shy right now—"

Amanda waved her hand in dismissal. "While he's my attending, it's a moot point." Why was she suddenly so frightened? Was it because she now realized that Lucas Stone wasn't just a fantasy, but a flesh-and-blood man with feelings that could be hurt?

She changed the subject. "Tell me about this patient with symptoms similar to Tracey Parker's and Becky Sanborn's."

SEVENTEEN

Thursday, 8:41 P.M.

THERE WAS JUST SOMETHING ABOUT A COLD beer and steaks done on a grill, Gina thought, tipping back her bottle of Yuengling to get the final drop. Better than any four-star gourmet meal at Christopher's. Especially now that it had finally cooled down a little since the sun went down. Not much—it was still muggy, and clouds hid the moon—but at least it felt more comfortable. She was actually starting to believe in the whole global warming nonsense—AccuWeather said they were due to break another record high tomorrow as well.

Lydia's crazy cat, the one that looked like a panther escaped from some jungle, curled between Gina's legs as it made its way over to Lydia. The cat hadn't shown itself much during dinner; instead it had amused itself by yowling from the shadows at irregular intervals, as if calling to the women to play hide-and-seek.

It felt so—to use one of her mother's favorite terms—*civilized* to sit back and enjoy a good meal with good friends. Well, friends minus one. Damn Lydia for getting in her face like that. She was almost as angry at Lydia as she was at Ken Rosen for dragging her into Homewood this afternoon. His attempt at shock therapy might have been well intentioned, but she could do without it. What a waste of time, all these months thinking he had the answers, building up her courage to go see him.

She took another bite of her steak and sighed in contentment as she chewed and swallowed the juicy morsel. Despite being pissed as hell, somehow she felt relief that Lydia knew her secret—as if a weight had been lifted. She didn't have to pretend anymore, didn't have to be in control of anything. For the first time in days, she not only enjoyed her meal but had no compulsion to purge. And better yet, no guilt about eating or enjoying eating.

See, she *could* be normal, damn it.

Sudden laughter from Amanda startled her, and she thought for a moment everyone was laughing at her. Acid soured her taste buds.

"No Name, scat!" Lydia was saying.

They were all laughing at the cat. No Name had toppled Gina's empty beer bottle over onto its side and was spinning it, catching the drops that flew free with its paw, then licking them. The cat resolutely ignored the humans around him, claiming the picnic table for his own, until Lydia scooped him up.

He screeched, an unearthly sound that made Gina's flesh crawl, raising the hair on her arms, but he didn't show his claws to Lydia. Instead he glared at her as if they shared an unspoken language. Lydia set him out in the yard and turned the sprinkler on, aiming it so that it wouldn't drench the women on the patio.

"Only cat I've ever seen who likes getting wet," Amanda said, taking another sip of her Merlot.

The beer and two glasses of wine she'd had were flushing her cheeks and nose. It was good to see her relaxed, acting like a girl instead of a walking, talking textbook. Girl studied more than anyone Gina had ever met, as if her life depended on her grades.

Nora handed Gina another bottle of beer and offered one to Lydia, who shook her head no. "If you're going to keep him, you should take him to the vet, get him all his shots, maybe declawed or something."

"I'm not keeping him," Lydia said as she resumed her seat, sending a fond glance in the direction of the cat. "I think it's more like he's decided to keep me. He hates Trey, but whenever I'm around he stays close like a dog."

"He protects you because you feed him," Nora suggested.

"It was Trey who started feeding him—he's got the scratches to prove it." Lydia shook her head. "I don't know. But I can't see getting him in a cage to go to the vet."

No Name seemed to sense they were talking about him. He stopped in the middle of the sprinkler, water flying from his fur, and raised his head to stare at them. Then he raised his tail, turned, and stalked away, disappearing into the arborvitae hedge.

"You don't let him inside, do you?" Gina asked, noticing that the branches didn't seem to move as the cat flowed through them. As if he were a shadow or something.

"Don't have to," Lydia said. "He finds his own way, in or out. I haven't figured out how."

"Animals are smart," Amanda said. "Look at Nora's dog—"

"Ex-dog. He's Seth's now."

"Oh, right. Anyway, we had this beagle once who was the laziest dog you ever met, but he could sniff out folks with cancer."

"Come on, really?"

"Really." Amanda waggled her wineglass in emphasis, making the Merlot dance. "Chigger would sniff at a person and give a little whine and they'd rush off to the doctor, find out they had cancer. Got to the point where folks were coming from miles just to let him smell 'em. They'd figure, why bother with the doctor unless they were sure there was something wrong. Doc Hadley got so mad 'cuz folks wouldn't want to pay him when they could let Chigger sniff them for free. And Chigger was so accurate that they sometimes would just go home and put their affairs in order, instead of going to the doctor at all."

"I can't believe a dog would be more reliable than blood work," Nora argued. "Surely he was wrong some of the time. I mean, even lab results are wrong a percentage of the time."

Amanda was shaking her head vehemently. "No, ma'am. He was dead right every time. And you know, someone sneaked in one night and poisoned him because of it? My dad figured it to be Doc Hadley—hard enough to make a living without some old hound dog stealing your customers. But we could never prove it."

Lydia leaned forward, fists on the table. "He killed an innocent dog? What the hell kind of doctor does that?"

"Doc Hadley didn't kill Chigger. Just poisoned his nose. Poor old boy couldn't smell anything after that—no good at hunting, no good at anything. My folks still kept him—he just ate and slept on the porch or down at the docks until he died of old age."

WHILE THE OTHERS WERE STACKING THE dishes, Amanda's cell phone rang. A normal ring, like a normal phone, thank goodness. She checked the number and recognized Dr. Nelson's clinic. Could he have her lab results back already?

She edged out to the living room, out of earshot, and answered. "Hello, it's Amanda Mason."

"Amanda, it's Faith."

"Faith, hi. Do you have my lab tests back already? Any idea what's wrong with me?" The words poured out as if she'd turned on a spigot; she put a knuckle between her teeth to stop herself and give Faith time to answer.

"Amanda, dear, don't worry. I'm sure there's nothing wrong with you that a few good meals won't take care of.

In fact, we should schedule a date for you to come to the house for dinner soon. I wanted to let you know that I did some checking about that other girl, your patient."

"Tracey Parker?" Amanda forced herself to relax. Faith was right; she was overreacting.

"You wanted to know if she was a study patient?"

"Right. Her boyfriend said she was, but he didn't know which study."

"Well, I don't know if it helps or not, but she actually came to only two clinic appointments—dropped out of the study almost immediately. And that was several months ago."

"Okay. Thanks, Faith. I appreciate your looking into it."

"No problem. And get some rest—that will do you more good than anything, I guarantee it. Good night." She hung up, and Amanda returned the phone to her pocket.

Well, that ruled out any problems with a research project gone awry. Not that she'd really thought that was possible—there were too many checks and balances.

Which meant they still had no way of connecting the three patients—or Amanda.

Lydia and the others joined her in the living room. Gina took the overstuffed chair by the window, Amanda and Nora sat on the couch where they could have easy access to the patient files, and Lydia leaned against the fireplace mantel.

"Which patient was first?" she asked. "How did they present?"

"Becky Sanborn. I was there when she came in," Amanda answered. "Presented to the ER unresponsive with what appeared to be focal seizure activity but was later determined to be myoclonus and muscle fasciculations. She was nineteen, a student at Carnegie Mellon, no history of drug or medication use, no past medical history other than asthma as a child, no allergies, no family history. She died the next day without regaining consciousness. Her symptoms began several weeks prior, and she was seen at the neurology clinic by Lucas Stone. Evaluation negative and no gross findings on the postmortem, but microscopic results are still pending—we're hoping to have them tomorrow."

Lydia nodded at her presentation. Amanda felt pleased with herself; it had been short but covered all the relative points—without any of the emotional turmoil she'd felt while watching Becky die. Maybe she *could* learn to detach herself, treat patients as patients instead of getting too involved.

"And the second patient?"

Nora shuffled the papers in front of her. "Michelle Halliday. Twenty-two, grad student at Pitt, presented to the ER with sudden onset of muscle weakness and numbness after a workout. Muscle fasciculations noted in the ER." She looked up. "Gina, you were the resident on her case."

Gina jerked herself as if she'd been asleep. "I was?" Nora passed her a copy of the ER record. Gina scanned it and shrugged. "Guess I was. Looks like I turfed her to neuro right away; it was an obvious admit."

"Admitted to Lucas Stone's service, workup negative," Nora continued. "He tried chelation therapy when a urine screen came back borderline positive for mercury."

"Mercury? Could she have been poisoned?" Gina said, interested enough to reach for the case file and begin to riffle through it.

"Further testing said no. And the chelation didn't work," Nora said. "She showed improvement for approximately twenty-four hours, then died of sudden cardiac arrest. Autopsy negative. Also no past medical history, no meds, no history of drug use, no family history."

Gina tossed the chart to Amanda, who was sitting closer to her than Nora was. It fell open and Amanda found herself staring at a familiar face. She froze, her finger covering the patient's name: Michelle Halliday was Shelly. Shelly, the assistant manager of the boathouse. Shelly, who had died a few weeks ago from some unknown illness.

"Mercury, that would be environmental exposure, right?" she asked.

"Almost always," Lydia answered. "Is there a place all three patients have in common?"

"But Lucas ruled out mercury poisoning," Nora said just as Gina also sat up to protest. "Besides, mercury might explain some of their symptoms but it wouldn't kill them."

"You're right, it wouldn't explain their deaths." Lydia rearranged herself, not quite fidgeting but also not standing still.

"Becky and Shelly—er, Michelle—both used the Washington's Landing boathouse," Amanda said, her voice low, her gaze still focused on Shelly's chart. She wanted to be wrong, hoped she was wrong.

"They did?" Nora asked, leafing through the chart.

"Becky was on CMU's crew team and Shelly worked there."

"What about Tracey?" Lydia asked.

Amanda remembered Jared lamenting that his girlfriend was a runner, strictly a landlubber, hated the water. "She didn't row, but her boyfriend works at the boathouse."

"Well, now we're getting someplace," Gina said. "The boyfriend is playing Bluebeard, slipping them all mercury cocktails."

"Gina, be serious." Lydia bent to rub No Name's belly. "You're right, mercury couldn't have killed them, but maybe there's another link. Tracey and Michelle both presented after exercise. What was Becky doing when she presented?"

"Not exercising," Amanda said. "It was three in the morning. Her roommate said she was pulling an all-nighter, studying for a test." She thought for a moment; her own symptoms were often worse when she was stressed out or tired. But of course she didn't have anything like what these three patients had. Definitely not.

"Maybe it's not exertion but fatigue that brought on their symptoms?"

"Maybe," Lydia allowed.

"Everyone gets tired. They don't go all spastic and drop dead from it," Gina put in, always the life of the party.

"She's right," Nora said. "There has to be something else these girls had in common, something that made them vulnerable."

"Vulnerable to what?" Gina asked. "How can you figure out what triggered their symptoms when you don't even know what killed them? You're chasing in circles."

"Let's look at the symptoms," Lydia suggested. "What's our differential?"

"Parkinson's, multiple sclerosis, Guillain-Barré," Nora said.

"Huntington's, myasthenia, rabies, stroke," Amanda volunteered. "Also botulism, maybe West Nile virus?"

"No, Parkinson's isn't fatal, and myasthenia wouldn't kill this fast," Gina argued.

"Forget the timetable for now; just concentrate on the symptoms," Lydia said.

Gina leaned forward, finally getting into the spirit of things. "Okay, then, you'd better add the mercury thing. And how about ciguatera poisoning?"

"Only if they all ate exotic fish a few hours before their symptoms."

"Still, the symptoms fit."

Lydia nodded as Amanda added it to her list. "Don't forget neuroleptic malignant syndrome, progressive multifocal leukoencephalopathy, thalamic lesions, and shattered nerve syndrome."

Trust Lydia to come up with diseases Amanda never even heard of. She was going to have a lot of research to do. Gina frowned at Lydia's list as well. "You made that last one up."

"Nope. Shattered nerve syndrome is real. It's a form of spinocerebellar ataxia where the beta spectrin proteins degenerate and form deposits. It's what Abe Lincoln had, why he walked so funny."

Amanda wrote as fast as she could, trying to keep up.

"Okay, then," Gina countered. "How about idiopathic generalized dystonia?"

"Now, *you* made that one up," Nora protested. "That name translates to 'muscle problems anywhere in the body from unknown causes.' "

"No, Gina's right," Lydia said. "It *is* a disease category. Mostly older folks, but there's an early-onset variant."

Gina smirked and swung her legs over the arm of the chair. "Anyone else got one?"

They all shook their heads. Amanda glanced at the list she had scribbled onto the back of a HIPAA form. Most of the diseases had no common origin: some infectious, some inflammatory, some genetic; some were side effects of medication, others idiopathic.

"Now," Lydia continued, "what have we already ruled out?"

"Lucas did a pretty comprehensive workup," Nora said, thumbing through the charts. "And it looks like he thought of everything we did, plus a few things I've never heard of." She went through the diagnostic evaluations each patient had, all with negative results.

Amanda crossed off each diagnosis in turn. They were left with a handful of rare diseases, including Gina's ciguatera poisoning and Lydia's shattered nerve syndrome. And mercury toxicity.

"Did he test anyone besides Shelly for mercury?" Lydia asked.

"No, not Becky," Nora said, shuffling through the pages of Becky's chart.

"He did send a urine mercury level on Tracey," Amanda said. "I remember wondering why. It won't be back for a day or more."

"And the autopsy tests on Shelly's tissue won't be back for weeks."

"Besides," Gina said, "if it was this boathouse, there'd be tons of young women showing symptoms. How many women go there, Amanda?"

Amanda shrugged, uncomfortable as everyone turned to stare at her. "Gina gave me a membership two Christmases ago," she muttered. "All the colleges use the boathouse for their crew teams, some of the local high schools as well. And there are tons of rowing clubs . . ."

"See? We're talking hundreds of people—but only two with symptoms and a third whose only connection is through her boyfriend? It doesn't add up."

"Okay," Lydia conceded. "What else, besides mercury?"

"Lucas wants to do a Tensilon challenge tomorrow," Amanda said, circling myasthenia gravis. It was an autoimmune disease where the body attacked the nerve endings secreting the chemicals needed to stimulate muscles. If the patient did have myasthenia, the Tensilon would jump-start those nerve endings by flooding the body with the needed chemical.

"I still say the timing isn't right. And the symptoms are too extreme for myasthenia," Gina argued.

"Sudden-onset generalized myasthenia does occur. It's rare, though," Lydia conceded. "And for three women to all present that way?" She shook her head. "You'd have better odds hitting the lottery without buying a ticket."

"Other than being women, young, and living within thirty miles of Pittsburgh, they don't seem to have anything in common," Gina said, standing and pacing behind her chair, zigzagging between the numerous plants Lydia kept near the window, "except the kinda-sorta-quasi connection to the boathouse. Becky was originally from Ohio. Tracey was born and raised in Millvale. Michelle was married and from Wheeling, West Virginia. Becky was a student, Tracey works at Westinghouse."

"Maybe the slides from Becky's tissues will show something," Amanda said.

Lydia didn't look satisfied with that answer. "Let's hope so. A trip out to that boathouse to investigate any environmental factors would be worthwhile."

Gina stopped abruptly, swinging back around to stare at the other women. "Wait. They do all have something in common. They all had Lucas Stone as their doctor."

EIGHTEEN

Thursday, 10:51 P.M.

FOR SOME REASON THE OTHERS DIDN'T WARM up to Gina's announcement of the obvious: that all the women who had died were patients of Lucas Stone.

Nora had grown downright surly, grudgingly dividing up the patient charts so that Lydia and Amanda could do more research tomorrow. Though Lydia said nothing, Gina had the feeling that she'd been thinking along the same lines as Gina—or had at least entertained the thought.

Amanda had surprised her, vehemently defending Dr. Stone. "You can't go around saying things like that," she'd told Gina as they walked out to Gina's car. "What would people think?"

"I don't know, that it's the truth?"

"But still—"

"A fact is a fact, Amanda. There's no arguing that Lucas Stone is a common denominator between these women."

"*After* they had symptoms."

"*Before* they died," Gina reminded her. Amanda

slammed the passenger door and slouched in her seat. Gina continued, "Before they died of unknown causes."

Amanda maintained an uncharacteristic silence as Gina drove them to the Angels employee garage where Amanda had left her VW parked.

"I'll see you at home," Gina said as Amanda got out. "Jerry will be working all night, I'm sure."

Amanda nodded, twisted the keys in her hand, then shoved them back in her pocket. "I think I'll spend the night here. Make sure my patients are okay."

"You're on elective, Amanda, you don't have to take call." Gina really, really did not want to go home to an empty house. Not after her visit to Homewood today. And Jerry's place was out of the question—when she'd talked to him earlier, he'd made it clear that he'd probably be at the station all night, working those dead bodies he'd dug up out of some yard in East Liberty. She'd be lucky if she saw him for days. "What good are you going to do running yourself ragged?"

"Tracey's all alone. At least if she does wake up again, even if she can't move, she'll know there's someone there for her."

"Sometimes you sound more like a nurse than a doctor." Gina pulled out her Gitanes and shook one free of the pack. She'd been dying to light up for ages but knew better than to smoke around Lydia. "Look, I'm sorry about what I said about Lucas Stone."

Amanda didn't answer. Gina lit the cigarette and took a deep drag. Ahhh, that was the ticket. "Oh, come off it. Grow up, Amanda. Tracey's not going to even know you're there, and all the compassion in the world isn't going to help your grade on this rotation. Who are you really showing off for?"

Amanda flushed, opened her mouth, closed it again, then stomped off toward the stairwell. Gina gunned the engine, tires leaving rubber behind as she sped down the ramp. Seemed like nobody gave a shit about what was going on with *her*. Nobody except maybe the half-gallon of Cold Stone she'd stashed in the freezer.

She left the top down, but despite the AC on high, the night air hit her like a warm, wet wall of humidity. Heat lightning and thunder rumbled in the distance, echoing like the sound of gunshots. She clenched the wheel, pushed the car, skirting yellow lights and dodging traffic, ignoring the curses and honking of other drivers.

Let her get arrested. Wouldn't that just be the icing on the cake? Being forced to choose between pulling Jerry off his precious homicide investigation and waking the great and mighty Moses Freeman from his prescribed eight hours of slumber.

The dreadful thought for some reason filled her with a rush of anticipation. Awful, yet tempting. Like standing on a cliff and stepping out to the edge, looking down and wondering what it would feel like to jump.

Who would she call to bail her out?

She let off the accelerator, her stomach sinking, the lingering taste of Yuengling turning rancid in her mouth. Would either of them care enough to come for her?

AMANDA ENTERED THE MEDICAL ICU AND wasn't too surprised to find Lucas asleep in the visitor's chair beside Tracey's bed, a nursing chart facedown on his lap, perilously close to sliding off. She'd been working so hard to avoid him ever since their encounter down in pathology that he was basically all she'd been thinking about.

Better than thinking about where she was going to come up with another two hundred dollars a month now that she was out of the study, or what her labs might show, or how she had no time to take off if she was sick—which she wasn't—or Gina and her tantrums, or even the mysterious ailment that had taken Becky Sanborn and maybe Michelle Halliday and now Tracey . . .

the ailment that Amanda most definitely, absolutely did not have.

She blew her breath out in a frustrated sigh, too soft to disturb Lucas. His glasses had slid halfway down his nose. He had thick and wavy hair, the kind that got curlier as it grew, and he was definitely past due for a trim. She opened and closed her hand, stretching her fingers, knowing just how good it would feel to run her fingers through his hair . . .

Stop it, Amanda. Not the time or place.

The last guy she'd dated seriously had been right before leaving for med school—her brother Andy's best friend, Justin. They'd known each other for ages, practically grew up together, so she hadn't been too worried when things turned more serious. But Justin had other ideas, taking her out on the boat one day, proposing to her—only to return to the marina to find her mother and both their families, all their friends, the entire town practically waiting to celebrate. But she had turned down Justin's proposal, to the everlasting shame of her mother.

No one seemed to understand that she didn't want to settle down and have kids—at least not right away. She wanted to do something with her life, see the world, meet people. Learn things.

She thought she had everything figured out. Until now. Lucas Stone confused her—compelling and infuriating all at once. Add to that a silly-schoolgirl-falling-in-lust feeling and it was a recipe for bad juju. Right now she had more of that than she could handle.

Okay, this was a huge mistake, coming here. Especially after two glasses of wine and a bottle of beer—more than she usually drank in an entire month.

She turned and crept away. Until the shrill tones of "Free Bird" sounded from her pocket. Damn it. She snatched at the phone, answering it without looking to see who Gina had programmed the ring tone for. Skynyrd—it could only be the other "free bird" of the Mason clan, her middle older brother, Anthony. The one brother she might enjoy hearing from, Tony had been her defender against Adam's tyranny and Andy's tormenting.

"Hey, sweetie pie," he said by way of greeting. "How's my favorite Baby Girl?" You could hear his smile in his voice, even a thousand miles from home. Tony was always smiling. So laid back that she often had to resist the urge to poke him with a stick just to see if he was still breathing. Andy used to torture him mercilessly, trying to get a rise from his big brother and always failing.

She edged farther away from Tracey's bedside, darting a glance over her shoulder. Too late. Lucas was awake, glasses back into position, rescuing Tracey's chart and climbing to his feet to follow her as she crossed through the ICU.

"Hey, Tony. I'm just fine, thank you. How's it going? Everything okay with Becca and the baby?"

Tony wasn't fooled by her lilting voice or lies. She could tell by the pause before he answered. "Everything's fine down here—no matter what Mama told you. Don't let her guilt you into doing something that's going to hurt your schoolwork."

At least Tony saw what she did as some kind of work rather than a childish fit of pique. Even her father didn't understand why she'd been driven to leave South Carolina and the family.

"How's the Love Bug? It getting you around okay up there in the snow and all?"

Coming from a family of mechanics had its benefits—Tony had rallied her brothers and father to restore a pink 1972 VW Bug and give it to her as a going-away present when she left for Pittsburgh over three years ago. "It was eighty-five degrees here today, Tony. Not a snowflake in sight."

Footsteps approached from behind, and a hand brushed against her arm. Lucas. She shivered and pulled away—

not sure whether the heat slip-sliding from her belly up her chest was embarrassment or anticipation.

"You still there, Baby Girl?" Tony's voice reached out to her.

"I have to go now, Tony. Give Becca and the baby a kiss and hug for me."

"I will. Love ya—don't you forget that."

She folded the phone closed and tucked it back into her pocket before turning to face Lucas. "I was just on my way home."

He said nothing, but merely nodded toward the small conference room the nurses used for report. Amanda held her ground. He finally broke the silence. "We need to talk. Now."

How dare he treat her like he had any right to order her around? "No. I don't want to talk about it. I'm fine, and Dr. Nelson's taking care of everything. There's no need for you to get involved."

She remembered what Nora had told her about Lucas and Dr. Nelson and regretted her words. But she didn't back down, staring at him, meeting his gaze even though she had to tilt her head back to do it.

"You made that perfectly clear, Ms. Mason," he said, his words clipped with annoyance. "It may be difficult for you to believe, but the topic I wanted to discuss was our patient, Tracey Parker. Not you."

He stalked past her down the back hall to the conference room. As he stood there, holding the door open, waiting for her to join him, she realized that all the nurses were staring at her. At them. Embarrassment flooded over her, burning her cheeks.

Damn it, why couldn't she and Lucas Stone have a rational, adult discussion? She walked down the hall, following in Lucas's footsteps, trying to keep her chin high, dignity intact.

Until she stumbled as she crossed the threshold. Lucas

righted her with a hand on her elbow, closing the door behind them as she sank into a chair. The conference room had windows for two of its walls, so they had no real privacy, although no one could hear them.

"I'm just tired," she muttered as Lucas stared at her. Again. He was a man of few words, but his expressions spoke volumes.

She remembered that was what had attracted her to him in the first place. The way he could focus so intently on a problem, on helping a patient. She had wondered what it would be like to be the object of that kind of singular attention—but hadn't bargained on his seeing her only as a scientific conundrum rather than a woman.

Lucas relaxed, leaning back against the door. "You took my notes on Becky Sanborn and then vanished for the day."

"Jim sent me to do a consult on peds." It was strange, but she owed Jim for that one.

"Jim is not in charge. I am." His lips twisted from side to side as if tasting something bitter. "Maybe we should make some changes around here. As of tomorrow you can work with Dr. Hansen in the clinic."

That brought her to her feet again. "You're punishing me for not allowing you to interfere with my personal life?"

"No. I have to put the welfare of my patients first."

"Now you're saying I'm incompetent, a danger to patients?"

"No—I . . ." He trailed off, shaking his head. He pushed off from the door, rubbing his face between his hands. When he looked up, his eyes were clouded, and for the first time she had a glimmer of hope that Nora was right, that he had noticed her. "You're not incompetent, Amanda. Far from it. But I don't think I'm the best attending to teach you."

He leaned against the table's edge, his body seeming to sigh with the effort of remaining upright. His arms were crossed against his chest—warding off any chance of his touching her again.

"I can't be your attending any longer." He paused, the silence heavy as she tried to unravel the nuances of his expression. "It's a conflict of interest."

"Why?" she demanded, taking a step closer so that she was directly in front of him. Now it was she who blocked his escape. "What conflict?"

Her voice dropped, and she was certain it betrayed everything she felt. If only she could figure out *what* it was she felt. Sweat pooled between her breasts, and she felt hot and moist all over—kind of tingly as well, sensations that most definitely were neither professional nor ladylike. Blame it on the wine—better than admitting the real cause: Lucas. Conflict of interest? Did that mean he was as interested in her—her, Amanda, the woman, not the patient with strange symptoms—as she was in him?

"There are—rules."

He stared at her, waiting. As if she were the one in charge, the one with the power here.

The thought charged through her and she straightened, daring to reach out and brush her fingers against his sleeve. "Lydia didn't follow the rules when she started the hypothermia protocol—you said she probably saved that baby's life. You didn't follow the rules when you tried chelation therapy on Michelle Halliday."

He jerked his chin up at the mention of Michelle. "You know about her?"

"I did my research. Trying to find other patients like Becky and Tracey. Why didn't you tell me?"

"I didn't want to scare you. I was already having a hard enough time getting you to trust me enough to tell me your symptoms." He frowned, shaking his head ruefully. "Still am, it seems."

"I'll tell you everything if you don't make me spend

the month in the clinic." She tried her best to summon up one of Mama's best Sunday social smiles. "Please."

She was surprised to see him squirm. She'd seen Gina have this kind of effect on men, and her mother as well, but never expected that she could wield such power. Warmth flooded her. Spending the last year on the wards, trudging into the hospital before dawn and home hours after sunset, she'd forgotten what it felt like, feeling like a woman, like someone desired *her*—not just her ability to start an IV, draw blood, or run errands.

She wanted nothing more than to hike her dress up, slide onto his lap, and kiss him in a most unladylike and scandalous fashion.

His lips parted slightly and she could hear his inhalation. If it weren't for the glass walls surrounding them . . .

The moment roared through her mind like a summer squall across the ocean. Her smile deepened, no longer one she'd copied from Mama, but a genuine one that was all hers.

Then the storm crashed down on her. His gaze met hers and his expression was one of dismay. No, horror.

"I think we have a misunderstanding here," he said, shoving his hands deep into his pockets. "You're my student, Amanda."

She fled through the door and raced out of the ICU before he could finish. Her heart was pounding and the blood rushing through her felt like molten lava. Good gravy, had she just tried to seduce an attending physician?

No, it was insane, against all the rules; her foolish actions could end her career—or worse, his. What if she got kicked out of school, was sent home in shame? What would she tell people?

NINETEEN

Thursday, 11:22 P.M.

"IS THE COAST CLEAR?" TREY MEANDERED through the French doors to join Lydia on her patio, where she was watching the stars from one of her chaise longues, absently stroking No Name into a purring frenzy loud enough to disturb the corpses in the graveyard beyond. She wasn't too surprised to see Trey—unlike her, he wasn't suited to long periods of solitude.

He sat down beside her, ignoring the swipe of No Name's paw as the cat protested the disturbance. "Did you guys finish your chart review? Solve the mysteries of the universe, or whatever else you women do when you get together?"

"I think I got through to Gina," she said, watching as he and No Name played Whack-A-Mole, the mole being Trey's hand as it tried to settle on her thigh. "We'll see how she does tomorrow."

Trey made a noncommittal noise. He shifted his weight so that they now lay side by side on the chaise longue. No Name meowed—a sound like a garbage disposal on overload—and finally conceded, leaping gracefully to the ground with a baleful and superior glance back over his shoulder.

"And Nora's patient she was worried about?"

"Turns out there's more than one patient. I don't know—things don't add up, but I have a few ideas I want to look into tomorrow."

"Sounds like you're planning to spend your day off inside the hospital." He reached behind her to massage the taut muscles along the back of her neck. She relaxed into his touch, amazed once again by how he knew exactly what she needed.

"It's okay, I have a patient I want to follow up on." She didn't add that the patient came with a great-grandson whom she'd promised to take care of. Still wasn't sure how she was going to pull that one off without violating hospital rules or CYS regulations. Probably she'd ignore both . . .

He slid his hand down her arm, entwining it with hers. His hazel eyes twinkled in the light coming through the window. Then he wagged one eyebrow in a melodramatic leer and stood up, pulling her to her feet. "Let's go upstairs, try out that new bed of yours."

"Can't. The sheets are dirty." It was a lie. The sheets were new—she hadn't even slept in them herself. She couldn't meet his gaze as she pulled away from his grasp. The thought of *her* sleeping in that bed—much less in that bed with *him*—panicked her. Probably why it had taken her so long to find the right bed.

It represented a huge investment in this place, in this man, in a future here. She'd never had a home or family other than her mother, never had to make a commitment before. She couldn't do it now, not just on a whim.

"I don't mind." He pivoted her so that her back was to the French door and kissed her.

She tried to respond fully, but her pulse still surged with fear. She had to tread carefully here or she could hurt them both.

He raised his head and regarded her with a serious expression. "Do you have a problem with me staying the night?"

"You can stay all night any night you want. You know that."

He pulled back, caging her in his arms, his face hovering inches above hers. "No, Lydia, I don't know that. I wouldn't have asked if I did."

She bristled at the hurt in his voice. Damn it, was she supposed to be a mind reader or something?

"Well, now you know." She rose up on tiptoe to catch him with a kiss, but he turned his head away. "Trey, really, it's fine. Stay the night."

The sound of No Name tumbling through the sprinkler saved her. The big cat stopped and looked over his shoulder at her as if inviting her to come and play. Not a bad idea.

"Come with me." She ducked beneath Trey's arm and tugged at his hand.

One of the things Lydia loved about her house was its privacy. Originally the cemetery caretaker's cottage, it was built at the end of a cul-de-sac, the only house there, surrounded by tall hemlocks on three sides. The backyard faced the cemetery with its century-old trees and bushes, providing absolute silence and privacy unless you were a ghost.

No Name frolicked, chasing the dancing drops of water. The sky had cleared of storm clouds, allowing a half moon to shower a dim, otherworldly light down on the cat.

"The night's too nice to be cooped up inside. Are you staying?" she asked Trey, holding his hand.

A small furrow of a frown appeared on his forehead, but by the time she slid her hand free and pulled her shirt over her head it had vanished, replaced by a wide grin that showcased the dimple on his left cheek.

She couldn't resist that dimple, and he damn well knew it. He hugged her tightly, then danced her backward through the wet grass into the path of the sprinkler.

"I'll stay."

She interlaced her fingers around his neck, and he lowered her into a dip, her hair brushing the wet grass. He was laughing so hard she was surprised he didn't drop her. No Name took that moment to slink beneath her, his tail brushing her bare skin, tickling her, and she began to laugh as well. Water glistened on Trey's face, making him look like something from a fairy tale. Prince Charming in the moonlight.

"Your cat's crazy, you're crazy, and I love you, so I guess that makes me crazy as well."

Lydia jerked her head up, startled by his words. Water from the sprinkler pummeled them both, making her gasp as the cold sparked against her skin. By the time she caught her breath, she could almost believe she'd imagined his words.

The cat screeched louder than a hoot owl, a sound worthy of a graveyard animal, and Trey laughed again, collapsing them both to the ground. Before she could ask him if he meant what he said, before she could even begin to imagine the implications of his words—if she hadn't imagined them—he buried her mouth with a kiss.

NORA CLIMBED THE OUTSIDE STEPS TO HER second-story apartment and let herself inside. The house was vintage Victorian with spacious rooms, high ceilings, hardwood floors, and large leaded-glass windows that rattled in the slightest breeze. Nora had the entire second floor to herself, with a private entrance outside as well as one leading downstairs through the waiting room to Mickey Cohen's law office.

It made her feel important, being able to help the lawyer. Mickey was semiretired; she'd been a law professor, but now she focused on part-time work, her health permitting, for the ACLU. Nora had been here almost four months now and found that Mickey's independent, argumentative spirit added a spark to what would otherwise be empty nights spent missing Seth.

But now Mickey was away on vacation, leaving Nora alone in the empty house, nights filled with strange noises, moans and groans amplified by the silence.

Nora tossed her keys down and clicked on the lights. Everything in its place, just the way she liked it. Still, she felt compelled to adjust the towels hanging from the oven door, aligning them perfectly.

She rinsed out the empty sink; wiped the canisters on the countertop, followed by the countertops themselves; flipped up the burners to scrub beneath them, even though the stove hadn't been turned on all week; and then cleaned the front of the refrigerator and microwave.

The mindless motions soothed her racing thoughts, edging out concern about Seth, anxiety that she'd forgotten something vital to a patient, fear that Lydia and Gina were heading toward trouble on their own reckless paths, and worry that something was wrong with Amanda.

By the time she finished, her mind had quieted and she felt that maybe she could fall asleep without too much effort.

She went to the bathroom, scrubbed her teeth clean for the prescribed two minutes with her sonic toothbrush, washed her face, and changed into her nightgown. After double-checking her locks and leaving the bedroom door open and the lights on—Nora did not sleep with the lights off—she crawled beneath her covers. She'd just eased herself back, breathing deep until her shoulders slumped in relaxation, and closed her eyes when the phone rang.

She bolted upright, blinking twice before she remembered that the phone was on the table beside her. Her fingers and lips tingled with the familiar early signs of hyperventilation by the time she picked up the receiver. "Hello?"

"Nora? I didn't wake you, did I? I know you're usually such a night owl and I didn't know who else to call after

Gina didn't answer, I think she's pissed at me anyway, or maybe at Jerry, I'm not sure. Definitely pissed about something, probably Lydia giving her an ultimatum and making her go to work with EMS tomorrow. Anyway, I thought you'd still be up. I didn't wake you, right?"

Nora took a beat to process Amanda's tumbled words, all the more difficult to understand because her Southern accent was also on overdrive. "Amanda, what's wrong?"

"Wrong? Well, nothing's wrong. I guess. Maybe. I'm sorry, I never should have disturbed you. Go back to bed."

"Amanda—"

"I kinda tried to kiss Lucas Stone and he was so totally not interested, you should have seen the look on his face, you'd think I was a swamp monster or Cujo or something, his eyes got so big, and he practically threw me out of the ICU and now I don't know what to do, oh God, I'm so embarrassed. Nora, what should I do?"

Nora sank down onto her bed, her breathing finally slowed back to normal. "Slow down and tell me exactly what happened."

"We were in the ICU—the conference room, you know? The one with glass walls—oh my God, everyone could see us, they were probably all laughing at me—"

"You were in the ICU and . . ."

"We were talking about Tracey Parker—oh heck, I forgot to tell him about the ideas Lydia had—anyway I tripped and he kind of caught me, and we were standing really close and I had this idea that maybe he was interested and I—I—I—"

"What, Amanda? Did you kiss him?"

"No. But I wanted to." The medical student's sigh rattled through the airwaves.

"Did he kiss you? Do anything inappropriate?" Nora couldn't imagine it, not of Lucas—but then again, her judgment about men hadn't been very accurate lately. She couldn't help but remember what Elise and Gina had said earlier about his being the only common factor in the deaths of two patients.

"Lord no! If you could have seen the look on his face! He was shocked, horrified—Nora, I disgusted him! He said I should leave the service, work down in the clinic, that it was inappropriate. Do you think he'll call the dean? He could get me kicked out of school. Nora, I couldn't bear that, I just couldn't. What would I tell my folks?"

"Calm down, Amanda."

Usually Amanda was the quiet one, but when she got to talking it was like trying to stop the Johnstown Flood with a spatula. Nora threw the covers off and bounced to her feet, happy to have someone else's problems to think about. "If I know Lucas, he's more embarrassed than you are. Probably blaming himself for giving you the wrong impression."

"He didn't, honest, he didn't. It was all my fault."

"It was no one's fault. These things happen. You both were tired, working so close together trying to help a patient, it's easy to get your signals mixed up."

"Really? So you don't think I'll get kicked out of school or anything?"

Nora paced past the windows looking out over the back of the house. She stopped, drew back the edge of a curtain. There was a man walking across the backyard.

"No, you're not going to get kicked out of school. Do you *want* to go down to the clinic for the rest of your rotation? It would get you away from both Lucas and Jim Lazarov."

"Jim. Yuck. If he hears about this—" Amanda interrupted herself. "No. I don't want to leave my patients. I want to stay on the floors. Even if it means working with Lucas and Jim."

The man in the backyard stopped at the base of her steps. Nora craned her head, watching from behind the curtain so he couldn't see her if he looked up. He didn't walk up the steps, but instead crouched down as if placing something there.

Son of a bitch. Seth, the lying bastard. Leaving her more flowers—after she specifically told him to stop.

"Amanda, here's what you do. Don't mention it. Act like it never happened. Lucas will do the same."

"He will?"

"I guarantee it. Don't worry, everything will be all right." As she spoke, Nora jogged through the house to the back door and unlocked it. She flicked on the outside light just as she jerked the door open. "I have to go now. Bye."

Still holding the phone, telling herself she'd call 911 if Seth tried to do anything, she ran down the steps. The lights caught the glisten of florist cellophane and the bright colors of a bunch of daylilies lying on the grass. The man was already almost to the curb.

"Seth!" she shouted. A dog barked in the distance. "You bastard. Go ahead and run—and don't you ever come back!"

The man paused but didn't turn around. He was too far away for her to make out any features other than that he wore jeans and a dark hooded sweatshirt. He kept going, out of sight around the corner of the house. A few moments later, there was the sound of an engine gunning and the squeal of tires.

Nora grabbed the bunch of flowers and whacked them against the railing of the stairway, quickly decapitating the delicate blossoms and venting her fury as the petals exploded around her.

TWENTY

Friday, 6:17 A.M.

SOMETHING COLD BRUSHED AGAINST AMANDA'S arm, and she startled awake. She'd fallen asleep at a computer in the hospital library. She brushed her hair away from her face and looked around. Then grimaced.

Lucas Stone stood over her, offering a can of Dr Pepper. She accepted it without thinking and took a gulp to cover her embarrassment. She'd retreated to the quiet refuge the library offered and had spent the rest of the night researching Tracey's symptoms and trying in vain to correlate them with anything she could have been exposed to through Jared or the boathouse.

Well, most of the night. Her fingers mashed at her face, tracing the imprint the keyboard had left behind on her cheek.

"I noticed you seem to like the sweet stuff. You know, that's got more caffeine than coffee," Lucas said, leaning against the back of a chair. "Looks like you might need it, though."

She looked at him with suspicion. "Are you here to tell me I'm suspended?"

Ignoring her question, he rustled through the stack of articles she'd printed out. No answers yet, but lots of theories to consider.

"Good work. I disagree with Friedman and there's no evidence of heavy metal toxicity, but this article about lupus and progressive multifocal leukoencephalopathy could be promising. Wow, you even got into beta spectrin degeneration; I'm impressed." He squinted at her over the top of the sheaf of papers. "Guess maybe you're better off with me than stuck down in the clinic."

"Is Tracey okay?" She started to stand, but her foot was asleep and she stumbled, almost spilling the Dr Pepper on Lucas.

Lucas stepped forward to catch her, then froze, leaning back as she steadied herself on the back of the chair. Like he was afraid to touch her. Who could blame him after the way she'd acted last night? She was never going to mix beer and wine again, she swore.

"No change." Handing her the papers, he spun on his heel, not waiting as she grabbed her lab coat. "C'mon, I'll buy you breakfast. Then we need to make rounds."

He was acting as if nothing had changed—yet it also felt as if everything had changed. No surprise after her blatant display of hussiness last night.

Her neck flushed with embarrassment, and she gulped the Dr Pepper, barely tasting it, but the fizz and cold brought her fully awake. Buttoning her lab jacket over her rumpled scrubs and shoving her notes into her already bulging pockets, she hurried to catch up.

Then she took a breath and forced herself to slow to a more professional pace. If he could ignore what happened last night, so could she. Nora had been right—*it never happened, it never happened* was her new mantra. She couldn't afford to embarrass either herself or Lucas again, not if she wanted to pass this rotation. A mask slid down over her features as she strolled down the corridor beside Lucas. Two professionals going to breakfast, that's all this was.

If only her heart would stop galloping so hard that she was sure it was ready to burst free from her chest.

NORA WAS LATE. SHE WAS NEVER LATE. SHE HAD slept through her alarm—she never slept through her alarm. Heck, usually she woke five minutes before the alarm went off. But last night had been one of her worst nights since she'd left Seth: restless, jittery, barely drowsing, waking every few minutes with a panicked lurch, her heart double-clutching, until sheer exhaustion took over.

She grabbed her car keys and ran out her door and down the steps that led from her second-story apartment to the rear of Mickey's house. Almost tripped and fell down the last few when she saw what waited for her below.

The steps were garnished with bouquet after bouquet heaped together, bright colors popping out from under greenery, the morning sunshine glistening on the cellophane.

Lavender daylilies. Her favorite. She crouched beside the mountain of color and rustled through the arrangements. No card. Again. But there was no need for a card. Seth knew how much she loved daylilies and that lavender was her favorite color.

She'd probably heard him returning during the night; that was why she'd kept waking. Had he been watching her? After she'd already run him off once?

Crushed petals tumbled through her fisted fingers. Nora stood, stomping through the floral offerings as if they weren't there, and stalked to her car. Her fingers shook as she turned the key in the ignition.

This had to stop. She blinked in fatigue, trying to summon the energy to drive the two miles to Angels, not to mention working a twelve-hour day. He had to leave her alone. She couldn't keep living this way.

TWENTY-ONE

Friday, 6:51 A.M.

GINA STOOD POISED IN THE DOORWAY TO HER bedroom, smoking a cigarette. She'd avoided temptation all night—other than a shot of Maker's Mark to help her sleep. Now she was up and fully dressed, even had her Kevlar on.

She took another drag and blew it out in a stream of smoke, imagining Greta Garbo—now *there* was a woman with attitude.

All she needed to do was walk out the door and drive over to meet Med Seven. Prove to Lydia Fiore once and for all that Gina could handle it, that she was in control. She could do it. She would do it—if only to show Lydia how wrong she was, threatening to dump Gina from the residency program.

After all, Gina was the goddamn Hero of Angels, wasn't she?

She didn't move. Imagined falling back onto her king-sized bed with its thick handcrafted mattress and silk sheets, the weight of her ballistic vest pulling her down, the soft folds of sheets billowing over her, sinking,

sinking . . . finding that warm safe place where nothing could touch her, where she was bulletproof from everything and everyone.

The temptation was overwhelming. She tugged at the Velcro of her vest, shuffled one step forward. Bed was where she'd spent most of her life lately. At least the hours when she wasn't marking time at work or with Jerry.

Jerry. Visions of herself, regal and elegant in a white flowing dress, Jerry beaming at her as they exchanged vows, children racing around, filling a house with laughter as he wrestled with them. . . . She shook her head. Jerry would make a wonderful father, the best. But she didn't have what it took to be a wife or a mother. She barely had what it took to take care of herself, much less someone else.

She crushed her cigarette into her Murano ashtray. The bed filled her vision once more. Another step and she was almost there, had almost escaped. Part of her despised the weakness, the surrender. Most of her was too numb to care. She ripped another swath of Velcro open.

The phone rang, and her stomach jumped with guilt. She grabbed it. "Hello?"

"Gina, it's Trey Garrison. Look out your window."

Puzzled, she crossed the room to the front windows overlooking Gettysburg Street. Double-parked in front of her house was an ambulance. In front of it, waving up to her, stood Trey Garrison, dressed in his district chief's uniform. Beside him, slouched against the driver's door, his trademark Oakleys shielding his eyes, was Scott Dellano—better known as Gecko—one of the paramedics who'd been with her during the drive-by shooting.

"Trey. What are you doing here?"

"Heard you needed to get back on the streets or you'd never finish your EMS rotation. Figured the least I could do was come along on your first shift." His voice was jovial, more inviting than pressuring.

She shook her head, recognizing Lydia's guiding hand.

Lydia might be new to Angels, but she sure as hell seemed to have Gina's number.

Gina wasn't sure whether to be insulted or touched. It wasn't every day a district chief of Advanced Life Support escorted an emergency medicine resident on a ride-along.

"How can I say no?" she said, forcing lightness she didn't feel into her tone. No, she didn't feel light at all; she felt bloated and heavy, weighted down. "I'll be there in a minute."

She hung up and walked out of the room with one last glance at the bed. As she closed the door, gunfire echoed through her mind, along with the grit of the pavement as she dove for cover, the gleam of the bullet caught by the Kevlar vest.

Pausing in the hallway outside her bedroom, she bowed her head, sucked in a breath that swelled her chest until her vest tightened like a boa constrictor. She could do this. She could.

Acid bit her throat. She sprinted down the stairs and out the front door before she could change her mind.

DURING THE SHORT TIME THEY'D BEEN WORKING together, Amanda had figured out a lot about Lucas Stone. For starters, he was more than a tiny bit compulsive. He was downright germophobic—something manageable on the wards, where sinks and soaps and antibacterial foam dispensers were in easy reach. But here in the cafeteria?

Breakfast was the one meal when the cafeteria could be counted on to prepare something that tasted better than sautéed cardboard, so it was always the most crowded time of day. When they finally found an empty table, Amanda sat down with her tray piled high with eggs, hash browns, sausage, oatmeal she tried to pretend was grits, and a glass of milk.

Lucas, on the other hand, balanced his tray on the flat

of his palm with one hand as he efficiently wiped his side of the table before sitting. His breakfast consisted of a packaged blueberry muffin, a banana, and a cup of coffee, along with a package of plastic silverware and a stack of napkins.

Amanda dug in, watching as Lucas stirred a package of sugar into his coffee, then unwrapped a straw.

"I've never seen anyone drink coffee with a straw," she said.

"Doesn't burn your mouth this way." He gestured to the length of the bendy straw. "Gives it time to cool."

"Right. Surprised more people don't use straws with their coffee."

He glanced around the crowded cafeteria, flinching as someone sneezed at the table beside them. "So am I."

He ate his banana first, finishing the entire thing without putting it down. "Did you find anything?"

She was halfway through a mouthful of eggs and sausage and had to swallow before answering. "About Tracey?"

"Or the others."

From the way he stared at her, she had the feeling he was trying to decide whether to lump her in with Becky and Michelle. She started to tell him about the possible connection to Jared and the boathouse, but stopped. It was too vague. She'd just regained his trust; she couldn't afford to look like a fool.

"No. Nothing fits. That case study of shattered nerve syndrome was the closest thing I found."

He didn't look too surprised at the unusual diagnosis. What was she thinking, that she could come up with something that Lucas Stone couldn't? The man was a genius, and everyone marveled at his diagnostic acumen—if he couldn't figure out what was wrong with their patient, what hope did she have?

"What about your symptoms?" He fiddled with his straw, gazing into the coffee cup as if it held the answers.

"Don't you think it's about time you told me what's going on?"

"*Our* patients"—she stressed the pronoun—"had a much more precipitous course. I'm sure I have nothing in common with them."

"Why don't you let me be the judge of that?" he snapped, jerking his chin up in irritation. "Damn it, Amanda, why won't you trust me, let me do my job?"

"Maybe because my symptoms *aren't* your job. Besides, Dr. Nelson is taking care of things."

His face clouded and a flush colored his cheeks, highlighting the early stubble of a beard, reminding her that she wasn't the only one losing sleep over their patients. "You trust him more than you'll trust me?"

She laid her hand flat over his and felt his muscles bunch as he suppressed a flinch. She pulled away, chiding herself. Everyone in her family was always touching, hugging, reaching out—but now it was a dangerous habit. She had to make him see her as a professional, a colleague. It should be easier because it was so very obvious he had no interest in her, but it wasn't.

"I trust you, Lucas. But we need to focus on Tracey—I don't want my little medical student hypochondriasis or stress or whatever to distract you."

He narrowed his eyes at her, well aware that she had avoided his question.

"Did you talk to Tracey's boyfriend, Jared?" she asked, hoping he'd change the subject.

"He was gone last night, but left a message that he's coming back this morning. We couldn't find any other family." His eyes took on a faraway expression and his mouth tightened. "I'm hoping that maybe I can give him some good news when he gets here, but—"

"Hey, no change *is* good news." Amanda wondered at her need to comfort him. He was an attending, had probably lost more patients than she had seen in her short career, but he just seemed so vulnerable. As if it were his fault Tracey wasn't better. "At least she's stable, not deteriorating like Becky did."

"For now. Who knows for how long." He took another sip of his coffee and tossed his still-wrapped muffin from hand to hand, crushing the poor thing to a mass of sticky crumbles. "I asked Ken Rosen to consult."

"He's an immunologist, right?" The one who'd been with Gina during the drive-by shooting last summer. Amanda had often wondered about the man but hadn't met him herself.

"Pretty smart guy. I asked him to set up some special immunofluorescent stains from Becky's tissue specimens. They should be ready for us to review later this morning. Hopefully they'll show us something we—I—missed. Or at least point us in a definite direction."

Amanda liked it when he used the plural pronoun; it felt like she was an important part of the team, not just a student there to do scut work. Or worse, a liability.

"Lydia and I were talking," she started, hoping that by invoking another attending's name she wouldn't look too foolish, "and she suggested you might look at environmental causes. Maybe mercury toxicity."

"*Lydia* said that?" His tone made it obvious that he'd seen through her. "What's going on, Amanda? If you found something—"

"It's nothing, just a rough theory. Not even a theory."

"Tell me."

"We were going through Becky's and Michelle's charts and realized that they both rowed."

"Rowed?"

"You know, like crew? Becky was on CMU's team, and Michelle worked at the same boathouse."

"Hmm . . . a boathouse? I guess they might have cleaners and other chemicals. But that doesn't explain Tracey or her symptoms."

"Jared, Tracey's boyfriend, works at the same boathouse." She plunged on. "So when we saw that Michelle had an elevated mercury level—"

"I'm waiting on Tracey's test results, but I'm sure you're well aware that mercury doesn't explain their deaths."

"Well, not alone. Maybe there's something else?"

"Leaving us exactly where we started." He looked downright glum.

"So you're still going to do the Tensilon challenge this morning?" She hated the thought of Tracey waking up, paralyzed, unable to communicate, but they had run out of options.

"Yes. Jim's getting everything ready upstairs." His pager went off. He glanced at the readout and cursed, almost dumping his tray as he jumped up. "It's the ICU. Tracey Parker is crashing."

TWENTY-TWO

Friday, 7:14 A.M.

EMMA GREY'S PACEMAKER SURGERY WASN'T scheduled until nine, giving Lydia enough time to check on her patients in the ICU before she retrieved Deon.

Spending her day off babysitting a kid wasn't top of her list of things to do—she had planned on spending the day in the medical library or pathology, looking into the cases Nora had brought her to review.

What the heck was she supposed to do with a ten-year-old kid, anyway? She could barely take care of a cat—and No Name wasn't even her cat, pretty much fended for himself.

But she had taken care of her mother for all those years—that gave her hope that she wouldn't screw up too badly. Besides, it was only for a day or so, how bad could that be?

Maybe Trey had left one of his shoot-'em-up movies at the house? No, too much violence. She'd ask the folks in Child Life to recommend one that was age-appropriate. Besides, it was too warm to keep a kid inside. But she doubted a ten-year-old street kid would like to go for a run—much less keep up with her seven-minute miles. Hmmm . . .

The nerve-grating, low-pitched subliminal buzz that permeated the peds ICU pushed all thoughts of Deon from her mind. She hated this place with its bright, cheerful colors surrounding families hovering between hope and despair. Hated the careful whispers, the smiles the nurses wore like death masks, the too-tiny beds eclipsed by machinery and monitors.

Here and the neonatal ICU were the two places Lydia usually tried to avoid. But she wanted to see how Alice Kazmierko was doing, if her gamble had paid off.

There was no one else at the baby's bed space. She grabbed the flow sheet with the information collected overnight. Not good; Alice's EEG showed slowing and minimal variability, and her sodium was dropping—a sign that her brain was going into SIADH and producing the wrong hormones.

Lydia dropped the clipboard back on the table and washed her hands. She automatically reached for the stethoscope hanging from the monitor railing but then pulled back. This baby didn't need someone else listening to her heart. Her heart was fine.

Instead of examining the baby, Lydia simply laid her palm over the girl's forehead, taking care not to disturb the EEG leads. She stroked Alice's leg with her other hand, hoping the human touch might do more than the machines had.

"Dr. Fiore." The pediatric fellow joined her at Alice's bedside. "I'm going to have to ask you to leave."

"Why? Are you planning a procedure?"

"No." He shifted his weight, obviously uncomfortable.

"It doesn't look good, does it?" For the first time, Lydia gave her doubts a voice.

"Dr. Stone hasn't made rounds yet this morning, but he's probably going to get an MRI angio later today." A test for brain death. Lydia blinked hard and kept her face as neutral as possible. "We knew the odds were overwhelming," he continued, almost as if trying to comfort her. "Before anyone even touched her, it was too late. That's why it's so hard when you guys in the ER do something heroic like this. Makes the family think there's hope."

"Is that why you want me to leave? Because I tried to save her?"

He shook his head, frowning. "No. The father has gotten a lawyer. They have a restraining order against you."

Lydia straightened so fast she jerked the pulse ox monitor off. She replaced it before the machine could alarm. "A restraining order?" It was crazy. "Why? How could they? The courts aren't even open yet."

He shrugged. "I guess it's not officially a court order. Just a letter on her chart from a law firm. A man brought it this morning, made the charge nurse sign for it. Looks pretty serious to me."

"They're going to sue me? For trying to save their baby?" The lights and monitor tracings all blended together in a cascade of colors, as if she'd stepped into an alternative reality.

"You gave the family hope. So when things go wrong, it makes you an easy target. The mom's bad enough, all wailing and gnashing, but the dad"—his frown deepened to a scowl—"he really has it in for you, claims you assaulted him. Way he talks, you're worse than the driver of the car that hit him."

"You mean the car *he* hit—after running a red light and being drunk enough to have a BAC three times the legal limit."

"I can't judge him. All I can do is take care of their child and help them begin to understand the reality of her condition. But for Alice's sake, I really do have to ask you to leave and not come back."

Lydia drew in her breath, ready to argue. But the sight of the little girl, still as death, quieted her anger. "Okay. I have my cell—will you ask Lucas Stone to call me, keep me updated?"

"I will." Lydia began to walk toward the door when he called out, "Be careful of Mr. Kazmierko—I don't think this is the end of it."

LUCAS SPRINTED UP THE STEPS TO THE ICU SO fast Amanda wasn't sure his feet ever touched the ground. By the time she followed him into the ICU, her breath was coming in heaving gasps, but he was already at Tracey's bedside, surveying the situation and calmly giving orders.

"Get me a gas, lytes, calcium, and magnesium. What's her bedside glucose? How long was the seizure?" he asked as he examined Tracey.

"Generalized seizure, two minutes, preceded by a spike in blood pressure," Jim Lazarov answered. His voice was nowhere as calm as Lucas's. He sounded jittery, like a high-tension wire vibrating in the wind.

Lucas grabbed the EKG rhythm strip revealing the electrical spikes that drove the heartbeat and scrutinized it. "Bradycardia preceded the seizure." Then he turned to the EEG machine. "Except there's no sign of seizure activity in her brain."

"What the hell? I saw it, it looked exactly like a seizure."

Amanda thought about Becky Sanborn and the way she'd presented to the ER. "Myoclonus and muscle fasciculations," she suggested. "Severe enough, they'd look like seizures."

"Myoclonus doesn't cause a spike in blood pressure or EKG abnormalities," Jim snapped.

Lucas wasn't buying any of it without evidence. Amanda watched as he checked and rechecked the EEG and monitor leads, glanced through the nursing notes, and even checked Tracey's IV.

"Who added bicarb to her IV?" he demanded.

"You did, Dr. Stone," the nurse said. "Pharmacy sent it up last night; the order was processed"—she flipped through her chart—"at eleven forty-four p.m."

Lucas was shaking his head, his glasses seesawing on his nose. "Let me see that."

She shoved the chart at him. "According to the pharmacy it was a faxed order, came directly from you."

"I never—they must be mistaken, gotten the patients mixed up."

Now the nurse looked alarmed. "No. Look, it was confirmed with her patient number—it's all straight from the computer."

"Then the night nurse made a mistake, took the order from a different doctor—I didn't order any changes, certainly not at eleven forty-four last night."

The clerk rushed up, handing Amanda a lab slip. "Her blood gas is back. The pH is seven point four eight; she's got a definite metabolic alkalosis."

"Switch the IV to normal saline; let's run a bolus, get me a repeat gas in an hour." Lucas tapped his fist against his lips as he concentrated on Tracey's motionless form. He thought for a few moments, then raised his face to laser in on Jim's. "How much did you give her total?"

Jim startled, and Amanda was surprised to see him look away, unable to meet Lucas's gaze. "I don't know what you're talking about."

"The EKG shows that this all started with a run of bradycardia. A sign of Tensilon toxicity."

Jim shuffled back as if Lucas's low tone were a barrage. "I didn't do anything wrong."

"How much did you give her?" Lucas enunciated each word sharply enough to make Jim flinch.

"I followed your protocol. Started with point one milligram, went up to one milligram, then three and then five when she showed no response." Jim straightened his shoulders and whirled on Amanda as if this were somehow her fault. "I told you it wasn't myasthenia gravis."

"So you gave her only a total of nine point one milligrams?"

"Right. Strictly per your protocol. All I was doing was saving you time. I had everything under control."

Lucas raised an eyebrow and kept his gaze directed at Tracey without saying a word.

"Jim, you could have killed her," Amanda protested.

"The main risks of a Tensilon challenge come from airway control and possible anticholinergic syndrome. We have her airway secured, and other than the bradycardia—which responded to a single dose of atropine—she showed no other symptoms. You can't blame the alkalosis on me; I'm not the one who added bicarb to her IV fluids."

"No, you're just the one who almost killed our patient," Amanda snapped.

To her surprise, Lucas didn't back her up. Instead he was concentrating on the latest lab results. "He's right. It's not myasthenia. We need to resedate her and start over." Jim practically preened, but Lucas ignored it, swinging around to focus on them both. "You two, get down to pathology. Ken Rosen should have those slides ready for us. I'll join you as soon as I'm sure she's stable."

Jim slumped, his face twisted into a scowl of insubordination—he obviously expected some kind of medal for breaking the rules and doing the Tensilon challenge on his own. The scowl quickly vanished as Lucas edged a glare in his direction. "Come on, Amanda, don't dawdle."

NORA RAPPED ON THE TRAUMA RESIDENT CALL room's door, trying to ignore the churning in her stomach. It was in the room right next door that she had found Seth and Karen, the bimbo nurse anesthetist, together. Naked. Memories ricocheted through her mind: Karen's smug smile, the way she flaunted her too-perfect-to-be-natural body, her expression of superiority, laughing at Nora . . .

and then Seth, waking up, the look of surprise and guilt on his face—right before Nora slammed the door on him and their future together.

Nora took a breath, holding fast to her resolve. She had to end this cleanly, now, before it started interfering with her work.

Seth's intern said he was here, but Seth wasn't answering. Did he know it was her?

She rattled the doorknob of the stout old oak door. It turned easily, but something else was holding it in place. Residents weren't allowed to put locks on their call rooms—they had private lockers for that.

Nora pounded with the side of her fist, hard enough to rattle the door in its frame. "Seth! Open up, it's me. We need to talk."

After a moment she heard furniture moving, being dragged across the floor. Then the door opened and Seth appeared, looking rumpled and haggard as if she'd just woken him. Impossible. He was a surgeon, would have been in the hospital by five-thirty, making rounds. And surgeons didn't nap, especially not less than two hours into a workday.

As he ran his fingers through his hair, trying to smooth it down, she wondered if maybe the door had been blocked because he wasn't alone. She craned her neck, trying to look past him, but he was too tall.

"Did I come at a bad time?"

"Uh, no. Of course not." He rubbed one cheek, his fingers tracing fresh sheet impressions. "I didn't get much sleep last night, was just trying to get caught up."

"I'll bet you didn't get much sleep. What did you do? Ransack the gift shop and all the patients' rooms?"

His forehead creased. "What did I do?"

She knew it was going to be painful, but she had to see for herself. She pushed past him, stomping into the room, ready to confront Karen or whoever the bimbo of the week was.

The room was empty. The sheets were tangled on the bed, Seth's shoes sat beside his OR clogs, and his lab coat was draped over the back of the only chair in the room. The door to the minuscule bathroom was open and it was obviously unoccupied.

Unless Karen was hiding under the bed with the dust bunnies, Seth was alone.

Nora was surprised at the disappointment she felt. This time she'd been ready—instead of the speechless, stunned, simpering fool she'd played last time, this time she knew exactly what she wanted to say. Only there was no one to say it to.

Robbed of her chance to confront Karen, she whirled on Seth. "This has to stop. Now."

He turned slowly, holding onto the door. "What? Nora, I don't know what you're talking about."

"The flowers. You. Standing around, watching my house all night. Stop it."

He shook his head, a stray lock of hair falling unnoticed into his eyes. "I haven't been watching your house—well, maybe I've driven by Mickey's a few times, just to make sure you were all right . . ." His voice trailed off.

"Seth, don't play games. I know you left them." She took a step back. "If you don't stop, I'm going to the police."

"Nora." He straightened, lumbered toward her. "Do what you have to do." He spoke slowly, resignedly, as if each word were painful.

His expression was serious, his voice level, his gaze open and without deceit. Exactly the way he had looked when he assured her that he and Karen weren't sleeping together.

She bit her lip, as angry at herself for being sucked in by his Huck Finn gosh-shucks playacting as she was at him. "Go to hell, Seth."

Stalking past him, she took advantage of the solid oak door and slammed it. Hard. A satisfying bang echoed down the hallway, but it did little to quiet the turmoil that raged through her. She saw the elevator doors begin to close down the hall and sprinted, catching them just in time, and found herself alone inside the steel box with its mirrored walls.

The woman who faced her was a stranger. A stranger with the bruised look of a victim.

Nora turned her back on that strange woman and pounded the button for the first floor with her fist.

TWENTY-THREE

Friday, 7:47 A.M.

"I CAN'T BELIEVE YOU DID THAT," AMANDA told Jim as they rode the elevator down to the basement.

"Hey, I did my homework. I knew Stone was being overly cautious by insisting that he be there for the challenge. I might have saved her life by ruling out myasthenia before we wasted any more time on chasing zebras."

"Zebras are all we have left."

"Says you. Maybe Lucas Stone isn't the genius everyone makes him out to be. I've heard he's lost other patients lately."

"Which is why we need to help him figure out what's wrong with Tracey."

"Please," he said, rolling his eyes and using a mock Southern accent. "You mean it's why you want to help *him*. You don't really give a shit about our patient."

"How dare you! Of course I care about Tracey."

"I know what you're doing and it won't work." He snatched the sheaf of articles from Amanda's lab coat and thumbed through them with disdain. "You're wasting your time."

Amanda retrieved her research and shoved it back into her pocket as they exited the elevator. She was barraged by smells of mold, burned laundry, and a sickly sweet scent that she suspected meant a rat had died somewhere nearby. She hated being down here, and she was annoyed with Jim and worried about their patient. It was clear Tracey was starting the same downward spiral that had led to Michelle Halliday's and Becky Sanborn's deaths. "I have no idea what you're talking about."

"Sure you do." Jim stopped at an intersection where two large steam pipes branched out overhead. "Lucas Stone. You're trying to seduce your way into a good grade. Too bad he's gay."

It took a second for Amanda to process what Jim was saying. He started down one corridor, stopped, turned around and began down the opposite one, Amanda rushing after him.

She'd never seen anyone sputter in indignation before, but she was pretty sure that was exactly what she was doing. Wouldn't be surprised if there was steam shooting out her ears like in the comics. Only problem was, Jim didn't seem to notice or care.

"First of all, it's none of your business. Second of all, you're an idiot. Third, that's rude, crass, insensitive, and ignorant. And finally—" She broke off, her thoughts galloping faster than her words. "And finally, you're an idiot."

Jim only smiled. Smug, superior, confident—not even a smile, a smirk. "Whatever." He stopped again, straining to read a faded sign. "Shoot, this isn't right, we're heading toward the cemetery."

"Cemetery?"

"Sure. See that dark tunnel with the low ceiling and brick walls? In the old days, they'd bring the corpses directly from the hospital over to be buried. Saved time, especially during times like the Spanish flu and polio epidemics when folks were dropping like flies."

She backtracked, throwing a worried look over her

shoulder toward the darkness that lingered behind her, ready to pounce on unsuspecting medical students. "You're just trying to scare me."

He stopped and flashed a toothy grin at her, one that didn't make it to his eyes. "It's working, isn't it? Never knew you were superstitious. Or is it claustrophobic? You've been skittish ever since we came down here."

"I just don't like wasting time, is all. Tracey Parker is counting on us to find the answers we need to help her."

"Tracey or Dr. Stone? I told you, it's a lost cause. I'm more his type than you are."

"What's with you and this obsession with Dr. Stone's sex life?" she asked as he led her down another corridor, this one more modern and brightly lit.

"Hey, I just call them like I see them. Makes no matter to me—I can get any woman I want, anytime I want."

"Right. Mr. Studmuffin." Amanda laughed, picturing the blueberry muffin Lucas had crushed into a blob during breakfast this morning. A soft, doughy blob with blueberry pimples—that's what Jim reminded her of. Despite his clean-cut preppy good looks, he really was just a blob. No one to take any account of.

"What?" he demanded, his voice bouncing off the concrete walls and echoing down the corridor. He spun on his heel, trapping her against the wall. He hadn't touched her, but his body was so close she could count the pores on his cheeks, see the faint stubble his razor had missed. "You don't believe me? What are you laughing at?"

Jim seemed to feel that the rules didn't apply to him, that he had the right to badmouth the hardworking people around him, but he was really an arrogant, lazy ignoramus who took credit for other people's work while avoiding his own and who didn't give two shakes of a possum's tail about his patients.

She straightened, meeting his gaze dead on. "You, Jim Lazarov. I'm laughing at you."

He raised his hand, and she realized too late that his

eyes had narrowed. Before she could move, he grabbed her arm.

Amanda reacted instinctively. She shoved off the wall, driving her knee into what she hoped were Jim's genitals. He squealed—a real, honest-to-goodness full-blown hog squeal—and let her go.

Jim slumped against the wall, both hands hugging his crotch. "What the hell! I was just trying to help you—your hand, it's twitching."

She looked down at the arm Jim had grabbed. Muscle fasciculations rippled below the skin, coiling up and down the back of her left hand and forearm. Gingerly, she touched her hand. It was numb. She tried to make a fist but couldn't; instead, the movement produced shocks of electricity spiraling into her elbow.

Amanda stood rigid, the adrenaline that had propelled her moments ago flushed away by embarrassment.

"What's wrong with you?" Jim asked, barely able to stand upright.

She wasn't sure whether he meant her reaction to his touch or what was going on with her arm. "Everything's fine."

She shook her arm from the elbow, let it hang for a moment, and slowly feeling returned. She made a fist, released it, and wiggled her fingers. No more tingling; everything seemed to be back to normal.

"Didn't look that way—looked a lot like what that patient had."

"It's nothing. Just forget about it."

Jim managed to stand, although he still leaned against the wall. "Not very likely. That was some kick. Maybe I should press charges or something."

"Wuss," she muttered. Any one of her brothers could pound him into the ground without breaking a sweat. "Heck, my great-aunt Nellie could whoop you. Even without her white cane."

"Still, I'd bet Stone would like to hear about your

'nothing' symptoms. Especially the way you tend to overreact when someone tries to touch you. What if I'd been a patient?"

"Patients don't usually go around insulting and grabbing me."

Before Jim could retort, Lucas and another man rounded the corner ahead of them. They were about the same age and height, but there the resemblance stopped.

Lucas had thick, sandy-colored hair and wore a crisp pale blue shirt, neatly knotted tie, and an even crisper lab coat, free from any stains, pockets empty except for a stethoscope, two pens, and a reflex hammer.

The man with him wore jeans, a polo shirt, sneakers, and a rumpled lab coat with pockets overflowing with debris. His hair was long, dark, and scraggly, as if he'd tried to trim it himself but had given up halfway through.

"You two do realize you're headed the wrong way, don't you?" Lucas said as they came abreast of her and Jim. Then he stopped to scrutinize them.

Jim was still pale, barely able to shuffle without a wince, and Amanda knew she looked flustered. She hastily tried to straighten her hair and smooth her lab coat, but it was in vain.

"What's going on?" Lucas asked, his voice edged with suspicion.

"Nothing," Amanda said at the same time as Jim.

The man behind Lucas hid a smile behind his hand, rubbing at his face. Lucas assumed a stern expression. "We have patients who need our full attention. Are you two ready to get back to work?"

Jim glanced at Amanda, his expression one of lethal intent. For a moment she was certain he was going to tell Lucas everything, but instead he stood up straight and gave Lucas one of his shit-eating simpers. "Yes sir. It was just a misunderstanding."

"Amanda? If you can't work with Jim, you can be reassigned to the clinic."

"No." It was so unfair, being the low man on the totem pole, the one most likely to get sent off to the Siberia of clinic-land. She stopped short of begging. But she needed to stay with Tracey, see her case through. She felt like she was close to finding the answer; she just needed a little more time—and fewer distractions from Jim. "No, thank you, Dr. Stone."

Besides, Jim was right—nothing really had happened, other than her being frightened out of her wits. She'd overreacted, let her fear and anger take control—some would say she might even owe Jim an apology. Her mother, always aghast at Amanda's inability to behave like a proper lady, would have been the first to insist on it.

Adrenaline leached from her, leaving her trembling and feeling a bit sickened by her actions. Last thing she wanted was more questions, more attention.

"All right. Jim, go up and check on our baby in the PICU. See when radiology can get her in for her MRI and let me know. Amanda, come with us." Lucas motioned for her to join him and the other man.

"This is Dr. Ken Rosen." Lucas introduced him as they continued down the hall to the pathology suite of labs.

Ah, so this was the mysterious man who had saved Gina's life. He didn't look like much, although Gina had said he was some kind of research whiz kid, bringing in almost as much grant money as Dr. Nelson.

"Ken's found something interesting in Becky Sanborn's tissue samples."

"Something that might help Tracey?" Amanda asked, hoping there was more to Ken Rosen than his appearance suggested.

"Not sure. The pathologists thought they might be postmortem changes, not clinically significant."

Dr. Rosen moved with an easy lope down the hall, a counterpoint to Lucas's rushed stride. "I've never seen protein deposits like that before," he said with confidence. "Not premortem or postmortem."

"Do you know what caused them, Dr. Rosen?"

"It's Ken. We found them in both her striated and smooth muscle tissue as well as in the basal ganglia and on sections throughout the nervous system. If it weren't for Lucas ordering the extra immunofluorescence stains, we never would have found them at all."

"But you know what they are, we can treat them, right?"

Both men stopped and stared at her. Ken was rubbing his hand over his chin as if he'd recently shaved off a beard and was missing it. Lucas merely shook his head, not meeting her eyes.

"These tests will take weeks to get results, Amanda. It's going to take time."

The fury she'd felt at Jim returned, only now she had nowhere to direct it. What was the good of getting angry at a disease that you didn't even have the name for? Her cheeks burned as she blinked back tears. "Tracey doesn't have time to spare."

TWENTY-FOUR

Friday, 8:11 A.M.

AMANDA WALKED INTO PATHOLOGY WITH LUCAS and Ken. The two men were animatedly discussing new variants of FAB staining and which technique gave the best results. They could have been speaking Greek for all the good it did Amanda. Yet again she was reminded that even though she was less than a year away from graduating from one of the best medical schools in the country, there was still a universe of material for her to learn and master.

Once she graduated, was a real pediatrician, kids' lives would depend on her not just knowing the facts but knowing what to do with them. And if these two men, both obvious geniuses, were uncertain about what to do next to help their patient . . . the challenge seemed overwhelming.

She slumped into her chair between them as they scrutinized some glowing blobs projected onto the video screen by the microscope. They had the lights turned low, casting the path lab into shadows, and the air conditioning was running full blast. Amanda felt her eyelids droop, the sluggish weight of fatigue drawing her into its embrace.

Lucas's beeper went off, snapping her awake. He stood and crossed the room to the phone. Ken frowned at the screen.

"Hate to say it, but the pathologists might be right. These deposits are too irregular, don't fit any pattern."

"So we don't know anything more than we did yesterday." She blew her breath out in a sigh so forceful it fluttered her bangs.

"Some things you can't rush. We definitely know more than we did yesterday. Just nothing that will help your patient anytime soon." He paused and pulled away from the microscope far enough to make eye contact with her. "Guess I understand your impatience. But even a medical student should realize how unprofessional it is to consult with another doctor behind her attending's back."

"Excuse me?" Amanda glanced at Lucas, still engrossed in his conversation.

"Lucas told me you got Lydia Fiore involved, reviewed his charts."

"He said I was unprofessional?"

"No. He was intrigued that she also thought mercury toxicity might play a role. *I'm* the one calling you unprofessional. And it comes very close to being a breach of HIPAA rules as well."

Amanda didn't know what to say. She couldn't very well tell him that it was Lydia who had come to her—or about their impromptu brainstorming session last night. Taking medical records out of the hospital had to be a violation.

"I'm sorry. I was just trying to do what's best for my patient."

"As long as you understand that Lucas is as well. He's the attending. If anything goes wrong, it's his responsibility." He turned back to the microscope, cutting off any further discussion.

Lucas hung up the phone. "We need to go; Tracey's

boyfriend just got here." He nodded to Ken. "Let me know if you think of anything."

"No problem," Ken said, fully immersed in the microscopic world of nerve endings and muscle fibers. Then he abruptly looked up. "Nice meeting you, Amanda."

Amanda followed Lucas out as he led her through the maze of tunnels back to the elevators. As they rode upstairs, he leaned against the corner in a very uncharacteristic slouch.

"I apologize if I broke protocol by looking into Becky's and Michelle's cases," she said, hoping to clear the air. He hadn't seemed upset when she mentioned Lydia this morning, but Ken was right; it was unprofessional not to involve him from the beginning.

He frowned, as if her words surprised him. "I told you to look into Becky's case. I should have told you to add Michelle's to the list myself. Would have if I hadn't been distracted."

He glanced at her leg, as if checking for more fasciculations, and she shuffled her feet. The door opened before she could think of some way to salvage the situation.

"Which reminds me," he continued as they walked down the hall to the family room. "We need to get you tested for mercury poisoning." He paused, his hand on the door. "Just in case."

LYDIA WAS LATE GETTING TO EMMA AND DEON Grey—no time to stop at Child Life and ask for advice or even to pick up a new book for Deon at the gift shop. She rushed in to the telemetry room, still flustered by the idea of a father threatening to sue her over trying to save his daughter. Misplaced guilt; she was certain nothing would come of it, but still it gnawed at her.

As she skidded into Emma's room, she felt off balance, anxious to regroup. "How are you feeling today, Mrs. Grey?"

The older woman looked up with a pinched, worried expression. "You haven't changed your mind, have you? There's no time."

Lydia *was* having second thoughts. What if something happened while Deon was in her care? Or worse, what if she was being set up for a lawsuit or some kind of blackmail—hustling on the street with her own mother, she'd seen worse. And the one thing Lydia had always vowed was to never be a patsy, a rube.

"There's still time for me to call social services. Maybe one of the nurses or doctors is on the emergency foster care list—"

"No." Emma's voice cut through Lydia's with authority.

Lydia straightened and glared at the old lady—she was the one who usually used that tone; she wasn't accustomed to being on the receiving end.

"No, please. You promised. I trust you; I don't trust any of those others. They'll take him away from me and I'll never see him again."

Deon remained silent, his gaze fixed on a spot between his purple-and-green-checkered dollar-store sneakers.

"Maybe we should discuss this in private," Lydia hedged, still unsure about the whole situation. It was against all the rules—a physician taking a patient home to spend the night? An unaccompanied minor at that?

"There's nothing to discuss."

Lydia rocked on her toes and forcibly relaxed her clenched fists, spreading her fingers wide. Trey was always saying she needed to learn to trust—hell, that's what all the men she'd been involved with said. No time like the present.

"You're right."

Emma sank back, looking relieved. Lydia crouched down so that she was at Deon's level. "What do you want to do today?"

Before he could answer, the nurses came to transport Emma up to cardiology. Emma pulled Deon into a fierce hug, kissing him on top of his head, then placed his hand into Lydia's. "You take care now. Both of you."

"Yes'm," Deon mumbled, swiping a tear from his cheek with his free hand.

He and Lydia stood, side by side, as they wheeled Emma out. Suddenly the room felt cavernous, overwhelming with the vacancy she had left behind.

Too late Lydia remembered that she'd meant to ask Emma to put something in writing—small protection against wagging tongues and the rule-mongers, but at least it would give her some credibility if anything happened.

"She's going to be all right, isn't she?" Deon asked, still gripping her hand.

Lydia couldn't restrain herself. She pulled him close into a hug. "She's going to be fine. Everything's going to be fine."

Making promises she couldn't guarantee. Breaking her own rules. Getting involved. What the hell was she doing?

TWENTY-FIVE

Friday, 8:26 A.M.

JARED WAS WAITING FOR AMANDA AND LUCAS IN the ICU waiting room. "They wouldn't let me go in to see Tracey this morning." He leaped up from the sagging and dispirited couch. "What's happened? Something went wrong, didn't it?"

Lucas motioned to Jared to sit back down. The couch sighed with his weight. Lucas pulled up a straight-back chair to sit opposite. Amanda hovered in the background; she was never sure how much she should contribute to these family meetings, and it still felt weird, knowing Jared and being privy to the intimate details of Tracey's treatment.

"Tracey's stable but in serious condition," Lucas began. He leaned forward but kept his hands folded on his lap, giving him the appearance of an older man. "We're doing everything we can, but any information you can give us could make all the difference."

"Anything," Jared said. "What do you need to know?"

"Has Tracey been sick at all lately? Maybe a rash or complaining of numbness or tingling in her hands and feet?"

"No rash. I remember a few times she said her foot fell asleep, but it was after she was sitting for a while, seemed normal. Oh, and she started doing this kicking thing at night, like she had that restless leg thing."

"Headaches, nausea, vomiting?"

"No, I told you all this yesterday. Nothing like that."

"How about you? Have you been sick at all?"

"Me? No, I'm fine. Haven't been sick since spring when my allergies always act up." Jared stared at Lucas. "Why are you asking about me? Does Tracey have something that's spreading?"

"Did Tracey go to the boathouse often?"

"The boathouse? What's that got to do with any of this?" He turned to glance at Amanda. "I told you Tracey hated the water—she was a runner. She couldn't even swim."

"Did she come visit you there?" Amanda asked. "Maybe use the exercise equipment or something?"

He frowned, considering. "Maybe once or twice last winter when the weather was bad. Not in a long while. Except to shower and change after a run if we were going out." He rocked back. "Oh my God. Does she have the same thing Shelly had? Is she going to die, too?"

Amanda had no idea what to say, but thankfully Lucas took over. "Jared, we're looking into every possibility. That's why we need to check everything."

"Okay. I guess. I brought all her medicines and stuff," Jared said, nodding to a brown paper bag sitting on the side table. Amanda began to go through it, handing off anything interesting to Lucas. "I grabbed everything, didn't know what might be important."

"Birth control pills, acetaminophen, ibuprofen, antacids—"

"Those last are mine," Jared put in. "But you said bring everything."

"What are those?" Lucas asked as Amanda pulled out a prescription bottle with a bar code across the label. He took it from her, frowned, and shook out a few shiny golden perles into his palm. "She was in one of Nelson's studies."

"No. I asked," Amanda said. "Tracey dropped out months ago, right after she started."

Jared was shaking his head. "She told me she went every month. Loved those pills, said they were helping her train for her next marathon. Called them her Energizer Bunny food."

Lucas twisted the bottle in his palm, reading the numbers beneath the bar code. "The date is four months ago. Maybe she'd found something else to give her energy." He looked at Jared. "You said Tracey is a serious athlete. Has she ever taken steroids? Sometimes they're found in natural health supplements or herbal preparations?"

Doubt crept over Jared's face. "Maybe. She was into natural healing. I'm not sure." He didn't meet Lucas's eyes as he asked, "If Tracey wasn't going into the city to see the doctor every month, who was she seeing?"

Lucas was still focused on the bottle in his hand. He stood, and Jared mirrored his movements. "When you go home, maybe you can check her appointment book, see if she had found someone else to help her with her training. Maybe a nutritionist. If you find anything, let me know." Jared nodded. "In the meantime, wait here while I talk to the nurses and see if I can get you in there to see Tracey."

Amanda followed Lucas out into the hallway. He stalked a few steps toward the ICU, then spun on his heel, turning on her. "You knew she was a patient of Nelson's but you didn't tell me?"

"All I knew was that she was in a study. It didn't seem important, not after I found out she'd dropped out."

"That's not for you to decide. *I* decide what's important about my patients. What else haven't you told me?"

"Nothing." She remembered her episode when she was down in the tunnel and realized she was lying. No matter, Lucas wasn't her doctor; it was Dr. Nelson she needed to call.

"I want you to send those pills down to the lab. Make sure they test for mercury contamination as well as other heavy metals."

"Lucas, that's ridiculous. There are thousands of people around here in Dr. Nelson's studies. If there was something wrong with them, we wouldn't have three patients, we'd have dozens."

The glare Lucas gave her could have sliced through a diamond. "I didn't ask your opinion, Amanda. Just do it. And while you're at it, go home. Get some rest. I don't need you back here until tomorrow morning."

"What about Alice's MRI? I want to be there—"

"Jim can handle it. You go home. Now." Before she could protest, he turned and stalked away, hands thrust deep into his pockets.

NORA CHECKED IN WITH RACHEL, WHO WAS covering the ER for her. "It's pretty quiet," Rachel told her when she called. "Take your time. I'm stuck here finishing the schedule anyway."

"Thanks, Rachel. I'm just going to grab some breakfast and I'll be right down."

As a supervisor, Rachel was very understanding. She knew that her nurses routinely put in unpaid overtime, and she didn't hound them when they needed to take a few minutes of personal time. Nora was still jumpy after her confrontation with Seth—kept expecting him to come up behind her, wanting to talk. Worse still was anticipating the new bout of gossip that would soon be humming through the hospital grapevine.

She grabbed a sausage biscuit and cup of coffee, then added a chocolate chip cookie to her tray. Protein to get through the shift, caffeine to keep her awake, and chocolate to soothe her tattered nerves. Breakfast of champions.

The white-hot flash of anger that had seared her while she'd confronted Seth was fading. Her hands no longer trembled; she trusted her legs to get her to a table. Then she saw Lydia and Deon at a booth beside the windows.

"Shouldn't he be in school?" she asked. Damn it, she hated how her voice sounded—shrill and judgmental when that wasn't what she meant at all. After last night and this morning, she'd really wanted the comfort of one thing going as predicted. Just one little thing, sitting down and eating breakfast, was that too much to ask?

"Not while Gram is sick," Deon said, hunching over his eggs and bacon as if he feared she might steal them from him.

Lydia slid out a chair for Nora. "Figured he wouldn't be good for much worrying about Emma. But as soon as she's out of surgery, I'll take him over for the rest of the day."

Nora settled into the chair. "So he does go to school."

"Sure he does. Tell her what you guys are studying, Deon."

"We're constructing a computer model of the fossil record, and then we're going to debate the theory of evolution and its alternatives. My team is doing the coolest—we're gonna prove that spacemen from another planet brought the dinosaurs!"

Nora had to smile at that. Working in the ER, the theory of human evolution—or lack thereof—explained a lot of what she saw on a day-to-day basis. "What's your gram think of that?"

"She says since God's behind it all, doesn't matter what story we put on it. She says even the Bible is a story—that you have to read the truth between the lines, can't take stuff for granted just 'cuz someone wrote it down."

"A wise woman," Lydia said, handing Deon a spare napkin to wipe chocolate milk from his chin. "You should listen to her."

"I always do."

Nora started with her cookie, even though she knew it was a terrible example to set for Deon.

"You okay?" Lydia asked her.

"Fine, why?"

"You look tired, is all."

Nora shrugged at that, filling her mouth, hoping it would prevent any more questions. Probably not, but Lydia's cell phone ringing did.

"Yes?" Lydia answered, obviously assuming that whoever called her didn't need any formal greeting. "Everything's okay? Sure, I can meet you there in a few minutes." She hung up and repocketed the phone.

"Is it Gram?" Deon asked.

"No. It's Jerry Boyle. They caught that kil—that guy they were looking for."

"Yancy?"

"Yeah. Boyle messed up his arm, wants me to take a look at it real quick."

Nora gathered the trash onto her tray and stood up. "You're not on duty."

"I don't mind. Except," she nodded to Deon. "I don't suppose . . ."

"No. No way. The ER is not a day care. I told you, this is why you need Tommy Z's help. He could have arranged all sorts of help for Deon and Emma."

"I'm not a baby. I can take care of myself," Deon interrupted, standing on his tiptoes in an obvious ploy to look older and taller than he was.

"I don't need a lecture, Nora." Lydia looked down at Deon. "You have a choice, Deon. Do you want to learn some medicine or wait at the nurses' station? Maybe Jason will let you play his computer games."

"You can't let him watch you treat a patient, Lydia. It's, it's—" There were too many words describing how wrong it was to pick from.

"It's educational," Lydia said as they dropped off their trays and left. "I'm sure he's seen worse out on the streets."

"Still. The ER is no place for a ten-year-old. He could get hurt."

"I'd rather watch," Deon put in.

"Watching it is," Lydia declared, ignoring Nora's frown. "Let's go."

GINA SWAYED AS THE AMBULANCE BOUNCED over potholes. Their first patient of the day was a "Surf 'n' Turf"—Gecko's slang for chronic patients whose regular doctor didn't want to deal with them on a Friday, in case they interfered with the doctor's early escape to the Jersey Shore for the weekend.

In other words, a dump. In this case, the patient was a woman in her seventies, currently babbling to Trey about an ancient Fred Astaire–Ginger Rogers movie—something about Rio or Macedonia or Argentina, Gina wasn't sure—who had kept them almost an hour at her house while she fed the cats, double-checked the locks, and packed her bag.

The monitor showed atrial fibrillation, and from her swollen ankles, Gina was sure she was in early stages of heart failure, but there wasn't much other than oxygen and monitoring that they could do for her.

A freaking taxicab, that's what they were. Not to mention baggage handlers.

Med Seven hit another pothole, and Gina's aggravation spiked. She didn't understand why Lydia was so insistent she finish this damn rotation—she'd learn more and do more good in the ER where she belonged. She glanced up to see Trey scowling at her manicure.

Remembering Lydia's reaction last night and wondering whether Lydia had shared Gina's secret with Trey, she waved her fingers before him. "It's a new color from OPI; you like?"

His frown deepened. "You know that's against regulations."

"Hey, Gina, you still gonna talk to us peons after they give you the key to the city?" Gecko called out from the driver's seat. "It was on the news this morning that they're giving you a Carnegie Medal."

Thinking about the ceremony soured Gina's mood even more.

The patient grabbed Gina's arm, drawing her close and squinting at her. "Hey, I know you. You're the girl saved all those babies last July. They gonna give you an award, sweetheart? Good for you."

Gina pulled away, leaning back on the bench seat and crossing her arms over her bulky vest. *Yeah, right. Good for her.*

TWENTY-SIX

Friday, 9:22 A.M.

AMANDA WALKED OUT OF THE HOSPITAL AFTER dropping Tracey's study medication off at the lab. Another hot, muggy day with dark clouds pressing down so hard they were giving her a headache. This Indian summer seemed destined to go on forever. It was warmer here this week than it was down home. Despite the heat, she pulled her lab coat around her, as if it could mask her shame. Worse than being exiled to the clinic, Lucas had kicked her out of the hospital for the day.

A rumble of thunder sounded overhead. The air shimmered as if it were about to start raining, and black clouds obscured the sun. She crossed the street and entered the employee parking garage.

She needed to get back into Lucas's good graces so that she could get back on the wards, be with her patients. The best way to do that would be to find out everything she could about the boathouse and any potential toxins that might be hiding there.

Amanda reached her pale pink Love Bug. She slid onto the black vinyl driver's seat, wincing as the heat permeated through the thin cotton of her scrubs, and cranked down both the driver and passenger windows before turning the engine on. The old VW didn't have air conditioning, but other than that it was perfect for her: reliable, economical, cute, and best of all, paid for.

After giving the fan a few minutes to chop through the wall of humidity that had filled the car, she put the clutch in and shifted into reverse. The clutch felt mushy—Gina must have been driving it again. Amanda blew her breath out in annoyance. Gina wanted to learn how to drive a straight stick and Amanda was glad to teach her, but she had a bad habit of riding the clutch. And like most of her bad habits, Gina found it easier to ignore than to fix.

Amanda pulled out of her parking space and had to double-clutch to shift into first. Gina had promised to pay for a new clutch if need be—she might take her up on that. Now that she was out of Dr. Nelson's study, she didn't have money for luxuries like car repairs. Or food. She was going to have to find work that she could juggle between her clinical duties. Maybe the medical records department would hire her back as a data-entry clerk.

As she steered down the steep corkscrew turn leading to the exit, she gnawed over her options. Gina would let her slide with rent and her share of the utilities—Gina didn't need a roommate for financial purposes, she just hated living alone—but Amanda refused to take advantage of that. She'd pay Gina back. Even if it did mean going back to work in the dark dungeonlike cubicles of data entry.

Amanda hit the brakes to slow as she rounded the final curve. Her stomach somersaulted in surprise as her foot went all the way to the floorboard. She pumped hard, trying to find some braking power, but the car accelerated down the steep hill.

Don't panic, she told herself even as her heart began to race. The concrete walls on either side of the barricade were looming as she hurtled toward them. She tried shifting down.

Nothing except the engine revving in rebellion. She yanked up the emergency brake, producing a screech and the smell of burnt rubber but not slowing the car.

Beyond the exit barricade was Mathilda Street, bustling with traffic—both vehicular and pedestrian. Even if she survived a collision, there was a risk she could kill someone else. She couldn't take that chance.

The other parked cars were a blur in her peripheral vision as she focused on her new target. She decided to ram the concrete wall, try to swerve at the last minute, and hope for a glancing blow that would stop her without causing too much damage.

The wall was speeding toward her—she knew it was the other way around, but it felt as if she were immobile, trapped in a bubble of time as the rest of the world moved around her. *Don't tighten, don't tighten,* she thought, trying to force her arms to relax, not hyperextend at the elbows. *Too fast, too fast*—she'd kill herself, there was no air bag, nothing but her seat belt, she was going to die. . . .

She wrenched the wheel to one side, spinning the VW into a skid with only inches to spare. The car stood poised, fighting gravity and velocity, for one sickening moment, then spun sideways into the wall. Sparks flew as metal struck concrete, the sound of the car's death throes high-pitched as a dying animal's wail, metal straining, then buckling in surrender, collapsing around Amanda.

IN THE END, JUST AS LYDIA KNEW SHE WOULD, Nora had taken charge of Deon and parked him with his Harry Potter in a chair beside the ward clerk with strict orders not to move. Deon had protested; he'd been looking forward to seeing some blood and guts—but once Lydia explained that Boyle was a police officer, his street kid aversion to authority figures had triumphed over his young boy's bloodlust.

Lydia both loved and hated how much Deon reminded

her of herself. At least Emma was a better role model for Deon than Maria had been for Lydia. She pushed through the door into the suture room, where Jerry Boyle waited, his arm stretched out over a procedure table.

"So we got the bastard," he said, his eyes aglow with adrenaline.

"Yancy?"

"Yep. Found the bodies of three women buried in his backyard. Finally caught up with him after pressuring the guys who owed him money. Best way to find someone you want to put away—go after the folks who'd stand to gain if they're behind bars." He puffed out his chest, then winced as Lydia probed at the separated edges of his arm laceration.

"You tore two of my stitches."

"Yancy didn't exactly come easily. Had to tackle him. He's getting checked out next door—don't want any charges of police brutality messing with my case."

Lydia poured some Betadine over the wound and scrubbed it clean.

"Talked with Gina," Boyle went on, studiously looking anywhere except at his arm. "She said Trey was riding with her today. Is that normal? I mean, I thought he cruised around in that fancy Suburban looking for trouble."

"I asked him to keep an eye on her."

He glanced at her, silent until she raised her gaze to meet his. "Thanks. I appreciate that."

"No problem. It's part of my job, taking care of the EM residents." She returned her attention to the laceration repair. "I'm just going to put in one staple—it's been too long to replace the stitches, we risk infection."

"Sure, whatever. Just make it fast, will ya?"

She grabbed the surgical staple gun. "No problem." She aimed the gun and pulled the trigger. A loud report echoed through the room and Boyle jerked.

"Hey!"

"All done." She quickly reapplied a dressing. As she

was sealing the tape on the edges, one of the nurses poked her head in.

"If you're finished, we need this room. It seems a medical student ran her car into the parking garage wall."

TWENTY-SEVEN

Friday, 9:32 A.M.

AMANDA WAS JERKED ABOUT WORSE THAN A dinghy riding out a hurricane. Her head hit the steering wheel, her neck was wrenched in one direction and then whipped in another, her knees collided with the underside of the dash, and one arm was nearly impaled by the gearshift.

Everything stopped. There was quiet, long enough for the ringing in her ears, the echoes of metal shrieking, and the hammering of her headache to fade. Only to be replaced by the shrill tones of "The Devil Went Down to Georgia."

Amanda brushed a shaky hand against her forehead, assessing the damage. Nice goose egg, but no bleeding. Everything moved all right, although with protesting aches. She blinked several times, surprised by tears manufactured by her adrenaline, and looked around.

The roof of her beloved Bug had crumpled along the midline, folding inward, hanging down like a stalactite beside her. Her car was almost half the size it once had been, now folded like origami.

The Charlie Daniels Band interrupted her reverie once more. The sound was coming from below her. As she heaved in a breath, her chest recoiling with pain, she inched her hand across her lap to unfasten her seat belt—and found her cell phone.

She needed to call someone—wasn't quite sure who. A tow truck? Gina, to give her a ride? No, Gina was working today—Lydia was off, she could call Lydia, Lydia would know what to do.

More tears came as she realized that she would need to abandon her beloved Love Bug. The engine ticked unsteadily, finally sputtered, and then stalled, smoke billowing from below the hood.

"Hello," she said, trying to remember if she'd called someone or if they had called her.

"Hey, Baby Girl, what the hell you doing?" Andy's too-cheerful bellow blew through her with hurricane ferocity.

Her hand holding the phone was shaking, the smoke was making her cough and cry harder, and the seat belt wouldn't let go.

"You know you made Mama cry, don't you? You can't be doing that. You have to come home, make things right."

Through the haze of smoke, Amanda saw figures running toward her. Two security guards, a paramedic, and Nora. *Nora! Thank God, she'd take care of everything, Nora was so good at that.*

Amanda slumped against her seat, pressing the phone against her cheek. "I can't talk now, Andy."

"Of course you can. This is our mama we're talking about—family trumps any emergency you have going on up there. Besides, it's not like you're a real doctor or anything. They can do without. You get behind the wheel of your car and haul your bony butt down here; stop making Mama cry. I'm telling you, Baby Girl—"

The guards and paramedic were trying to pry open Amanda's door from the outside. Nora was saying something, obviously concerned, but Amanda couldn't make out her words. Not with Andy's voice rattling through her brain. "Andy?"

"You're going to be home by morning, Baby Girl. I'll tell Mama."

"Andy." He paused long enough for her to speak her mind. "Go to hell."

The door popped open and Amanda tumbled out into the waiting arms of a security guard, the phone skittering to the concrete floor and skidding below the wreckage that had once been her car.

GINA AND MED SEVEN LEFT ANGELS AND WERE heading to the station when another call came in—possible jumper, Smithfield Street Bridge.

"Finally, a live one," Gecko said with gusto, revving the engine as they ran Code Three, lights and sirens and air horn honking at drivers reluctant to give way to the speeding ambulance. Trey was busy packing and checking gear boxes and didn't even look up as they rattled over a set of railroad tracks and then onto a rough, potholed road.

"You can swim, can't you?" Gecko shouted back from the driver's seat as they took another jarring bounce over a curb.

"Off with the vest," Trey ordered. "Too heavy. You can't wear it under your PFD."

The ambulance screeched to a halt just as Gina processed his words. She took off her bulletproof vest, hesitating before leaving it in the ambulance and joining Trey and Gecko outside.

They were on the edge of the Mon wharf, surrounded by police cars and two fire trucks. Waiting for them was a boat with twin engines howling, spitting out diesel fumes, like a racehorse eager to break free of the gate.

Gecko grabbed a bright orange flotation vest and jumped on board, not bothering with the small gate that led onto the rear deck. Trey handed Gina a similar vest, then fastened his own tight. Waves lapped against the wharf, driven by the wind. It wasn't raining yet, but the air felt heavy, water-soaked.

"Perks of being a district chief," Trey yelled over the noise as he handed her into the boat. "Usually River Rescue would handle it alone, but since we were close enough to meet them, I thought you'd like to see some real action." He deftly climbed in after her and waved to their pilot.

They cast off, Gina still staring at the rapidly receding shoreline. "If they jump, we don't have to go in after, do we?"

"That's our job," a man's voice came from the cabin behind her.

She turned and saw two men inside the cabin suiting up in wetsuits bearing the River Rescue logo. They were both extremely fit and grinning as the boat pounded through the choppy water. Like Trey and Gecko, no one would ever peg these guys as office workers. It was obvious they lived for this shit.

"Who's our mascot, Chief?" one asked.

"Behave yourself, Gordon. This is Dr. Freeman, doing a ride-along."

"Picked a good day for it. I've got odds this one is gonna go."

The boat bounced to a stop, engines backing down to a low growl, idling. As they waited, Trey squinted into the wind, climbing up to look above the cabin at the man on the bridge above them. Flashing lights, a police barricade, and official vehicles surrounded him. The man looked to be in his late forties, bald except for a too-long comb-over that the wind was whipping into every direction.

"Hmmm. Who's the negotiator?"

"Sanders."

"Shit, this guy's as good as gone already," Gecko put in. "Wish they'd let Jerry Boyle come back."

"That's only because you won enough money off him," Gordon said.

"Man had a silver tongue, could talk the stripes off a leopard."

"Jerry Boyle?" Gina asked. The men tore their gazes away from the jumper, looking around as if they had forgotten her. "Jerry was a negotiator?"

"Yeah, back when he worked SWAT. About two, three years ago now."

"He never told me."

"He didn't exactly leave under the best of circumstances. Almost lost his badge," Gordon said. He reached for a pair of binoculars and trained them on the would-be-suicide's face. "Hey, put me down for twenty. This guy is going to go for a swim, I'm sure of it."

"You two good to go?" Trey asked, inspecting the rescue team's preparations.

"What happened?" Gina interrupted, ignoring the drama on the bridge above her. "Why did Jerry almost lose his job?"

Gordon opened his mouth to answer but shut it again when Trey shook his head. "Let's focus on the job here, folks."

Gecko grabbed the binoculars, obviously impatient with the long wait and inactivity. "Hey, Gordo, I'll take that bet. Look at how he's clinging to that strut, he's ready to wet his pants and come on home to Mama."

"Why don't you give Gina the glasses?" Trey said. Gecko reluctantly passed them back to Gina.

She craned her head back so far that her neck muscles cramped. "How high is it?"

"About forty-eight feet. Most folks who jump don't die on impact, usually just fracture their legs, sometimes their spine," Trey answered as she focused on the man above.

The wind was buffeting the man even as the crowd around him grew. His mouth was moving and he would gesture with one hand, only to wobble and grab back onto the metal beam he was clinging to.

"What usually kills 'em," Gordon said, finishing Trey's lecture, "is drowning. They can't kick after the impact shatters their legs, and they drop like stones. Which is why we're here. We go in, fish 'em out, hopefully fast enough to save 'em. Easier in the winter when the water is colder—gives us longer if they swallow some. But this chop"—he gestured at the turbulent water, opaque and murky—"is gonna make it tough. Poor visibility and a wicked current." He shook his head. "Not such a good combo."

Gina kept her gaze fixated on the agitated man balanced on the side of the bridge. Tears streamed down his face, and he kept releasing his grip to wipe his nose. A suited man on the bridge, obviously the negotiator, took a step toward him as the man nodded vehemently.

"I think he's surrendering," she shouted.

"I'll be damned. Sanders pulled it off."

The suited man was gesturing, talking to the man on the bridge, motioning him to come forward. The man kept nodding, sliding his foot off the high girder, precariously balanced as he began to climb down. He raised a hand to swipe at his eyes and nose.

He teetered, and the policemen rushed forward, reaching toward him, but then he lurched backward, hands flailing for the beam, as he fell.

TWENTY-EIGHT

Friday, 10:11 A.M.

BETWEEN NORA, THE MEDIC, AND A HANDFUL of other medical workers, Amanda was quickly transported to the ER, clad in a patient gown—which was ridiculous because she was fine—and left to wonder whether her student health insurance would cover the bill.

She was waiting for her discharge papers—the ER doc had found nothing wrong with her that a hot bath and a few Advil wouldn't cure—when there was a knock on the door. Lucas Stone appeared, frown lines edging his eyes deeper than ever. He'd better be careful or they'd become permanent.

Amanda hid a giggle behind her palm. She'd been feeling giddy ever since the accident—trying to avoid the truth that her only means of transportation was destroyed, that she had told her youngest older brother to go to hell, and that once again she had failed Lucas.

"I'm sorry," she said. "I should have told you about what Jared said."

Lucas did what he always did: stared at her. As if she

were a specimen he was worried would wiggle away before he could figure her out.

"I'm fine," she said in a rush, the word echoing through her brain as if that would scare away the shakes that had taken over her insides. She plastered one of Mama's smiles onto her face, trying to bolster her declaration. "I'll be back upstairs to help with Alice and Tracey in a few minutes. Just waiting for my paperwork." Damn the man, why did he constantly turn her into a babbling idiot? He didn't care about her paperwork, only about her doing her job—something she had failed.

"Can't go home—I don't have a car anymore." Again the impulse to either cry or laugh hit her. One look at Lucas's earnest face squelched it.

"Are you sure you're all right? How did this happen? Was it your leg again?" he asked.

"Stop looking at me like that. I told you, I'm fine." *Fine, fine, fine.* Not scared or shaken or worried. Well, except about poor old Love Bug; how on earth was she ever going to find another car as good—or as affordable? "It wasn't me. The brakes on my car failed."

Before she could say more, the door opened. She straightened, hoping it was the nurse with her discharge paperwork. Instead, it was Jerry Boyle accompanied by a uniformed officer.

"Jerry?" Maybe she did have something to worry about. Was she in trouble? "Surely they didn't send a detective for my fender bender."

Jerry didn't smile—and Jerry was almost always smiling, at least with his eyes. Instead he looked as worried as Lucas did.

"What's wrong?"

"Amanda, this is Officer Smith. He just heard from the mechanic that towed your car. This wasn't an accident."

"I know. I didn't have any choice but to hit the wall; it was the only way to keep from rolling into traffic and maybe hurting someone else. That's not against the law or anything, is it? Is the hospital going to sue me or something?" That would be just perfect.

"No." Jerry blew his breath out, one hand rubbing his forearm as if fighting the urge to scratch an itch. "Smitty, tell her what you told me."

Lucas had moved to stand at her side, between her and the police. Amanda shot him a glare; she didn't need his protection, most certainly not from Jerry.

Officer Smith flipped open a small notebook and began to read. "On inspection of the undercarriage of the 1972 Volkswagen in question and on further inspection of the fluids left in evidence—"

"In evidence? Evidence of what?" Amanda asked, not sure whether she was in trouble.

"There was a puddle of fluid at the space where you parked," Jerry explained.

Smith continued, "There was evidence of multiple lacerations made by a sharp object as yet undetermined in proximity to both the brake lubricant lines and the clutch, suggesting manipulation of the vehicle's ability to perform, specifically to brake." He flipped the notebook closed and gave a short nod.

Amanda merely stared. "That makes no sense."

"Amanda, he's saying someone tampered with your car, tried to kill you," Lucas said.

"I know what he said. But it's crazy." Her insides felt as if they'd spun out of control, just as her Love Bug had, coming down that ramp. Kill her? No. Things like that didn't happen, not to girls like her. Gina and Lydia, maybe—they went looking for trouble. Amanda did as she was told, followed the rules—who would want to kill her?

"No one said anything about anyone trying to kill her," Jerry put in. He nodded to Smith, who disappeared, presumably to go gather more evidence. "But it does appear that the vehicle was tampered with. For whatever reason."

Amanda shook her head, ratcheting the pounding in it up to a level she was certain could be heard by everyone in the room. She rubbed her palms along her thighs, leaving sweat stains on the patient gown, and clenched her fists tight to hide the trembling. "Could I please have some privacy so I can get dressed?"

"I need to ask some questions—"

"Jerry, please. Just give me a minute, please."

"Can't you see she's been through a lot?" Lucas said, pivoting to face Jerry.

She wondered at his protectiveness, but didn't have time to dwell on the question. Not when there were so many other questions ricocheting through her brain.

Like who was trying to kill her. And why?

TWENTY-NINE

Friday, 10:28 A.M.

GINA'S STOMACH HURLED HEAVENWARD, BILE and acid scratching her throat as she watched the man fall through the air. It could have taken only a few seconds at most, but everything seemed to happen in slow motion.

The pilot launched the boat forward. The River Rescue divers slapped on their regulators and had the dive door open as they prepared to jump into the water. Trey and Gecko leaped into action, Trey talking into his radio as they both opened trauma kits and got ready for their patient.

Somehow, even as all of this kaleidoscope of action was happening in Gina's periphery, what she registered was the look of shock, then terror, chiseled onto the man's face. He swung his arms and legs, but as he fell backward, his head was below his feet.

His solitary hank of hair was now streamlined, plastered across his face. His tie, a hideous shade of purple shockingly vivid against the gray sky, billowed out.

His scream lagged behind his body, then gained momentum, like a freight train roaring through a tunnel.

She didn't just hear the slap of his body hitting the water, she felt it slam through her body and almost fell as she stumbled back. She staggered against the railing. In that fraction of a second, the man had vanished below the surface.

"Where? Someone give me a twenty!" Gordon called out, waves slapping against his body.

"Gina!" Trey's voice penetrated her awareness. He yanked the binoculars away from her face and she blinked, blind for a moment. "Where did he go in? You were tracking him."

She shook her head, unable to admit she hadn't been tracking him—only watching him, too mesmerized to be of any help. Her hesitation lasted only a second, but it was a second too long.

"I don't know," she mumbled.

It was too late. Trey had already turned away and was taking coordinates from the first mate, who *had* been doing his job and had tracked the man's fall. The divers splashed overboard, and Trey watched them through the binoculars.

Gina strained to see, but all she could make out were the bright yellow air tanks bobbing through the water. Thunder clapped overhead and rain began to pelt her.

Then a diver's head appeared, followed by another. The man, pale and limp, the boat's spotlights gleaming on his bald head, was ferried back to the boat by the divers, kicking hard. Gecko pushed Gina aside to climb up to the cabin roof, grabbing a backboard equipped with flotation devices. He and Trey maneuvered the backboard vertically into the water, and the divers positioned the man above it. The board floated up to meet their patient at the diver's door, and Trey snapped a cervical collar into place around his neck.

Together the men leveraged their patient on board without risking further injury. They laid him out on the aft deck and began working on him immediately.

"Left pupil's blown, respirations irregular," Gecko called out as Trey grabbed the bag-valve mask and handed it to him.

"Pulse good. How's his airway?"

"Clear. Any pneumo?"

Trey listened to the man's lungs as Gecko breathed for him. "Nope, nice and equal." He grabbed an IV as one of the divers ripped open the man's shirt. The boat made an abrupt turn and began to speed back toward the dock and the waiting ambulance. Gina clutched the railing, not for balance, but to keep her upright, afraid that without that grip she'd hurtle backward into the water just as the man had.

AMANDA SLOWLY CHANGED INTO A PAIR OF clean scrubs, her movements hampered by muscles already knotting with pain. She slid her lab coat on, but the added weight from her brimming pockets acted like a yoke on her neck muscles. Rubbing her trapezius, she tried to massage away the coiled knot of tension that had settled into the muscle. She'd always thought whiplash was just a ploy for sympathy until now.

"Moist heat tonight." Lydia Fiore's voice came from behind her. "I can write you a script for some PT—ultrasound, hot tub, massage. And you won't be wearing this for a while." Without asking, Lydia slipped the heavy lab jacket from Amanda's shoulders. "Damn thing weighs twenty pounds."

"I need that."

So typical of Lydia—no knocking, just waltzing in and doing what she damn well pleased, taking charge . . . oh, and damn it, being right about the weight of the lab coat making things worse.

Lydia laid the jacket on the gurney and began sorting through the contents of its pockets. "You get checked out?"

"Yes. I'm fine."

"Good. I heard Boyle say someone did this on purpose? You're not going home alone, are you?"

Why did everyone assume she couldn't take care of herself? Amanda stopped herself before she could stamp her foot in irritation. This whole situation was too bizarre—it was all some kind of crazy mistake. It had to be. "Yeah, he said that. But it doesn't make any sense. Why would anyone want to hurt me?"

"You're working with Jim Lazarov this month. You know he gave Nora a hard time when he was in the ER."

"Jim's an ass. That doesn't make him homicidal. Besides, he was with me all morning."

Lydia said nothing as she grabbed a clipboard hanging on the wall, stripped it of its inventory sheets, and replaced them with Amanda's stack of research papers and patient notes. She clipped a pen to the top and returned the clipboard and the now lighter-than-whipped-cream lab coat to Amanda. "Try that."

"Better," Amanda admitted, shrugging into the coat, now burdened only by a spare pen, reflex hammer, penlight, and stethoscope. "But I need those." She pointed to the tower of pocket manuals.

"No. You don't. Especially not with Lucas—he loves teaching. If you don't know something, just ask. Besides, these were outdated before they were even printed. You'll learn much more by watching Lucas."

Amanda gave a grudging nod. Lydia was right. Again. She was only five years older than Amanda, but Amanda had the sinking feeling that she'd never achieve Lydia's sense of confidence or half of the attending's abilities, no matter how many questions she asked.

"I'll go put these in your locker," Lydia said, gathering the books into her arms and exiting with one last concerned glance over her shoulder.

Another knock on the door, and Jerry Boyle appeared again. At least *he* knocked first. "Good news. Kind of. We found a bunch of other cars that appear to have been vandalized as well. All parked on the same level as yours."

"So I wasn't the target." Relief swept through her, steadying her. She knew it had to be a mistake.

"We don't know who or what the reason was. Traffic will be taking over the investigation, but if you see anything out of the ordinary—"

"I'll give you a call." She straightened her lab coat—time to get back to work, to her normal life.

Jerry didn't look entirely convinced. "I'm going to follow up with Traffic myself."

Amanda gave him a hug and a quick peck on the cheek. "Seriously, I'm fine. I have to get back to my patients. Thanks, Jerry."

She left the exam room and hadn't gone more than a few steps down the hall when she ran into Dr. Nelson. He was rushing down the hallway, pausing to look in each patient's bed space, whisking curtains aside, leaving them swinging in his wake. Then he saw Amanda and skidded to a stop, his face suffused with color.

"Amanda!" He sped forward, pulling her into a bear hug. "They said you were hurt in an accident. Are you okay? What happened?"

Amanda inhaled his citrusy scent, felt his strong arms encircling her, and the roller coaster of emotion created by the morning's events overwhelmed her. Tears seeped from her eyes as she returned his hug. Dr. Nelson never went anywhere in the hospital except the clinic—at least not in the two years she'd known him. Since his baby boy died, he had plunged his energy into his research.

"Norman, give the girl room to breathe." Faith's voice came from behind him, sounding tight, choked with emotion as well.

Reluctantly, Amanda pushed free, swiping tears from her cheeks. "I'm sorry," she blubbered. "I just need a moment."

"Dear, you take all the time you want," Dr. Nelson said

even as Faith took her hand and led her into a vacant suture room. "We were so worried."

"Are you okay?" Faith asked.

"I'm fine. Just a few bruises."

"You had us scared to death," Dr. Nelson said in a tone that sounded like a child's even though his face had more wrinkles and shadows than ever. He shook his head, saying nothing more, shoving his hands into his pockets.

Amanda leaned against the counter and used a paper towel to clean her face. Then she glanced up at the two of them, both looking so worried. Surely they hadn't both left their busy clinic just to check on her. Unless . . . there was bad news? Had something horrible shown up on her lab tests?

Icy fingers skittered their way down her spine. She sucked in her breath, but it didn't fill the sudden emptiness that had hollowed out her chest. "What is it? What did the tests show?"

"What?" Dr. Nelson asked, a frown creasing his brow.

"Her lab work, dear." Faith took a slip of paper from her pocket. Unlike physicians and med students, her lab jacket was a pale gray that suited her, made her look professional yet more warm and approachable than the stark white did.

"Your tests are fine, Amanda." Faith handed her the lab report.

"Except the potassium, don't forget the potassium."

"I didn't." Faith pulled a dark brown pharmacy bottle from her pocket. "Your potassium is a little low—"

"Borderline," Dr. Nelson put in. "Borderline low. But I want you to take this potassium chloride, two pills every six hours." He took the bottle from his wife and folded it into Amanda's palm, gripping her hand tight. "I'll see you back next week, repeat the tests."

"That's it?" Amanda asked. "Just some low potassium?" She felt lighter, as if she were floating a few inches on the other side of her skin as relief flooded over her.

"That's it," Faith said with a smile, patting her arm reassuringly.

"Now, young lady, you need to take this seriously," Dr. Nelson said. "Hypokalemia can cause weakness, muscle fasciculations, decreased reflexes. And if it persists, I'll need to do some further testing. Might be Charcot-Marie-Tooth, familial periodic paralysis, or the like."

Amanda found herself nodding in agreement. Those diseases were rare but not life threatening. And none had the protein deposits Ken Rosen had found in Becky's path results. "Yes, sir. Thank you." She smiled at both of them, blinking back more tears. "Thank you both."

"You need to take better care of yourself," Faith said, already edging toward the door.

"Yes. You should get plenty of rest and eat healthy." Dr. Norman remained where he was, at Amanda's side. "Faith, we should have her over for dinner this weekend."

"I thought the same thing. How about Sunday afternoon? Come to the house around four; I'll make my pot roast, and apple pie for dessert."

Images of Amanda's home in South Carolina, live oaks draped in Spanish moss, bright sunshine splashing on the water, filled her mind. Just the thought of home was enough to calm her. And now, she realized, she had a home here in Pittsburgh as well. She didn't need to travel a thousand miles to find people who cared about her. "Thank you, that would be lovely. I'm looking forward to it."

THIRTY

Friday, 10:51 A.M.

THE RAIN CONTINUED AS THE BOAT HURTLED over the waves, speeding back to the pier where Med Seven waited. Gina was soaking wet, her body trembling despite the ninety-degree heat. She tried to tell herself it was seasickness, but even she didn't buy it—would Trey and Gecko?

The pilot throttled back and gently nudged them against the bumpers. Gordon leaped out and secured the boat, and within seconds they were back on solid ground. The four men raised the corners of the stretcher, and Gina automatically stepped up to reach for the bag-valve mask to keep breathing for their patient.

A flash began to strobe, and she looked up. More flashes. A crowd of reporters had gathered behind a police barricade. The men loaded their patient in the back of Med Seven while Gina waited her turn to climb in. As she tugged her life vest off, she heard her name called.

"Hey, hey Gina!" The photographer lowered his camera and came running, outflanking the police officers guarding the ambulance.

Gina groaned. It was Pete Sandusky, a blogger who claimed to be Pittsburgh's equivalent of the Drudge Report. Last summer, Pete had made her the front-page, prime-time Hero of Angels with his video of her carrying a baby to safety.

"How is he?" he called out, aiming a tape recorder her way. "Did he say why he jumped?"

"He didn't jump, he fell," she said.

"Really? Surrounded by cops and he fell—that's fantastic!" His face lit up like a kid at a magic show. "Tell me more."

Trey's hand clamped down on her shoulder, hauling her into the ambulance. Pete snapped a few more photos before the doors slammed shut.

"You any good at lines?" Trey asked as he climbed past Gecko to the head of the bed and prepared to intubate the patient. Gordon had taken over driving duties, playing the air horn like it was improv night at Heinz Hall.

Anxious to redeem herself, Gina grabbed the IV kit and began to work on a second IV. The man's veins were for shit, and being tossed about in the back of an ambulance doing sixty over potholes wasn't helping. Still, she managed to get a sixteen-gauge into the antecub without blowing it.

"BP still falling," Gecko reported after they pushed two liters of saline.

"We're here," Gordon called back as they turned the corner into Angels.

They backed into the ambulance bay, and the doors were opened by waiting ER personnel. Trey and Gecko jogged alongside the stretcher, heading into the ER.

Gina found herself alone in Med Seven, surrounded by the detritus of a resuscitation. Her Kevlar vest had gotten shoved under the bench seat. She pulled it free, smoothing the embroidered letters spelling out her name, rubbing away a mud stain.

The ER's entrance sign cast a bloodred glow into the

ambulance. Gina shuddered, shrugged back into her vest, and climbed down from the ambulance. She hesitated before the doors, but the electronic, all-seeing eye caught her presence and whooshed them open, expelling the raucous jungle noises of an urban trauma center.

Zipping the vest tight, so tight she could barely breathe, Gina went inside.

FAITH AND DR. NELSON LEFT AMANDA IN THE exam room as they returned to their patients at the clinic. Amanda took the time to check her appearance in the mirror above the sink. She had red eyes, a red nose, and a goose egg forming on her forehead from where she'd hit the steering wheel; she'd probably have a black eye in a day or so. Smoothing her bangs over the lump, she tried out a smile. It wasn't all that hard—the news that there was nothing seriously wrong with her made up for the loss of the Love Bug. Well, almost.

She poured two of the pills into her palm and swallowed, washing them down with more water. She should try to follow Dr. Nelson's orders and splurge on a real meal in the cafeteria. Tapping her numb foot against the floor, she marveled that a simple little electrolyte imbalance could cause so much worry. Bananas, they had lots of potassium; she'd see if the cafeteria had any bananas.

Ignoring the dull ache that was already creeping up her neck muscles, she left the room, smiling and feeling better than she had in a while.

At least she was until she met Nora at the nurses' station. "Here's all the paperwork from the tow truck and the police," the charge nurse told her. "And they fished this out of the backseat." She handed Amanda her bag with her dress and nice shoes. It seemed so long ago that she'd picked the blue dress from her closet and been so excited about wearing it to work yesterday. "Want me to call you a cab?"

Right. She'd been dismissed for the day. Amanda rubbed the side of her neck, kneading the muscle knots already forming. What was she going to do, lie around and watch soap operas?

"No, thanks. But could I borrow your car?"

"I don't think you should be driving."

"Why not? I didn't have a concussion, just a little neck strain." She straightened to prove her point. "I'm fine. I'll ask Gina to come by to pick you up after your shift." Nora didn't look convinced. "Please. I promise, I'll drive extra careful."

"It's not my car I'm worried about." Nora scrutinized her with one of her patented don't-give-me-any-BS looks. Amanda simply smiled. "Okay." Nora handed her the car keys. "I'll see you tonight."

Amanda walked out the door, slowing considerably once she was out of Nora's eyesight. Nora's gray Honda Accord was parked in the employee garage on the first floor, around the corner from the skid marks that were all that remained of Amanda's Love Bug. She drove out of the garage, quickly learning to turn her entire body to check her mirrors, not just her neck—too painful.

She hadn't intended to lie to Nora, but she couldn't stop thinking that she'd let Lucas and her patients down. She'd allowed her own worries about her symptoms to cloud her judgment and maybe had sent Lucas on a wild-goose chase. After all, she'd seen herself as part of the pattern linking Becky, Shelly, and Tracey to the boathouse. But in reality it was only two out of three patients, with Tracey having a more tenuous connection.

Instead of turning toward the house she and Gina shared in Point Breeze, she turned down Penn Avenue and toward the boathouse on Washington's Landing. In a small city like Pittsburgh, the boathouse seemed less a connection and more an innocent coincidence. Least she could do before taking the day off was to check it out—one way or the other.

THIRTY-ONE

Friday, 11:18 A.M.

GINA HOVERED OUTSIDE THE CRITICAL CARE room, listening to the familiar cadence of a full trauma resuscitation. Airway, breathing, circulation. ABC.

"I'm thinking spinal shock in addition to the head trauma," Seth Cochran said after completing his assessment and stepping outside as the X-ray techs wheeled their portable machine into the trauma bay. "For what it's worth."

His tone was grim, and with good reason. Gina winced, remembering the sound the man had made when he hit the water. Almost as loud as the sound of a gunshot. No surprise his spine had snapped.

"The boys stick you with the paperwork?" Seth said with a smile, gesturing to the chart Gina clutched. "Don't worry. It's a rite of passage. They'll let you on board for the fun stuff if you don't whine too much, be a good team player."

She nodded, his words passing her in a blur. The X-ray techs finished shooting, and he disappeared back inside.

She hugged her arms around her chest, leaning against the wall, avoiding eye contact with everyone.

Trey and Gecko emerged from the room, hauling their stretcher. She hadn't had the guts to go with them into the room, but had waited here in the hall. Useless.

"Cops said he has a wife, two kids," Gecko told her. "Said he'd just lost his job, lost their house, everything. Gambling." He shook his head. "Don't see how killing himself was gonna solve any of that."

Gina decided she was better off not knowing the intimate details of the man's life. Treat 'em and street 'em—that was the ER way. No need to get involved. She scratched at the inside of her wrist, staring at the red welts her fingernails produced.

Trey said nothing, his focus on Gina. Finally the weight of his gaze forced her to look up and meet his eyes. "Gina, we usually do a critical-incident debriefing after a case like this."

He surprised her. She'd been waiting for him to ream her a new one.

So she did it for him. "I don't want to sit around talking about a dying man and how I screwed up."

Gecko did a double take at her raised voice. Trey gave him a nod and he scurried away, taking the stretcher with him.

"Why do I get the feeling you care more about how you screwed up than you do about that man's life?" Trey asked.

"Because it's the truth. I don't know him—I don't need to know anything about him. Why should I? Why should I give a damn? People want to throw their lives away, go drinking or gambling or jumping off bridges or shooting at each other, what's it to me?" She was close to shouting. Close enough that Tommy Z emerged from the family room across the hall, frowning.

Gina whirled, ready to unleash more of her pent-up frustrations, only to see Lydia coming from the nurses' station. Damn it, wouldn't you know Lydia would show up on her day off, just in time to hear about Gina's screwup? Or had Trey had something to do with that?

Trey stepped back, arms open wide as if giving up on her, letting Lydia take the lead.

"Sounds like a tough case," Lydia said. Sympathy from her only made things worse. "Maybe we need to talk about taking you off the streets."

Translation: take her out of the residency program. Warmth crept up Gina's neck, a slow burn that added to her anger. Damn it, she'd thought Lydia actually cared, gave a shit what happened to her.

"You can't do that! I'm the best damn resident you have."

"Not right now you aren't," Lydia snapped back.

Gina opened her mouth, ready to spew out a probably career-ending retort, when Tommy Z stepped into the fray.

"Gina was just getting ready to join me for her stress debriefing," he said, smoothly pivoting her toward the family room. "I'm sure everything will be fine."

Lydia glared at the social worker, obviously skeptical. "All right. We'll give that a try."

"I don't need any debriefing," Gina protested, tired of people treating her like a child.

"Can I have her for a few minutes, Trey?" Tommy asked, ignoring her.

"She's all yours. I'll let you know if we get a call."

Gina started to balk, saw the look on Lydia's face, and stomped past Tommy into the family room. Tommy closed the door and turned to face her. "So. Where should we start?"

She straightened to her full height, rocking her weight forward. Usually a five-foot, ten-inch black woman scowling at them intimidated men, but Tommy seemed impervious. Just as Ken Rosen had yesterday. Damn, she *was* losing her touch. "How about we start with you telling everyone I'm fine so I can get back to work?"

He shook his head. "Why are you in such a rush to get out on the ambulance anyway? Haven't you been shuffling shifts to avoid it?"

"Who told you that?"

"Does it matter? You know, Gina, during debriefings lots of people will talk about anything except the elephant in the room."

Elephant? Exactly what she felt like, stumbling and bumbling and fat, everyone staring at her, most jumping to get out of her way when she went on a rampage. Most—except Jerry. Seemed like he was the only one left who really gave a damn about her.

She lost the staring battle with Tommy. To cover it, she dumped herself into a chair, hanging her legs over the arm. Her best defense against most headshrinkers—pouty silence. It both irritated and agitated them. Shrinks were used to asking all the questions and getting answers. In Gina's experience, they didn't handle silence all that well, despite their protests to the contrary.

And she'd had a lot of experience with them. She kept her face blank as Tommy slid into the chair opposite her. Her fingernail scratched a furrow on the inside of her wrist, out of his sight. The stinging pain felt good, let her breathe.

"Nice vest. Did Jerry Boyle give that to you?" Tommy's voice broke into her thoughts.

She hid her triumphant smile. Tommy was no better than the expensive shrinks her parents had smuggled her to after she almost flunked out of college sophomore year. Her fingers traced the monogram on her new Kevlar vest. It was heavy and hot, but one just like it had saved her life back in July. No way she was going out on the streets without it. She'd joked to Jerry that she might just start wearing it to the grocery store.

Jerry's laugh hadn't made it all the way to his eyes. Instead, he'd given her that worried look, the one that said he'd do anything to have been the one under fire, the one who had gotten shot at. A guy like that, she had to be crazy not to marry him, right?

"What's your position on mixed couples?" she asked Tommy.

He took the non sequitur in stride. "You mean different races? Like you and Jerry? I don't think there's a problem as long as both parties are prepared to face any obstacles together. A united front, so to speak. How do *you* feel about a mixed marriage?"

She hadn't been thinking about the race thing at all. More the "my family has money and are a bunch of self-righteous pricks and yours aren't" kind of thing. Or something along the lines of "I'm so screwed up, used to having everything my own way and done for me, but you're so damn sweet and normal and sane and loving. . . ."

She sat up straight, the vest bunching up around her throat threatening to strangle her. She tugged it back into place. "I'm against them. Don't think they're a good idea at all. You'd have to be crazy to want to live that way the rest of your life."

She paused, scrutinizing Tommy's face. He caught her gaze and returned it with that smug and superior "go on" look common among shrinks. Hah. He had no idea what she was talking about. She bounced to her feet; she didn't have time for this shit. "Who in their right mind would want to live that way?"

She was out the door before Tommy could answer.

TREY WALKED BACK WITH LYDIA TO THE nurses' station. She leaned her elbows on the countertop, watching Deon zap space invaders on a handheld game that Jason, the ward clerk, had lent him. She still didn't have a plan for Deon, and with Tommy Z on the prowl, she'd have to get him out of the ER. Maybe she could con a nurse into letting him sit with her while Lydia got some work done on those strange neuro cases. Except she really should talk with Gina again . . .

She didn't realize that she was bouncing on her toes until Trey laid a hand on her shoulder, quieting her. "Hey, relax. It's your day off."

She scrunched up her face, reaching a hand up to cover his, intertwining their fingers on her shoulder. She twirled beneath their joined hands in a move he had taught her, and was rewarded with a smile. "How bad did Gina do?"

"Not too bad, considering."

Lydia translated that as pretty darn bad—Trey had a soft spot for Gina.

"She froze," Trey conceded. "But not everyone's equipped for life on the streets. Not to mention the sight of a guy falling from a bridge and landing right in front of them."

"You're saying I should cut her a break?"

"I'm saying maybe you should back off. Give her a little breathing room. I'll talk to her if I need to."

She considered that. Backing off wasn't in her nature, but she could trust Trey. "Okay."

The door to the family room opened and Gina bounded out just as Trey's radio sounded. "Gotta go," he said, planting a kiss on her forehead. Gina didn't make eye contact but followed Trey out without a word.

Lydia watched the doors swish shut behind them and hoped Trey was right about Gina.

THIRTY-TWO

Friday, 12:27 P.M.

AFTER GRABBING A BASKET OF CHICKEN nuggets and some hot-mustard sauce from the cafeteria, Nora made her way to the office of the head of the ER, Dr. Mark Cohen. Mark was off today, and the office provided peace and quiet as well as enough room to spread the nursing schedule out across his desk.

She'd barely started when Lydia and Deon arrived. "Mark said Deon could watch some videos while I go through our patient charts," Lydia said.

Deon shrugged out of his backpack and sidled up to Nora. "Hey, you got chicken nuggets, too! Aren't they good?"

Nora didn't know whether to hide the unwholesome and wholly addictive processed, battered, and fried meat or offer him one.

"Don't," Lydia said. "He already conned me out of a serving of chicken nuggets, a piece of pie with ice cream, and two helpings of onion rings." She sighed. "Emma's gonna kill me."

Nora smiled. At least she wasn't solely responsible for

the downfall of America's nutritional status. She gave Deon another chicken nugget. "Comfort food. Besides, he's too skinny."

"No, I'm not," he retorted, standing up on his tiptoes and making a muscle with his bicep. "Gram says I'm just right."

"Then you are," Lydia said. She crouched down, examining the tapes on the bottom shelf of the TV/VCR stand. "What will it be? *Fantasia*, *Beauty and the Beast*, or *Cinderella*?"

"No thanks. I'd rather read." He pulled out two books, each carefully encased in zip-top bags, and curled up in the chair beside Nora. Opening a book of Sudoku puzzles, he leaned forward on his elbows. "Gram says TV gives your brain cavities."

"Can't argue with that," Nora said.

Lydia joined them at the desk, taking Mark's battered leather chair across from them. "Nope. Deon's gram is a very smart woman."

He tilted his head up, squinting at the clock behind her. "Is it time to check again?"

"Not yet. I just called a few minutes ago." Lydia turned to Nora. "Emma's pacemaker insertion got bumped for an acute coronary syndrome, so she's still in the anesthesia holding area."

"Looks like you're going to miss the whole day of school," Nora said, watching as Deon quickly filled in the blanks on his puzzle. It took her hours to do one of those. And sometimes she cheated, got help by looking at the answers.

"That's okay. School's boring." He let loose an operatic sigh.

"I thought you liked school." Lydia powered up Mark's computer.

"I do, but the best part is telling everything to Gram after. Then she tells me all the stuff the teachers got right and what they got wrong and we make a list to look up at the library. I love the library," Deon exclaimed. "You can learn everything—even stuff about other countries and outer space and the ocean and stuff and you never even need to leave Pittsburgh!"

"I like libraries too," Lydia said with a wistful tone.

"Gram used to work there."

"She did?" Nora asked.

"She was a librarian." He said the word with a reverent hush. "Till they 'tired her. I told her I want to be a librarian when I grow up, but she says I should be some kind of professor."

"Emma was a librarian?"

Uh-oh; Nora could see from the expression on Lydia's face that she was up to something. Bad enough they were breaking the rules having Deon here at all.

But then Lydia turned her attention to Nora. "Thought you were on duty."

"Rachel switched with me. She's working my shift in exchange for my finishing the schedule for her and the nursing, EMS, and physician QA."

"Sounds like you got the bad end of that deal."

"It's not so bad except this schedule." She gestured to the color-coded spreadsheet lying across the desk. "It's a mess."

"You have nurse G working two places at once," Deon piped up.

"What?" Nora slid her finger down the list of nurses. "You're right. Darn it."

"If you move her to here"—Deon pointed to an open shift—"and nurse L to here and switch these two, it will work."

Nora squinched up her nose as she tried to follow him. "He's right. It works."

"Kid's a genius. In fact, I'll bet he'll do the whole thing for you, wouldn't you, Deon?"

Deon had already rolled his chair closer to scrutinize the spreadsheet. "Sure. It's fun. Like a puzzle."

"Deon, you're hired. What do I have to lose?"

Lydia laughed. "You're not afraid of Rachel finding out you let a kid make the schedule?"

"Heck no. He does a good enough job, she'll probably put him on retainer." Nora leaned back, her eyes fluttering shut for a moment.

"You okay?"

"You asked that before. I'm fine."

"Seth?"

Nora didn't answer for a long moment. Her neck muscles clenched, grinding her molars together.

"It's nothing," she said, opening her eyes. "Let's get to work. We know what Lucas ruled out and what they don't have."

"But do you trust that Lucas isn't covering something up?" Lydia replied.

Nora frowned. She refused to believe that the fault lay with Lucas. "Now you sound just like Gina. You guys don't know Lucas like I do. Once when he and Seth were kids, they went on a field trip to a dairy farm. Before they left, Lucas sneaked away and opened all the gates. Then he stood there, waiting for the cows to stampede to freedom, but instead they just chewed their cud and stared at him. Seth said he cried on the way home, sad for the cows who didn't even realize there was a world outside their fence. Lucas has been a vegetarian ever since."

"Not exactly serial-killer material," Lydia said dryly.

"Serial killer? Stop joking, Lydia. There has to be another explanation."

Lydia didn't look like she was joking. In fact, she looked like she was giving the problem serious consideration. "You know what I tell the EM residents."

"Oh right, the infamous Fiore rules of emergency medicine."

"Rule number three: everyone's an assassin, out to get your patient."

"You're too young to be so cynical. Here, you take the

nursing notes, I'll go through the orders." She divided the papers and passed a stack to Lydia. "Besides, what about your rule number two?"

"Think twice, look twice, act once." Lydia shuffled her stack of papers and settled back in her chair. "That's why we're here."

AMANDA DROVE OVER THE 30TH STREET Bridge and onto Washington's Landing, a small island in the middle of the Allegheny River. The boathouse was a modern, two-story cement-block-and-brick building with large garage doors on the first level leading to where the boats were stored.

It felt strange, coming here in the middle of the day, wearing scrubs, looking for clues to a mysterious illness. She climbed out of the car, unleashing a new wave of aches. Mysterious illness . . . sounded like something from a TV show. But there had to be an explanation for her patients and their symptoms.

Her tennis shoes crunched over the gravel of the parking lot. It was warm but cloudy, and there were puddles. Sometime while she'd been trapped in the ER, it must have rained. And from the looks of the clouds, it might rain again—which meant there wouldn't be many people trying to get in an hour of rowing over lunchtime. And anyone looking for a workout would be across the river at the newer and larger Millvale boathouse, where they had indoor practice tanks.

Indeed, the only folks she found inside were the two clerks at the desk when she signed in and an older man who was working out in the weight room. Jared was probably still at the hospital with Tracey. She had the place pretty much to herself. After reassuring the clerks, both college-aged kids probably working in exchange for free membership privileges, that she didn't need help taking a boat out, she went downstairs to the boat storage area.

The high-ceilinged garage with its concrete floor that slanted down toward the river was eerily quiet. With the three sets of garage doors shut, shadows cast by the overhead bare lightbulbs gathered at odd angles below the racks of upside-down boats.

The air smelled musty, damp, shut in. Amanda walked past a rack of privately owned sculls and turned the corner only to stumble back as a huge beast lunged at her from the darkness. She rocked against the storage rack, releasing a deep *boom-boom* echoing through the cavernous space, a deep-sea monster sounding its war cry.

Her hand pressed against her chest, heart pounding beneath it, she laughed. The strangely shaped shadow was cast by one of the club's two dragon boats—large boats that held crews of twenty and had signature monster figures decorating their bows and bass drums to keep the crew's rhythm.

Patting the dragon on its head, she turned into the narrow space behind it to the storage closets. One held water gear: PFDs, oars, paddles, and so on, The other was marked EMPLOYEES ONLY. If any chemicals or other toxins were stored in the building, they would be behind that door.

Amanda tried it, expecting it to be locked. But rowers were trusting souls, no doubt expecting people to obey the sign as well as they obeyed the rules of water safety or the calls of their coxswain. She found the light switch and entered the small cinder-block-walled room.

She turned around in a circle. The place smelled fresh and clean, like a Laundromat. Metal shelves held industrial-size bottles of laundry detergent—biodegradable, in keeping with the club's philosophy, and which explained the scent—as well as a can of mineral spirits, a gallon can of Gel-Gloss, some rubbing compound, and a bottle of waterline algae cleaner. The familiar products reminded her of home—her father used them all at their family's marina.

On the other set of shelves were stacked paper towels,

toilet paper, soap for the bathroom dispensers, and spray bottles of biodegradable multipurpose cleaner. A mop, bucket, plunger, assorted chamois and rags, and some basic tools took up the rest of the space.

Not exactly the toxic cesspool she'd imagined, and no evidence of anything with mercury in it. She glanced at the ingredients of the Gel-Gloss: carnauba wax. No idea what that was, but her father swore by it. The rubbing compound was basically liquid sandpaper, that she knew. And the waterline cleaner—she opened the bottle cap, yep, the same minty smell as the one her dad used—was a mix of hydrogen chloride and phosphoric and oxalic acids, which could burn but shouldn't cause neurological or long-term symptoms.

All were properly stored, there were no signs of spills or any puddles of chemicals mixed together into some kind of toxic witches' brew, and nothing looked unusual or sinister.

Maybe the boathouse was a wild-goose chase after all.

She clicked the light off and left, closing the door behind her, her eyes blinking in the sudden murky darkness. Before she could move, a hand landed on her shoulder and a man's voice said: "What are you doing in there?"

THIRTY-THREE

Friday, 12:38 P.M.

AMANDA FELT HER BREATH ESCAPE AS SHE opened her mouth and nothing came out. It was Jared. Suddenly she wondered whether she should have been looking for *who* had caused the symptoms rather than *what*.

He came closer, his hand swinging toward her. She flinched, unable to move, pinned against the door; all she could do was bring her arms up and try to defend herself.

There was a *click* and banks of overhead industrial lights snapped on, flooding the cavernous area with light. "Amanda," Jared said. "You shouldn't be down here, alone in the dark. You scared the death out of me."

She didn't want to think about what he'd scared out of her. Her heart was speeding along like a freight train, and her mouth was so dry she couldn't talk. Then things went from bad to worse.

Lucas Stone came down the aisle behind Jared. "Amanda, I thought I told you to go home."

Busted. Big time. Both men stood across from her, staring at her like she'd escaped from the loony bin.

"I thought I'd check to see if there was any mercury or other toxins—"

Jared looked from her to Lucas. "I thought you said that was what *you* were looking for."

"It is. We got our signals crossed." Lucas stared at Amanda, his expression a mixture of exasperation and anger. "Amanda, wait for me upstairs while Jared shows me his chemical inventory."

"I already checked," she said. "There's nothing in there that would cause the symptoms."

"And you know this how?"

"I know this because my family runs a marina and boatyard down home in South Carolina. I've worked with all these chemicals before myself." She opened the door to the storage room and gestured inside. "See, nothing but mineral spirits, some cleaners, rubbing compound. No heavy metals, nothing that would lead to neurological symptoms."

Lucas strode past her, examining the various containers himself. Jared grabbed a clipboard from the wall beside one of the shelves and handed it to Lucas. "Here are all the industrial safety guides and our inventory sheets. There's nothing missing." He blew out his breath, rocking back against the doorjamb. "Wish there were—if it would help you figure out what's wrong with Tracey."

Lucas was frowning. "I can't believe it's a coincidence. All four have ties to here."

Four? Damn, he was still considering her one of the patients. "Dr. Nelson said the only thing my tests showed was low potassium." That reminded her, she should try to eat lunch and maybe take another potassium pill. Her foot was doing that numb and tingly thing again.

"Amanda, you're sick, too?" Jared sounded genuinely worried. "Could it be Legionnaire's or something like that? In the ventilation? Should we shut down?"

"You could move operations across the river to the Millvale building," Amanda said. "Give us time to check this one out, see if there is anything."

"Hold on, don't go jumping to conclusions." Lucas handed the clipboard back to Jared. "Let me look around first, see if there's anything obvious."

Together they went back upstairs. Amanda's left foot kept banging against the risers, forcing her to stare down to make sure she had them both firmly planted with each step. Damn, she needed to get her potassium up; this was getting ridiculous. And she didn't want a repeat of yesterday when her leg had frozen with fasciculations—not in front of Lucas.

"I'm just going to use the restroom for a moment," she told the men, leaving them examining the exercise room.

The women's locker room was brightly lit with white-tile floors and nautical-blue shower and toilet stalls. She ran the water cold and cupped her hand to scoop enough to swallow two of her potassium supplements. That should do it—especially once she got something to eat.

Her head felt heavy, her neck protesting having to hold it up, so she took the opportunity to gently stretch her neck and shoulders. As she tilted her face back, she noticed the glass-and-wood barometers hanging between each mirror.

Pretty. Her father had inherited a few barometers like that from his dad—they were as accurate as the ones the National Weather Service used.

She straightened quickly—too quickly for her bruised muscles, releasing a wave of pain. Ignoring the pain, she ran back out to the meeting space. "You need to see this. I think I found your mercury."

Amanda pushed open the door to the locker room and gestured for him to go inside. Lucas hesitated, and then both he and Jared moved past her.

"You tested Shelly for mercury poisoning," she said. "This is where she was exposed."

She raised her hands, indicating the dozen or more old-fashioned barometers and temperature gauges that hung along the walls. "Don't these all use mercury?"

Lucas stood, head craned as he examined the devices. "They do. We'd have to get them tested, see if there are any leaks, or enough to cause toxicity."

The door opened and a woman stepped inside, looking at them with a puzzled expression. Lucas smiled at her and escorted Amanda back outside. "Does the men's room have any of those?" he asked Jared.

"No. They have old oars and yacht flags. Shelly found the barometers at a flea market last spring; she was so excited, she cleaned, polished, and hung them all herself."

"That would explain her rash and borderline high mercury level." He frowned. "It doesn't explain the others, or why Becky showed symptoms first."

"They're glass," Amanda said. "Maybe one dropped and the mercury escaped. You know how hard that stuff is to clean—in fact, if someone tried to sweep it up, it might have only spread. There could be mercury hiding under a locker or in any of a hundred nooks and crannies."

"You're right. And the hot and humid conditions would release the vapors into the air anytime someone took a shower. But why only four of you with symptoms—"

"Three," she said firmly.

"How many female members do you have?" he asked Jared.

"Over two hundred. And we also have nonmembers who use the facilities—school teams, rowing clubs."

Lucas frowned again, doing the math, shaking his head. "It doesn't add up, but it's a start."

"Does this mean you can fix Tracey? Get her better?" Jared asked.

"I'll start her on chelation therapy as soon as we get back to Angels," Lucas assured him. He looked at the women's room door again, his frown deepening. "Let's hope it works."

THIRTY-FOUR

Friday, 2:11 P.M.

A SHORT WHILE LATER THEY STOOD OUT IN THE parking lot, watching as the Allegheny County hazmat team scoured the building.

One man clad in a white Tyvek jumpsuit, rubber boots, and gloves and wearing a respirator emerged, consulting with his teammates. They huddled over a small box, reading it, and then one of the firefighters came jogging over to Lucas. "You're right. We've got readings near the drains and showers of the women's locker room. The EPA will need to resuscitate the building before they can resume occupancy."

He left again, and Amanda glanced at Lucas, who didn't look very happy with either her or the situation.

"What's wrong?" she asked.

"Mercury toxicity can't explain it all. Some of their symptoms, maybe. But not their deaths." His scowl deepened. "Michelle had the more serious mercury exposure, but why did Becky get her symptoms first? It doesn't make sense."

Amanda blew her breath out. There was just no satisfying the man. "But they all had the boathouse in common. What else is there?"

He shrugged. "There has to be some other connection between all the women."

"You mean besides being young, female athletes with connections to the boathouse and exposure to antique mercury instruments?" She shrugged. "Seems like maybe you have a lot of connections, just none of them related to what killed them."

"That's what worries me. What if I was wrong?"

Silence lingered between them as thunder grumbled overhead. "You mean what if they all have different diseases?"

"Diseases I failed to diagnose." His words were almost swallowed in the sounds of the hazmat RV's engine starting.

"Lucas, I don't believe that. You're an excellent doctor. We just need to keep looking."

Before she could say anything else, the sounds of "Dixie" rang out from Lucas's pocket.

"I forgot," he said, handing her her cell phone. "Jerry Boyle gave it to me to give to you."

"My mom." She opened the phone and glanced at the calls she'd missed while in the ER. Andy. Mama. Andy, twice more. A break with no calls—lunch, no doubt, which reminded her that she still hadn't eaten. And now Mama again. She hit the button. Better to face the music now. "Hey, Mama. I can't really talk right now."

"Amanda Camille Mason, what did you say to your brother? He's threatening to cancel the entire bridal shower. Whatever you said, you apologize right away, young lady."

"Mama, I'm not coming to the shower. And honestly, I don't think I have anything to apologize for."

"What do you mean, you're not coming? Amanda, I'm counting on you—"

Lucas walked away, opening the driver's door of his Camry. Amanda rushed after him. She wanted—no, she needed—to get back to work.

"Mama, I have to go now. Love ya, bye."

She hung up. Ice water flooded her veins as she realized the implications. She'd hung up on her mother. The boys were bad enough, but Mama? She half expected the ground beneath her to crack in two as she plummeted straight down to hell.

"Lucas, wait," she called out. He stopped and turned. "Where are you going?"

"It's almost time for Alice Kazmierko's MRI. I need to get back to Angels."

"I'd really like to be there for that too."

He nodded grudgingly. "It's in thirty minutes. I'll see you back at Angels."

She drove Nora's car back to the hospital and rushed up to the PICU. Outside its glass doors, she stopped. Why was she so excited? In a few minutes she might be giving a little baby a death sentence.

She sobered, tucking in her scrub pants, taking a moment before going inside. Mr. Kazmierko wasn't at Alice's bedside. Inside the mother waited there, openly sobbing, a wadded-up tissue in each hand. "You're going to be all right," she crooned to her baby. "Everything's going to be all right."

Alice didn't move, other than the slight expansion of her chest as the ventilator blew air into her lungs. Mrs. Kazmierko held tight to the edge of the crib, refusing to let go until Amanda gently separated her fingers from it.

"We'll be back soon," she told the mother, taking care not to promise anything. She knew the pediatric intensivists had given up on Alice, but Lucas seemed to hold out some slight hope.

Good to have something to hang on to until they knew for certain. The nurse and respiratory therapist began to steer the crib out of the unit. Lucas followed them, his attention divided between Alice and the transport monitor that hung from the side of the crib.

Amanda hurried after them, her numb left foot catching as she crossed the threshold. She stumbled but didn't fall, catching herself quickly. Sharp electrical shocks flared through her leg and thigh, this time reaching all the way up to her lower back. She felt her muscles quiver with fasciculations, that gruesome writhing-snake's-nest feeling beneath her skin.

She stomped her foot, hoping to dispel the fasciculations. They'd lasted only a few moments yesterday and earlier today. This spell seemed worse; it wasn't going away. Lucas and the nurses had reached the patient transport elevator and were waiting for it.

Hiding her limp and pain as best she could, she hustled down the hallway. The fasciculations stopped during the elevator ride down to radiology but the pain persisted, spiraling up her spinal column, finding new and unexpected places to torment her.

Stupid, she chided herself. She'd missed lunch—her potassium was probably back down again.

Jim was waiting for them in radiology. When he saw Amanda, he buttoned his lab coat as if worried she would kick him again. Ha. She could barely stand; the pain was like lightning dancing over her nerves.

There was a water fountain outside the exam room. She let the others go ahead as she gulped down another potassium pill, hoping it would raise her potassium faster and take away the pain that was now creeping up her arm. They were only twenty milliequivalents each, and she'd just pee out any extra. She flexed and extended her fingers. Still working fine. By the time the test was over, she'd be back to normal.

At least she hoped so.

* * *

MED SEVEN BOUNCED TO A STOP, ITS TIRES scraping the curb. Gina couldn't tell where they were from looking out the back window—it was all a haze of dingy gray to her. Maybe somewhere in Garfield or East Liberty. Who knew?

Who cared? Her brain spun; her stomach was knotted with adrenaline; her pulse hammered so hard that she felt it in her fingertips, making it hard to focus on much of anything.

The call was for a drug OD—which usually meant puke and shit and urine and steps to climb and patients who would be less than thrilled to see them, if they were even awake or alive.

Her Kevlar vest felt heavier than ever, pulling her shoulders down, making her drag. It had nothing to do with her attitude, she told herself as Trey wrenched the rear doors open, glaring at her for not already being out the door with their gear. Both medics were giving her the silent treatment, watching warily as if she posed a threat.

She let Trey and Gecko wrestle with the equipment. Instead of helping them, she climbed out of the ambulance and surveyed the scene. A single-family house, gray with old-fashioned tarpaper siding that looked like it belonged on the roof instead of on the exterior walls. It sat alone on a lot, making its neighbors—a long line of rowhouses—look like ugly stepchildren crowded together. And to be uglier than this squat dog of a house, that was a lifetime achievement—more than most in this neighborhood could boast of.

A chain-link fence surrounded the house on its pitiful postage-stamp yard. Remnants of bright yellow crime-scene tape billowed in the wind like streamers left over from a party. Cops had been here recently—a lot of them, from the looks of the trampled and muddied front yard. No sign of them now, though.

"What do you think?" Gecko asked, pushing his ever-present sunglasses higher up on his nose. He nodded to the crime-scene tape. "Maybe she was DOA and they forgot to call us?"

"Who'd the call come from?" Trey asked.

"Anonymous—no surprise."

Trey nodded, raising his radio to his lips. "Dispatch, what's the twenty on our LEO backup?"

Gina paced along the sidewalk, her steps jittery as she regarded the house warily. It was standard procedure to dispatch the police along with a medical unit to an anonymous 911 call. Especially in this neighborhood. Goosebumps marched along the back of her neck and down her spine as she felt the stares aimed at them from behind closed windows.

"It's just another junkie," she muttered. "Why should they care? Why should anyone care?"

"What the hell's wrong with you?" Gecko asked.

She couldn't see his eyes behind his Oakleys—who the hell wore sunglasses on a dreary, rainy day like today anyway? What'd he think he was—some kind of rock star?

Gina scowled, her lips twisted tight, and resumed her pacing in front of the house. She felt ready to shatter with tension. Better to do something, anything, than just stand here. She rattled the gate. It opened without a sound, swinging back and forth despite the fact that the wind had died. "Hell with this. I'm going in."

JIM GOT TO THE CHAIR WITH THE VIEW OF THE MRI monitor before Amanda did, and Lucas was sitting with the radiologist. Which left Amanda pacing the back of the small room, praying for a miracle for Alice.

Her pacing was interrupted by calls from all of the oldests: Andy, then Adam, Andy again, Tony, and Andy one more time. She let them all go to voice mail and turned her phone to vibrate instead of ring. Guilt at ignoring her family gnawed at her, but she needed to concentrate all her attention on her patient.

The MRI chunked and clunked and made angry machine noises. Poor Alice was swallowed up inside the belly of the beast. There was a pause as they reset everything for the angiogram part of the study.

"Looks like reduced ADC with cellular edema," Lucas announced after reviewing the first set of scans. The radiologist nodded his agreement. "The angio will tell us for sure."

Cellular edema was a sign of diffuse damage—damage that may be permanent. Or not. It was hard to predict in babies. But the angiogram would show the amount of blood flow to the brain. Normal flow was good. Too much meant a risk of swelling and secondary inflammatory damage—exactly what Lydia had attempted to prevent with the cerebral cooling.

And no blood flow, well, that was bad. No blood meant no brain left to save.

Amanda watched as the tech injected the dye. The potassium seemed to be working; the electrical shocks had disappeared, although her hand was still tingly and numb along the pinkie finger. No big deal, she didn't need a pinkie finger for anything anyway.

Her phone rang twice more, buzzing through her lab coat like a hungry locust. She ignored it, trying to get a glimpse of the computerized results. She couldn't see anything past Jim and Lucas, and their expressions gave nothing away.

Finally the clanging stopped and the scan was over.

"Amanda and Jim, help them get her ready for transport while I go over these," Lucas ordered.

Amanda wanted to stay behind and see the results, but the grim look on his face changed her mind. A few more minutes of denial wouldn't hurt anyone.

She joined Jim and the transport nurse outside the scanner where the transport ventilator, monitor, and bed waited.

The MRI magnetic field was always on, so transporting

patients in and out of the scanner took several steps. First, the respiratory tech, who wore scrubs and carried nothing with her, took an MRI-safe bag-valve mask into the room and helped the MRI nurse extricate Alice from the machine.

"I'll lift her out of the scanner if you get ready to hook her back up to the vent," the nurse told the tech as Jim and Amanda watched from outside. It was a delicate procedure with all the IV lines, monitor wires, and endotracheal tube connected to Alice. The respiratory tech disconnected Alice from the MRI's ventilator and bagged oxygen through Alice's endotracheal tube and into her lungs.

The nurse skillfully scooped Alice into her arms, taking care not to tangle any of the many wires and tubes. She did a graceful pirouette and carried Alice out of the MRI field to the transport crib. She laid Alice onto the crib, where the respiratory tech bagged a few extra breaths into her.

Amanda held the PICU's ventilator extension ready. Once the respiratory tech pulled back, Amanda reached for Alice's endotracheal tube with her left hand, ready to switch the baby back onto the breathing machine.

Her numb pinkie finger brushed the tube, setting off a lightning storm of electrical shocks that made Amanda's entire arm jump, knocking out the endotracheal tube.

Without the tube, Alice had no oxygen.

Fear clenched Amanda's gut, twisting it mercilessly. *Damn.* "Someone grab a mask, bag her."

The respiratory tech was already replacing the endotracheal adapter with a mask to force oxygen through Alice's mouth. Amanda reached to stabilize Alice's head, but now both her hands were quaking with myoclonic jerks.

"Amanda." Jim pulled her away from their patient before she could do more damage. "What the hell is wrong with you?"

Amanda tried to answer him but her breath was coming in gasps, choking her. Her vision blurred and she realized she couldn't blink. Her entire body felt as if it were sparking with pain, muscles firing haphazardly, jerking uncontrollably.

She fell to the ground, her last vision the worried look on Lucas's face as he ran in from the outer room.

THIRTY-FIVE

Friday, 3:29 P.M.

STRONG ARMS CRADLED AMANDA. DADDY? NO—he was a thousand miles away, back home. She forced her eyes to focus. They seemed to be stuck open; everything seemed blurry unless it was right in front of her. She tried to blink but couldn't. A face appeared. Lucas?

Good God, it *was* Lucas carrying her. She tried to squirm free but her legs wouldn't move; they felt disconnected from her body, her muscles gyrating like a bucket full of worms trying to avoid the fishhook.

Something had crawled inside her throat, sealing it shut. She couldn't speak. Even swallowing was hard to do, as though she had a big old cat's-eye marble trapped in her windpipe.

Panic surged through her as she tried to move, to shout, to scream. Nothing. She was trapped, locked in as certain as when Andy had trapped her in that hateful attic trunk so many years ago. At least then she could fight. This time she was helpless.

Terror made her retch on her own secretions. Lucas

looked down at her, his face creased with worry. "Don't worry; everything is going to be all right."

The same words he'd whispered to Tracey Parker. He pushed through a door, and voices barraged her with the force of an ocean wave. The ER.

Other hands, strangely disembodied because she couldn't focus past Lucas's face, began to touch her, drawing her down onto a hard surface, wheeling her down the hall, fluorescent lights rippling through her vision.

Lucas never left. Her hand was numb, but if she forced her vision down—strange how much work it was shifting her eyes—she saw his hand gripping hers.

The baby—was Alice okay? Had Amanda killed her when she extubated her? Guilt and shame flooded over her. How could she have let her pride risk a patient's life? She should have listened to Lucas last night when he'd questioned her ability to safely care for patients. What kind of a doctor was she, putting herself before her patients?

A little baby—innocent, deserving of her best—could be dead because of her.

"Alice is fine," Lucas reassured her, but his worried look didn't ease. "We reintubated her and she's back upstairs."

Amanda swallowed hard—this time her throat was blocked by tears. She couldn't blink, so she tried to move her eyes up and down, as if they were nodding her understanding. It didn't feel like they moved at all, but Lucas seemed to comprehend.

"Don't worry about Alice," he said as the stretcher came to a halt beneath the glare of lights in an examination room. "We need to find out what's wrong with you."

"Amanda." Nora's voice came from her other side, but it was just too much effort to shift her eyes over that way.

"What happened?" Lydia asked, also out of eyesight.

"Fasciculations, myoclonus, paresthesia." Lucas rattled off her symptoms. "She collapsed in radiology."

"Sounds a lot like Tracey Parker."

Vaguely, as if her arms and legs were a long distance away—all the way back home even—Amanda felt strange hands brush against her skin and realized they were undressing her. Shame threatened to smother her. She couldn't let Lucas see her naked, not as a patient. Things would never be the same between them again.

There was a pinch and a flood as ice filled her veins. An IV, fluids wide open, she understood. Who knew room temperature actually felt freezing cold to a patient? More fumbling, disembodied hands jerking her arms and legs, thumping, rearranging, pushing, poking, prodding. Being a patient was bad enough, but feeling all these sensations and not being able to protest, to cooperate, to give consent . . . it was maddening.

Through it all Lucas remained constant. He'd disappear for a moment, and she would hear his voice giving commands, but he'd always return, standing directly over her face where she could see him. After the initial flurry of activity, he began to talk her through everything, his voice punctuated by the regular bleep of her heartbeat on a monitor out of sight.

Amazing how quickly her other senses chimed in. The smell of Betadine as they prepped her arm for an arterial blood gas. The sounds of footsteps, voices, the monitor beeping, IV dripping. All of these helped her fill in the missing blanks. But none of them could replace losing her voice, not being able to express her thoughts, feelings, desires, pain . . . Ouch! Like the stab of the second IV being started.

"Why's she so damn alkalotic?" Lucas asked, vanishing from her narrow field of vision.

"She must have been hyperventilating." Jim's voice came from her left side.

Great, Jim got to see her stripped almost naked, lying

here helpless. He'd better not try anything . . . the thought faded as she wondered at their initial question. Alkalotic? That meant her blood pH was high—that wasn't linked to a low potassium, was it?

Tracey had gotten worse after the accidental dose of bicarb had raised her blood pH. Amanda tried to keep the thought in her head, to remember later when she could ask Lucas about it. But then everything went woozy.

"Just a little Versed to calm you down," Lucas whispered in her ear. "You're doing fine. We're not going to have to intubate."

Not yet. The words remained unspoken.

Despair crashed down on Amanda. Was she going to end up paralyzed, trapped in her own body, like Tracey?

Then the drugs took effect and washed her away on a wave of numb denial . . .

"GINA, WHAT THE HELL ARE YOU DOING? WAIT for backup." Trey's voice sliced through the air in a tone of command.

Gina stopped halfway to the house, her boots sinking into the mud. "You and Lydia keep telling me I have to think of my patients first, forget everything else. So here I go—be sure to include it in your report to Lydia if I get killed."

It took Trey only three long-legged steps to reach her. The clouds parted, a stray shaft of light streaming down between them. "Stop being childish. We clear the scene first."

Gina was sick and tired of people telling her how to act and what to do—and even more tired of feeling afraid and uncertain and cowardly. Fear and panic whiplashed through her. "If someone inside there needs help, we're here, let's do it. I'm not gonna stand around out here twiddling my thumbs. C'mon, Trey, you're a tough guy; let's go risk our lives for whatever strung-out, skanky crack whore lives here. It's what heroes do, right?"

Trey gave his head a quick shake as if her words needed straightening out. Maybe they did. Gina was on full-tilt mode, not quite sure of what she was saying until she heard the words sputter from her mouth. To hell with words. What good had ever come of talking stuff to death? Gina spun on her heel and stalked toward the house.

There was a screech of brakes behind her, followed by the sound of car doors slamming just as she hit the front porch. Trey stayed with her; he probably would have tackled her or shoved her aside if he'd seen any hint of danger.

"The cops are here. Let them do their job, Gina." He laid his hand on her shoulder, adding to the weight of her bulletproof vest.

Her bravado was spent. But not her anger. That was growing, churning like the storm clouds overhead, waiting for lightning to spark.

She stood sweating beneath her layers of Kevlar as the uniformed officers jogged up and pounded on the door. They opened the wrought-iron screen door, revealing a large yellow sticker slathered across the opening edge of the inner door.

"What the hell," the first officer said. "Looks like the detectives sealed this place not three hours ago. Seal's broken now."

The second officer was on his radio. "Major Crimes was here—dug up a few bodies in the backyard yesterday."

Oh yeah, Gina thought, remembering Jerry's case. So this was where Jerry spent last night. Didn't look like a serial killer's house—didn't they all live in creepy Victorians with rocking chairs silhouetted by cobwebs?

The officer looked up again, reholstering his radio. "Dispatch confirms this is the address of the nine-one-one call. Unresponsive female, probable drug OD."

The first one frowned. He drew his gun. "You two, back to the curb. We'll check it out."

Trey grabbed Gina's arm, giving her no choice. She allowed him to lead her into the yard as the officers busted through the door, shouting at any inhabitants to show their hands. A few minutes later the second one poked his head out through the doorway.

"It's clear. There's a woman down—needle beside her—she's alive, I think."

They followed him inside, Gecko joining them with the airway and drug bags. The interior of the house was a contrast to the dilapidated condition of the outside. Shiny gold wallpaper flocked with red velvet covered the foyer walls; the front room had an actual chandelier hanging from the ceiling and was crowded with overstuffed leather furniture, as well as a bar in the corner with a widescreen TV.

All the other rooms had been converted from their original purposes into bedrooms. Some had been sectioned off from larger rooms, such as the former dining room, into small worklike cubicles each containing a bed, mirrored walls, and a single straight-back chair.

Gina guessed the front room represented the courtship phase where the customer was wined and dined, separated from his money, and offered his selection of girls. After that it was all work, no play. Gina's boot got tangled in a discarded fake-silk kimono, and she paused to shake it free, not wanting to touch the walls to keep her balance, not wanting to touch anything here. The entire house reeked of cheap perfume, booze, marijuana, and sex.

She caught a reflection of herself in one of the many mirrors that lined the haphazard arrangement of rooms. Dumpy cargo pants, baggy T-shirt, bulky vest, clunky boots; she looked fat and ugly. If she worked here, no man would choose her—hell, she'd probably have to pay to sleep with them.

"She's back here." The first cop appeared in front of where the partitions took a crazy turn.

The house was a maze of mirrors. She'd never find her

way back out of here again. Trey and Gecko moved faster than she did through the labyrinth. By the time she turned the corner, they were already bagging oxygen into a skinny black girl and starting an IV. The cop hovered a few feet away, keeping his distance. He held a small plastic bag containing rubber tubing used as a tourniquet and a syringe.

"She must have waited for the detectives to leave and come back to get her stash," Gina surmised.

"Nope. They cleared the house with the K-9 drug unit before they left," the cop said. "She brought it herself."

"Or someone brought it for her," Trey said. "Look, bruises on her arm. Someone held her down and shot her up." He reached for the Narcan from the drug box. "I can't get a vein. Gina, keep looking while I give her the Narcan IM."

Narcan was the universal antidote for opioid overdoses like heroin. It worked very fast, reversing the effects of the drugs. Sometimes too fast.

Gina knelt beside the patient as Trey injected her thigh with the Narcan. As Gina searched for a vein on the too-skinny arm scarred with old track marks, the patient suddenly sat up, pushing Gecko and the breathing mask aside in one violent movement—like a mummy coming to life.

"Don't you hurt my baby, you goddamned bitch!" she screamed, smashing her fist into Gina's face.

The cop and Gecko leaped forward to pin the girl's arms down while Trey held her thrashing legs. Gina lashed out, pure adrenaline-fueled reflex, and raised her hand as if to strike back at her assailant. She stopped herself, pain and fear and anger all surging through her hand, freezing it in midair.

"Gina," Trey shouted, now kneeling on the girl's legs. "Give us a hand here."

"My baby, don't hurt my baby," the girl was moaning, tears streaming from her face.

Gina rocked back and scuttled away to sit on the floor,

one palm pressed against her jaw. She wasn't sure whether she was more frightened of being hit or the fact that she had come perilously close to striking back.

Nausea surged through her, but she clenched her jaws tight, refusing to surrender to it. She'd never hit anyone before, had never come that close to committing any kind of violence.

And she'd never been hit before, not by her parents, not by anyone, certainly not punched in the face with a closed fist. Pain stabbed through her jaw and cheek. Cautiously, she opened her mouth, slid her jaw side to side. Nothing broken, no loose teeth. But *goddamn*, it hurt.

The girl was calm now; the men had released her. She was sobbing and talking quietly, nodding at something Trey said.

"It was Chevette," she said. "She told me Yancy had money stashed here—she ought to know, she ran this place for him. Said she'd split it with me if I helped her come get it. But when we got here, she hit me, held me down, shot me up." A strangled cry escaped her, and she grabbed onto Trey's arm. "My baby, did she kill my baby?"

Gecko sidled past Gina, not even looking at her, as he left to get the stretcher. The weeping girl was now fully entangled in Trey's arms, tears and snot staining his uniform. But he didn't push her away; instead he held her as if she were a child and let her cry.

"It's okay, Tanesha. We're going to Angels; the doctors will check you and your baby. Everything's going to be okay."

"She—she tried to kill me."

The cop was on the radio, giving Chevette's description to the dispatcher as Gecko and the second cop returned with the stretcher and loaded Tanesha onto it. As they wheeled her out, she still clung to Trey's arm. The cops followed, and Gina was left alone in the empty room, swimming in the scent of stale sex and fear.

THIRTY-SIX

Friday, 3:57 P.M.

"IS YOUR FRIEND GOING TO BE ALL RIGHT?" Deon asked when Lydia returned to Mark's office. He'd done what she asked—stayed put while she and Nora ran down to the ER to check on Amanda.

"I hope so," she said, wishing she could give a more definite answer. She bent over his shoulder to examine his work.

"I finished the puzzle," he told her, smiling as he spread the schedule in front of her. Not only had he finished it, he had adorned the outer margins with pictures of stars and comets and spaceships blasting off.

"Wow, nice job."

"Do you think Miss Nora will like it?"

"I think she'll love it. Let's pack up your stuff."

He said nothing, but merely carefully folded Nora's schedule and presented it to Lydia, then hopped off the chair and swiftly gathered his pencils and books into his knapsack. "Your friend, she's really sick, isn't she?"

"Yes, she is." Lydia supposed she should have lied to him, painted a pretty picture, but it just felt wrong.

"I thought so. You look scared."

She knelt down beside him on the floor, taking his hand in hers. "I am. A little. But she has really good doctors taking care of her."

"Doctors like the ones taking care of Gram?"

"Just as good. And"—she straightened, lifting his knapsack onto her own shoulder—"that's the reason why I'm back. I got a call. Your gram is out of surgery. She did great. Want to go see her?"

His face lit up with a smile that was blinding in intensity. "Yes!"

"All right then, let's go."

He slid his hand into hers, in a trusting gesture that threatened to break her heart—or at least dent it a bit. She guided them along the back hallway to the elevator bank, the long way around but away from the ER's R-rated hustle and bustle.

"So she has a machine instead of a heart now?" he asked, his face squinched up as he imagined it. "Like the Tin Man in *The Wizard of Oz*? Will I have to wind it up and stuff?"

They climbed onboard the elevator, joining a couple arguing about paying the bills and a sad old man.

"Not instead of her heart, to help her heart," Lydia corrected. She'd shown him pictures and explained everything. She knew he was just letting his imagination wander free. "And everything's inside her; you won't see any machine."

He nodded, an impish smile on his face. "But if it was windup, then I could forget to wind it on Saturday nights, and we could sleep in on Sunday instead of going to church."

"No, you go to church with your gram and you listen." Strange words from someone who was an atheist four days out of seven. But Emma had done a wonderful thing raising Deon; the kid was bright and articulate and kind and thoughtful. Lydia didn't want to undermine her.

"You sound just like Gram," he said, tugging on her arm as the elevator doors opened on the fourth floor. "Cardiac care unit," he read the sign, "this way."

They turned down the hallway. The pediatric ICU was between them and the CCU. In front of it paced an angry man, flailing his arms as he muttered to himself. Alice Kazmierko's father.

Kazmierko caught sight of Lydia and froze, his foot planted in front of him like a bull ready to charge. "You," he shouted. "Are you happy now? Your little experiment killed my daughter!"

Lydia's fists clenched as she stepped into a fighting stance. Her instincts were to face Kazmierko head on. But she had Deon with her. She pulled the boy behind her, urging him backward toward the elevators.

"I want to see Gram," Deon said, as close to a whine as she'd heard him make.

"In a few minutes," she said, gauging her options. "Go wait by the elevator. Count the angels in the cemetery."

Deon resisted but then obeyed. Just in time, because Kazmierko was now striding down the hallway, his fists held at his waist, arms bent, ready to swing. She'd almost love to see him try something—she was certain she could take him, and it would give her an excuse to have him locked up. But she didn't want any violence in front of Deon.

Kazmierko's face was slick with tears. He was crying unabashedly, his nose red, choking with sobs so that his words were almost incomprehensible. "She's dead, my baby's dead because of you, bitch. What are you going to do about that?"

What could she do? She wasn't God. If there was a God.

She stood still, weight balanced in a fighting stance just in case. Kazmierko kept coming, closer, closer, until he finally pulled up short, just inches away. He still wore the same clothes from yesterday, still reeked of Southern Comfort.

"It's all your fault," he was sputtering. "You're going to pay for this, I'm going to see to it. You killed my baby. Do you understand me? You killed my beautiful little baby girl!"

Lydia had no words to offer the grief-stricken man—no one did. All she could do was to stand there and let him vent his rage.

That seemed to be enough, because after a few moments he caught his breath and raised his fists to swipe away his tears. He stood, eyes covered by his fists, swaying. "She's dead, my baby's dead, she's dead."

Lydia risked reaching a hand out to him, placing it on his arm. He shrugged it off, pivoted on his heel, and staggered away, still mumbling. She watched until he vanished into the PICU family room and then dared to turn her back on him.

"I can see eight angels," Deon said when she joined him at the large picture window overlooking the cemetery. "I was praying to all of them. To watch over that man and his little girl."

Lydia crouched down and pulled Deon into a tight hug. He let her squeeze him tight for a long moment before pushing away. "Can I go see Gram now?"

AMANDA WOKE TO THE SOUND OF VOICES. SHE couldn't see anything. Panic overtook her, flooding her with adrenaline that left a copper taste in her mouth and thundered through her head. Then she realized someone had put lubricant ointment into her eyes and taped her eyelids shut while she was asleep.

If she couldn't see, she was totally cut off. Trapped. Back in the darkness of that attic trunk where Andy had trapped her as a kid. Her skin crawled as she imagined unseen insects creeping over her naked flesh.

She tried moving, tried speaking. No sounds emerged no matter how hard she tried to force her lips and tongue to make them. But she could move her lips and tongue—that was definite progress. And at least they hadn't needed to intubate her.

Then she realized someone had placed a Foley catheter into her bladder. Oh God, had Lucas watched? She had never understood before the indignity of being a patient, stripped of all privacy.

Unable to see or move, she focused on the voices. It was Nora. Speaking in a hushed whisper, over in the corner of the room it sounded like from the way her voice echoed.

"If anything happens to her under your care," Nora was saying, "they'll crucify you."

"Nothing's going to happen," Lucas protested. "I'm going to get to the bottom of this."

"In time to save her? Or Tracey Parker?"

Silence. Amanda could almost see Lucas jamming his hands into his pockets, shoulders hunched, frowning so hard that the little worry knot bulged out in his forehead. It was obvious that whatever was happening to her and Tracey, what had killed Becky and Michelle, was a complex and rare disease process, out of the realm of ordinary medical diagnostics.

She wished she could tell him this, reassure Lucas that she had faith in him. She strained to bring her mouth under her command and was rewarded by creating a choking noise that sounded like a frog getting its neck wrung. As she struggled, she found she was able to move her fingers and rattle the pulse ox probe that was attached to one finger, making the monitor alarm.

"Amanda." Footsteps rushed to her side. Lucas pried the tape from her eyes and she was able to open her eyelids—a major triumph.

"You're moving," Nora said, reaching beyond Amanda to shut off the monitor.

"Try to move your feet," Lucas commanded, pulling back the sheet and leaving her legs exposed to the chilly air conditioning.

As Amanda strained, she raised her head, but her vision was too blurred from the ointment to see beyond a few inches. She focused on her feet, trying to wiggle them, and felt the sheet brush against her right foot, followed by Lucas's reflex hammer as he thumped on her Achilles tendon. Her left leg remained frozen, numb like a chunk of dead wood.

"That's good, that's very good."

Nora appeared in her vision. "You're going to be all right, Amanda. Lucas is taking good care of you."

"No." The word was barely a strangled whisper. She stopped and gathered her strength. It was like trying to talk after the dentist shot you up with Novocain; everything felt heavy. "Not Lucas. I want Dr. Nelson. He's my doctor."

"Amanda, are you sure?" Nora asked, her face filling Amanda's entire field of vision.

It was like looking through the wrong end of a pair of binoculars; everything felt small and wavy and so far away.

"I don't want Lucas taking care of me." She swallowed; it was hard work. Almost as difficult as rejecting Lucas and his help. But the best way to protect Lucas, no matter what happened to her, was to keep him off her case. That way if something went wrong, he wouldn't be blamed.

Nora pulled back, revealing Lucas standing behind her, staring at Amanda. His face was contorted with anger and hurt, so much so that his glasses had slid halfway down his nose, unmasking his glare. A glare so icy sharp it sliced through her like a laser.

She couldn't feel his fingers dropping her foot, but she felt the chill of their absence, her vision dimming as he turned his back and stalked away.

THIRTY-SEVEN

Friday, 4:11 P.M.

AFTER CALLING ADMISSIONS AND LEAVING A message for Dr. Nelson, Nora had returned to complete Amanda's nursing assessment. "Any meds?"

"Really, you all don't need to fuss," Amanda protested, her voice stronger, back to normal. "I feel better already, now that my blood pH is almost back to normal—I must have been hyperventilating like crazy to get it that far out of whack."

"That was more than just hyperventilation and you know it. Medications?" Nora repeated.

Amanda looked like she was going to balk at answering any more questions, then gave in. "I'm in Dr. Nelson's study—well, I was before yesterday. But turns out I was only getting the placebo, so I guess that doesn't count anyway."

"Anything else?"

"Potassium supplements. I just began those today. Dr. Nelson checked my electrolytes yesterday and my potassium was a little low; he thought that was the reason behind my symptoms."

"Symptoms? Amanda, how long has this been going on?"

"Since March. It was no big deal, just the occasional numbness or tingling, a dizzy spell back in July. Nothing ever lasted long enough for me to get it checked out."

"Until yesterday?"

"Well, yes. I had a couple spells of muscle fasciculations in my legs and arms. Maybe they lasted more than a few moments. I guess."

Nora dropped the pill bottles into her pocket so she could check them later against the *Physician's Desk Reference*. It was a habit hammered into her from years of dealing with patients who were taking the pink pill for sugar and the blue pill for blood pressure when in reality they weren't supposed to be taking either or had their meds hopelessly mixed up.

After she checked a patient's meds, she'd relabel them, print out an easy-to-read information sheet, and return them to the patient. So many people didn't realize that good nursing was really all about paying attention to details and taking the time to put things right.

She still couldn't believe Amanda had had symptoms for so long and hadn't told anyone. Especially after knowing what happened to Becky and Michelle. "Does Lucas know about this?"

"He's seen a few of my spells. But Dr. Nelson checked me out and everything was fine. It doesn't match their symptoms, waxing and waning like this. The others went steadily downhill."

"You got better after we brought your blood pH back to normal." Nora thought hard, picturing Michelle's nursing notes in her mind. Hadn't there been a notation about a high blood pH on that last day, right before she died?

"Did Lucas send a mercury level with my labs? We found high levels in the women's locker room at the boathouse, and I took a shower there yesterday."

"Yes. And he ordered chelation therapy—of course

that was before you fired him as your doctor. Did Tracey have a high mercury level?"

"I don't know. And Lucas said mercury wouldn't kill them." Amanda closed her eyes for a moment. "It's all so confusing."

"Maybe it's more than one thing—maybe the mercury is combining with something else?"

Amanda shook her head, obviously puzzled and worried. High time she started worrying, in Nora's opinion. Didn't she realize she could have died?

"Lucas and Dr. Nelson will straighten it out, I'm sure."

"Do you remember if any of the other patients had a high blood pH?" Nora asked, certain she remembered seeing that in Michelle's chart.

"Tracey did this morning—but we found out it was a pharmacy mix-up. She had bicarb added to her IV and she shouldn't have. Her pH was normal when she came in yesterday. Why?"

"Nothing. Just grasping at straws, I guess. Do you want me to call anyone? Your family?"

"Lord, no. I don't want to tell them anything until we have some answers."

"Are you sure?"

"I'm sure."

"Well, your cell phone is here with the rest of your belongings." Nora tucked the bag between Amanda's feet.

"Nora?"

"Yes? Do you need something?"

Amanda's blush burned her cheeks all the way up to the tips of her ears. "Who put the Foley in?"

Nora gave her a reassuring smile and patted Amanda's hand. "I did. And I cleared the room first. Figured you'd like some privacy."

"Thanks."

There was a knock on the door, and the transport attendant arrived, carrying Amanda's chart. "Looks like your bed is ready. I'll come by and visit before I go home tonight."

Amanda nodded, but her lips had gone pale. "Don't be scared," Nora told her. "I can stay the whole night if you like."

"No. I'll be fine."

Nora watched the transport attendant wheel the stretcher out the door and wondered how long Amanda had been lying to herself.

ONCE AGAIN GINA WAS BANISHED TO THE nurses' station and paperwork as Trey and Gecko were in the exam room with their patient. She squinted at the run report on the clipboard in front of her, tempted to slap off sarcastic answers to the multitude of inane questions.

She came to the next question: limb integrity. A paramedic had once told her about a pileup on the parkway that left a truck driver in several pieces scattered over the roadway. As the medics cleared the scene, parts of him were transported in different ambulances—each requiring their own run report. He'd ended up with the torso and had filled out his report as *limb integrity: none* and documented the absence of a signed consent to transport with *no arms, legs, fingers, toes, or pulse, thus unable to hold pen and sign consent.*

Unfortunately Tanesha's case didn't give her the opportunity for such witticism, so she wearily checked the "Intact" box and moved on.

She moved on to the next question on the EMS assessment: patient occupation. Biting down on the pen cap, she considered for a moment, and then wrote *crack-whore addict, skank, lazy-ass slut.*

That ought to cover it.

The words swam in her vision as she realized it wasn't her patient she was hurling insults at, it was herself. She violently scratched out the hateful words, burying them in ink, tearing through the top layers of the run report until it was shredded and torn.

She glanced up to find the clerk staring at her. "Rough day?"

Drawing in a deep breath, trying to purge herself of this maelstrom of emotion, she nodded. "I think I'm going to need to start over."

He swiveled in his chair, opened a file cabinet, and emerged with a fresh run report. She took it, surprised to feel tears burning her eyes as she accepted his offering and gave him the ruined report.

"What should I do with this?" he asked.

"Shred it."

She had resumed filling in the mundane details of Tanesha's near-death experience when she heard a familiar voice.

"Tanesha Grant, she's a patient." Jerry was at the other side of the nursing station.

"Jerry, what are you doing here?"

He looked up and rushed over to her. "Did you transport Tanesha Grant? Is she okay? I got a call that she was here—"

"She's fine. Or will be with a few more doses of Narcan. Why did they call you?"

"She's a witness in my homicide case. What happened?"

"Heroin OD. Trey thinks someone gave her a hot shot, but I saw track marks. I'm not so sure."

"Those are old," he said, dismissing her judgment. "Damn it. She's pregnant, you know."

"So she said." How the hell did Jerry know so much about this witness? Sounded like he was more concerned about Tanesha than he was about Gina—hadn't even noticed the bruise on her jaw. She was sure there had to be one; it still felt sore. "She also packs a mean punch. Got me good when we gave her the first dose of Narcan."

"Yeah, that happens sometimes," he said, his gaze sweeping the closed exam room doors. "Can I see her? Which room is she in?"

"Help yourself," Gina said, giving her voice an edge he seemed oblivious to. "Room eight."

"Thanks, Gina." He gave her an absent peck on the cheek—her bruised cheek, but he didn't notice her wince—and left. Gone to take care of his witness. As if she needed taking care of more than Gina.

Then Jerry turned back to her and seemed to actually see her for the first time. "I'm glad you got the call. Tanesha couldn't have been in better hands."

Right. If he only knew the kind of care she'd provided. Well, hell. This day just kept getting better and better. She was just so damn happy Lydia had made certain she got to work it. Oh yeah, that Lydia, she was a real peach.

Jerry wavered then stepped closer to her. "Hey, are you okay?"

He cupped her chin in his palm, and the simple, gentle movement completely undid her. She nodded yes even as her tears betrayed the truth, and she threw her arms around him.

"I miss you," she whispered into the crook of his neck, inhaling the musky scent that was all Jerry. *I need you*, was what she meant. He seemed to translate, pulling her tighter.

"I'm sorry." He teased her hair with his fingers. "Work. It was just one night."

Her tears flowed faster. She turned away, taking him by the hand, and blindly led him to the stairwell behind the nurses' station. No one ever used the stairs, but as a precaution she led him down to the basement level. Their footsteps echoed through the otherwise silent airshaft towering over them.

Her need had no words. She pushed him back against the cinder-block wall, her hands slipping inside his suit coat even as her lips tangled with his, her body pressed against his. They melted into each other, kissed so long that there were spots before her eyes when she opened them again.

"I want you." Her voice was a hoarse whisper, her tears burnt away by desire. She yanked at the Velcro and zippers that secured her vest, her breasts aching for release. He helped, removing the weight from her shoulders. It fell to the concrete floor with a thud.

"Here?" he asked, nuzzling her neck, tugging at the T-shirt she wore beneath the vest. He quickly gave up on the sweaty cotton, instead sliding his palms against her flesh, one coming to rest over her breast, the other circling behind her, locking her into place.

"Here."

He spun her against the wall as she unzipped and pushed her cargo pants down. She didn't care that there was no time to get undressed, didn't mind the pinch of zippers and buckles and seams pressed against her. All she knew was that she needed him. Inside her. Part of her. Now. Right now.

THIRTY-EIGHT

Friday, 4:38 P.M.

IT WAS A TESTAMENT TO DR. NELSON'S INFLUence that he was able to arrange for Amanda to be admitted to a monitored bed in a private room on the med-surg floor. He and Faith arrived just after the nurse finished her assessment.

"No sense taking chances," he said, when she protested that she now felt fine, except for not being able to move her leg. She didn't even want to be admitted at all, much less take up a precious—and expensive—private, monitored bed.

"Nonsense," Faith had said. "Just relax, Norman will take care of everything."

"I spoke with Lucas Stone. He appears to have done a decent evaluation on his other patients. A bit of a shotgun approach. And mercury poisoning? That really doesn't fit. But with these new protein deposits Ken Rosen found, maybe I can zero in on what's really going on."

The knot in Amanda's stomach tightened at Lucas's name. Could she have messed things up worse than they already were? Not even if she had tried. But there was no way Lucas could be her doctor; she couldn't stand the thought of him seeing her weak, vulnerable.

"So what's the plan?" she asked Dr. Nelson, fighting to put on a false mask of bravado that she was certain everyone saw through.

"The plan, young lady," he said in a hearty voice, "is for you to rest comfortably while I arrange for some further tests. I'd like to start with a nerve conduction study and muscle biopsy."

The same tests Lucas had performed on Tracey, but the results had been equivocal. Of course Tracey hadn't been able to respond; she'd been under sedation—with Amanda awake and alert, maybe they'd get some conclusive results.

"Okay, bring on the needles," she said, her fingers massaging the sheet into a knot.

"That's the spirit."

"Don't worry, Amanda. Norman will figure this all out." Faith patted her arm. "And I'll sneak some real food in for you. If I have time, I'll bake some of those mincemeat cookies you like so much."

Amanda blinked back tears. "Thanks." She squeezed Faith's hand. "Really. I don't know what I would do without you two."

"I hate to see you here all alone," Dr. Nelson said. "Do you want me to call your family?"

"No. Please. I don't want to worry them—not until we have a better idea what's going on."

"One idea coming up. You just lay back and rest—doctor's orders."

He took Faith's arm, and they strolled out of the room as if they were promenading on a boardwalk. Dr. Nelson unabashedly wrapped his arm around Faith's waist, she paused to straighten his lab coat, and the smile he bestowed on her in thanks was brilliant. Amanda sank back against her pillows, wondering if she'd ever find a man like that.

* * *

AFTERWARD, GINA AND JERRY SAT TOGETHER on the steps, trying to reassemble their clothing into some semblance of order. It was hard when they couldn't seem to stop touching each other.

"So, you going to tell me what that was all about?" Jerry asked, one finger tracing circles on her kneecap. "Not that I'm complaining, mind you."

She blew her breath out and laid her cheek against his shoulder. "I had a rough day."

"The jumper?"

"Uh-huh. Among other things."

"But, hey, you're back on the streets where you belong. And they're gonna give you a medal." He kissed the top of her head. "The Hero of Angels. I'm so proud of you."

She pulled back. "Would you be proud of me without the medal?"

"Of course. You've been my hero since the night we first met. When you saved that girl's life. You know that."

A smile slowly spread across her face, bringing with it a warm feeling that filled the hollow of her stomach. She did know that—but sometimes she let other voices, like her father's, drown out Jerry's. "Thanks."

She kissed him again, parting only after her phone rang. He got to his feet as she answered it. A text message from Pete Sandusky, the reporter who had started all this hero BS.

"Secret admirer?" Jerry secured his gun on his belt, then bent over and picked up her vest.

Gina wrinkled her nose. "Pete Sandusky. Wants to meet me tonight."

"About what?"

"He doesn't say. But I'd like to talk to him, see if he can back off on all this 'hero' stuff—maybe cancel the medal."

"You sure about that?" Together they began up the stairs.

"No. My dad had a hand in it, and you know what he can be like. I'm not certain it's worth disappointing him—especially in public."

"It's your decision. You know I'm behind you all the way." They stopped outside the door to the ER. He kissed her on the forehead. "I have a witness to interview and you have more lives to save."

To her dismay, he eased the vest back onto her body. As the weight fell against her shoulders, so did her spirits. "Can't we just go home? Janet can talk to your witness—"

She knew it was hopeless before she finished. Jerry wouldn't shirk his duties, let a witness down. Or his partner. Didn't he realize she needed him too? That she couldn't face going back out on the streets again?

He said nothing, but merely shook his head, waved good-bye, and disappeared through the door. Gina didn't follow, but contemplated escaping through the tunnels and never showing her face inside the ER again.

She reread Pete's text message. *Meet me at Diggers, 8 pm, important story you can help with.* For a reporter, Pete sure didn't have a way with words. She sighed, pushed through the door, and reentered the ER.

Trey was waiting at the nurses' station. "We need to talk."

She laughed, a brittle, tinny sound that escaped before she could stop it. Trey didn't look like he was in a laughing mood. The time with Jerry had almost made her forget her screwup with Tanesha, the way her anger had almost overcome her. Trey obviously hadn't forgotten that—or anything else she'd done wrong today.

She sauntered over to him, trying to act nonchalant. After all, she was in her territory. Here in the ER, she was the boss. Attitude, it was all about attitude. "You breaking up with me, Trey, sweetie?"

"Gina, this is important. You're halfway through your residency; it's time that you made a choice." His grave tone forced her back a step until she hit the wall. He stood up straight, hands on his hips as if addressing his troops.

"In case you've forgotten, I'm the doctor here." She knew instantly it was the wrong thing to say.

"That is the problem, *Doctor*. You need to make a choice. Are you going to merely call yourself a doctor, or are you going to start acting like one and stop sleepwalking through your shifts?"

"What the hell are you talking about?" she snapped, trying to ignore the sudden flip-flop in her stomach. He'd seen through her act. First Lydia and now Trey. What the hell had she been thinking, that she could fool them all?

"I don't care how rich you and your family are, I don't care about what's going on in your life outside the hospital, but I sure as hell care if you come ride on my rig and don't bring everything you have to the game. You're smart, Gina. Damn smart. But you put on the white coat like it's a costume. You're playing dress-up to impress Daddy and the crowd. You need to start acting like you actually give a shit about what you're doing instead of how you look doing it. You need to put your patients first. I don't want you working with my guys until you do."

His words barely reached her. She was numb, protected by her Kevlar. He stared at her, waiting for a response. He was going to be waiting a long time. She spun on her heel and walked away. Her shift had three hours left, but the hell with that. She was finished.

Gina thought about Lydia and the way she fought for every patient that came into her care, the passion she exhibited every time she took someone's life into her hands. Did she have that passion? That strength? The courage to get involved no matter the risk or odds against you?

Maybe her parents were right, she should just quit. She wasn't cut out for this job. She pushed through the doors, hitting a wall of humidity and storm-tossed wind. Maybe it was Jerry who was the fool, blind to the truth everyone else seemed to see. Blind to the kind of person she really was: a no-good, gutless coward.

BEING A PATIENT WAS PRETTY MUCH THE MOST boring thing Amanda had ever done—worse than shucking pecans or helping her mama polish the silver.

She couldn't sleep, not with everyone poking and prodding and machines yipping all around. She couldn't do anything but sit there, ice-cold fluid seeping through her from the IV, which was basically a straw floating around inside her vein, jabbing her from the inside every time she moved her hand. She had no books, no music, nothing but time to ponder her situation. She tried the TV, but it carried only the local channels and they all had the afternoon news on, which made her even more depressed. She clicked it off and forced herself to sleep, managed to doze for a short while, only to wake to find Lucas sitting beside her—wearing the same worried expression he had when he'd held vigil over Tracey.

"What are you doing here?" she asked, coughing out a frog the dry air had left in her throat.

He stood and reached across her for a small plastic glass of water with a bendy straw. The bedside table was on the same side as her hand with the IV, so he held the glass for her as she leaned forward and drank. "Thanks."

"How are you feeling?"

She started to force a smile, realized he would see right through it, and decided it wasn't worth the effort. "Okay. A little scared. Maybe. How's Alice? I didn't hurt her, did I?"

"It wouldn't have mattered. The scan showed no blood flow." He looked away, concentrating on centering the cup exactly back in the water ring it had left behind. "Her parents are deciding on organ donation and when to withdraw support, but she's essentially gone already."

Amanda fell back against the pillow, her eyes sinking closed, fighting against the overwhelming wave of grief.

She squeezed the tears back. She didn't want to cry, not in front of Lucas—besides, she was supposed to be a professional. She took a deep breath and managed to look back up at Lucas. "I'm sorry."

"We did everything we could."

"Does Lydia know?"

"Unfortunately, yes. The father practically attacked her in the middle of the hallway outside the PICU."

"I tried to explain to him that it wasn't her fault, that babies' brains are delicate—"

"He doesn't want an explanation. He wants a target. And Lydia makes an easy one." He stopped fiddling with the cup and turned back to her.

"Are you mad at me? For choosing Dr. Nelson instead of you?"

"I was. Then I realized you were trying to protect me in some kind of misguided gesture. That's why I came, to let you know that there's nothing to protect me from. I haven't done anything wrong, Amanda."

"I know. But this way so will everyone else."

He frowned at her logic but then shrugged. "I called your parents. Told them you'd call yourself when you could."

"Lucas, how could you!" She grabbed the bed rail and hauled herself up straighter, trying without success to erase the disadvantage that lying in bed, being seen as a helpless patient gave her. "Fine time to start breaking the rules. That's a HIPAA violation, you know."

All she needed was Mama or one of her older brothers showing up, trying to persuade her to come home. Daddy wouldn't come or call. Since the stroke he didn't drive and never called. "Seriously, Lucas, you shouldn't have called them."

"Why not? You're obviously close; they call you all day long. What's the problem? Don't tell me you're upset because of any silly patient privacy regulations."

"You wouldn't understand."

"Try me."

"Do you have brothers or sisters?"

"One of each."

"But you're the oldest, aren't you?"

"How'd you know?"

"Believe me, after a lifetime of being told my brothers got to do things I didn't because they were the oldest, I've made a study of birth order."

"Baby Girl," Lucas murmured. "That's what your brother—one of them—called you. His voice carries."

"Yeah, I'm the baby. But also the only daughter. Which means I was pampered, treated like china—"

"Why do I get the feeling you rebelled against that?"

"Much to my mother's dismay. You see, I was her last and only chance. She wanted to make me into a proper lady, someone she could be proud of, who would take care of the family when she's gone."

"A lot to ask. What if you wanted to live your own life?"

Amanda sank back against the pillows, her breath escaping in a sigh. "Exactly. Which is why I'm up here among strangers a thousand miles away from home."

"You miss your home, don't you?"

"Yes. And I miss my family—even though they can never understand me or what I want or why I do what I do. I can't help but hurt them, but I need to live my own life.

"Last Christmas I finally made it home for a visit. The day after Christmas, my daddy had a stroke. Not too bad—he's back at work, motor skills are fine. His speech is still a bit weak, so now he just about never talks, especially on the phone. Not that he ever talked much to start with—Mama always did all the talking for him."

"I'm guessing they wanted you to stay home, help take care of him?"

"Yes. He was fine, already walking and doing most everything on his own when I left to come back to school, but—"

"They thought you were betraying them by leaving." His tone made it sound like he knew exactly what he was talking about.

"Abandoning them, that's what Mama said. Said no job was more important than family. But it's different for my brothers—they all work at our marina, live less than a mile from home. They never want to leave; to them life is perfect just the way it is."

"But you have bigger dreams. You want more."

"Mama says that's my failing. Always wanting more. Guess she's right."

"Amanda, don't you ever let anyone try to box you in. Some people need to dream big, to work for those dreams even when no one else around them understands—or forgives." A shadow crossed his face.

She remembered what Nora had said about Lucas's father, the garbageman with the genius son. Lucas did understand what it was like not being able to explain his dreams to his family, the sense of betrayal that leaving them behind entailed.

"Anyway, I can't ask them to come up here. Daddy never leaves the marina or talks to outsiders, and Mama couldn't leave him behind alone. She doesn't even let him go out on the boat anymore, not after the stroke."

"I'm sorry I called them. I just didn't want to see you go through this alone."

"I'm not alone. I have Dr. Nelson and Faith, my friends, and you." She paused while she screwed up the courage to ask what she really wanted to know—the reason behind the fake smile plastered on Dr. Nelson's face. "Besides, it's not that bad, is it? I mean, Tracey stabilized and I'm nowhere near as bad as she is."

He was silent for a long moment. Then he did the one thing that proved to her that things were worse than she thought. He reached over the bed rail and cradled her hand in both of his, his face lined with concern. "Tracey's in a coma."

"The locked-box syndrome?" She shivered and pulled the covers tighter.

"No. A real coma. Her EEG shows diffuse slowing."

She looked away. She'd thought there was nothing worse than the locked-box feeling, but she was wrong. If she had told Lucas about her symptoms sooner, could he have helped Tracey? But he hadn't been able to help Shelly or Becky.

"Dr. Nelson will find something," she said, placing her hope where she could. "You'll help him, won't you?"

Lucas stared at her, his eyes clouded. Then he dropped her hand and walked away, his shoulders rigid. He didn't even bother to stop and wash his hands.

He didn't look back before disappearing out the door, either.

Amanda sank back against her pillows, realizing for the first time just how alone she was.

THIRTY-NINE

Friday, 7:22 P.M.

ONCE SHE'D CONVINCED EMMA'S NURSE THAT IT was in her patient's best interest to let Lydia sneak Deon in for a quick visit, he'd seemed like a new boy, bouncing with energy. Afterward, Lydia had taken him to Diggers, the restaurant/bar across the street from the hospital with a menu laden with comfort food, and let him order anything he wanted, even down to the banana split for dessert.

Then they'd walked the two blocks to her house, and he'd discovered another treat: No Name. Lydia had been cautious at first, knowing how the cat treated Trey, but No Name had taken to Deon immediately and soon the two were racing around the backyard, playing a strange variation of tag. Deon had even christened No Name with a new name: Ginger Cat.

" 'Cuz he looks like a gingerbread cookie, all sorts of shades of brown," he explained, stroking No Name until the cat released a loud roaring sound that was his attempt at a purr.

She watched Deon and the cat and felt a bit guilty.

What if No Name—er, Ginger Cat—scratched or bit the boy? She'd be responsible. But it wasn't her cat—or was it?

The cat was a stray, had lived here before she did. What right did she have to take a free animal and put it in a cage, torture it with trips to the vet, needles, and the like?

The thought of being responsible for a living creature—not just for the few minutes that patients were under her care in the ER, but for . . . forever? . . . sent chills through her.

When she was little she used to beg Maria for a pet, longed to take care of something, someone other than her mother. But now she was an adult and she knew how heavy a burden that was.

"Bedtime," she announced at seven thirty.

Deon didn't protest; in fact, he looked ready to fall down where he stood. He shuffled off to the bathroom to brush his teeth and change into a pair of Toy Story pajamas that were worn thin at the seams. Freebies from the shelter, no doubt. Lydia made a note to take him shopping before they went to see Emma in the morning.

In the bedroom, Lydia flipped back her sheets, a soft mauve and made of Egyptian cotton. Even getting them on sale, half off, marked for clearance, she still felt a thrill of extravagance every time she touched the softly brushed cotton. It was the first time in her life she'd ever had sheets that matched—and she hadn't even slept in them yet. Deon would have that honor.

Before climbing into bed, Deon prowled around her room, stroking the handmade quilts and burlwood furniture she'd bought at a farm auction, much as he'd stroked the cat. Ginger Cat followed, his nose almost touching Deon's calf.

"I like the swirls in the wood," Deon eventually announced in approval. "It's like going to bed surrounded by nebulae and galaxies."

"Why, thank you," Lydia said, adding a trip to the bookstore to their itinerary for the morning. "Climb on up."

"Not yet. Prayers first." Deon bowed his head and folded his arms on the bed. "Dear God, please watch over Gram and keep her safe. And help out Lydia's friend—"

"Amanda."

"Amanda, and let everyone know how special they are and how lucky they are to be alive, and oh, please let Mrs. Bradley not be mad that I'm turning in my science homework late. Thank you. Amen."

"Amen," Lydia echoed with a smile.

Deon climbed into the bed and snuggled down. The cat leaped up next to him and perched with its front paws on Deon's hip, watching over the boy with a fierce yellow-green stare. Didn't look like she'd have to worry about the cat getting in any trouble tonight. Or anything bad happening to Deon. Not with Ginger Cat on the job.

She turned and closed the door partway, then crept down the stairs, leaving the hall light on in case Deon woke up.

"NORA, HEARD YOU DID THE NEW SCHEDULE," Melody, the night-shift charge nurse said. "Thanks for getting me that Sunday off I needed."

"No problem," Nora said with a grin, remembering how excited Deon had been about finishing her "puzzle."

"Not that I mind the help, but what are you doing here so late?"

"Just finishing a few things before I go visit a friend upstairs." Nora emptied her pockets and found Amanda's pill bottles. She'd forgotten all about them. Well, she had to finish her nursing notes anyway and get them into the computer.

She quickly transcribed her nursing assessments, reproducing what she'd written by hand on the paperwork that had gone upstairs with Amanda. Computers—seemed like they tripled the paperwork she had to do despite promising to cut it in half.

When she finished, she grabbed the pill bottles. She tipped one of the research pills into her hand. Tiny. Amanda said she was taking the placebo, but if the real pill contained the same amount of supplements that Nora gagged down daily with her horse-pill-sized vitamins in such a small package, then Dr. Nelson had another gold mine on his hands.

Amanda had said this study was targeted specifically at women of childbearing age, with a supplement designed to increase energy, stabilize hormones, prevent osteoporosis, and help maintain a desired weight. Hell, if it did all that, Nora would be the first to sign up to try the pills. Of course, they'd probably be priced out of her range, like most of Dr. Nelson's products.

She replaced the small perle back in the bottle and examined the other prescription bottle. Potassium, twenty milliequivalents. Strange, the pills didn't look like any potassium supplements she'd seen before. She shook a few into her hand, turning them over. They were large white tablets, scored into quarters.

"Melody, could you hand me that *PDR*?"

Melody handed her the thick *Physician's Desk Reference* manual. The book contained information on prescription medications including a section that had colored photos of the pills. Nora quickly scanned the pages until she found the pills Amanda had been taking.

That was weird. They weren't potassium supplements at all. Instead they were a diuretic: Diamox.

How on earth had the pharmacy mixed the two up? There was no way. She grabbed the phone and dialed the pharmacy.

"I'm trying to help a patient, Amanda Mason, with what appears to be a medication mix-up," Nora told the clerk who answered. "She has a prescription from Dr.

Nelson for potassium chloride, but the pills she received are actually Diamox. Could you check on it, please?"

"Sure, hang on." She heard the sound of computer keys clicking as the clerk hummed. "You're right, ma'am, there was a mix-up."

Nora relaxed. At least she could cross conspiracy theory off her list of possibilities.

While she waited for the pharmacist, she kept reading the *PDR* description of Diamox. It was more than a diuretic, it also was used to prevent altitude sickness by causing hyperventilation and raising the blood pH.

That explained Amanda's high blood pH. She tapped her finger on the pill bottle. But it didn't explain why Amanda's symptoms got dramatically better once the pH was returned to normal.

She grabbed the medication orders from Becky's and Michelle's charts. She'd been carrying the damn things around all day, but now she finally knew where to look. Flipping the pages, she scanned them. There. Both had received infusions of bicarbonate—a drug designed to raise the blood pH. Both patients deteriorated shortly afterward.

The high blood pH was linked to Amanda's symptoms—and if so, could someone have slipped the Diamox to her on purpose?

Maybe the same someone who had cut the brakes to Amanda's car?

"Yes, ma'am." The pharmacist returned on the line. "The prescription for Diamox was meant for Norman Nelson. I'm so sorry; if you have the patient bring the bottle back, we'll correct the situation immediately."

"Has Dr. Nelson picked up his prescription yet?"

"Let me check. We sent both prescriptions directly up to his office. We often do that for his study patients. That must have been why the mix-up occurred. Wrong label on the wrong bottle."

"Thanks." Nora hung up the phone, stunned. She shivered, wrapping her arms around her. Someone *had* switched the medications. Someone who knew that increasing the pH of a patient with these symptoms could be deadly.

Dr. Nelson had tried to kill Amanda.

She sprang to her feet, grabbed the bottles and her paperwork, and ran down the hall to the elevators, arriving at Amanda's room at the same time as Lucas. He was smiling for the first time in days. They entered together.

"I think Ken Rosen and I have this about figured out," he told Amanda. "He found trace levels of mercury in Becky's tissues—part of those protein deposits we saw. You and Tracey have tested positive for mercury as well. Not as high as Shelly, but it's still detectable."

Nora hovered in the doorway, listening, hoping he'd found something to disprove her theory. After all, why would anyone want to hurt Amanda? It made no sense.

"The protein deposits are an idiosyncratic reaction; we found oversulfated chondroitin sulfate in Nelson's supplements. It's the same contaminant that caused problems with reactions to heparin last year, but combined with the other ingredients in his supplements and the low levels of mercury you and the others have in your system, it's causing different symptoms."

"But Dr. Nelson said I was on the placebo," Amanda protested. "And Tracey dropped out of his study."

"He must have been wrong."

"Or he lied," Nora put in.

Lucas continued, "I checked with Becky's roommate and Michelle's husband, and they were both in the same study. Michelle began taking the study drug only a few days before she died."

Amanda was frowning. "Idiosyncratic protein deposits. Like those babies with the calcium and antibiotic interaction."

"Babies?" Lucas asked.

"Yeah. They've been using ceftriaxone in newborns at risk for sepsis for decades; it's saved thousands of babies. And lots of those really sick newborns also get calcium. Recently they realized that a small number of deaths seemed to occur if the two drugs were given within forty-eight hours of each other. Some kind of genetic predisposition, probably. Anyway, those babies died because of protein deposits."

"Okay, same idea. I didn't know about the babies. It was your research into shattered nerve syndrome that gave me the idea. Only Ken and I aren't sure yet how to reverse things. Chelation may help. We think the mercury is what triggers the deposits to leave the bloodstream and collect on the muscle and nerve fibers—which would explain why Michelle's symptoms came on faster once she was exposed to the study drug. But"—he shook his head, and the worry-knot between his eyebrows reappeared—"none of that explains why the patients suddenly decompensated and died. Ken thinks something caused a cascade reaction, and their systems were overwhelmed by the formation of the protein deposits in their bloodstream."

"What about a change in the blood pH?" Nora asked. "Doesn't being exposed to either an acidic or alkalotic environment change the solubility of some proteins?"

"Yes."

"Tracey got worse after the bicarb was added to her IV," Amanda said.

"Becky and Michelle had bicarb added to their IVs as well," Nora told them.

"They did? When? Who ordered that?"

Nora frowned at Lucas. "According to their charts, you did."

"I didn't."

"It's your signature on the orders faxed to the pharmacy." Nora handed him her copies.

Lucas shuffled them, frowning, then passed them to Amanda to examine. "But I didn't—"

"I know," Nora said, still not believing the implications. "It must have been the same person who gave Amanda Diamox instead of potassium supplements."

"Diamox?" Amanda asked, a puzzled frown on her face. "I've never had Diamox."

Lucas spun to face Nora, his face knotted with fury. "Who gave Amanda Diamox?"

"Dr. Nelson."

FORTY

Friday, 7:51 P.M.

TREY WAS WAITING FOR LYDIA ON HER COUCH when she came downstairs from putting Deon to bed. He was wearing pressed khakis and a red polo shirt that set off his dark skin tone, making him look good enough to eat. She yearned to curl up in his lap, wrap his arms around her, close her eyes, and rock away the cares of the world.

She settled for plunking down beside him, stretching her legs across his lap. Who knew that watching a kid all day could be so exhausting? Trey didn't reach for her, but he did lay a palm on her knee.

"Guess you forgot about dinner with my folks." His tone wasn't accusatory, more like someone accepting the inevitable.

Shit. She still hadn't gotten used to the idea that inviting Trey into her solitary existence also meant opening the door to his large and loving family.

She'd never dealt with things like weekly family dinners before now. Hell, she'd never dealt with a family before. Years of living on the street with her mother followed by years in the L.A. County foster care system hadn't prepared her for any of this.

"I didn't forget," she lied. "I just forgot to call you to cancel."

"Uh-huh. Want to tell me what was so important that you forgot?"

She regarded him through half-closed eyes. For a laid-back kind of guy, Trey could be funny about following rules. Not as bad as Nora, but close. "Not really."

He arched an eyebrow at her. "Maybe there wasn't anything so important?"

His tone was still totally nonjudgmental—just trying to get a lay of the land. Yet it rankled her. More because she was angry at herself for forgetting about dinner. Even worse was how much she had come to enjoy the weekly get-togethers with his family. She didn't need a family, didn't want that kind of complication, entanglement in her life.

The silence lengthened. He shifted her feet to the side as he slid out from under her and stood. "I'll see you tomorrow. Or maybe that's too far ahead to plan?"

Ouch. The offhand tone he delivered his question in only made it worse. "When we met, you said you didn't want to put down roots, didn't want to be tied down to any one place—or one woman."

He stared at her, his posture rigid, hands fisted as if he were holding back. Then his face twisted and he turned away. "Maybe I've changed my mind."

"Damn it, Trey. Don't walk away."

"No, you're right. You don't owe me any explanations."

She grabbed his arm, but stopped short of actually spinning him around to face her again. Instead they stood there, touching but not together. She didn't know what to say or how to say it. So instead, she slid her palm down to his hand, grasped it firmly, and began to lead him up the stairs.

"Sex isn't always the answer, Lydia," he said, stopping halfway up.

"Shhh." She tugged, and he gave in and followed her up to the bedroom. She nudged him so that he could look through the half-open door.

"Who the hell is that?" he whispered. "Lydia, why is there a kid sleeping in your bed?"

AMANDA STARED AT NORA IN DISBELIEF. "NO, I don't believe it. Dr. Nelson would never do anything to hurt me—to hurt *any* of his patients."

"Do you have proof?" Lucas asked, although from the tight tone of his voice and the way his face had gone blank—too blank—Amanda could tell he was holding back, forcing himself to be rational.

"No. It could have been a pharmacy mix-up. But I doubt it." Nora explained what the clerk had told her.

"And there's your signatures on the bicarb orders," Amanda reminded him. "If you didn't write those orders, then someone forged them. Maybe it's someone trying to undermine Dr. Nelson's research?"

Lucas began pacing, hands dug deep into his pockets, swinging his coat wide with each turn in the tiny space. "No. Nora's right. It has to be Nelson. He must have realized that there was a small subset of patients who reacted adversely to his supplement. What he didn't realize is that it wasn't because of any fault of his but rather the cross-contamination of the mercury and the chondroitin."

"No, not Dr. Nelson. If he saw something wrong with his supplements, he would have stopped the studies, analyzed everything. . . ." Amanda sat up straighter, a sudden chill overcoming her, settling deep inside her. "Oh my God—it's all my fault. I recruited the volunteers from the boathouse. If I hadn't posted those notices, Becky and Shelly might still be alive. Tracey wouldn't be dying."

Lucas strode to the head of the bed, taking her hand in his. "You can't blame yourself, Amanda. No one could have seen this happening."

His words did little to stop the guilt washing through her. She was partially responsible for the deaths of two girls. Amanda closed her eyes, trying to force back the wave of nausea generated by the thought. They had to find a way to help Tracey. And to find out who was really behind this—she couldn't believe it could be Dr. Nelson. She opened her eyes to find Lucas staring at her, his hand squeezing hers, his gaze clear, reassuring.

"It will be okay," he said in a low voice. "We'll figure something out. I promise."

They were only words, but somehow they made Amanda feel better. She tried to smile and failed, so she nodded grimly.

"The important thing is, if we know the trigger is having an alkaline pH, can we reverse it?" Nora asked. "Amanda got better pretty fast once we got her pH back to normal—should we try to make it more acidic?"

"I don't know," Lucas said. "When Ken and I found these proteins they were already deposited in the tissues. We need to find some way to dissolve them, break them down without damaging the nervous tissue."

He released Amanda's hand and began roaming the room, not touching anything, his gaze darting every which way as if seeking inspiration. Nora started to say something, but Amanda held up her hand, motioning her to silence. Suddenly Lucas stopped, his stare fixed on the oxygen supply valve.

"Hyperbaric oxygen. That might work." He frowned. "Or it might make things worse."

"I doubt that," Amanda said, gesturing to her dead leg.

"No. Seriously, it can have complications. Pneumothorax, blindness, brain damage. We'd need to try it first, maybe on an animal model, get approval from the Institutional Review Board and the ethics committee."

"Lucas." He stopped his rambling, his gaze returning to fix on her. "We don't have that kind of time. Tracey is in a coma—if she follows Becky's pattern she won't make it past morning." Amanda didn't add that there was a good chance she'd soon follow. From the expression on his face, she didn't have to. It was funny. She was the one who should be scared, but she felt strangely calm, as if all this were happening to someone else.

"At least let me try—"

"No," she interrupted him. "You can't waste time. And you can't risk trying it on Tracey first. Tonight. You'll try it on me. Tonight."

He spun around, staring at the wall, his shoulders hunched.

Nora sat down on the bed beside her. "Amanda, do you know what you're asking? Lucas could lose his job, maybe even his license, if he uses the chamber without authorization. And the risks to you—"

"I don't care about the risks to me. I just want this over. I want you to keep your promise to Tracey," she said as Lucas slowly spun around, hands free of his pockets, hanging empty at his sides. "We can't let her die, Lucas. Not if there's a way we can save her."

He blew out his breath then nodded. "Let me see what I can do. In the meantime, I'll start you on the mercury chelation protocol."

She watched him leave, finally able to relax once the door shut behind him. Nora took her hand and squeezed it tight. Amanda felt relieved that she could feel Nora's touch—that hand was following the same intermittent pattern that her leg had before it went totally dead.

"Are you sure?" Nora asked.

Amanda nodded, unable to speak as the fear she'd been waiting for sneaked up and choked her into silence.

FORTY-ONE

Friday, 8:18 P.M.

GINA HAD CALLED HER FATHER'S CAR SERVICE to drive her home after leaving the ER. It wasn't like she could ask Trey to drop her off in the ambulance, not after he'd practically fired her. As the driver sped her through the streets of East Liberty and to her house in Point Breeze, she wondered if she still had a career—probably not, not once Trey tattled to Lydia about kicking her off his squad. Lydia would make good on her threat to fire Gina if Gina didn't get her act together. No second chances there. She should know better. Moses was right: you have no one you can count on but yourself.

She couldn't help but wonder if this was all part of Moses and LaRose's plan to free her from her squalid existence as an ER doctor. But no, there was no one to blame but herself.

Her cell phone rang several times: Lydia and Nora. She didn't want to talk to either of them, so she let the calls go to voice mail without listening. When the car pulled up in front of her house, she jumped out without waiting for the driver to open the door, left it hanging open, and didn't look back as she bounded up the steps and into the house.

It was empty. Shit. Where the hell was Amanda? Probably still playing Mother Teresa at Angels.

Gina paced through the house, denying herself the pleasure of ice cream or even a beer. She took a long shower, hoping to wash off the stench of the brothel, and changed into jeans and a tank top. Still no calls from Amanda—although there was one more from Nora. Seemed like Lydia had given up on her; no surprise there.

She tried Jerry's cell, but it went to voice mail. Too busy to talk with her. Great.

The house echoed with self-pity. She stamped down the steps, grabbed her car keys, and headed over to Diggers, the dark and dingy tavern where most of the workers from the medical center hung out. The food stank and the atmosphere was nonexistent, but it offered plenty of privacy and the drinks weren't watered down.

There she found the usual crowd following the change of shift at the hospital. She toyed with the idea of joining a few other EM residents in a game of pool, but instead took a booth in the back where she could get down to some serious eating while waiting for Pete Sandusky.

"Gina!" Pete emerged from the shadows surrounding the bar and approached her, carrying a mug of beer. "Glad you could make it. Seems like I'm persona non grata at Angels, thought maybe you could fill me in. How's your patient?"

"The jumper?" Gina realized that she didn't even remember the man's name. *Lydia would have,* a tiny whisper taunted her from the guilt center of her brain. She shook her head, to both clear her thoughts and express her sorrow. "Didn't make it."

The reporter shrugged, sliding into the booth, taking the side facing the door and the crowd. "Too bad. I'm guessing the *Post-Gazette* will still be putting your picture front and center. They should after what they paid for it." He stopped and looked her up and down. "You look beat. Let me buy you a drink."

She considered. Jerry wouldn't be home for hours—if he made it home at all. And who knew what Amanda was up to? Probably curing cancer or the like. She loved Amanda, but sometimes it was damn tiresome living with a freaking saint. "Sure, why not?"

"What will you have?" Pete asked, settling himself back in his seat and waving over a waitress.

He was one of those average white guys—not too tall, not too skinny, not too handsome. His main features were his salt-and-pepper hair and craggy eyes, both reminiscent of George Clooney in a vague sort of way. What George might look like if he were a normal guy.

"Maker's Mark." Gina's father hated bourbon almost as much as he detested beer. She glanced at the menu even though she knew exactly what she wanted. She'd promised Lydia she wouldn't purge, but she didn't remember saying anything about bingeing. Anyway, it wasn't really bingeing if she hadn't eaten all day.

Like a dull itch just below the surface, aching to be scratched, adrenaline buzzed through her. What Lydia didn't know wouldn't hurt her. Besides, it was Gina's life—Lydia had no control over what she did, no right to interfere, much less try to dictate to Gina or threaten her career. As she stared at Pete, a glimmer of a plan began to form. Lydia couldn't very well fire the Hero of Angels, could she?

It was a plan that stood for everything she hated. A plan her father would have been proud of. She'd hit some lows in her life, but this was scraping bottom.

Pete was prattling on about something to do with his blog and freelance work and the rich and famous Pittsburghers he hobnobbed with. Gina caught just enough to realize that the world of freelance journalism mirrored her father's world: "friendships" based on favors owed and disdain.

The waitress brought their drinks, serving Gina a Jim Beam. That was all Diggers carried, but still she always asked for what she wanted, even if she knew she'd be destined to settle for less.

Irritation, anger, adrenaline, and need combined into an intoxicating mix stronger than the bourbon. Gina found herself ordering food despite the nausea that wracked her at the thought of eating it and the knowledge that she'd feel awful—bloated, fat, defeated, dirty, a failure—afterward. It couldn't be worse than how she felt already.

Pete stopped talking as the waitress brought the food, filling the table with plates piled high with potato skins laden with cheese, bacon, sour cream, and chives; deep-fried pierogies stuffed with onions and cheese; chicken wings slimy with sauce; a mountain of French fries; and deep-fried mozzarella sticks coated in bread crumbs, cheese oozing from the ends, congealing on the plate.

"Great idea," he said, digging in and matching Gina bite for bite. For a while. Then he sat back and sipped at his beer as she continued her death march through the jungle of grease.

"Don't know how you do it," he said, starting on his second beer. "You're as skinny as a model from one of those fancy magazines." He tilted his head at her. "Why didn't you become a model? Why a doctor—and at Angels of all places? With your dad's money you could have done anything you wanted."

She smiled around a mouthful of pierogi. "What makes you think I haven't? Done exactly what I wanted."

"Dunno. You just don't seem to quite fit in around there. Too polished, too smooth. But at least for all your money, you're not a snob. Not like Lydia Fiore. You know she won't even take my calls or give me a heads-up on stories? After all I've done for her." He shook his head. "If I weren't such a nice guy, I'd take it personally, feel betrayed. I helped her out and this is the way she pays me back?"

Gina grabbed another wing, popped it in her mouth before the sauce could drip, and sucked the meat from the bone. Pete had gotten her a second drink—or was it a third? She couldn't remember, her senses overwhelmed by the food. Resentment flared through her at Pete's words—he wasn't the only one who had stood by Lydia before.

"Sometimes I don't think she's a team player," she admitted, flashing on the memory of Lydia telling Gina she'd drop her from the residency program if Gina didn't follow her rules. "Lydia always has to go it alone, be right about everything."

The same had been said of Gina, often, but she brushed that thought aside.

Pete leaned forward. "So, what can you tell me? My sources tell me Lydia tried some experimental procedure on a baby and killed it. Is that true?"

"What sources?"

He smiled, revealing brilliant white teeth. Too bad they were a bit crooked, marring the image. "Kid's own father. But I need confirmation from someone objective. Someone who knows medicine. Like you."

Gina paused in her eating to take another drink. She already felt bloated, acid burning her esophagus, her face smeared with grease. There was a piece of chicken gristle caught in her teeth and she picked at it with her fingernail, its painted surface reminding her once more of Lydia, the dictator. "What kind of confirmation?"

"Just background information. I wouldn't use your name or anything. I just want to be sure of my facts—have to be responsible about these things, you know?"

That seemed reasonable. "Well . . ." She took another sip of the cheap bourbon. It didn't taste so bad now. "I wasn't there, but this is what I heard." And she told him what little Nora and Amanda had told her last night. Which wasn't that much, really—certainly nothing confidential if he'd already spoken with the father.

"So she actually froze the girl? Right there in the ER?"

He seemed excited as he scribbled notes on a cocktail napkin. A small digital recorder had also appeared on the table. "Freaky."

Gina found herself basking in his attention. Maybe it was the bourbon. Or the afterglow of bingeing. Either way, she began to fill in as many details as she could—wishing that she had gotten Nora or Amanda to tell her more.

"So would you say Lydia was incompetent? A menace to her patients?"

Gina frowned, her vision swimming in front of her. She could barely breathe, she was so stuffed. She swallowed hard, but acid and bile kept backing up in her throat like a toilet overflowing. That's what she was, a human toilet, letting herself get so out of control like this. What the hell was wrong with her?

"I wouldn't say that," she hedged.

Despite her anger at Lydia, she drew the line at declaring another doctor incompetent. No amount of bourbon could force her to go there—doctors had lost their licenses for less. It was one of the tactics her father used all the time. Another wave of nausea hit her, and she wondered whether maybe Lydia had been right. Maybe Gina should have listened to her. "I wasn't there."

"Here's Michael now," Pete said, waving to a man behind Gina, indicating the empty seat beside him. "He can tell you more than I can."

"Why?"

"He's the kid's father."

FORTY-TWO

Friday, 8:42 P.M.

NORA WAITED WITH AMANDA UNTIL LUCAS returned. Apparently he'd consulted with Ken Rosen, who'd agreed that hyperbaric was a feasible treatment. He'd also found out that the chamber would be empty that night.

"We'll have to wait until after nine, when they're done with the last patient," he told them.

"Nora, can you help?" Amanda asked. She didn't seem to notice that her left hand was writhing with fasciculations, but Nora couldn't stop staring at it.

"Amanda, you can't ask her—she could lose her job and her license," Lucas protested.

"Just like you."

It went against every instinct in Nora's body, breaking all the rules, flouting the safety regulations. The hyperbaric chamber was to be used only by trained technicians and doctors granted special permission by the hospital's Institutional Review Board. But it was even more risky for Amanda if Lucas tried to treat her alone.

"I'll be there," she promised. She turned to Lucas. "But how are you going to get into the chamber? That area is locked down tight when it's not in use." Hyperbaric chambers with their concentrations of pure oxygen under high pressure were considered potential targets for terrorists.

"I have the security codes from a few months ago. I was one of the investigators on a study using hyperbaric oxygen on patients with Parkinson's. That's when I took the training course, so don't worry"—he patted Amanda's shoulder—"you're in good hands."

Nora stood. She had time to try another option first. "I've got to go," she said. "I'll see you two at nine, down in the basement."

"Thanks, Nora." Amanda actually smiled—how could anyone facing a death sentence smile like that, just because a friend was willing to break a few rules to save her? Nora tried her best to smile back, faltered when she glanced at Amanda's hand twitching. Instead, she nodded at Lucas, and left.

She stopped at the nurses' station to leave a note, sealed it in an envelope, and then slid it inside an interdepartmental envelope addressed to Lydia. She wouldn't get it until tomorrow, but if Nora's plan worked, she wouldn't need it. The note was just a precaution. After all, she couldn't go to the police; there was no tangible proof, other than what seemed to point at Lucas.

There was one more thing—it wasn't quite proof, but it would tie up some loose ends. She grabbed the phone and dialed the operator.

"Hi, it's Nora from the ER. I have a fax here and it's unreadable. All except the fax number it was sent from. Can you tell me who sent it so I can call and ask them to resend?"

"If it came from here in the medical center, I can track it for you."

The number on the bicarb orders faxed in the middle of the night to the pharmacy looked like an Angels extension. Nora read it to the operator and waited.

"That fax machine is Dr. Nelson's. Do you need his number?"

"No thanks, I have it." Nora hung up and stared at the phone for one long moment. She hadn't wanted to believe Dr. Nelson could be behind this, but now she was certain. It might not hold up in court, but it was proof enough for her.

She added the faxed orders to her packet, dropped the envelope off in the clerk's outbox, and headed to the elevator. A few minutes later she was in the foyer of Dr. Nelson's private clinic. It was pretty spooky, with only one light on above the receptionist's desk, the hallways dark. Empty.

Except for a stream of light coming from under a door down the left-hand hallway. She approached it warily and saw that it was Dr. Nelson's office. Her heart was pounding, her palms sweating, but she wasn't panicked. No, she refused to panic. She needed to do this right, for Amanda's sake.

Without knocking, she opened the door.

"SO WHAT'S THE KID'S STORY?" TREY ASKED AS they sat on Lydia's couch, sharing a beer.

Lydia curled up against him. "He's the great-grandson of a patient."

"A patient? Lydia, you can't go bringing patients or their families home with you. He's not a stray cat. He's an unaccompanied minor. What if something happens, if they make up some horrendous story and it's your word against his? I can't believe you did this."

"I made a promise." Trey's agitation was making him less of a cuddly pillow, so Lydia sat up, tucking her legs under her. "They aren't going to sue or make up stories or file a complaint."

"How can you know that? What made you risk your career for this kid and his grandmother?"

"Great-grandmother." She slid the beer from his hand, took a small sip, and returned it. She wasn't much of a drinker, never anything more than beer, seldom finishing an entire bottle herself, but tonight it really hit the spot. "Trey, there are a lot of things you don't know about me."

"That's okay, there's tons you don't know about me."

She doubted that—Trey was frightfully easy to read. Her mother would have taken him for everything he had and he would have walked away smiling about it. No way she could tell him all the details of her past, but . . . "When I was a kid, my mom and I lived on the street for a while."

"You were homeless." He set the beer on the floor and turned to her, pulling her close, his hands massaging her arms. "This was before your mom died and you went to foster care?"

She'd let him know the barest of details. He had no idea that she and Maria had been on the streets for the first twelve years of her life, or that her mother had been a con artist, or how she'd died. There was so much he didn't know, it was overwhelming.

"Yes," was all she said. "Emma, my patient, is an older woman, seventy-one, and she's the only person her great-grandson, Deon, has."

"What happened to his folks?"

"Dad's nowhere to be found, mom's in prison, grandmother dead." She gave him the details she'd pried from Deon while plying him with French fries, pierogies, and cheeseburgers at Diggers. "Emma worked as a librarian at Garfield High until they forced her to retire. They lived on her savings and Social Security for a while, but then she lost her subsidized housing this summer and—"

"And you can't collect SSI without a permanent address." He nodded. It was a vicious cycle. "So she and Deon have been on the street since the summer?"

"Despite that, Deon is top of his class and hasn't missed a day of school until yesterday, when he tricked his gram into coming into the ER. Good thing he did, too. Emma has Brugada's, previously undiagnosed—she got her pacemaker today."

"Which means she'll be in the hospital another day or two."

Lydia shrugged. Honestly, she was just taking things one day at a time. "I'm not working again until Tuesday. She was going to refuse the surgery unless I promised her that I'd take care of Deon."

"Did you at least get anything in writing? Something to keep Children and Youth off your back?"

"No. But I trust her."

He stared at her in surprise. "Isn't your first rule of ER medicine 'Trust no one, assume nothing'? It took you a long time to trust me. But just like that, you're placing your career in the hands of a woman you never met before?"

Lydia pondered that. It was gut instinct, not rational thought. And in a way, she owed it to Maria, for keeping her safe all those years on the street.

After spending just one day with Deon she now realized just how difficult that must have been. Maria could have easily left her with Family Services, moved on with her life without the burden of a child, but she hadn't. They might not have had the perfect life, but Maria had always made sure she was there for her daughter, right up to the day she died.

Trey chuckled. "Knew you were a soft touch, Lydia. The way you always get involved, get so passionate about things no one else gives a damn about."

"I am not a soft touch," she protested, bristling at the insult. No one who had seen what she had seen, done the things she had done, could ever be labeled soft.

"Don't worry, your secret is safe with me." He leaned back, his thumb tracing circles over her neck and hairline. Just where Maria used to rub to erase her tension and worries. "So Emma needs a place to live. A job wouldn't hurt either, I'm guessing."

"I think I have an idea for that. They need someone to get the family library at Angels back up and running. The girls at Child Life said they have grant money but can't use it without a trained librarian."

"One problem solved." He kissed the back of her neck, sending a tingle through her. "How about if you let me work on the other one?"

She smiled and curled further into his embrace. "I was hoping you'd say that."

He stroked her hair, then slowly untangled his body from hers. "I'd better head over to my folks' and apologize for being so late if I'm going to help your lost cause."

DR. NORMAN NELSON WAS SEATED BEHIND A large Brazilian heartwood desk. The desk was empty—no papers, nothing except a phone, a lamp, and a framed photo. Nora stepped inside the room but left the door open behind her.

"Dr. Nelson, I don't know if you remember me?"

"Of course I remember you. Nora Halloran, from the ER." His voice was crisp and clear, in contrast to his appearance. He looked haggard, shoulders slumped, lips turned down in a frown. Hard to believe this was the same man she'd seen in the ER a few hours ago.

He swept his hand, lovingly caressing the desktop. "Do you like it? My wife, Faith, gave it to me. After we lost our only child. This place"—he looked up, nodded to the far corners of the room—"this work, it has sustained us since then. Until now."

Nora stood a few feet away, uncertain how to proceed. Dr. Nelson made the decision for her. He brought out his other hand, the one hidden below the desktop, and revealed a large, chrome-plated gun. At least it looked large when he pointed it at her.

"The pharmacy called, told me you were asking questions about the mix-up with Amanda's prescription. Then I checked with medical records and found that you've been checking up on some of my clinic patients. You've been quite busy, Ms. Halloran."

FORTY-THREE

Friday, 8:54 P.M.

GINA FORCED HERSELF TO LOOK UP FROM HER cheese sticks to greet the man Pete had invited to join them. She'd reached the state in her binge when every swallow threatened to come back up, when every breath hurt because there was simply no more room left inside her.

Michael turned out to be a man in his late twenties or early thirties, with red-rimmed eyes and hollowed cheeks. "Gina," Pete made the introductions, "this is Michael Kazmierko, Alice's father."

Michael shook her hand desultorily, slid into the booth beside Pete, then downed a shot of what looked like tequila. He nodded to the waitress, who soon returned with a new round of drinks for all of them.

"I'm sorry about your daughter," Gina said, sipping at her bourbon.

Michael gulped down his new shot, rapping the empty glass on the table as if commanding their attention. "Yeah, right. Everyone's sorry, but no one does a damn thing about it."

"They just decided to harvest Alice's organs for donation," Pete put in. "But Michael got thrown out of the hospital."

"Thanks to your doctor friend, the one who killed Alice. My little girl is going to die tonight and I can't even be with her."

Gina's mind was buzzing with endorphins from the food and alcohol. She wasn't quite following the conversation—Lydia was off today; how the hell had she gotten someone thrown out of Angels? But somehow it made sense.

"She should be home by now," she said, hating the tears that flowed down Michael's face and searching for a way to get rid of him. The man was pathetic. "I'll bet if you asked her, she'd talk to security."

"I doubt it," Michael said with a pout. As if she'd taken the edge off his rant and he wasn't too happy about it.

"Suit yourself, but she lives just a few blocks away."

The waitress distracted her with another round of drinks and food. She ignored her drink as she shoveled more food in, to the point where she no longer tasted it and every bite was a chore to force down. Michael kept the waitress hopping, throwing back shot after shot of tequila.

"The important thing," Pete was saying when she came up for air, "is that we find a way to make Alice's story public. To prevent any other family from needlessly suffering this tragedy." He raised his untouched glass and intoned, "To Alice."

Gina and Michael clinked glasses at that. "To Alice."

"My poor dead baby girl," Michael moaned, tears flowing freely.

She lurched out of the booth. Finally, it was time to purge. "Excuse me."

Gina plowed through the crowd at the bar to reach the ladies' room behind it. She locked the door, turned the water on full blast, then fell to her knees in front of the toilet.

She held on for a second, just to prove to herself that

she could, to imprint the memory of this awful-bloated-corpse-about-to-explode-in-a-thousand-pieces feeling.

Then she stretched out her middle two fingers and let herself do the thing she'd been dreaming about all day.

"OTHER PEOPLE KNOW ABOUT THIS, SO YOU CAN put the gun away," Nora snapped, using her best trauma-command tone. The one that made even surgeons jump.

Dr. Nelson looked at the gun as if he hadn't realized it was in his hand. He laid it down on the desk, his hand still holding it tight, but at least it wasn't pointed at her. "Sorry. I didn't mean to scare you."

Right, like pointing a gun at someone wouldn't scare them.

"It was another gift from Faith," he continued, examining the gun as if it were a prized possession. He jerked his chin up. "You need to know she wasn't a part of this."

"I don't care. I came to find out how to reverse it. Amanda Mason and Tracey Parker are dying, and you can save them."

He frowned, looked close to tears. "No. I'm afraid I can't. It's too late."

"No. It's not. Just tell me what you know about the protein deposits. How can they be removed, the process reversed?"

"My dear, if there were a way to reverse the process, do you really think I would have let any of those girls die?"

Silence as she struggled to think of a way to persuade him to help. "Then you've done research on it—share it with me; maybe Lucas Stone or Ken Rosen can find a cure."

He almost responded to that and straightened for a moment, looking hopeful. Then he slumped in his chair again, cradling the gun thoughtfully. "There is no cure. It's impossible. I'm sorry I ever started this clinic. I truly wanted to make the world a better place. Tell me you understand that."

He jerked the gun so it was pointed in her direction.

"I understand. Just as I understand that Amanda looks up to you like you were her father. She once told me that it was because of you and your wife that she chose pediatrics. Because of how you lost your son."

"That's when we first met Amanda. She was visiting the neonatal ICU, shadowing a doctor who worked there. Joey was only three days old, so tiny, still hanging on. Amanda began talking to us; she was so hopeful, so earnest. She offered us comfort when all we had was despair. She was there the day Joey died—two weeks later. She'll make a wonderful physician some day." His voice drifted off into a wistful silence.

"Help her become that physician," Nora urged. "Put down the gun and help her. You can save her life, I know it. She's defending you—even now, knowing everything, she doesn't believe you could hurt anyone. Prove her right."

She thought she was getting through to him when he removed his hand from the gun and picked up a picture from the desk. "Amanda took this. Faith and I holding little Joey before he died. He was so tiny, so very tiny." He looked up, his eyes blazing with clarity. "Tell Faith everything I've done, I did for her."

Before Nora could move, he raised the gun and placed it to his temple, pulling the trigger.

FORTY-FOUR

Friday, 9:12 P.M.

"WE CAN'T WAIT ANY LONGER FOR NORA," Lucas said, glancing at the clock on the wall of the office shielded by thick glass. The hyperbaric chamber was in the basement, on the other end of the hospital from pathology and much creepier. They were in the control room just beyond where the two single-patient chambers sat. "I guess she changed her mind—sure you don't want to as well?"

Amanda did. She'd seen pictures of hyperbaric chambers before, but had never realized how small and claustrophobic one was until she got up close.

She crossed into the other room and tapped the thick glass wall of the torpedo-shaped cylinder. The sound had the same hollow thud as clods of dirt hitting a coffin. She shivered, pulling her patient gown tighter. No metal was allowed in the hyperbaric area, nothing that could potentially create a spark or any static electricity. All the better not to blow up the hospital.

She shook herself, pushing her fears aside—although

she was certain they weren't out of reach. "No. Let's do this."

"You didn't tell me you were claustrophobic."

"Guess it shows, huh?"

"Only the pulse throbbing in your neck, the fact that you're suddenly paler than my lab coat, and the sweat breaking out—"

"Ladies don't sweat, we perspire." Bantering with him was easier than imagining herself squeezing inside that tiny circular coffin. Once inside she wouldn't have room to move, her face would be only a few inches away from the walls, and she'd be strapped to a stretcher.

"Maybe we should wait."

"No. You saw how fast Tracey and Becky went downhill. We can't risk waiting if we're going to save Tracey. And the IRB won't give you approval, not without proof."

"At least let me sedate you."

"Then you'll lose your neuro exam." She faced the chamber and tried to ignore her heart, which was pounding so hard it was choking her. "I can do this."

"You sure?"

"It's the only way." With his help, she climbed onto the stretcher that lay on rails extending from the outside world into the airtight chamber. He slid her inside but didn't strap her down or close the door. Even knowing that escape was mere inches behind her, she still began to hyperventilate with panic.

Her breath fogged the glass immediately before her, making her feel as if she were suffocating. Her lips grew numb; her fingers began to curl into futile claws, numb from hyperventilating; and her heart thudded against her chest wall.

As her vision dimmed, she heard the whisper of well-oiled ball bearings and suddenly fresh air blanketed her.

"Slow down, Amanda, you can't let yourself panic." Lucas's voice filled her awareness.

Slowly her vision cleared again and she saw his face staring down at her in concern as he raised her hand. His fingers on her pulse were warm, steady.

"If you hyperventilate, you can precipitate more protein deposition. You have to calm down, breathe slowly. In, out. That's it."

She matched his slow deep breaths, and the panic subsided.

"That's better. Can you squeeze my hands? Any aftereffects?" He quickly did a neuro assessment. No change. Her left leg was still useless, her left arm numb and weak.

"I'm okay now. I just need a minute." She hated lying here, so vulnerable. Hated even more the worry that consumed his expression.

"No. We can't risk it. If you have a panic attack and hyperventilate it could be devastating."

Lethal was more like it, but she was glad he hadn't chosen that adjective. "I won't panic." She wished she sounded more confident—then maybe she could convince herself. "Let's go."

His fingers taking her pulse slid around to grasp her hand and squeeze it. "Amanda. We're talking about your life here."

"And your career—if anyone finds out that you circumvented the Institutional Review Board, it will mean your job."

He shrugged. "That's not important."

"I can do this, Lucas. I know I can."

"Okay. But listen to me on the intercom. I'm going to give you a few minutes to acclimatize before I seal it."

Once the double seals on the door were applied, the chamber was unable to be opened from the inside. She'd be totally helpless, locked inside the glass tube smaller than a coffin. She tried to swallow but her mouth was too dry, so instead she nodded her understanding. He slid her inside once more, closing the hatch without locking it.

"Can you hear me?" His voice came over the speaker.

"Yes." She felt the panic rise, pounding against her like hurricane-driven waves against the shore.

"Focus on my voice and your breathing. Doing okay?"

His face was oddly distorted by the thick glass that encased her, making his features look like an anxious old wise man from a fairy tale. *Guess that would make me Sleeping Beauty.* She giggled—laughing seemed to ease the panic.

"I'm okay."

"Good. We'll take it slow. Try putting the mask on. Let's make sure you're okay with that."

She fumbled for the black mask—it was thick and bulky and looked like what a fighter pilot would wear. Once the chamber was flooded with pressurized hundred-percent oxygen, she was at risk for oxygen toxicity, so Lucas would monitor her status and send regular air through the mask when she needed it. The mask felt heavy on her face, clammy with her sweat, and smelled like a rubber dog toy, slick with doggy spit.

At first the smell made her stomach roil, but she simply closed her eyes and thought of home. The way the sun made the salt marshes shimmer like sapphires and the spartina grass became waves of emerald and gold spun from magic. The graceful glide of a blue heron, the lazy-dazy roll of dolphins in the surf, the tickle of sand between her toes. In her mind she was walking on the beach near home—and Lucas was there with her, strolling at her side, holding her hand.

"Everything all right?" he asked.

She nodded, relaxed and blissful, then realized that it was the real Lucas who had asked—and there was no way he could see her nod beneath the mask. She opened her eyes. The overhead light framed him in a rim of silver. "I'm fine."

"Give me a minute to set up the computer and we'll get started."

He vanished from sight. She lay there, trying to be

patient when all she wanted was for this to be done with. She'd have a few hours trapped inside the chamber; she hoped her imagination was strong enough to keep her mind occupied and panic-free that long.

"How much air does this thing hold?" she asked, not certain she wanted to hear the answer. "I mean, if the oxygen cut off, how long would I have?"

"We could find out if you like." Faith Nelson's voice cackled through the intercom. Then her face appeared, grotesque and contorted by the glass separating them.

Amanda tried to squirm around, but ended up with the mask falling to one side and her palms pressed against the glass above her. "Where's Lucas?"

"Incapacitated. I don't think it's permanent. Yet."

Faith's face grew larger as she peered down at Amanda. Her eyes were impossibly wide, the whites showing all around her irises, and her cheeks were flushed crimson red. It was the face of a madwoman, not the Faith whom she'd come to rely on as her surrogate mother. This wasn't the woman who had steered her to pediatrics, brought her homemade cookies at Christmastime, given her a calendar filled with beach scenes to ease her homesick heart. This woman was a total stranger . . . and appeared completely insane.

FORTY-FIVE

Friday, 9:52 P.M.

AFTER TREY LEFT, LYDIA SURPRISED HERSELF BY falling asleep. At first she'd paced, racing up the steps at every slightest sound, checking on Deon. But somewhere along the line she'd finally collapsed on the sofa and dozed off.

Until a large furry mass hurled itself at her, landing with a thud on her chest.

"No Name, get off," she moaned, trying in vain to roll over and dislodge the heavily muscled and extra-large cat. No Name stayed with her, balancing like a lumberjack dancing on logs. "Okay, okay, Ginger Cat, get off," she tried again. No luck.

Then the cat sank its claws into her arm, bringing her fully awake. Deon. Was something wrong?

The cat jumped silently to the floor, mission accomplished, and she sat up, listening intently. No noise from upstairs, but there was a strange shadow flitting past the front windows. Good thing the lights were off so whoever it was couldn't see her. Bad news: she'd left the phone in the kitchen—the other end of the house from where Deon slept upstairs.

Not wasting time on debating her options, she crept through the shadows to the stairwell and silently jogged up the steps.

"Deon, wake up," she whispered, nudging him awake with one hand while the other reached for the bedside phone. No dial tone and her cell was downstairs charging. Fear hummed through her, but she refused to let it hijack her focus.

She needed to protect Deon. That had to be her first priority despite the tightening of her gut and the spark of adrenaline flaring along her nerves.

He came awake quickly and silently. Long nights sleeping in a crowded shelter taught you to sleep light.

"Is it Gram?" he asked in a whisper as noiseless as her own.

"No." The sound she'd been straining to hear came—the creak of the French doors immediately below them being forced open. "There's someone in the house. I'm going down to distract him and when I do, I want you to go out the front door. You go through the backyard and cross the cemetery, you run until you find someone—there will be people at the ER in Angels, there's plenty of lights on over there, you can't miss it."

His head was bobbing with her every word, eyes shining wide in the scant moonlight creeping in through the curtainless window.

"Can you do that?"

He nodded, his Adam's apple bouncing as he gulped. "Did I do something wrong?"

"No, baby." She hugged him close, quick and hard. "No, you didn't do anything wrong. You just do as I say and run and get help, okay?"

Another nod as he slipped from bed and stepped into his sneakers. Together they crept down the steps. She held him back on the landing, listening to the intruder's footsteps thud against the linoleum. The intruder had turned on the kitchen light but not the dining room's.

"Go," she mouthed.

He squeezed her hand and as she flicked on the living room light, he ran to the front door, No Name following close behind.

"Who's there?" she called out, covering the noise of the door opening.

Deon ran out into the night. The cat paused on the threshold, tossing her a glance over its shoulder, then vanished as well.

Deon's safety assured—at least as sure as anything could be—Lydia closed the door. She sidled across the living room, grabbed the fireplace poker, and positioned herself against the wall at the edge of the large archway separating the living room from the dining room. It was on the opposite side from the staircase, so hopefully on the intruder's blind side. His footsteps were now in the dining room, but she didn't think he'd seen her.

She flattened herself, poker at the ready, waiting. She didn't have to kill him, only slow him down long enough to allow Deon to escape. The familiar thrill of adrenaline surged through her veins. She didn't *have* to kill him—but damn she wanted to, for terrorizing her and Deon this way.

"Now, don't you make me chase you down," a man's voice cut through the dark. "I'd like to take things slow. Just like the way my baby is dying. Nice and slow."

Kazmierko? Damn the man, she'd never thought he'd get violent. How the hell had he learned where she lived?

Adrenaline sharpened her senses, slowed down time. She focused on the target area, waiting for him to get close. Heard the creak of his step getting closer. His shadow loomed.

C'mon, c'mon. Just one more, one more step.

* * *

"DO YOU KNOW WHERE I'VE JUST COME FROM?" Faith demanded, pounding on the hyperbaric chamber.

"Faith, what's wrong?" Amanda asked, panic seizing her. She was sweating, had her palms pressed against the glass, straining to see beyond the confines of the hyperbaric chamber. Then she saw what Faith was banging on the chamber with—the butt of a pistol.

"I just came from Norman's office," Faith continued, not waiting for Amanda to answer. "Where I arrived just in time to find him with his brains splattered all over creation."

"Dr. Nelson's dead?" *Why? How?* Amanda's thoughts were buzzing faster than she could process. Why did Faith have a gun, why was she angry at Amanda, where was Lucas?

"He killed himself. Your friend Nora saw it, told the police that before he did, he confessed to killing the other women in his study, the ones like you. She also told them all about your little adventures in research, how you found out about the side effects of Norman's newest project."

She pounded on the chamber wall again, producing a shock wave that made Amanda's ears ache. "He died because of you, Amanda! After everything he did for you, you killed him!"

"No," Amanda protested, still trying to comprehend everything that had happened.

Damn it, if only she were outside where she could face Faith, try to explain. Instead she lay here helpless, a wall of glass between them. Not to mention a gun. Faith was the most rational, calm, caring person she knew—even when her baby had died, it was Faith who had offered comfort to Dr. Nelson.

"Faith, let me out of here so we can find the truth. Dr. Nelson would never hurt anyone."

Faith's face morphed into something from a childhood nightmare as she pressed it against the curved glass. "Of course he never hurt anyone. I did what had to be done to protect him."

Amanda sucked in her breath, tasting the rubber from the mask that still covered her face. No. Faith couldn't mean what she'd just said. Could she?

Faith continued, "When Lucas Stone developed the perle manufacturing process, I saw the future. I did what Norman needed. When Norman needed capital to fund his research, I was the one who slept with two of the hospital trustees and blackmailed them into supporting him. Not that they haven't profited handsomely from their investment. And when Norman's latest creation had some unexpected side effects—side effects that affected a minuscule portion of the population—I cleaned up the loose ends. As usual."

"You killed those girls?" Amanda blurted the words out without thinking, too stunned by Faith's confession. Despite her shock and fear, she felt a surge of anger at Faith's betrayal. Amanda had looked up to Faith, accepted her as a surrogate mother. Damn it, she had trusted this woman.

There was a long pause, and Faith's expression softened. She looked like the Faith Amanda knew, the person to whom Amanda had confided her fears and dreams, her hopes and aspirations. "No. I was trying to help, to find a way to reverse the effects. But everything I did made things worse, and the first one died. One death is all it takes to shut down a study, so after that . . ."

Her voice trailed away as she eyed the oxygen supply lines. "Now Norman's gone and there's nothing left. Thanks to you."

"Faith, no. Think of Dr. Nelson. He wouldn't want this." Amanda's voice sounded weak and pitiful through the intercom.

Faith merely smiled sadly, shaking her head. Then she jerked her chin, looking over her shoulder as if something had startled her.

"Poor Lucas is starting to wake up. Let me take care of him. Then you're next."

FORTY-SIX

Friday, 10:11 P.M.

BY THE TIME GINA RETURNED TO THE TABLE both men were gone, sticking her with the bill. Or rather, her father. She handed the waitress Moses's platinum AmEx and waited for the prerequisite electrons to filter through the phone lines and back again to Diggers's ancient computer system.

"It's not your name on the card," the waitress said, digging around in her mouth with a toothpick that had bright red plastic furls twitching from its end. "Says Moses Freeman Esq."

Gina scooped up a handful of the chalky pastel mints from beside the cash register. Yum. Powdery mint, stomach acid, cheap bourbon, and chicken fat. Mm-mm-good.

"Never heard of a name like that before. Esq." The waitress stared at Gina with bug eyes.

"It's Inuit," Gina told her. "We're part Eskimo."

"Oh. Well, good for yunz." The computer finally spit out its approval and a receipt for Gina to sign. The waitress craned her neck, watching as Gina painstakingly wrote *Gina Freeman Esq*, with a flourish curling off the *q*. "Have a nice night."

Gina nodded her thanks. She was all talked out for the night, swimming with her binge-induced endorphin fest. She pocketed the slip of paper for Moses, who would find some way to use it as a tax deduction. Most of her life she'd been saving tiny slips and proofs of her existence so he could write her off.

She giggled as she opened the car door. She was just a little tipsy. Maybe she should call her father's car service again.

Her father. Well, at least she had one. But she didn't have a Daddy like Amanda. Or a Dad like Nora. Real men, involved in their lives. People who had earned a nickname for themselves. A nom de guerre.

Unlike Lydia. Lydia didn't seem to have anyone, never talked about family. Gina had seen a picture of Lydia's mom—looked just like Lydia only paler—but she had the feeling that Lydia was even less acquainted with her father than Moses was with Gina.

For some reason, thinking of Lydia didn't make her feel as angry as it had before the four—or was it five?—shots of bourbon. Lydia. There was something nagging, something about Lydia, something important. . . .

"Oh shit!" No one was around to hear her shout. She pulled out her cell phone and hit the speed dial for Jerry.

"I'm a little tied up right now, Gina," he said when he answered, his voice heavy with fatigue.

"Jerry, I think someone's going to hurt Lydia." She rushed the words out; the sooner they were out, the sooner someone would do something about them and they'd no longer be her responsibility. But, shit, it *was* her responsibility. She'd practically drawn Kazmierko a map!

"Who?" his voice was still distant as if he were only half listening.

"Michael Kazmierko. The guy who tried to attack her at the hospital earlier. He knows where she lives."

AMANDA'S BREATH CAUGHT AS SHE BRACED herself, listening for the sound of a gunshot. Visions of Lucas's bloody body filled her mind. She pressed her palms against the glass walls surrounding her, straining to see past the chamber and into the control room where Lucas and Faith were. If Faith used the gun there, would it be enough to blow up the chamber?

No sound came. Could Lucas still be alive? The hope flared through her, bringing life back to her numb hands. If he was, then she was his one last chance. She had to get out of here, somehow get Faith away from Lucas, away from the hyperbaric chamber where she had the potential to blow up the entire hospital.

Wriggling her arms up over her head, Amanda pushed against the hatch. Lucas hadn't sealed it shut yet, but Faith obviously didn't know that, had assumed that with the mask over her face and the hatch closed, Amanda was already locked in.

Amanda had to shove hard with the poor leverage her position put her in, but was rewarded when the hatch sprang open and the cot slid along the well-oiled railings, popping her free of the chamber.

She looked around as she climbed down from the stretcher. Faith was in the glass-walled room that held the controls for the hyperbaric chamber. Lucas was slumped in a chair and Faith was doing something to him—but at least he was still alive; otherwise why would Faith bother to move him?

"Faith," she called out, wishing there were some kind of weapon in the room. But the room was purposely kept spartan—nothing metal, nothing that could potentially cause a spark or any random static electricity. "If you want to avenge Norman's death, come and get me!"

FORTY-SEVEN

Friday, 10:14 P.M.

LYDIA'S VISION HAD NARROWED TO A BRIGHT tunnel where everything sparked in perfect focus. Kazmierko took a step into the living room and she swung the poker, aiming at his chest. It would have been a stunning blow if he hadn't been holding a baseball bat that deflected it with a dull *thwack*.

He spun to face her. She pulled back, ducked as he aimed a swing at her, and darted past him into the dining room, where there was more space to maneuver. Lots of empty space—nothing here except her long board. He tried again, moving faster this time.

"You wanted her dead," he accused her. "To cover up your mistakes. You told them to kill my baby!"

No use reasoning with him, so Lydia saved her breath for fighting him. She'd been in street fights before, some vicious, but she'd always been able to walk away without killing anyone. Until tonight. Kazmierko might give her no choice.

He swung again, forcing her to dodge his longer reach, backing her into the corner. She needed to negate the advantage of his longer arms—either move in close or extend her own reach more than the short poker allowed her to. If she had a knife, she wouldn't hesitate to move in closer, but Kazmierko, despite his drunkenness, had the well-muscled look of a brawler. If they began to grapple, she'd be forced to go for a killing blow.

The bat whistled through the air, accompanied by his laughter, and she realized he was toying with her. He aimed at her legs and she easily sidestepped, but this dancing around wasn't doing anything except buying time for Deon. Surely he would have reached Angels by now.

Kazmierko had her backed up against the corner, her back to her long board with its bright sunset swirls of purple, ruby, and gold. He was grinning, not out of breath, enjoying himself as he hefted the bat against his palm.

"Now, we're going to have some fun."

AMANDA RAN THROUGH THE PATIENT ENtrance to the chamber and down the tunnel, taking any turn that led away from the hyperbaric chamber. *Tottered* might have been a better term, as her entire left leg dragged behind her, keeping her constantly off balance as she looked back over her shoulder, hoping Faith was following but not close enough to get off a clean shot.

The tunnels were deserted, so there was no use screaming or hollering or any of the things young ladies being chased by murderers did in the movies. Besides, she didn't have the breath to waste on silly screams—she was too busy trying to run and look for something she could use as a weapon.

She crossed an intersection, then stumbled to a stop and backtracked. Down a dark tunnel, an old one with peeling paint, brick walls, and a cement floor, sat a yellow FLOOR IS WET caution sign. She pivoted and began to limp down the tunnel. Beside the sign was a janitor's bucket and mop propped up against an open door. Escape—and hopefully a burly janitor to tackle Faith, hold her while the police came.

The floor was still wet, so the janitor couldn't have gone too far. She slipped in a puddle just as she heard Faith behind her.

"You can't hide from me, Amanda."

Good. Last thing she wanted was for Faith to get bored with chasing after her and go back to Lucas or the hyperbaric chamber. The tunnel sloped up, then ended in a small landing.

Amanda pulled the heavy metal door the rest of the way open. It made a loud squealing sound that was more like a wild animal than an inanimate object. She glanced back over her shoulder and saw Faith, backlit by the brighter light of the main tunnel, the silhouette of the gun appearing large and deadly.

Faith spun toward her, taking aim, but Amanda slipped through the door.

She was inside a small room, maybe ten by ten with a high arched ceiling. The only light came from the single bulb at the end of the tunnel behind her. In front of her a large oak door that looked like it belonged in a church stood open. She crossed through it. Moonlight and the lights of the medical center illuminated pale gray specters rising from the earth.

Amanda startled, then realized that the doorway was bordered by statues and granite columns. She was in the cemetery across the street from Angels.

There was no one to be seen. No one living, at least.

Amanda shoved her weight against the heavy wooden door, trying to shut it and buy a few seconds before Faith and her gun arrived.

"Hello," she called out. "Help, I need some help here!"

It sounded lame even to her. No wonder the safety courses always said to yell *Fire!* if you were attacked. But who would believe there was a fire in a graveyard?

Still, she gave it a shot. "Fire!"

To her surprise, a man's head popped up from behind a tombstone several yards away. "Hey lady, what the hell you doing? Get away from that door, you got no right to be around there."

Amanda hobbled off the granite landing and into the grass. His mouth tightened into an expression that made it clear he thought she was a psych patient run amok.

"Please, I need your help."

"Wait on, you just wait on, I've got my hands full right now." He jerked his head around, then disappeared again as he dove behind a statue of a mother holding a baby. "Where are you, you varmint?"

Surreal panic engulfed her, swirling through her with the speed of a riptide as she wondered if he was related to Elmer Fudd. Just her luck, a killer behind her and a janitor-slash-graveyard-rabbit-hunter in front.

"Ah-ha, now I've got you!" he shouted.

The door to the small building housing the tunnel exit began to inch open, squealing with each grudging millimeter. That was good because it meant Faith was far away from Lucas, but it was bad because Amanda could now barely walk and her janitor-psycho-rabbit-hunter had vanished.

"A graveyard, how convenient," Faith said as she appeared in the doorway, aiming the gun at Amanda, who was now hopelessly exposed, standing in moonlight, her patient gown billowing around her.

"Hey, this one belong to one of yunz?" the janitor shouted, appearing from behind an obelisk holding a squirming boy by the elbow.

Before Amanda could say anything, Faith pivoted and fired. The sound snapped through the night like an elastic band stretched past its breaking point. Not loud, not thundering like in the movies. Amanda had fired guns back home, but somehow she'd expected the sound to have more of an impact when you were on the receiving end.

Shouldn't she feel something? Amanda wondered. She

looked down, didn't see any blood, didn't feel anything. Then she looked behind her.

The janitor teetered for a moment, looking surprised and dismayed as a dark stain began to spread over his abdomen. The boy wrenched away, rushing to stand beside Amanda, grabbing her arm. The janitor reached out to her, sinking to his knees. His mouth was opening and closing as if he were holding a one-sided conversation with her, but no sounds emerged. Then he collapsed on the grass.

A tiny noise, like the whimper of a rabbit caught in a snare, came from the boy beside her. "I'm sorry," he said, his whisper shredded with fear. "I'm sorry, lady. I'll go, I won't cause no one any more trouble, I promise."

He dropped Amanda's arm and took a step forward, toward Faith. Faith whirled on him, leveling the gun. Her hands were trembling, her eyes wide and panicked.

"Faith, no!" Amanda grabbed the boy's shoulders and pulled him back, shielding him with her body. "He's just a little boy."

Faith looked at her as if not recognizing her—as if Faith didn't even realize what she was doing. For the first time Amanda began to have a glimmer of hope that she might be able to take control of the situation.

She gauged her words carefully. "Just a little boy. He means you no harm. Think of your own little boy, Joey. You wouldn't want anyone hurting him, would you?"

Her tone was a gentle singsong, a lullaby without a tune. Faith began to sway back and forth in time with Amanda's cadence. Amanda tried to shoo the boy away, but he clung to her waist. She wanted to shout at him to run but didn't dare break the uneasy trance. Faith still held the gun, and she'd already proven that her aim was deadly.

"What would Dr. Nelson think if you hurt a little boy? How would Norman want to be remembered? Surely not for this." Amanda gestured with an open palm.

Faith wavered and stepped away from the open tunnel

door. Was that movement in the shadows behind her? Amanda could only hope and keep talking.

"Dr. Nelson believed his work would live beyond him. How can we keep that promise to him, Faith? Not like this. Put the gun down and we'll find a way."

"No. We can't. He's gone." Faith stared into the distance as if perplexed that her husband wasn't there. "He's gone," she repeated, her voice choked. "Because of you. All because of you."

FORTY-EIGHT

Friday, 10:16 P.M.

KAZMIERKO FEINTED FROM ONE SIDE TO THE other, taunting Lydia. The poker wouldn't do her any good, not while he had the reach on her, so Lydia tossed it aside, hoping to distract him.

Instead, he laughed, reading her action as fear or desperate surrender. He didn't notice that she had stepped forward or that her hands had reached behind her to grasp the edges of her long board. She didn't have to slide her palms far to get the grip she wanted, she and that board had plowed through miles of surf together. It was a Kalama eight-foot, six-inch board with a polycarb tri-fin. Lethal to waves and just as deadly as a weapon.

She took another step forward, gauging the space on either side of her and her distance to Kazmierko. Perfect.

He was grinning, hefting the bat onto his shoulder like Barry Bonds preparing to knock the leather off a curve ball. "No more games."

Lydia didn't waste time answering. She launched herself forward, swinging the long board around, using her body as the pivot point, aiming three razor-sharp, virtually unbreakable polycarbonate fins at Kazmierko.

He tried to dodge her blow, but she was too fast, slamming the board into his belly with all her strength, following through as if he weren't even there. His feet flew out from under him. He thudded to the floor, his head cracking against it, the bat flying from his hands.

Lydia released the board.

"I wouldn't move that if I were you," she said as she raced from the room to grab her cell phone and call for help.

He stared after her, the longest fin impaled through his stomach, his hands flailing around as his chest heaved up and down.

"I'll be back." She ran through the French doors, retracing Deon's steps as she gave 911 the information they needed.

Kazmierko should live—if he didn't do anything stupid like remove the surfboard himself. She climbed through the bars of the wrought-iron fence, arborvitae branches whipping her face. Kazmierko was the least of her worries. "Deon!"

GINA'S BMW BARELY HAD TIME TO WARM UP during the short drive to Lydia's place. Other than Lydia's Ford Escape in the driveway, she didn't see any other cars around—but Michael Kazmierko could have easily walked from Diggers. The living room light was on, but she didn't see any movement through the windows.

Hell. Had she pulled Jerry away from his murder investigation for nothing? Or was Michael inside with a gun, Lydia already dead or dying?

She drummed her nails against the steering wheel, needing some sound to ease her nerves in the all-too-quiet night. Anxiety skittered under her skin, adding to the tingling the bourbon had left in its wake.

Wait for Jerry. Secure the scene—just as Trey had reminded her earlier today. That was the smart thing to do, follow protocol.

She unbuckled her seat belt, flinching at how loud the click sounded, and eased herself out of the car, leaving the door open. Too late she realized her headlights had already announced her presence to anyone inside the house—including any homicidal fathers.

Fear gathered itself in a knot stuck in her throat, refusing to budge. It was difficult to swallow around it, much less catch her breath as she crept toward the house.

This was stupid, stupid . . . as stupid as leaving the safe confines of an ambulance to race out and save a stranger from a drive-by shooting. As stupid as Ken Rosen trying to save the life of that driver. But all she could see was Lydia, lying in a pool of blood. All she could hear was the roar of gunshots that drowned out any sane counsel her mind conjured.

The humid night air caressed the fine hairs on her arms, leaving them quaking and standing upright. She was almost at the porch, able to see through the front windows. Still no movement inside the house, but a trickle of blood, a thin stream of scarlet against the golden glow of the oak floors, sliced into her vision.

She turned the front doorknob in her hand. Open. No more excuses.

Gina opened the door and ran inside just as she remembered she didn't have Jerry's bulletproof vest to protect her. Not this time.

FORTY-NINE

Friday, 10:24 P.M.

GINA RAN INTO THE DINING ROOM AND THEN stumbled to a stop. It wasn't Lydia lying on the floor bleeding. It was Michael. Impaled through the abdomen by a surfboard.

She shook off the surreal image and crouched down beside him, checking his pulse and respirations.

"That bitch," he mumbled, his eyes slit half open.

"Where's Lydia?"

"She's going to pay." His eyelids fluttered and he became unresponsive.

Resisting the urge to shake him until he told her what happened to Lydia, she looked around for something to stabilize the surfboard. The fins impaling Michael were at one end, leaving the rest of the board angled against the floor. The slightest motion could cause worse damage to Michael's vital organs. She'd never realized how long the board was until now—well over eight feet. How the hell had a woman Lydia's size managed that?

The front door burst open and a man stormed in, shouting, "Police! Show me your hands!"

Startled, Gina rocked back on her heels, hands up. It was Jerry—but it didn't look like Jerry; at least she'd never seen him with that look of fierce assertiveness before. A look that said if it came down to him or the bad guy, then the bad guy had better start praying.

He halted, scanning the room with his eyes, his gun resolutely trained on Michael. "Gina, what the hell?"

"I saw the blood, thought it was Lydia."

"Anyone else here?"

"I don't know."

The sound of sirens echoed through the night, accompanied by the squeal of brakes. Two more uniformed police officers rushed through the front door, relaxing the smallest bit when they recognized Jerry.

"Search the house," he ordered, finally holstering his gun. "There might be another victim, a woman, five-five, dark hair. Once it's secure, get the medics in here." He squatted to join Gina on the floor beside Michael, but his gaze continued to scour the area, never relaxing their vigilance. "He gonna make it?"

"If I have anything to do with it."

"Can you get him talking?"

"Hold the board for me." Jerry took over stabilizing the precariously positioned surfboard while Gina palpated below it. "Pulse is good, so's his breathing, but his belly is distended. Probably perforated his intestine. I need to cut the board before we can transport. Did you say there were medics here?"

"They can't come in until the scene is secure. You shouldn't be here either." He leveled a glare at her.

Where was her Jerry? The kindhearted, understanding guy whose shoulder she could cry on? Although she had to admit, this take-charge warrior aspect of his was kind of sexy. Compelling.

"I'm not leaving my patient." As she spoke the words, for the first time in months she felt like a real doctor again. Not someone merely going through the motions.

The uniformed cops thundered down the steps. "No one."

"Get the medics in here to help me," Gina ordered. The cops looked to Jerry, who nodded his assent.

"Where the hell is Lydia?" Jerry asked. "Dispatch said she made a nine-one-one call right after you called me."

A sharp crack of thunder sounded nearby. Jerry leaped to his feet, gun appearing in his hand without Gina even seeing him make a move toward it. A uniformed cop ran in, his gun also drawn.

"Call for backup," Jerry ordered. "Shots fired in the cemetery. Let them know a plainclothes officer is on the scene."

He was already yanking the French doors open. Gina glanced at him and realized he wasn't wearing his vest—detectives rarely did.

"Jerry, wait!"

He didn't turn back but did stop and look over his shoulder. His eyes had a distant look as if he were already planning tactics, thinking two steps ahead. She wanted to say so much. Tried to form the words and couldn't. "Be careful."

The uniformed cop smirked, but Jerry ignored him, his expression softening the slightest bit, his gaze now focused solely on her even if only for the moment. "Always."

THERE WAS A SKITTER OF MOVEMENT ABOVE Faith. The roof. No help coming from that direction, Amanda realized, her hope sinking. Her leg was shaking; she wasn't sure how much longer it would support her.

If she fell, how could she protect the little boy?

Faith took a step forward, leaving the shadows of the building, moonlight making her face seem unnaturally pale. She raised the gun.

Amanda tried to push the boy away from her—what if

the bullet went through her and hit him? But he clung to her, his arms wrapped around her waist from behind. She wasn't sure who was supporting who, felt sure that without his weight anchoring her, she would have already fallen.

"Faith, think about what you're doing," Amanda tried one last time. "Let me help you."

"You've done enough, Amanda."

A flurry of movement and something—or someone—launched itself from the roof onto Faith. The gun went off, shattering the night. A large, dark-colored animal fell to the ground, not moving.

"Ginger Cat!" the boy wailed, abandoning Amanda to rush toward the cat.

It looked like No Name, but Amanda didn't have time to work out how the boy knew Lydia's cat. Without the boy behind her, supporting her, her leg gave out and she crumpled to the ground.

Faith was swearing, her words an incoherent muddle. Blood streamed from her face and arm where the cat had clawed her. Amanda crawled along the dew-slicked grass, desperate to reach the boy. Faith shook the blood from her eyes and raised her gun, this time aiming at the cat.

"No!" the boy said, covering the cat with his own body.

Amanda struggled, pulling her body along with her arms. "Faith, no! Look at me, Faith. It's me you want to hurt—not him. He's just a boy, Faith. Think of Joey. Think of how much you loved Joey."

Faith's expression went from murderous to confused. The gun wavered, aimed at Amanda, then the boy, then back at Amanda.

"Please, don't hurt Ginger Cat," the boy pleaded, his voice calmer than any of the adults'. "Don't hurt Ginger Cat." He huddled over the cat, staring up at Faith with wide eyes.

Faith met his gaze, and her entire body began to tremble.

"Joey?" she whispered, a faraway look in her eye as she remembered her baby.

Good, it's working, Amanda thought. She had to keep reminding Faith of the love she'd felt for Joey, try to get her to connect that feeling with the boy.

The boy said nothing but seemed to realize that it was important not to break the spell. He nodded slowly.

Amanda reached him and rolled onto her side to face Faith, putting the boy behind her once more. Lying on the ground with Faith standing over them didn't exactly give her a strategic advantage, but at least she was between the gun and the boy.

"Faith. You don't want to hurt him. Put the gun down."

Faith didn't take her eyes off the boy. Tears streamed down her cheeks, mixing with the blood there. The hand holding the gun was just a few feet away from Amanda, but with one leg dead and the other trembling with fasciculations, she couldn't risk trying to lunge for it. So she used the only weapon she had: her voice.

"Remember Joey? How small he was? Your precious baby boy. Remember how he barely fit into the palm of Dr. Nelson's hand? He said it was because of Joey that he worked so hard, trying to save the world. Trying to help people."

Faith was weeping loudly but still held the gun, although it was no longer aimed at Amanda. Instead Faith dropped to her knees. "I did it all for him. For Norman. His work was all he had left after Joey—" She choked on her tears. "I had to protect his work."

"I know you did," Amanda said, inching forward and pushing herself to a sitting position. She took Faith's free hand in hers. "You did everything for Norman. Because you loved him."

"He was my whole world."

Amanda reached for Faith's other hand, stroked Faith's arm reassuringly, then held the hand with the gun. Faith didn't resist, but merely dropped the gun into Amanda's hand as she wept and rocked her body, embracing Amanda.

"He's gone. I've lost everything. They're all gone."

The sound of footsteps and men shouting echoed through the night as the door to the tunnel opened. Lucas appeared, surgical tape hanging from his wrists and blood streaming from the side of his forehead, leading three security guards.

"It's okay," Amanda told them. "Help the janitor, he's been shot."

The guards grabbed Faith, hauling her away. Amanda sat in the grass holding the gun in her lap.

"You okay?" she asked the boy.

He scurried back, giving the cat room to breathe. "I'm okay. I think Ginger Cat is too—look."

The cat shook itself, gave the boy a stern look of reproach as if saying *Of course I'm okay, didn't need your help, don't need nobody's help*, then began to walk around the boy, rubbing its body against the boy, who responded by stroking the cat.

"Deon?" Lydia appeared from the back of the graveyard. She ran to the boy and hugged him. "Are you all right?"

"Ginger Cat saved me," the boy said with a wide grin.

Lydia pulled back from the boy and looked at Amanda. "What the hell is going on?"

FIFTY

Saturday, 3:12 A.M.

AMANDA'S FIRST HYPERBARIC TREATMENT HAD been a haze, time speeding by as Lucas stayed at her side, only the Lexan walls of the hyperbaric chamber separating them. The director of hyperbaric medicine arrived, a short, pudgy man who looked sleep-tousled and disgruntled.

Until Jerry Boyle and Lydia cornered him. Amanda couldn't hear what they were saying, but she could see them pressed into the far reaches of the room, talking earnestly. Finally the director had nodded and scuttled into the control room, shutting the door behind him.

People buzzed all around: Jerry Boyle and other police officers interrupting to get on the headset and ask her more questions, Nora with an update on the janitor—who looked like he was going to make it—Lydia checking on her before she went home. But all Amanda remembered was Lucas and his voice, calming her, making the time and the walls confining her vanish.

They had talked about everything: his family, her family, Dr. Nelson and Faith, Amanda's dreams of becoming a pediatrician, her hopes to someday make her family proud even if she wasn't exactly the lady they expected her to be.

The first treatment took a little longer than two hours, but by the end she showed definite improvement. Although her foot was still numb and she couldn't properly flex it, she had regained sensation in her arm and upper leg. Best of all, the godawful fasciculations had stopped.

At the end of the treatment Lucas had slid her from the chamber, his face beaming down on her like the sunrise over the ocean.

"You did great," he said. "I'm going to take you back to your room while they set up for Tracey's treatment. After she's done, we'll do another treatment on you."

"Do you think it will work for Tracey?"

"I think so, yes. I'm surprised you made this much improvement with one treatment."

"I can walk," she insisted as he helped her into the wheelchair.

"Let's take it easy. Besides, this way I can keep an eye on you." He crouched in front of her and raised her bare feet onto the footrests.

Had his hands lingered a bit longer than necessary? She couldn't be sure—even after everything they'd been through, she still couldn't read him. But the fact that he had touched her spoke volumes.

"I have a surprise for you," he said as he wheeled her out of the chamber. Before she could reply, a familiar voice greeted her on the other side of the door.

"Amanda, darling. How's my favorite doctor?"

"Daddy!" Tears poured from her as her father scooped her up into a big hug.

He lifted her a few inches from the chair and squeezed her tight. Both arms were now almost back to full strength, she noticed, even though his speech was still a bit slurred compared to how it had been before the stroke. She didn't care; it sounded wonderful to her ears. "Daddy, you came! I'm so glad you're here."

"Of course we came," Mama said from behind her father. "Put her down, Adam, you're squeezing the life from her. We didn't come so far just to have her drop on us, now did we?"

He gently settled Amanda back into the chair. His nose was red and she sneaked a peek at his neck, checking his veins for any signs of the high blood pressure that had caused his stroke. Nope, they were flat. He wiped a hand across his face and she realized he was crying.

Crying? Her daddy never, never cried, not even when any of her brothers got married or when Tony and Becca had their baby or . . . well, ever.

Mama approached, looking impeccable and ready for anything in an ivory shirtwaist dress and salmon-colored jacket. She regarded Amanda with a discerning eye, then zeroed in on what was most important. "We really need to get you a better robe, Amanda. That pale gray, dumpy patient gown just does nothing for your color."

NORA PARKED HER CAR IN FRONT OF HER HOUSE and rested her forehead on the steering wheel. She'd finally hit her wall. Days without sleep, hours of answering questions, then worrying about Amanda, and the constant struggle to push the image of Dr. Nelson's final moments from her mind all combined to ambush her.

Tommy Z had tried to do the critical-incident stress debriefing thing with her, but Nora couldn't handle that, not yet, so she'd sent him to help Lydia instead. She couldn't face Lydia herself, she was too furious—Lydia had broken all the rules and it had almost gotten an innocent boy killed. Hell, she'd almost bitten off Lydia's head earlier when she'd called, asking for help getting Deon into Emma's room for the rest of the night.

And Amanda! What in the hell had possessed her to ignore her symptoms, put her patients at risk like that? Look how that had spiraled out of control. And now there was blood on Nora's hands.

She held her hands up before her eyes. They were raw from scrubbing; she'd lost count of the number of times she'd washed them after trying in vain to save Dr. Nelson. Clicking on the overhead light, she flexed and stretched them. She couldn't see any blood left, but she knew it was there.

Maybe she could wash it off in the shower, wash everything away.

She turned the light off, climbed out of the car, and trudged up the steps to her apartment. Her gaze was concentrated on ensuring that her feet actually hit each step; she was so exhausted she didn't have the strength to look up.

She almost kicked the latest bouquet of lavender daylilies before she saw them. She froze, staring at the small cellophane-wrapped bundle—breathed in, breathed out, not even having the will to summon anger. She just didn't have anything left. All she wanted was to clean up and start over.

Slowly, she bent and lifted the flowers. This time there was a card. She unlocked her door and brought them inside, turned the light on, and read it.

I'm sorry. So sorry. Live a good life. Love always, Seth

Time seemed to flow past her as she stood in her kitchen, one hand holding the flowers, the other the card. She stared at it so long her vision blurred. Then she sucked in a deep breath, straightening, letting it fill her up.

She took down a vase from the cupboard, filled it with water, carefully trimmed the stems, and arranged the lilies. Setting them in the center of the table, she picked up the card. *Live a good life.* Typical of clumsy-with-words Seth. But she understood him. She'd always understood him.

She left the flowers behind, took the card with her to her bedroom, and slid it into the corner of her dresser mirror, where she could see it every day. There were no tears—she'd cried them all already. No need for tears, anyway. She was starting over, starting fresh.

Nora stripped naked and stepped into the shower, turning it as hot as it could go. As the water pummeled her, she realized she didn't feel as empty or tired.

She felt . . . ready.

WHEN LYDIA HAD ARRIVED HOME AROUND TWO a.m., she'd collapsed onto the couch, determined to sleep all day. Nora and Tommy Z had persuaded the CCU charge nurse to allow Deon to stay with Emma, and suddenly the house seemed hollow and too quiet without him.

But almost immediately after lying down, she sprang back up, pacing through the house, Ginger Cat shadowing her. She stripped the barely slept-in bed and cleaned the blood and fiberglass remnants—all that remained of her long board—from the dining room, but still she was filled with a restless energy. Finally she'd given in and had gone for a predawn run.

With her schedule, she often ran in the night—she liked it that way. It was like a stealth attack, surveying her newly adopted city while it slept, absorbing its rhythms and cycles, making them her own. As if, by sneaking in under guard of night, she could take up residence without Pittsburgh or the people she was fast considering her friends and family noticing the stranger in their midst.

Like a benign tumor that the body allowed to grow without mounting a defense against it—as long as it remained benign and didn't cause any trouble. Which was exactly where her downfall lay. Tumult and chaos pretty much defined Lydia's world. Look at what happened tonight when all she'd tried to do was give a kid a roof to sleep under.

Lydia stubbed her toe on a curb and cursed. Tommy Z

would call her fears of abandonment, her desperate need to be embraced by those around her, and her need to find a home all part of an adolescent's need for acceptance. He'd tell her she wasn't living very high up on Maslow's hierarchy—although, compared to the struggle to merely survive that had colored her early years, she was slowly making progress.

She shook her head as her feet pounded the pavement. Stray beads of salt water stung her eyes. What were these, tears? She never cried. She pushed her pace harder, trying to shake the feelings that stalked her.

What would Tommy Z think of that, of her lying to herself? Hah. She was as bad as Gina, the reigning queen of denial and self-deception.

Lydia turned the final corner, passing the cemetery. Her gaze settled on the soft glow of light that surrounded her front door, and she headed toward home.

After her run, she'd found herself ravenous. She was in the kitchen stirring tomatoes and basil into a frittata when Trey entered through the dining room. She'd heard him come in the front door and wondered at his formality, but she didn't leave her cooking, certain he would find her. He always did.

"I have a few hours before my shift starts. I heard about Deon, from Nora. Thought I'd see how you were doing."

She heard the slight rebuke in his tone. Should have called him herself.

"I talked to my folks," he continued, hovering in the doorway—also not like him. "They have an empty property. It's within walking distance to the school. Would be perfect for Deon and his grandmother. Until they get back on their feet."

"Thank you." The words came out hesitant, felt weak compared to the emotions roiling through her. Last night he'd been upset about her getting involved with Deon and Emma, yet still he had helped them. Help that was so much more valuable than her own pathetic attempts.

He regarded her with a seriousness that was in contrast to his usual easygoing smile. "You're welcome."

Silence swirled between them like an electrical current. So many things unsaid, so many things she didn't have words to say.

"Smells good." He nodded toward the stove.

"I'd offer you some, but I made it with chorizo."

Trey usually ate vegetarian to appease his mother's worries after his dad's heart attack. One of the things she loved about him—if any man was a born carnivore, it was Trey. Usually she tried her best not to tempt him, but how the hell was she supposed to know he'd be popping in?

Irritation flared through her. It was her house, her kitchen. Was she supposed to stop cooking and eating what she liked merely on the off chance that he might be joining her?

He seemed to read her thoughts—one of the things that most annoyed her about him—and stepped forward to wrap his arms around her from behind. "You don't have to change anything for me."

Damn right she didn't. She'd fought all her life to be independent, not needing anyone. So why was it that his arms around her felt exactly like what she needed? She leaned back against him, reveling in his warmth. A surge of heat flared in her pelvis and she wanted more than just his arms around her. She wanted him.

Hell, this was bad. Very bad.

He nuzzled her from behind, his arousal evident, matching her own. "My God," he breathed into her ear as his arms wrapped around her. "Just the scent of you makes me hard." He reached past her and turned the burner off. "Breakfast can wait."

Something in his voice added an edge to his usual playful banter. She turned to him, the heat from the stove at her back, and pressed both palms against his chest. "What's going on?"

"I brought some things with me." He stared down at her, his hazel eyes not blinking. "To stay the night. A few nights. Many nights."

Lydia met his gaze, keeping her face and voice calm. Her legs felt unsteady, as if his innocent-sounding words had triggered an avalanche beneath her feet. "We said we'd go slow."

He kept his hands on her shoulders, propelling her away from the hot stove and into the dining room. "Lydia, we've been together almost every day, made love in every way possible. I'd say the only *slow* thing about this is the commute from my place."

She balked as he waltzed her toward the stairs. "No. Trey. I'm just—I can't—"

"Can't what? Make a long-term commitment? Risk hurting me? Hurting yourself?" He lowered his forehead until it touched hers, until his face was the center of her vision. "Because you know by now I'd never hurt you, right?"

Silent, she nodded, her gaze locked onto his. Her heartbeat tumbled, then slowed. "It's just that . . . you know nothing about me. I need . . ."

She straightened her posture, pulling away from him. When she glanced around, her house seemed large and empty, so much so that she suddenly felt dwarfed. Trey stood in the center of her barren dining room, the rosy dawn glow of light streaming around him, and it felt like he anchored the house. Like he anchored her.

He cupped her chin in his palm and raised it. "I don't need to know anything more than I already do, Lydia. Everything I need to know, I knew from the moment I met you." He flattened his other hand against his heart. "I knew it here."

Lydia felt her toes curl, knew she was ready to bolt. No. This was her house, her home; she'd come too far and worked too hard to run away.

Forcing a plastic smile onto her face, she stood on tiptoe to give him a quick peck on the cheek. "You're such a romantic. I'm going to finish breakfast."

She stepped past him, aiming for the kitchen and the sanctuary of a few seconds to rally her thoughts, secure her feelings.

Trey wasn't so easily dismissed. He took her arm, twirling her up against the wall, and before she could resist, he kissed her with an intensity that rocked her to her core.

Their tongues tangled as passion fired every nerve ending in her body. She reached one arm around his neck, dragging him down to her even as he was lifting her up to meet him. Their bodies pressed together, urgency communicated flesh against flesh.

Within seconds she had stripped him of his shirt, her fingers kneading the hard muscles of his chest and abdomen, taunting him as they moved lower to unfasten his belt. He groaned, his own hands busy sliding her T-shirt over her head.

She sighed, her breath rippling the hair on his chest. "Well. I guess if you put it that way, then you can stay."

His chuckle vibrated through her. "In the bed. Upstairs. Together."

"Upstairs. Together. In the bed."

"All night."

"All night." She raised her chin, met his gaze. "For as many nights as you want."

JERRY WASN'T HOME WHEN GINA GOT TO HIS apartment. He was still interviewing witnesses and untangling the events of the night—events that she had only heard tantalizing bits of, so she was counting on him to tell her everything when he finally did get home.

She used the time to take a shower and gargled and brushed her teeth three times, trying to expunge the taste of booze and vomit.

Remembering the look he'd given her before leaving her at Lydia's—a look of pride, certain that she had the skills to save Michael—she lay down in his too-small bed. No silk or Egyptian cotton here, just sheets from Wal-Mart, the scent of musk and man and sweat, and a lumpy mattress. It felt like coming home.

She inhaled deeply, drawing his scent into her, filling herself with him. Tears slipped past her defenses, and she pounded her fist into the pillow. What would he say when he learned she had told Michael where to find Lydia?

Jerry's key turned in the front door. She wiped her face dry and pretended to sleep. He said nothing as he entered, simply stripped naked in the dimly lit room and slipped in behind her, easing his arms around her, one arm under her body and one over the top of it. He hugged her hard. His heartbeat raced through her before finally it steadied and slowed to normal.

She relented and opened her eyes, turning her head to glance over her shoulder at him. "Hi there, stranger."

He nuzzled her neck, burying his face in her hair. "Hi."

Gina pushed him away, guilt not allowing her to continue the charade. How could she when Michael and Pete would be telling the police the truth—it might be mere hours before Jerry knew her part in last night's events.

"You going to tell me what happened? I heard bits and pieces while we were getting Michael up to the OR." He acted normal, not at all like he was upset with her. So he hadn't heard yet.

"Thanks for saving him—can't wait to see the DA kick his ass."

Whoa. There was more of that fierceness. As if he read her thoughts, he turned her to him and kissed her thoroughly.

When she pressed him for more details, he grunted, obviously a bit distracted as his fingers traced patterns over her breasts. "Damn Internet. Lydia's complete phone book listing and a Google map with directions to her place were on his cell phone."

Relief washing over her, she played dumb as he told her the rest of the story about Michael's attack on Lydia—hoping that no one remembered their drinking together at Diggers—and was honestly surprised when she heard Lydia had had a kid in the house with her. What the hell had she been doing with a kid? Then he told her about Amanda.

Gina rolled all the way over now, facing him. Jesus. She hadn't even known Amanda was sick, much less in the hospital. And it was hard to believe that sweet little Amanda had faced down a killer.

"So everyone's okay?"

"All except a janitor who got shot. But he'll make it." He yawned, not bothering to hide it. "God, what a day."

She traced his jaw with her fingertip. Dark shadows weighted his eyes, and his muscles were knotted beneath her touch. She'd never seen him this tired. "You need to get some sleep."

He pulled her tight, so tight she had to fight to fill her lungs. "I need you."

"Jerry—" He tickled the spot below her ear, and laughter broke past her barriers. "Now, don't go starting something you can't finish. Shouldn't you get some rest?"

"Plenty of time for rest later. Right now, you're all I need."

She couldn't stop the smile that filled her with warmth as if Jerry had lit a beacon within her. A beacon no one except him could ever see. She kissed his forehead and stroked her nails down his spine.

"Saw you on the news. With the guy who jumped from the bridge. You're quite the hero—again," he murmured as she felt the tension seep away from his muscles. "And the way you handled Kazmierko—it's not often I get to see you in command mode like that. Have I ever told you how proud I am of you?"

Yes, he had. He was the only person who ever had.

And it was a lie. She was no hero. It was just a farce Pete Sandusky had created, yet another role for Gina to play. Perfect daughter, perfect doctor, perfect hero.

Her stomach clenched with guilt. She would let him and the rest of the city believe the lies because they felt so good. All her life she'd dreamed of being the hero, being the person who people turned to, who could solve all their problems.

But she knew the truth, no matter how deep she tried to bury it. She was a coward, she wasn't anything like she imagined she was; she was a liar, a fake, a cheat.

Jerry could never ever know. She'd lose him if he did. No one could ever know.

Gina swallowed the truth and forced her smile even wider as she placed one palm over his heart and took his mouth in hers. The kiss made her dizzy as she tried hard to make up for her deception, to give him everything she had to give.

He returned her passion, then pulled back, looking down at her with a crooked, tired smile as he stroked a thumb along her jawline. "Marry me, Gina. Let me come home to this every day, let me take care of you, let me make you happy. Say yes and marry me."

And Gina knew that she could give him more—less than what he deserved, but it was all she had to offer. Her heart began to beat so fast she thought she might be stroking out, but no, you didn't feel this light and fluttery and happy if you were having a stroke. This was something else, like the feeling you had standing at the edge of the high dive, getting ready to jump into the deep end, no safety net, no one to catch you.

"Yes." The word emerged a high-pitched squeak. She swallowed and tried again. "Yes. I'll marry you, Jerry."

AFTER TWO HYPERBARIC TREATMENTS AND FINishing the mercury chelation therapy, Amanda was almost back to normal, although her left leg was still weak. And, best of all, Tracey had responded as well—she was awake and talking.

Lucas had stayed with Amanda throughout the lengthy hyperbaric sessions, even suffering her mother's inquisition.

"You'll need one or two more treatments," he said as she came out of the chamber and he checked her reflexes. "But I think we beat this."

Her heart sped up at his use of the plural pronoun. He helped her up from the stretcher and steered her toward a wheelchair.

"No wheelchair," she said. "I'll walk. You said the more I used my muscles the faster the proteins would be dissolved, right?"

"Right, but I was thinking physical therapy."

"No better therapy than walking. Give me that cane." She balanced on the tripod cane, then took off, feeling like a toddler taking her first steps as she hobbled down the hallway. He followed a step behind, waiting to catch her if she fell.

"Sure you don't want to take the elevator?" Lucas asked when she walked past the elevators toward the stairwell.

He had shoved his hands deep into his pockets and seemed to be forcing himself not to help her. She was quite proud of the progress she was making.

"No. I like the stairs."

She reached the door a moment before he did and opened it with her free hand, balancing with the cane. He gave her a slanted look but proceeded through the door. She closed it behind her and listened. They were alone—no sounds of footsteps or voices. "There's something I wanted to tell you, and this is more private."

He visibly gulped and backed up against the wall. Before she could say anything, the shrill tones of "Dixie" rang out from her bathrobe pocket. Amanda ignored it.

"Don't you need to get that?" he asked. "It's your mother, isn't it?"

"Mama can take care of herself."

She flicked the phone off and focused on him. She took a step toward him, her cane rapping on the concrete floor. Now they were only inches apart. Still he kept his hands in his pockets. Fine, she could make the first move. "I wanted to talk to you about the academic code of ethics."

He started, his eyes wide. She grazed her hand against his forearm. For once, he didn't flinch at her touch—but neither did he reciprocate.

"The code of ethics?" he asked, his voice choked.

"Yes." Her voice was firm, confident. She smiled as a flush swirled through her—she felt confident. No matter his response, she knew how she felt and what she wanted—and if he said no, that was all right; at least she would've made her desires clear.

"I did my research. Did you know that there are no restrictions against a student becoming involved with a faculty member as long as the faculty member isn't in the position of grading the student or giving them a recommendation or evaluation?"

He shifted his weight as she slid her palm from his arm to press against his chest. "No, I didn't."

Finally his hands came free from the lab coat, but instead of touching her, he let them hang by his sides.

"It's true."

"But I *am* grading you." His face was tilted down so that she was looking directly up at him. "*And* I'm your doctor."

"Not anymore. I'm finishing my rotation with Dr. Hansen, down in the clinic." She pressed up, using the cane for leverage to make herself tall enough to reach, and kissed him lightly on the lips. "Plus, you're fired. Ken Rosen will be my doctor."

"I'm fired?" he murmured, their lips almost touching.

"You're fired." She kissed him again, harder this time, thrilled with the sense of power, of taking control. "Effective now. No more excuses."

In answer, his arms circled her waist and he pulled her tight against him, sinking into the embrace, supporting her. It was a few moments before they parted again and she felt dizzy, as if she'd been dreaming. But it wasn't a dream; it was real.

"Did I ever tell you that you're a damn fine researcher?" he asked.

"I'm pretty good at other things besides research," she assured him, wondering at this saucy girl who seemed to be inhabiting her body. "If you give me a chance, I'll show you."

Before he could respond, she gave him a sneak preview, hijacking his mouth and his full attention.

NOTE TO READERS

I hope you enjoyed Warning Signs. *As with every novel, there are a lot of people I need to thank for their help and support.*

First, my tireless editor at Berkley, Shannon Jamieson Vazquez, and everyone on the Berkley team who helped bring Warning Signs *to life. Also, my agent, Anne Hawkins, who always watches out for me, pulling me back from the precipice when I've gone too far, and pushing me harder when I need to move out of my comfort zone. And finally, my critique partners: Toni McGee Causey, Kim Howe, Margie Lawson, and Carolyn Males. You guys make writing a pleasure.*

For research, I turned to the experts of Pittsburgh's River Rescue Team: paramedics David Naples and Anthony Weinmann, as well as hyperbaric nurses Julie Jacob and Georgia Siebenaler, and ER charge nurse/paramedic instructor extraordinaire Laurie Weaver.

Any deviation from reality is mine, not theirs. If you'd like to see what a real hyperbaric chamber looks like, or the River Rescue crew and their boat, please check out the Adventures in Research article and photos on my website, www.cjlyons.net.

In writing the Angels of Mercy series, my intent has been to stay as close to the medical realities as possible while still remaining entertaining. For more information on the medical realities that inspired the fiction, please check out my article "Warning Signs: The Medical Facts and Fiction" on the Extras page of my website.

Be sure to let me know what you thought of Warning Signs. *I look forward to hearing from you!*

As always, thanks for reading!
CJ

Don't miss the "gripping"* debut novel from

CJ Lyons

LIFELINES

Sometimes even doctors need saving.

On her first day at Pittsburgh's Angels of Mercy Medical Center, L.A.-transplant Lydia Fiore, the new ER attending physician, loses a patient: the chief of surgery's son. Now, to save her career, Lydia must discover the truth about her patient's death, even as it leads her into unfamiliar—and risky—territory.

At least she's not alone. There's med student Amanda, a sweet Southern belle with problems of her own; Gina, a resident with a chip on her shoulder; and Nora, the no-nonsense charge nurse with a cool head but a fiery temper. Not to mention the paramedic who'd like to try out his bedside manner on Lydia...

"Tense, whip-smart medical scenes."
—*Tess Gerritsen

"A pulse-pounding adrenaline rush... Reminds me of *ER* back in the days of George Clooney and Julianna Margulies."
—Lisa Gardner

"An exciting debut... engrossing [and] intriguing."
—Heather Graham

M332T0908